VOLUPTUOUS PASSIONS

Although Adam felt Gilliane's attempt to pull away from him, he did not heed it. Holding her with one arm, he tilted her face up with his free hand and kissed her. She struggled against him, one last convulsive effort to save herself; but his grip was inexorable, and the molding together of their lips and bodies was not affected by her pathetic attempt. "Please . . ." Gilliane sobbed, but Adam paid no mind, pulling the pins from her hair so that it cascaded down to her lips in shining chestnut waves, kissing the lobes of her ears when she turned her head and her nape when she tried to bury her face in his breast.

Fire coursed from Adam's lips over Gilliane's body. Dimly into her mind came the assurance that she had nothing more to lose. Adam already thought the worst of her. Why, then, should she struggle? Why should she not take her pleasure, since she had already paid the price for it? She raised her head to meet his lips and let her hands run feverishly over his back and shoulders, pulling him urgently onto the bed.

SWEET SURRENDER

Gilliane

Roberta Gellis

PLAYBOY PRESS
PAPERBACKS

GILLIANE

PRODUCED BY LYLE KENYON ENGEL.

Copyright © 1979 by Roberta Gellis and Book Creations, Inc.

Cover illustration by San Julian: Copyright © 1979 by Playboy.

Published simultaneously in the United States and Canada by Playboy Press, Chicago, Illinois. Printed in the United States of America. Library of Congress Catalog Card Number: 78-20321. First edition.

This book is available at quantity discounts for promotional and industrial use. For further information, write our sales-promotion agency: Ventura Associates, 40 East 49th Street, New York, New York 10017.

ISBN: 0-872-16531-0

First printing, June 1979.

CHAPTER ONE

Fear! Gilliane could scarcely remember a time when there was no fear. There was a vague memory of a man with a deep, warm voice who had tossed her in the air until she shrieked with laughter and had then folded her in his arms, who had called her his dark rosebud. But that had been long ago. All of Gilliane's more recent memories were of shrinking into corners, of hiding when possible if a man came into view.

Someone had said—that was long ago, too, soon after the warm, strong presence had gone out of Gilliane's life—that patience and resignation brought an end to fear. It was true and yet false. Perhaps if the fear had stayed the same, it would be possible to become accustomed, to become resigned. But it did not stay the same. It changed and changed, and with each change it pricked anew, so that again Gilliane was forced to try to avoid the pain. And there lay another source of her inability to become resigned. By and large, Gilliane had been successful in discovering ways to escape the fear—not completely, though, never completely.

Always the fear lay like a shadow over her heart and mind so that she could never be happy, really happy. Resignation might have been better than cleverness, Gilliane thought. The early fears, now that she thought back upon them, had been like pinpricks, although they had seemed huge terrors to a little girl. It was a black horror to have changed, in one day, from being the center of loving attention whose every action and word called forth delighted laughter and warm embraces, to being the focus of blows and curses. Cleverness had taught Gilliane to avoid drawing notice to herself and, more important, to read every nuance in the faces and voices around her. She had learned to efface herself when possible, and when forced momentarily into notice, to match her words and manner to the mood of others. The blows became less frequent, the curses changed to indifference. The agony of terror diminished to a dull misery.

Too soon the agony had been reawakened. Gilliane found she was no longer a child, that the dark rosebud was blossoming into a beautiful flower. She noted a new expression in the eyes of the men of the family and in the eyes of men who came to visit the keep. At first Gilliane had been pleased, thinking she had at last won approval. Her brief hope had been quickly dispelled.

It was the shock of disappointment, as much as the physical pain and shame, that had brought black terror into Gilliane's days and filled her nights with nightmares. Desperate for affection, she had responded quickly and openly to the sly, whispered praises of a young visitor to the keep. When he had begged her to meet him in the little wood a half-mile from the keep, she had agreed happily, thinking that there they would have freedom to talk, to gather spring flowers.

It was not that she was ignorant of the facts of life. Beasts coupled freely in the keep and on the demesne farms, and the servants coupled almost as freely and publicly. Merely, at twelve, Gilliane did not associate the act with herself. She was unaware of the invitation implicit in the small breasts that pushed out the front of her cotte, or the waist that had narrowed to emphasize the soft curve of her hips.

Thus, Gilliane was totally unprepared when she was seized and kissed hungrily. Surprise and a tentative gladness at what seemed for the moment a display of affection kept her quiescent at first. It was not until the tie at her neck was undone and a hand was thrust into her bosom that Gilliane understood the young man's intentions. Then she began to struggle. The delayed reaction communicated the wrong message. Because Gilliane had responded so eagerly to his words and to the suggestion that they meet, the young man thought at first that she was being playful. When it became clear that her struggles to free herself were in earnest, fury inflamed lust. This young man knew the right treatment for teases. He tripped her with a leg behind her knees, knowing that he would fall atop her, that she would be half stunned and bruised, while his fall would be cushioned by her body. In the few moments that Gilliane gasped helplessly for breath, paralyzed by shock and pain, he had her gown up, his chausses down to his thighs. Despite his success this far, however, the young man was not an experienced rapist. Before he could make good his threat and truly thrust home, Gilliane had recovered her strength and breath.

Until that moment she had fought in silence, more afraid of the punishment she would receive for having sneaked out of the keep and exposed herself to this situation than of the situation itself. The violence and pain tilted the balance of her fear in the other direction, however, and she began to scream for help. The sudden shrill cries and renewed frantic struggle disconcerted the would-be rapist enough so that Gilliane was able to twist out from under him, roll away, and leap to her feet.

Unfortunately, escape did not end the nightmare for Gilliane. Had it done so, the memory might have been more amusing than terrifying. She had been bruised, of course, but she was accustomed to being bruised, and fear had never destroyed her sense of the ridiculous. When the shock was past, she would have remembered the outraged cries, the limping pursuit that ended in a fall. A last glimpse over her shoulder as she fled showed Gilliane her attacker's hasty struggle to stuff himself back into his chausses and tie them. That, together with the satisfaction of having accomplished her escape, would have overlaid Gilliane's fear and made her cautious rather than bitter.

The real anguish began when she fled into the keep. Her distraught manner, the stained and disheveled clothes, the dirt, leaves, and twigs in her hair, told too plain a story. Still too shocked to think of an adequate excuse, Gilliane confessed the truth. She endured the beating she received stoically—being beaten was nothing new. What sealed horror into her mind was what followed. The questions were not so bad. Gilliane could answer those with truth; nothing had really happened, she had won free. However, her word was not accepted. She was stripped, spread-eagled, and questing fingers were thrust into her.

Revulsion had overwhelmed fear. Revulsion, too, would not allow the horror to pass from her mind. It returned again and again until, desperate to fix her thoughts anywhere else and unable to remove them from the central shame, Gilliane began to wonder why it should matter whether or not she was a maiden.

Little by little, from a remembered sentence, from a snide remark made by the daughters of the house, from misty memories, Gilliane pieced together her condition. She was an heiress! Not a great heiress, probably—she had no way of estimating what by law was hers—but enough of an heiress to make her a valuable pawn. Her father—that was the deep, warm voice, the tender, loving hands. Tears came to her eyes, although by twelve she thought she had been wept dry. She had almost completely forgotten him, suppressing the memory because it gave her such pain to compare her present condition with what it had been. Never mind pain—her father had been Guillaume de Chaunay and he had been pledged to . . . to King John, who was both Duke of Poitou and King of England.

In the beginning, those were the only facts Gilliane had, but clever, seemingly pointless questions and assiduous attention to what she had ignored previously gave her the story over the months and years. When Richard, who had also been Duke of Poitou and King of England, had died in 1199—the year after her birth and her mother's death—John had inherited the lands. But John was not able, as Richard had been, to keep the barons from fighting among themselves. Little wars had broken out all over Poitou, and in one of them Gilliane's father had died. She, the sole surviving child, had inherited the property.

For his services to the Comte de la Marche, Saer de Cercy had been given Gilliane as a ward. That meant that Gilliane's estate was managed by Saer, and that the revenues from that estate came completely into his hands, except for the amounts paid to the Comte de la Marche. That fact told Gilliane two things. First, her estate was not very large or she would have been taken into the comte's own household; and second, her life, as long as she had no children, was perfectly safe. She could be beaten and left hungry and cold, but she could not be killed or starved or frozen to death. As long as she was alive, Saer had the lands; if she died, they would revert to the Duke of Poitou.

The key word, however, was *children*. That was why she had been so eagerly examined. If she had been secretly acting the whore—as the incident might have led people to think—she might be with child, and that child would be her heir. A brief, vicious notion flicked in Gilliane's mind, but she knew it was hopeless; Saer would never allow any child of hers, except from a husband of his choice, to live. There was another key word—*husband*. By the time Gilliane had worked out her situation, she was well ripe for marriage—fifteen.

Fear—sharper, deeper fear than ever before stabbed her. Soon—soon Saer would choose a husband for her. Gilliane thought of the life his wife led and had to press her hands to her mouth to muffle her whimpers of terror.

For months after that revelation, Gilliane crept around the keep, trying harder than ever to be invisible. She also did her best to conceal the fact that she was now completely a woman. Previously, she had made her clothes to fit her neatly. Now she let out all the seams until the garments hung loosely upon her. No one seemed to notice. Marie de Cercy was too dull, too numb from years of ill-treatment and humiliation, to care what Gilliane did—unless, like the escapade in the wood, it brought her husband's wrath down upon her.

However, more months passed and no husband was brought forward. As her fear receded, Gilliane realized that Saer had no intention of marrying her to anyone, for as soon as he did, her revenues would go to her husband. Worse, the husband could ask for an accounting if the estate had been damaged or diminished. Gilliane guessed that Saer did not look forward to that. She was safe from the threat of marriage.

Perversely, once she was sure Saer meant to keep her unwed, Gilliane began to dream of marriage, of a strong man with a deep, rich voice who would protect her from her cruel warden. But the months slid slowly past and changed to another year, and no such romantic knight even passed briefly through her life to give form to her dream. Only the sound of a bass voice and a vague image of bigness drifted in and out of her night thoughts.

By 1214, it was not for the lack of seeing men that Gilliane's dream still had no form. In the spring of that year, King John came to France to win back the lands that had been lost to the French king since 1203. Saer and his sons rode out to war. Twice, battle was joined quite near the keep. The castle itself was not attacked, but after each battle the wounded were carried there for shelter, and Gilliane learned to sew and clean wounds and to brew medicines that cooled fever and dulled pain.

It was then that her ease with the lesser castlefolk and with the fighting men-at-arms developed fully. Gilliane had always liked them—they were the only people who did not hurt her or regard her with contempt. Now she learned how to deal with them. Because she was the least of the ladies of the keep, it fell to her to direct the servants who performed the foulest tasks and to treat the common foot soldiers. Fear had pricked her again when she was ordered to these tasks, but very soon she blessed her fate. The "gentle" knights cursed and struck their nurses, reviling them for clumsiness or slowness in attendance. The "brutal" men-at-arms knew their place. They might strike or revile the maids and womenservants, but for Gilliane—a lady of the keep—they had only soft words of thanks.

Warmed by appreciation from even so unworthy a source, Gilliane strove to deserve the thanks. She became deft and gentle and begged the leech and the priest to tell her the herbs that would best bring ease to her suffering patients. She learned to give orders with a kind of gentle authority that made the servants and men-at-arms desire to obey her and feel ashamed to be slack or coarse.

Gilliane was very sorry when she learned, in August of 1214, that King John had been driven off. It was not that she regretted the loss of her little power—she pitied the sufferings of those who had brought her the power too much to regret its loss. Her disappointment was only because she associated John with her father, who had been John's liegeman. Also, she had had a tiny hope that, if John won, she would be taken out of Saer de Cercy's hands. Perhaps she should have feared a change of guardians or a marriage to one of John's supporters, but hate had grown strong over the years and it seemed to Gilliane that her suffering in other hands—if she should suffer—would be amply repaid by Saer's loss.

Instead, it seemed that she had fallen even further into Saer's power. Emboldened by the part he had played in the destruction of John's initiative in Poitou, Saer applied to the Comte de la Marche for the right to marry Gilliane to his second son, Osbert. The fear that seized her when she heard this news made her past terrors shrink into insignificance. Of all that loathsome family, Osbert was the worst. The eldest son was like his father; he was cruel and brutal but not unintelligent, and he was a brave man with confidence in himself. Osbert, however, was a coward—stupid, incompetent, and insecure, which made him torture and bully those weaker than himself and snivel and abase himself before the strong.

Gilliane understood Saer's purpose in choosing Osbert to be her husband. On the one hand, there was probably no other way to provide for him. He was not a good enough fighter to win a prize of war or make a living out of tourneys. No one, not even a poorer knight than Saer, would want him as a son-by-marriage, so there was no hope of gaining a wife with a dower for him. On the other hand, Osbert was much too afraid of his father to question the condition of Gilliane's estate when it was his. In fact, by marrying her to Osbert, Saer could keep things exactly as they now were. Osbert would not even dare to suggest that he and Gilliane live in her father's keep or that they manage the property themselves.

One of the reasons Gilliane regretted that she had not become resigned was that the habit of struggling would not permit her to take her own life. She did think of running away, but Saer thought of that, too, and she was closely watched. All she could do was pray, and at first it seemed that those prayers were answered.

Permission was withheld. The Comte de la Marche did not refuse, he merely put the request aside because he was much busied with affairs of state stemming from John's withdrawal and the truce that was being negotiated between King John and King Philip. He would look to the lands, he said vaguely, as soon as he had time, and then give his decision. Saer cursed and raged and beat Gilliane until his eldest son intervened, pointing out that, if he killed the girl, Marche would be looking all the sooner at the property, and with a less indulgent eye. Gilliane was abed for a week but still considered herself blessed by God because she knew Saer would not press the marriage.

For a time, life seemed to grow somewhat better, except that Gilliane's anxieties were kept in the forefront of her mind by her need to avoid Osbert. He regarded her as his property and could see no reason why he should not use her while he waited for the official sanction of ownership. Fortunately, Saer ordered Osbert not to take her by force. He did not discourage his son from pursuing Gilliane; if Osbert could win her agreement, it would be a strong point in his favor. However, there was enough of a chance that the Comte de la Marche would ask her if she was willing and remove her from Saer's power if she complained to make Saer order that she be treated with consideration. The comte might not really care how Gilliane felt, but her objections would serve as an excellent excuse to give her to someone of his own choice.

Thus, 1215 passed in relative peace. Gilliane was no longer beaten or given the dirtiest work. She was taught to embroider and do other "lady's" tasks. No doubt Saer thought she was an idiot and would overlook years of ill-usage; Gilliane did not forget, but she did not give anyone reason to believe her hate was unchanged. In 1216, Saer's attention was diverted from Gilliane by the news from England. Ordinarily, he paid little attention to any political situation that did not affect him directly, but this one had interesting possibilities. The barons of England had become so dissatisfied with their king that they had sent messengers to appeal to King Philip of France to send his son, Prince Louis, to destroy John and take on the kingship of England.

Saer was indifferent to the relationship between John and his barons, but he knew, if Philip decided to let Louis go to England, the French king would be too wise to allow his son to depend on the good will of the rebellious English barons. Having broken their oath of loyalty once, they would find it easy to break it a second time and return to their allegiance to John. Thus, if Louis went to England, he would need a strong tail of good fighting men to back him. Moreover, it was those men in whom his trust would rest. When keeps were taken and men were needed to hold those keeps, it would be Louis's French knights who would be given the lands. Throughout the spring of 1216, Saer paid close attention to the news from the French court and discussed the risks and advantages exhaustively with his eldest son. To Gilliane's almost incredulous joy, when Louis went to England in late May, Saer and Osbert went with him.

During the spring and early summer of 1216, Roselynde keep lay tightly shut and doubled guards marched the great walls and watched land and sea for enemies. Within, Lady Alinor alternately cursed King John in language that brought admiration to the eyes of her foulest-mouthed man-at-arms and worried about her loved ones. Her husband, Lord Ian de Vipont, was with the king, who lay brooding in Winchester. Her daughter and son-by-marriage were locked into Hemel keep, far too close to the rebel stronghold of London. Worst of all, her eldest son, Adam—eldest by being the male first born of her but still very young in years— held his own lands centering on the castle at Kemp—a pocket of resistance to Louis, who controlled most of the southeast of England.

In fact, Lady Alinor had more to worry about in the case of Adam's well-being than she knew. In July, Gilbert de Neville, Lord of Tarring, had abjured his oath to King John and sworn allegiance to Prince Louis. He had received the reward for his treachery rather more quickly and completely than most others, however. Within a month of shifting his loyalty, he had died in a tourney designed to entertain the idle hours of the French and English barons quartered in London. If some of the English lords had a faint suspicion that the accident was not totally accidental, their suspicion was lulled by the contrition of Saer de Cercy, at whose hand Gilbert had died, and by the urgent need to believe that Louis would not countenance murder by his men of his English supporters.

There was comfort, too, in the fact that Louis had promptly dispatched men to help Gilbert de Neville's son when he sent word that he was being attacked. Anxiety was reawakened by the knowledge that Saer was chief of the men sent to help Neville and by the news that young Gilbert had been sorely wounded in the battle and was like to die. However, by the end of August, Saer was back in London, reporting triumphantly that he had redeemed his unintentional slaying of the father by saving the life of the son. It was true, he reported, that young Neville would never be a man. A severe blow on the head had addled his wits and he had lost his right hand and part of his left leg—but he was alive.

Now Saer proposed that, since young Neville's virility was unimpaired, he should be married at once so that he could breed up children. Thus, the lands would remain with the blood of Neville, and the father's death would bring no ultimate loss to the family. There were raised brows at this proposal, but Saer did not suggest a daughter of his own to be the bride, as many suspected he would. Instead he offered his ward, Gilliane de Chaunay, a girl of good estate and totally unconnected to him by blood.

There were grumblings and mumblings because it seemed to some that Saer would still be tied too closely to the Neville lands, but such questions faded into insignificance before the fact that King John was stirring again. There was word that the king was gathering men and supplies and would soon take the field. No one wanted the thankless task of defending Neville's property, which all knew bordered on territory controlled by a family that staunchly supported the king. In spite of angry looks here and there, no other solution to Neville's problem was offered. A marriage contract, which stated the case very clearly and bestowed the lands upon Neville's children should any be born, and upon Neville's wife should there be no children, was drawn up, signed and sealed with churchmen as its guarantors and witnesses.

His main purpose achieved, Saer returned to Tarring to survey his new domain. He found it incomplete. The port in a wide estuary some two miles south of the castle was endangered by a small keep on a rise of land called Telsey cliffs. No attack from Telsey had ever been launched on the harbor, but it was in the hands of a man opposed to Louis. Saer dispatched Osbert to bring Gilliane to England and determined to add a bit to the bride's estate while he waited for her to arrive. He opened the strongboxes of Tarring and with that money hired mercenaries, who were plentiful. Then he rode out to invest the keep at Telsey cliffs.

Saer was surprised and, at first, somewhat amused by the resistance he met. The little keep could not possibly hold out for more than a week or two without help—and what help could come? Saer had already determined that the overlord of Telsey's castellan was Adam Lemagne, a boy of eighteen who was shut up, apparently for his own safekeeping, in his major stronghold at Kemp, Saer knew also that the boy's stepfather, Lord Ian de Vipont, and his brother-by-marriage, Lord Geoffrey FitzWilliam, had the reputation of being redoubtable warriors and battle leaders. But the stepfather was with King John and the brother-by-marriage was protecting his own lands north of London. By the time either of them could come, Telsey would be safely destroyed. Not discouraged by the fact that his orders to yield were ignored and his first attack was beaten off, Saer settled his men for the night, determined that they would take the castle by assault the next day.

It did not work out quite that way. About an hour before false dawn, when the night was darkest and the sentries in Saer's camp were drowsy with watching and with confidence that no night attack would be launched from the keep, a whirlwind descended upon the besiegers. At its center was a giant with a voice like a trumpet.

"Lemagne!" the trumpet blared. "Lemagne!"

The appellation, Saer thought when he had time to think, was all too appropriate. "The Strong" fulfilled the promise of voice and name only too completely. Each time the sword he used was lifted, red streams ran down its blade, and each time it descended, a man died or was maimed. However, Saer and his men were not novices. In a few minutes, arms had been assumed, weapons snatched up, defensive groups formed. The toll taken by the whirlwind lessened.

As confusion in Saer's party diminished, confidence was restored. It soon became apparent that they were still by far the stronger. Slowly Adam and his men were forced back toward the walls of Telsey. Saer had a brief feeling of victory when it seemed that the castellan would not open the keep to take in his own overlord. At the last minute, however, the gates did swing wide— not, to Saer's fury, to give entrance to the fighters and possibly also to their pursuers, but for the garrison to pour out and fall upon Saer's force anew. So fierce was this second attack that Saer drew his men back to regroup and to offer the trap of seeming retreat. The bait was not taken. Instead, Adam and his castellan, Robert de Remy, called in their men and withdrew into the keep.

By then the sky was pink with the rising sun and Saer could judge the extent of his losses. He was furious and appalled. It was particularly galling because there was no way of hiding the damage done him and because it had been done by a mere boy. However, the dead were carried away, the wounded tended, and the camp put back in order. Before the work was quite complete, Saer was hailed from the walls. He hissed instructions to a group of men near him and rode forward, helmeted and mailed, with his shield raised to guard against arrows from the wall, to hear what the besieged had to say. The young giant stood on the wall, bareheaded, his straight black hair lifting in the morning breeze.

"You have made a mistake," Adam said calmly to Saer, "and have been punished for your foolishness. Now take your men and go. I give you leave and pass my word I will not pursue you if you do not despoil my people further."

Saer choked at the effrontery. Even considering his losses, the combined force inside Telsey was inferior to his own. The probability of his being able to take the keep was still high.

"Do not make another mistake," Adam warned, "or think me a vainglorious boy child. My other men are summoned and will be here in two days' time."

Saer laughed aloud. "You must really think me a fool to believe I would swallow so plain a falsehood. If men were coming, would you tell me?"

Adam shrugged. "I have given you the benefit of the doubt. It so happens that I have more important bones to crack than yours. You have, as yet, done me no real harm, so I am willing to allow you to depart in peace.

You will find—if you do not go—that I never lie." A chuckle shook the mighty frame. "Sometimes I am not quite so open as I have been . . ."

Three things happened simultaneously. Saer made a small gesture with his right hand, which he was sure could not be seen from the castle wall. The crossbowmen who had accompanied him threw down the shields behind which they had concealed their wound bows, raised them and fired. Adam dropped to a crouch behind his own shield, which had been leaning against the facing of the wall. Several arrows thunked into the shield. Several more flew just above it, where Adam's broad chest had been, and another few whirred by still higher, aimed at his head. Even while the arrows were in the air, Saer's party had set spurs to their horses and galloped away out of range of reprisal. However, no shafts followed them—only the sound of merry, contemptuous laughter and the trumpet voice calling, "I warned you not to make another mistake."

The laughter made Saer more uneasy than he would admit to himself. He kept his men hard at work through the rest of the day, finishing the scaling ladders and the ram for the gates, and he sent out small parties to scout the land to the west and north. To his captains, he said that one might *know* the cockerel was lying, but only an equally vainglorious fool would fail to take a cheap, easy precaution. It was most peculiar, however, that when the parties came back to report no sign of any force moving anywhere, Saer felt even less confident and sent other parties out to watch.

Within the keep there was also considerable activity, although some of it would have puzzled Saer had he a spy to tell him what was happening. Most of the men and women were occupied with the ordinary tasks of war. Weapons were checked and readied, oil and sand heated for pouring from the walls, poles prepared for pushing away ladders. However, other parties were more curiously employed. All day water was drawn from the deep wells in the bailey until every barrel, pot, pan, skin—anything that would hold liquid—was full. As fast as vessels were filled, they were emptied— slowly, carefully, so that as much water would soak in as possible and as little be wasted. The water was poured over every flammable thing, particularly the foot-thick planks and bars of the gates that closed the walls.

Toward evening, Saer's men had finished their work and gathered around the campfires for a well-deserved meal. They did not unarm or relax their vigilance. One surprise had taught them that much, and it was a common tactic of desperation to launch an attack when one's enemy was concentrating on eating rather than on fighting. They would have been even warier had they seen, as the sun set and the breeze began to blow off the land and out toward the sea, Adam and about twenty of his men stringing six-foot bows.

When the bows were strung, each man took a handful of shafts tipped not with steel but with pitch-soaked heads of soft wood, and, carrying clay pots filled with red coals, they mounted the walls. The breeze freshened, faded, at last blew steadily offshore. On Adam's signal, twenty shafts were thrust into twenty pots, lifted to the bows and sent flying out—out into the dry grass of the hillside on which Saer's camp lay. The sentries called a warning when they saw the shafts black against the sky, but the flicker of flame at the tips did not show and the men snickered with contempt when they saw how far short of the camp the arrows had fallen.

For a while, they continued to laugh as four or five more volleys followed, not coming much closer. It seemed a remarkably silly waste of arrows. The laughter checked when smoke began to rise from the hillside and little tongues of fire could be seen licking up from amid the uncut hay. The horses began to stamp and whinny as the smoke rolled down toward them, driven by the breeze. Some ran to quiet the horses, others to wet blankets to beat out the fire. Saer came roaring and cursing from his tent.

In the midst of the confusion, trumpets could be heard blowing within the keep. The men fighting the fire rushed back to help saddle the horses. The fire was not really dangerous. Obviously it was a device to disorder the camp so that another surprise attack could be made. Horses, however, do not like fire. They kicked and sidled, delaying a process that ordinarily took only a few minutes. Meanwhile, the gates of the keep had opened and a substantial troop had ridden out. Saer's men cursed but went on calmly enough with what they were doing. The fire worked both ways. If their horses were recalcitrant, so would those of Adam Lemagne's men be. They could never drive the beasts across the widening band of smoking, scorching grass in any kind of organized charge.

Calm purpose held until, suddenly, flaming pitch-headed arrows began to fly into the camp itself, setting tents and supply wagons alight, here and there striking a man or a horse so that shrieks and wildly bucking animals turned organized activity into panicky chaos. Those who could leapt into their saddles, but there was no way they could come at their tormentors directly, and, as they rode northeast to get around the burning area, they heard the laughter of Adam and his men drifting with the smoke on the seaward breeze.

Long before any of Saer's party could come upon them, Adam's troop was safely back in Telsey keep. They had the pleasure of standing quietly on the walls and watching the besiegers lose at least half of their tents and supplies and all of their night's rest while they fought the fires with inadequate means. Robert de Remy stamped his feet and slapped his overlord fondly on the shoulder.

"My lord, my lord," he laughed, "how did you think of that?"

Adam smiled also, but his hazel eyes were bright

and hard with anger. "The Earl of Leicester, who was my lord, God rest him, did not believe in expending men or money uselessly or in permitting his property to be damaged. If a subtlety could save lives or lands, he was not afraid to use it."

"A subtlety," de Remy chortled, "a sweet, hot subtlety, but I fear those who must eat of it will not be grateful for their dessert."

He was punning on the use of the word *subtlety* to describe the towering food sculptures that customarily were constructed by cooks and bakers to signal the end of each course in great state dinners. Adam smiled again in acknowledgment of the pun, but his eyes narrowed with consideration as he watched the activity in Saer's camp.

"Set a double watch," he said to de Remy, "and bid the men use their ears as well as their eyes. This device can work two ways—both are to our advantage, but we must be ready with the right action for either one. Perhaps that French reaver will lose his temper and come upon us tonight, as soon as they are safe from the fire, or perhaps he will wait over tomorrow to rest his men. If they come tonight, they will be half dead already from their labor and we will have no trouble casting them off."

"And if they do not come until tomorrow, we will have help from Devil's Dyke and Trueleigh," de Remy put in eagerly.

"So I hope. The weather has held well, but we must be ready to protect ourselves if some accident should hold back William and Hugh. Hmmm . . . I wonder . . ."

"Another subtlety, my lord?"

"Not so subtle and more dangerous, I am afraid, but if they do not come tonight, set some men to watch where they store the scaling ladders they have made. It may be, if they are not kept too deep in the camp, we can send men with skins of oil and set fire to those."

Saer was livid with rage when he took account of the
new damage Adam had done, but he was not so angry
as to lose his common sense. Not only were his men
exhausted from battling the fire while they kept one
nervous eye on Telsey, lest more deviltry emerge to
plague them, but they were beginning to feel inferior
in spite of their greater numbers. It would be better to
let them rest the next day while their captains inflamed
their tempers and their greed with talk of the fact that
they would be allowed to rape and loot unrestricted,
owing to Saer's anger. Nor did Saer forget, at mid-
afternoon of the next day, to broadcast the news from
his scouts that no force was approaching. Thus, either
Lemagne had lied, thinking he could frighten them, or,
better still, the men he had summoned had disappointed
him.

About the same time that Saer was announcing that
Adam's hopes of help would certainly not be realized
before the attack, Robert de Remy was slyly contesting
his lord's will. He had not been trained in diplomacy,
but he had lived thirteen years longer than his young
overlord and had younger brothers. Therefore, when
Adam said he would lead the raid into Saer's camp, Sir
Robert did not exclaim that it was too dangerous. What
he said was that Adam should have more consideration
for his men than to expose them to instant recognition.

"No one," he remarked dryly, "has seen any giants
among the serfs carrying wood and water in de Cercy's
camp. Perhaps, had you hidden yourself in the fighting the night before last, or listened to me when I
begged you to let *me* talk to him from the wall, the
sudden appearance of a mammoth among their servants might be overlooked. I do not say it is likely,
but . . ."

"Oh, I can bend over a bit, or . . ."

"Or walk upon your knees, perhaps?" Sir Robert
asked tartly. "Assuredly, no one would notice that!"

Adam laughed, even while he frowned with irritation. He was considerably bigger than the usual run of well-fed noblemen; he was gigantic compared to the usual serf who, aside from the castle servants, suffered constant low-grade malnutrition and occasional semi-starvation, which stunted the growth. The plan they had devised was to creep down to Saer's camp under cover of darkness dressed as servants, and try to fire the ladders at dawn in this guise. Meanwhile, another attack from the keep would divert Saer's men and, they hoped, permit the arsonists to escape. Adam had to admit that he would be more a danger than a help to his men if one of Saer's party noticed him—and he *was* hard to overlook. At last he conceded that Sir Robert must go, merely warning his castellan to keep his mouth shut because he did not speak English and his unaccented French would betray him as surely as Adam's size would identify him.

Just before sunrise, Adam ordered the gates opened and led the castle garrison and his own men down on the camp with the greatest amount of noise and confusion he could manage. Under the circumstances, it was no surprise to anyone that the attack was expected. Adam and his men were met with a fury bred of frustration tinged with fear, and were thrown back toward the keep. Had Saer been less angry, perhaps he would have wondered why his enemies were so much less hardy in this attack than in the previous ones. However, an automatic mechanism that equated *besieged* with *losses* and *weakness* combined with his rage and his desire and blinded him to this new trap.

A chance view of his own camp marked by eddies of smoke and flame where neither smoke nor flame should be dispelled the illusion. The revelation of the trick did not alter Saer's intention, as Adam had hoped. He did not rush back to his camp to put out the fires. He was old in war and knew he still had the advantage of numbers and situation. If his force could maintain close contact with Adam's party, either they could defeat them on the field or follow them into the keep when the gates were opened, which was a far easier method of taking the place than going over the walls. The fact that Adam and his men began to fight with more efficiency and ferocity at the same time was more of an encouragement. Saer read desperation into that fact.

Adam was not unaware of the danger. If they should be beaten back under the walls of Telsey, his men would sustain greater losses than he had planned. As he roared encouragement to his followers, he wondered where Sir William from Devil's Dyke and Sir Hugh from Trueleigh were. His instructions had been clear, and wind and weather had been consistent and favorable. Of course, there was always the possibility that another of Louis's men had attacked Trueleigh or Devil's Dyke at the same time de Cercy had attacked Telsey. If so, this was a concerted attempt to root out any opposition to Louis in the south of England—and it might well succeed.

In the end, Adam's worst fears were dispelled. Horns called from the walls of the keep and Adam drew back from the fighting to look toward Saer's camp and the sea. The camp was full of men, and the servants were fleeing it. In a few minutes, the men were through the camp and pounding up the slope toward the fighting. Aware of the cessation of Adam's voice encouraging his men, Saer thrust away his opponent and also drew back to look around hopefully. Perhaps his infuriating adversary had been killed or wounded. Instead, he saw the young giant staring out over the battle.

Saer did not need to turn and look. He knew that Adam had redeemed his promise; his men had come to his support in two days, as he had said. Saer even knew how he had been fooled again. The men had come by sea rather than across the land where his patrols had watched for them. They had landed farther down the coast and had ridden up through territory Saer thought he had secured to attack from behind.

Raging but impotent, Saer bellowed for retreat, spurring his horse frantically northeast into the narrowing area between Adam's troops and the oncoming group led by Adam's vassals.

CHAPTER TWO

For four months Gilliane nearly approached happiness.
Saer's wife and daughters now simply ignored her. Saer
had said she was to be treated with consideration, and
even when he was hundreds of miles away Saer was
obeyed by his deeply subjugated womenfolk. Gilliane
did not actually pray for Saer's and Osbert's death, but
only because she was aware that evil prayers often
rebounded. Nonetheless, she could not rid her heart
and mind of the hope that they would both die, and
the hope fed and grew on the fact that no word came
from England.

In September, Gilliane's peace and hope were destroyed in a single blow. Osbert returned to the keep.
Saer was not only in the best of health, Osbert reported,
but he had increased the family's fortunes tenfold, at
least, and looked to increase them even further.

"If we succeed," Osbert said, sneering slightly at his
brother, "you may have these lands and good riddance
to them."

The young Saer laughed. "I do not need quittance
from you, whom I can crush with my fingernail like a
louse. I will have them, will you nill you. But tell me,
if all goes so well with you, what brings you home?"
His eyes grew even harder. "I will entrust neither men
nor money to you, whether or not you say you have
my father's order for it."

"Do I look to you as if I need men or money?" Osbert snickered.

A considering expression came into the older brother's eyes. It was true that Osbert had come with ten well-armed, hard-faced mercenaries—in addition to the two devils who were his own servants—and that his armor and clothing were richer and more elegant by far than what he had worn when he left. Young Saer guessed that the feathers were borrowed—actually they were young Neville's, but he was in no condition ever to wear them again—but, all in all, he was not displeased. He was less greedy than his father, and his primary interest was in the lands he now held. If old Saer was winning a rich estate in England, he might well stay there. That would suit his eldest son excellently. Thus, instead of depressing his younger brother's pretensions, which he could have done with a single snarl of ill-temper, young Saer ignored Osbert's provocative remark.

"Very well, then, why have you come?" he repeated mildly.

"For Gilliane."

Young Saer cocked his head and a cynical smile twisted his lips. "You are welcome to her for all I care. God knows, she is eighteen years old and should have been married three years ago at least, but you will not marry her in this keep nor within—"

"I will not marry her at all," Osbert interrupted, but his eyes slid slyly away from his brother. "Here is my father's order, closed with his seal," Osbert added hastily before young Saer could protest. "Let someone run for the priest to read it to you."

While they waited, the young Saer examined the roll of parchment with great care. The contents did nothing to clarify the situation for him. As Osbert said, the letter merely ordered young Saer to give Gilliane to Osbert, who would bring her to England. No reason was given, and, although he wondered mildly what maggot had entered his father's brain, he did not care much.

When Gilliane was told, she was dumfound. She asked no questions because she knew it would be useless to do so. Marie de Cercy, the bearer of the news, was never given more than a bare order to do this or that. Trembling between hope and fear, Gilliane packed what was hers in a traveling basket and laid out her riding dress. Perhaps young Saer would tell her where she was going and for what purpose when she came down for dinner.

There was, of course, no need for him to tell Gilliane anything. When she saw Osbert, her lovely brunette skin—rosy golden in winter, and nut-brown when touched by the summer sun—went ashen yellow. Even her lips paled, and her huge deep-brown eyes seemed to glaze. No one addressed a word to her, which was just as well because she would not have been capable of understanding. Habit carried her to her usual seat at the end of the bench, and she managed to sink into it before her knees gave way. After that, she stared at the table. She did not reach for food, and no one served her or urged her to eat. Hard usage had not bred sympathy among the de Cercys.

By the time dinner ended, Gilliane had recovered sufficiently from shock to feel afraid. Strangely, this time the fear did not hurt; it did not make her heart pound or squeeze her throat and chest. Actually, it would have been closer to the truth, Gilliane thought, to say that she knew she was afraid rather than that she felt fear. She felt nothing. She felt as if she were dead already, beyond pain. Into the vacuum of feeling, hate flooded. In her extremity, the memories of her father came clear and strong, and another idea, one that had not previously occurred to her, took hold. If her father had died, then he was on the side that had lost the war; therefore, his daughter had been given as ward to one of his enemies, perhaps even to the man who had killed him.

In the instant, Gilliane became convinced that Saer had killed her father. In fact, he had not. Gilliane's father had not been on the side that had lost the war. He had answered the summons of his overlord, the Comte de la Marche, had died in battle, and the comte had fulfilled his obligations to his liegeman by confirming the estates to Gilliane and placing her where he thought she would be safe and best serve his purposes. The question of whether Gilliane would be happy never entered the comte's mind; it was totally irrelevant. Now, however, the unhappiness nurtured by years of abuse gave birth to a monstrous notion.

To kill oneself was the ultimate sin because it was a sin that could not be confessed, expiated, and absolved. To kill Osbert, however, could not be so dreadful a sin. Men killed each other constantly in war—killed women and children, too—and confessed, did penance, and were absolved. If Osbert attacked her, was she not in the same situation as any other person who must defend herself?

Like a sleepwalker, Gilliane rose from the table when the others did and retreated to the women's quarters. By the time the other ladies of the keep came up, she was abed already, seemingly asleep, on the straw-stuffed pallet near the door where she had slept since she was considered old enough to govern the maids and prevent them from sneaking out to lovers in the night. Later that night, however, it was Gilliane who crept out the door and down the stairs and picked her way across the small bailey to the shed where the captain of the night guard lounged away the dull hours. The man was surprised, but he did not protest against her request nor voice his opinion that what she asked for would be of little help to her. He liked Gilliane. If a long knife would give her comfort—for whatever purpose—she should have it.

Thus, Gilliane returned to her bed concealing a real killing knife and its well-greased sheath under her skirt. This was no eating toy with a four-inch blade and a jeweled hilt that interfered with the grip. What Gilliane carried was an eight-inch poniard, its thin, wicked blade honed to razor sharpness on both edges, its hilt wound with leather that had been shrunk firmly to the metal haft, smoothed and shaped to fit the hand. Such a knife, had she the courage to use it, could slide so smoothly between the ribs of a man while he slept that he would be dead before he woke.

Whatever the guardsman thought, Gilliane did not believe she would lack the courage to use her weapon. That she would certainly be caught, might be tried and executed for murder, did not trouble her at all. Death would be more of a release than a punishment to her, and likely would bring her additional pleasure from knowing that Saer would be deprived of her property.

In the event, neither guardsman nor Gilliane was proved right. Circumstances prevented a trial of Gilliane's strength of purpose. Osbert made no attempt upon her at all. He did not drag her before a priest bribed to ignore her protests and marry her; he did not attempt to use her without even making her his wife. He assaulted her only with words, sneering at her while he spoke of the "great honor" that was to be done her. But in among the sly hints and nasty innuendos, Osbert let slip the fact that he was taking her to England.

Underneath the fear a small, new seed of hope began to put out roots. England was where King John ruled. Gilliane's father had been King John's liegeman. Perhaps somehow she could escape from Osbert and Saer and throw herself upon the king's mercy. It was not a bright hope. Gilliane knew she had little to offer. Her lands were in France and King John had no way of profiting from them, but perhaps . . . Between the comfort she gained from the long knife strapped to her thigh under her dress and the little seed of hope, Gilliane found the journey almost pleasant.

They rode long and hard. For the first few days, Gilliane was nearly fainting with exhaustion when she was lifted from her saddle each evening. Naturally enough, she did not complain nor did she ever ask to stop and rest. The mercenaries, unaware of her background and not perceptive enough to recognize the sneering insults that lurked behind Osbert's talk of the good fortune that awaited her, were impressed by the lady's stamina. Then, as the days passed and Gilliane grew hardened, the men began to like her even better. First, they recognized her strong distaste for Osbert, and they were at one with her on that. Second, they discovered that she liked them.

No one misunderstood that liking on either side. Gilliane was a "lady," not meant for their kind, but she understood and respected what they did in their sphere of life. Often, when Osbert rode off with his two chosen companions, Pierre and Jean, to see if he could catch a serf girl to rape, Gilliane would talk with the other men. It began out of a desire to know something about England—and she learned a surprising amount about the political situation—but she also learned about the men and they learned to respect her.

What Gilliane did not ask and the mercenaries did not mention, because, naturally, no one had told them, was Saer's purpose in bringing her to England. That knowledge came to her on the seventeenth of September, the day of her arrival, when Osbert thrust her into Saer's presence.

"By God," the old man chortled, although there was a vicious undertone to his laughter, "the Lord of Tarring cannot complain about the woman we have chosen for him. I had quite forgotten how beautiful you are, Gilliane." Then he looked sharply at his son. "You have done her no hurt, have you? If she is not a maid . . ."

"It is no doing of mine," Osbert quavered, shrinking aside. "You can ask the men. I never touched her—not even to lift her to the saddle or take her down. I never came near her."

Saer stared contemptuously at his weak reed of a son and snorted his disgust. Nonetheless, weak reeds have their value. It would have been impossible for him to use the device he had planned with a strong-willed son. He looked back at Gilliane and his eyes narrowed.

"You have been brought here to be bride to the lord of these estates," he snarled. "It is useless for you to protest—your overlord is many miles and a sea away, in France. He will not come to England to listen to your plea."

"Yes, my lord," Gilliane whispered, thinking of the knife that now seemed almost a part of her.

"I'm glad you are so reasonable," Saer remarked, but he did not sound glad. He sounded as if he were sorry she had not protested so that he could beat her into submission. Saer had not been in a happy mood since he had escaped between the pincers Adam had devised to crush him. Then his rage eased and he grinned wolfishly. "You will not find your husband completely to your taste, perhaps, as he is a little deranged in mind and damaged in body, but he will do you no harm and is, I know, capable of his marital duties."

Gilliane was silent. There could be no answer to a statement like that and Saer obviously did not expect one, but he smiled at the expression on her face.

"Because of your husband's condition," he went on briskly, grinning sadistically, "his loving wife will rule his lands. However, at present there is war in England between Prince Louis and King John. Since no woman is fit to rule in time of war, I will rule for you. Do you understand?"

"Yes, my lord," Gilliane repeated in a stronger voice.

The seed of hope that traveling to England had

planted in her put out more roots. If there was war, Saer might have to leave the castle. Perhaps, just perhaps, Gilliane thought, she would have something to offer King John. Perhaps she could get a message to him and somehow, some way, yield the castle to him— that is, if she survived the handling of the monster to whom Saer planned to mate her.

"Come," Saer said, "I will introduce you to your betrothed."

Gilliane wavered on her feet, but Saer grasped her firmly by the arm and dragged her across the hall, thrusting her through an antechamber to face a closed door of which the upper half had been cut away and replaced by bars. As their shadows blocked the light, a snuffling whimper came from the inner room. Saer pushed Gilliane forward so that her body was against the bars. She stiffened with terror, expecting the hands of a madman to tear at her, but nothing happened, and, as her eyes became accustomed to the gloom of the wall chamber, she saw what was left of Gilbert de Neville of Tarring. Gilliane's heart contracted and she hid her face in her hands.

Misunderstanding the gesture, which was bred of pity rather than revulsion or fear, Saer laughed. "I imagine you cannot wait for the happy moment when you can be joined to such a husband. Well, well, no delay is intended. The summons to Neville's vassals and castellans and the invitations to the neighboring lords are all ready. They can go out tomorrow. On the tenth of October, your joy will be complete."

He paused, waiting for Gilliane to plead with him to spare her such a fate, but she was silent, leaning against the door, her face still hidden. He swung her around and slapped her brutally, forehand and backhand.

"Do not think you will defy me at the last minute," he snarled.

"No," Gilliane murmured, her eyes stubbornly on the floor. "I will do as you bid me, my lord."

It was fortunate that Saer was not a perceptive man or he would have heard a decided note of satisfaction in Gilliane's dulcet murmur. Once she had swallowed her pity for the poor, cowering, whimpering creature that had once been a man, she realized that there was a possible path to freedom. Certainly her way would not be impeded by the poor thing in the cell. Perhaps she could even do something for him. Sooner or later, Saer would leave, even if only for a few days. Then ...

"And do not think that becoming a great lady means that you may also become idle," Saer snapped, breaking into her thoughts. "I will expect you to see that all is made ready to receive the wedding guests."

Gilliane raised astonished eyes to Saer's face, scarcely believing her ears. "You mean you wish me to order the servants and see to the supplies?" she asked in a trembling voice.

If he would allow her to ride out, she could escape. Gilliane scarcely blinked at the slap Saer dealt her as he told her he would expect her to run Tarring as his wife ran his keep. Escape. *Escape*. She clung to the word until Saer released her to go up to the women's quarters. There she faced about twenty maids, all of whom were completely demoralized by fear and lack of discipline. That Saer and Osbert had made free with them was apparent from what they said, but Gilliane could offer them no hope of protection. All she could do was steady them by setting them to familiar tasks. She did not worry that Saer or Osbert would interfere with her handling of the maids. From what she had seen in Saer's keep, she knew that neither he nor his sons gave favorable treatment to the women they used.

It was not until that afternoon, when Gilliane went down to see what was being readied for the next day's dinner, that she realized she could not escape quite so soon. Until she was wife to the poor idiot in the castle, she would have nothing to offer anyone to induce him to protect her. Strangely, she did not feel crushed by this realization. She liked Tarring. It was much larger than Saer's keep in France and it was much easier to stay out of his way. She felt a sense of satisfaction in what she had accomplished among the maids, and even more satisfaction in knowing that there was no other woman about to give them contradictory instructions.

At first things continued to go well, but within the week, Saer had news that threw him into a thundering rage and caused Osbert to pale with fear. King John was not beaten, as all had assumed. He had relieved the siege at Windsor and was on the march toward Lincoln. Louis's contemptuous attitude toward the rebel barons had bred sufficient dissatisfaction among them that a few had gone back to their old allegiance and others had simply withdrawn their support from Louis. This cast a new light on the subject of Gilliane's wedding. First, there was no need to propitiate the English contingent of Louis's supporters; they could be little more discontent than they already were, and Louis did not seem to care. Second, it was more important to get Gilliane wedded and bedded than to enlist the support of Louis's French adherents by making them witnesses to the legality of the marriage. In all likelihood, the French knights would be too busy to come to Saer's aid if his possession of Gilbert de Neville's property was contested by war. On the other hand, the sanction of the Church was well worth obtaining. Saer told Osbert to close and guard the keep and rode out to make arrangements to get Gilliane well married before his position was endangered.

Four days later Gilliane was summoned from the women's quarters. She came braced for trouble because she was never summoned except to be punished for something, but she stopped dead in her tracks, gasping with shock, when she saw the assembly in the hall. There were two priests and, from the elegance of their garments, they were prelates of some weight. Beyond them were three men Gilliane had never seen before.

They were not so richly dressed as the priests, but they were clearly not servants or men-at-arms. But what caught and held Gilliane's attention was Gilbert, held upright by Osbert and a sixth man whom Gilliane did not know.

"Ah, here is the bride!" Saer exclaimed. Before Gilliane could utter a sound, he had come forward and gripped her brutally by the arm. "You are to be married today. Now," he growled in her ear. "Answer as you should, or you will scream and pray for death for long and long before that peace is granted you."

Gilliane nodded dumbly, but it was not pain or fear that locked her tongue. Hate and rage were what brought tears to her eyes. Again Saer had cheated her and shamed her. It was not the marriage she resented. She had set her mind to that already. Distasteful as it was, it was her one hope of freedom and revenge, and she did not hate or fear the mindless cripple. It was the cruelty of exposing her, all unready, in her soiled, common—work-a-day garments, without even a proper wimple—only an old cloth tied around her head to keep her hair out of her way. A mere ten minutes' warning would have given her time to put on her Sunday garments, to wash her face and hands and hang around her neck the pretty crucifix carved from a sea-shell that she had found in the chamber of the late Lady of Tarring.

Hardly realizing it, Gilliane allowed herself to be led into the chapel. She did not see one of the Neville vassals shake his head in sympathy or another shrug his shoulders. They were sorry for her, but, since Gilbert de Neville was dead and his son reduced to such a state, it was best for them to accept the terms Saer had offered for their continued loyalty. If they would accept Gilliane and her children as Neville's heirs, continue to pay their rents and do their service, Saer promised to protect them from attack by Louis's forces. They would not be asked to fight for Louis or take any part in the civil war unless they were attacked by John's men. In that case, Saer would expect them to resist and he would lead them and fight for them with his own mercenaries.

They watched as her hand was thrust into Neville's. One noted, with a flicker of surprise, that she voluntarily clasped her husband's hand when she felt it in hers. The brief sensation of surprise passed with the assumption that the girl's fear of Saer outweighed the revulsion she must feel for the idiot. In fact, Gilliane was not much repelled by Neville. She did not find his incoherent mumbling much different from Osbert's behavior when he was drunk, which was frequently—except that Neville seemed perfectly gentle. Several times, when Saer and Osbert were both out, she had gone to Gilbert's cell and coaxed him to crawl to the door where she had given him sweetmeats and talked softly to him.

At first Gilliane had been impelled by the spirit of self-preservation. If she was to be thrust into the cell with Neville or he was to be brought out to couple with her, she wanted to know whether he would be violent. Soon, however, pity made her wish to remove the poor creature's fear of her. When it was apparent that she was succeeding—he came quite eagerly when she called to him and seemed to recognize her—another idea came to her. If she were carrying Gilbert's child, she would have more to bargain with when she escaped from Saer.

It was not pleasant to think of coupling with Gilbert, but Gilliane was reasonably certain that Saer would force her to do that to validate the marriage. Moreover, she had an ugly suspicion that, if she resisted or frightened Gilbert away, Saer would arrange to substitute either himself or Osbert for her husband—and Gilliane would a thousand times rather have Gilbert, mad and deformed as he was, than either of them. Thus, when the ceremony was over, Gilliane took her husband's head gently in her hands and kissed his lips. He responded to that; in fact, had Osbert and Neville's chief vassal not been holding him, he would have grabbed her there and then. She repressed a shudder. Apparently there would be no need for a substitute in the marriage bed.

They came out of the chapel into the hall again, and Gilliane saw that the servants had cleared the low dais where the high table was usually set. It came to her then that the men she did not know must be Neville's vassals or castellans, and fury flooded her once more. Saer planned to go through some ceremony of swearing to uphold the marriage contract—and she dressed no better than the meanest serving wench. She would not endure it. She did not think Saer would dare to beat her before all these witnesses. Trembling because of the retribution that might later fall upon her, but driven by the need to salvage some remnant of her pride, she stopped short and curtsied.

"If you will excuse me, gentlemen," she began.

"You are needed here," Saer barked.

"Yes, my lord," Gilliane replied. Her voice shook, but she would not give up so easily. "I do but beg your indulgence for a few minutes. I wish to attire myself more fittingly. I did not expect, when you summoned me . . ."

To Gilliane's immense relief, Saer burst out laughing, but Osbert's voice rose before his father could answer her request. "To attire yourself fittingly for this wedding, you should roll in a sty."

Saer stopped laughing and glared at his son. Everyone could see what Neville was, but to speak open insult in front of the men who were pledged to uphold his honor was impolitic. Saer could sense the offended stiffening of Neville's men. To appease them, he smiled at Gilliane.

"I am sorry, Gilliane. I forgot women make a great thing of such matters as dress. I should have given you warning. Go, by all means, and change your gown, but remember that our guests do not wish to wait until dark for their dinners."

That last word made Gilliane gasp. If there was no dinner fitting for the guests, Saer would beat her half to death. It would not matter to him that he had not told her there would be guests. She curtsied again and fled—not up the stairs to the women's quarters but down, outside the building to the kitchen sheds in the bailey.

When she had instructed the cooks, Gilliane ran breathlessly up the stairs, tore off what she was wearing and drew on her best tunic and cotte. Between her hurry and exertion and the soft rose color of her gown, she was becomingly flushed when she hurried down to join the men once more. She uttered a low apology for her delay and was so relieved when Saer merely nodded that her eyes sparkled.

Now Gilbert was lifted from the chair in which he had been placed by Osbert and Saer and helped onto the dais, Gilliane following. Because she was particularly keyed up and not at the moment oppressed by fear, she listened closely to and understood what was being sworn. The four men, two vassals and two castellans, were doing fealty to the family of Neville, through Gilliane and her children. Gilliane obediently repeated the acceptance of this oath of loyalty in the words Saer told her to say, waiting for some overt sign that the swearing was really to him—but there was none. That was the doing of Gilbert's men. Saer had tried hard to convince them that he should be named in the oath as Gilliane's guardian, but they would not agree because they did not wish to be tied irrevocably to one of Louis's men. If the tide should turn in John's favor, they wanted a loophole through which to escape.

Several times Gilbert delayed the ceremony by trying to escape from Saer and Osbert. He was tired, unaccustomed to being held upright for so long. At last he burst into tears and wailed so loudly that the proceedings came to a halt. Osbert made a move to strike the poor creature. Saer managed to block the blow, but Neville's four men glared angrily. They could accept Saer, but they liked Osbert less and less every minute.

"Let him sit down," Gilliane begged softly, and, while a chair was being brought by one of the men, she sent a servant for sweetmeats.

Between these and her soothing voice, which Gilbert associated with comfort, he was quieted. Sir Richard, the chief of the vassals who held lands at Glynde, looked at Gilliane approvingly. He had been a friend as well as a vassal of old Gilbert de Neville and had been greatly saddened by his death—although the suspicion that it was not completely accidental had not reached him—and by young Neville's misfortune. He knew, of course, that his friend had died by Saer's hand, but such things happened, and it seemed to Sir Richard that Saer was doing his best to atone for the accident. Certainly he had chosen the right woman to marry the deranged and crippled son. No doubt it was the relative wealth and power of Neville's lands that she wanted, unless she was too afraid of her guardian to protest, but she plainly understood and intended to be kind to her charge.

As soon as the ceremony of swearing was over, Sir Richard voiced these opinions to Saer, which put Saer into so good a temper that he was actively pleasant to Gilliane. He waited patiently for dinner to be served. Also, he decided not to return Gilbert to his cell. Had Osbert not been such a fool, Saer could have put Gilbert into confinement with some excuse about his needing quiet. Now he did not wish to associate himself with Osbert's actions. He could see that it was of considerable benefit to him that Neville's men should believe as Sir Richard did.

Thus, Gilbert was seated at the high table between

Gilliane and Saer, whose purpose was accomplished by the kindness with which Gilliane cut up her husband's food, directed his wandering attention to it, and generally attended to him. Toward the end of the meal Gilbert began to whimper, and Gilliane begged that he be allowed to go back to his cell to rest. Saer frowned at the word, but found a way to turn even that to good account.

"I am sorry to keep him thus," he said to Sir Richard, "but I fear he will do himself some hurt. Sometimes a dim memory of what he was seems to come to him, and then self-hate seizes him—as can be understood. Once he nearly cast himself from a window."

Sir Richard sighed and looked away. Gilbert had crawled to a mattress on the floor and curled up on it in a fetal position; he was sucking his thumb.

Saer shrugged. "Perhaps you think it would be kinder to look away and let him do as he desires, but I have my guilt to expiate. If Gilliane breeds a son of him, then . . . I do not wish the blood of the man I killed to die out and thus to stain me forever. No, do not think I am too good to be true," Saer added cleverly. "If Gilliane breeds a son, I will have benefit all ways. My conscience will be clear and I will have the profit and governance of these lands until the boy is ripe to manage on his own. By then, I will be dead or too old to desire more than a cushioned chair by the fireside."

That brought a smile and a nod of true comprehension. Indeed, it was a most reasonable attitude. Saer had not mentioned Osbert or his purpose in these arrangements, but Sir Richard was not troubled by that. He had seen Neville's reaction when Gilliane kissed him and he assumed that Saer planned to provide for Osbert either by another marriage or a grant from Louis, if and when John was defeated. Perhaps Saer even planned to use Sir Richard and the other vassals and castellans to win Osbert a heritage. That did not bother Sir Richard, either. He had several neighbors he would gladly eliminate with Saer's aid, and as for Osbert ruling that land, Osbert could be got rid of easily enough, Sir Richard thought.

The other men felt less strongly than Sir Richard, but nonetheless had been aware of unease about accepting their lord's slayer as their present protector. Gilliane's appearance and behavior toward Gilbert had soothed their discomfort. Thus, all were in high good humor, eager to make themselves pleasant toward the bride and to assure her that they approved of her. There was to be no bedding ceremony as there could be no question of repudiation. Neville's deformities of mind and body were obvious and Gilliane had openly accepted them. Clearly, also, Neville was in no state to repudiate his wife. To expose her was then useless; to expose Gilbert would be a senseless cruelty.

Gilliane went to her chamber when Saer told her to do so and quietly made ready, with the help of the maids. She knew what was coming, of course, but she could not help being repelled and frightened, and she wept softly. It was dreadful to be married only because one was driven by hate and fear.

One of the women, who had acted as personal maid to her, pressed a small clay pot into her hand. "Anoint yourself below with this," Catrin whispered. "It will ease the pain. It will also deprive you of the pleasure— but there can be no pleasure with such a man. Poor lady. Poor little lady."

The sound of voices outside the room made the maids withdraw hurriedly. Gilliane stifled her sobs as well as she could and got into the bed, covering herself as completely as possible. She could hear the men come in with Neville, but they were hidden from her by the bed curtains. Suddenly there was the sound of a struggle and Gilbert screamed in terror.

"What is wrong?" Sir Richard asked.

"He is afraid to be naked. I do not know why," Saer replied harshly.

He did know why, but he was not about to admit that Gilbert's mindlessness was as much owing to the torture he had ordered inflicted as to the head injury—which he had also inflicted. Both torture and treatment, which was almost equally painful, were carried out when Gilbert was naked. Saer was too economical to ruin clothing.

"What the devil is now to do?" Sir Richard gasped, struggling to hold the squirming, screaming creature.

Gilliane was shaking with fear, but she could not endure the pathetic cries she heard. "Let him come to me as he is," she called. "I will try to calm him."

She sat up, clutching the coverlet to her, sobbing with a mixture of horror, pity, and grief over her fate, which seemed to grow ever more dreadful. Gilbert was dragged to the bed and pushed into it.

"Hush," Gilliane soothed, trying to steady her voice, "hush. No one will hurt you."

Again her voice seemed to exert a calming effect. As she repeated her assurances over and over, Gilbert stopped screaming and struggling to get to the floor. He lay quiet, panting with fear. Saer looked at Gilliane significantly. He wanted her to get on with disrobing Gilbert and then couple with her husband, but she would not do it. She lifted her head defiantly, uncaring of what the later cost might be.

Sir Richard put his hand on Saer's arm and drew him toward the door, whispering, "It is men he fears. Leave him with her. I do not believe he will hurt her and, in any case, it would be easy enough for her to escape him. We can wait outside if you wish. Lady Gilliane can call us if she needs help."

Alone with her husband, Gilliane let go of the covers. She felt no more shame at being naked before Gilbert than before a small child. "Gilbert," she murmured, stroking his hair, "do not weep. No one will hurt you. Come, you know me. I have never hurt you."

He quieted and his clouded eyes sought her face. Gil-

liane touched his cheek and forced a smile. Something
stirred in his usually vacuous face. He lifted his maimed
right arm as if he would imitate her gesture. Very gently,
Gilliane pressed it away and took his left hand, which
she put to her own face. The fingers touched her cheek,
moved to her hair, stroked the thick chestnut waves.
Pity for him and for herself brought tears again.

Fearing to frighten Gilbert, Gilliane did her best to
restrain her sobs. Again expression flickered in Gilbert's
eyes. He left off touching her hair and put a finger to
the tears coursing down her face. Then, suddenly, he
wriggled upright. Before Gilliane could stiffen with fear,
he had put his right arm around her shoulders and
drawn her against his breast while his left hand tried
to wipe the tears from her cheeks. Gilliane was so surprised that she stopped crying and looked carefully at
him.

What she had hoped for fleetingly was not there. It
was not a miraculously restored man who looked back
at her. Nonetheless, there was something in Gilbert's
face, a dim awareness of his own humanity and hers.
It was not much, but it gave Gilliane another thread
of hope to cling to. Perhaps with patience and kindness,
at least part of Gilbert's mind could be restored. If only
she had time. She sighed. Unfortunately, she could not
afford to wait. She had not forgotten Saer's glance. He
would be back well before morning to make sure she
had truly become Gilbert's wife. Swallowing nervously,
Gilliane lifted her face still further and touched her
mouth to her husband's.

CHAPTER THREE

On November fourth a complete family party was assembled before the huge fireplace in Roselynde's great hall. Lady Alinor's attention was divided between her eldest son, who was describing with great enthusiasm his knighting, which was one of the events that had taken place in conjunction with the coronation of the boy king Henry III on October twenty-eighth, and her husband, who was still thin and hollow-eyed from a desperate illness.

"I swear our troubles are over," Adam said, his voice a bass rumble in his effort not to shake the rafters as he sometimes did when carried away by excitement. "Many came who would not go near John. Some were there to swear who, I am sure, had already given oath to Louis—but they will not waver again. And this papal legate, Gualo, really knows the possible from the impossible."

Lord Ian smiled at his stepson but turned his head to look at his son-by-marriage, who was leaning over the back of the chair on which his wife, Joanna, sat. "Geoffrey?" Ian asked.

"Oh, you will never get Geoffrey to say *yea* without a little *nay* in it," Adam protested.

Geoffrey laughed and came around the chair—short step, long step—a limp that was a permanent memento of the disastrous battle at Bouvines, which had ended

John's hope of recovering the territories on the Continent that he had previously lost. As he passed his wife, he touched her gently. "I am not so bad as that," he said. "I will agree readily that those who have sworn to Henry at this crowning will hold by their faiths, and I agree, too, that among the legate Gualo, Peter des Roches, and the Earl of Pembroke, this land will have good governance. For all of that, it will not be so easy to rid ourselves of Louis. He is no fool. Perhaps he did not foresee John's death, but he saw most clearly that it would be unwise to place too much dependence on those that broke their faith, even to such a king as John. What he has taken is held by his own men, and they will not lightly yield."

"I know that," Adam remarked indignantly, "but I do not regard unseating them as trouble."

Lady Alinor sighed and Joanna said bitterly, "Oh no, killing is your favorite sport."

"Tush!" Adam responded tartly. "Do not be so womanish."

Ian and Geoffrey laughed aloud. "In heaven's name, bite your tongue," Geoffrey cried. "Do you think I wish to lie abed with a man? What should Joanna be if not a woman?"

"You know what I mean," Adam said, laughing also. Then he frowned. "And Jo knows as well as I that we cannot live in a land divided in this way, so what is the use of saying to me that I love killing—which is not true anyway. Since it is absolutely necessary to cast Louis out, and it cannot be done except by war . . ."

"Adam is right about that," Geoffrey put in.

"Fighting cocks!" Joanna spat. "You are all of a feather."

"There is wealth in this land," Alinor said slowly. "Has it been suggested to Gualo to offer Louis a bribe to go?"

Ian put out a hand and stroked his wife's arm. "Your heart is speaking, Alinor, not your head. Louis is here because the land is rich. He wants it all, and to offer him money now would be more of an encouragement to him to stay—as if we were crying aloud that we believe ourselves weak—than any inducement for him to go."

"Besides," Adam urged, "to rid ourselves of Louis would have little effect on the men who have taken keeps and are sitting in them. They would not go, even if the prince took the bribe. We would need to fight them anyway."

"And even if we, who still have our lands, should abandon our countrymen and agree that those who now hold the land should keep it—" Geoffrey began.

"No!" Alinor and Joanna exclaimed together, their eyes lighting with rage.

Ian looked at Geoffrey, whose face was perfectly expressionless except for the amused glow deep in his golden eyes. Too clever by half, Ian thought, he has picked the one note that can make fighting palatable even to Joanna. The possessiveness of the women of Roselynde was bred deep in their bones. The thought of giving up an inch of land or the least useful of their serfs could turn both of them into vindictive furies. It was not greed. Both women were generous to their dependents and charitable in general. Neither raised any protest over what her husband spent—although, Ian thought ruefully, it was just as well neither he nor Geoffrey had ever tried to include the cost of a mistress in his spending. It was almost as if the land and the people who belonged to it were a child that needed protection.

"We must be a little flexible about who holds the disputed lands," Adam remarked thoughtfully. "Those who have been deseisined must be restored, of course, but in some cases, the right is not clear. Some of the men who returned with Louis were first deseisined by John, and for no good cause. Some, also, were holders of the land before John lost Normandy and were forced to give up their English holdings to keep what was theirs in France."

"They may go back to what they desired, then," Alinor said sharply, but she looked at her son with amazed admiration.

Adam had always been so heedless and playful as a child that she had often despaired of his being willing to give serious thought to any subject. Yet here he was, sounding more and more like his father every day. (The word *tush*, that Adam had used a few minutes before, was Simon's. Ian said *peste* when he was annoyed.) More important, the delicate perception of shades between absolute wrong and absolute right was characteristic of Simon and must be part of Adam's nature because Simon had not lived long enough to teach Adam his marvelous sense of justice.

"What Adam says is true," Ian commented, shaking his head at his wife. She did not like France or the French, and anyone who chose lands in Normandy over lands in England was no loss to the country as far as Alinor was concerned. "But," he continued, before she could begin to press her point, "the question is of no immediate concern. What we must decide is whether to wait for Louis to move, whether to press Winchester, Gualo, and Pembroke to start an offensive, or whether to begin quietly to clean out our own part of the country."

"We can do nothing without first warning Pembroke what we are about," Alinor said quickly.

Joanna could not see her mother's eyes because they were lowered, but she knew how they would look—black pools of fear, all the gold and green light gone from them. King John had died on October eighteenth of a combination of dysentery and an affliction of the lungs. The latter had developed from nearly being drowned trying to rescue the baggage train, which had been caught in a sudden flood and sunk in the quicksands near Wellstream. Ian, wetted as thoroughly as the king, had also nearly succumbed to drowning inside his own body of the phlegm in his lungs. Fortunately, his men were able to bring him to Hemel, where Joanna's devoted nursing, his own strong body, and his intense desire to live had saved him.

Once over the worst, Ian mended fast, but he still did not have his full strength. Geoffrey and Adam had ridden to Henry III's crowning without him, while Alinor brought him slowly home to Roselynde. The journey had so exhausted Ian that he had spent the next two days abed, yet here he was, eyes bright with anticipation at the thought of going into battle, even though his breath still rattled suspiciously in his chest from time to time.

Her own husband, Geoffrey, was no better. Joanna watched him limp to the other side of the fireplace to refill his goblet from the flagon that stood on a small table near Ian. Not long in the past, Geoffrey had nearly died of the battle wounds that had left him lame. However, neither the pain nor the permanent injury had dampened his eagerness to thrust himself into the first line of any fight. As for Adam . . . Joanna uttered a disgusted snort as Adam confirmed her thought before it was clear in her mind. He smiled warmly at his mother and made a happy gesture, completely unaware that his words were like a knife in Alinor's heart.

"You need not worry that we will spoil any plan of Pembroke's, Mama," he said earnestly. "I made sure to speak to him of the matter and he said any disturbance we made here in the south would be most welcome to him because—"

"Welcome to him, indeed," Alinor snapped. "I never thought William would use us as a cat's-paw. But it is always so with men, who forget they have friends or family whenever a cause of honor comes before their eyes. Doubtless it will be useful to the king's cause if we draw Louis's full wrath upon us while—"

"Mother!" Adam exclaimed. "What makes you mis-

say Pembroke? I have not yet told you the full sum of
our talk."

Ian began to laugh and then to cough. Both Alinor
and Joanna jumped to their feet, but he waved them
back. "Sit. Sit. I did but choke on my own spittle because of laughing. And you need not doubt your mother's good sense, Adam. She is only doing what she accused Pembroke of. She is sacrificing his good name as
an excuse to keep me from doing what she thinks would
harm my health."

"Nonsense," Alinor rejoined, but she was gratified
to see the stricken expression in her son's eyes. Adam
adored his stepfather and would never knowingly do
anything that might hurt him. He would be more careful now. "What I said was perfectly true. I did not
mean that William would permit us to be overwhelmed.
If there was real danger, he would send help or even
come himself, but I cannot see why my lands should
be burned and battled over."

"It will not be your lands if we ride out to smite our
enemies," Ian remarked irritably.

"That is all very well," Geoffrey interrupted smoothly, thinking that Lady Alinor was not so far wrong. Ian
was not yet well, as the sudden sharpness so soon after
laughter betrayed. "But it will be necessary to choose
those enemies carefully." What Adam had not yet said
was that Pembroke, while agreeing that any action
against Louis's men would be of help, had urged that the
action be one that could be quickly ended or broken off
unfinished without hurt. "He already plans to march
against the prince in force and will summon us for that
purpose as soon as his plans are fully formed."

"What is soonest begun is soonest ended," Ian
pointed out.

"Yes, but not if one begins to besiege London," Adam
said, laughing, thereby redeeming himself in his mother's eyes. "Geoffrey is quite right, and I was just about
to say the same thing."

Ian looked from one young man to the other. "I was afflicted in the chest, not in the head," he said dryly. "What has given you both cause to think that a week in bed has driven all knowledge of war from my mind? I can bear to be treated like a half-witted child by my womenfolk because that is their way of love, but do not you two begin to cosset me. What news did the court have of Louis's actions?"

"The most important is that Louis called on Hubert de Burgh to yield Dover as soon as the news came that John was dead, and Hubert denied him with contumely, and so fiercely resisted the attack Louis began that the prince was finally convinced the city would never yield. Louis has withdrawn to London to lick his wounds."

"No," Alinor warned, "that cannot be."

Ian looked at her sharply, but he knew his wife. The warning was no further attempt to protect him from himself but a judgment on the news. "Do you mean you do not think Louis has given up hope of taking Dover?" he asked.

"As to that, how could I guess what is in Louis's mind? No, I meant he has returned to London, if he has returned there, for some purpose—not to lick his wounds."

To that all three men nodded agreement. "He has never held Dover and has lost little by raising the siege." Geoffrey voiced the opinion for all three. Then he caught and held Ian's eyes. "And I do not say this to cosset you, my lord, but because I really believe it. We must wait to see what Louis will do before we make our own move."

After a moment, Ian nodded. "Yes, at least insofar as direct action goes, we can wait for a little while. However, we are all agreed, are we not, that there will be hard war, and that unless the weather is far more severe than usual, it will be fought right through the winter?"

"Yes."

"Thus, to sit still is foolish," Ian continued. "We must begin at once to hire and train men. This will not be like an expedition to France or Wales, where we can call up our levies and draw men-at-arms from our own keeps. Each keep must be fully garrisoned, even when we ride out with a full tail of men."

"We will be hard pressed for battle leaders," Geoffrey pointed out. "For instance, I cannot take Sir Roger from Hemel because I cannot leave the keep, even fully garrisoned, without a man to lead."

"I can go to Hemel," Joanna said. "The men will obey me, and you need not fear I will yield the keep."

Geoffrey turned pale. "Joanna," he protested, "did you not tell me you had a hope you were breeding?"

"What has that to do with anything?" Joanna asked tartly. "Since when has a full belly made a woman unable to guard what is hers? I will be all the more careful to preserve the patrimony of my child."

"Let us count up what we have before we come to any hard decision," Ian suggested hastily, seeing the agonized expression on Geoffrey's face and fearing he would say something that would precipitate his headstrong wife into stubbornness.

"There will be two knights from Iford," Alinor began. "Sir Giles and one of his sons can go, leaving one son to hold the keep. Sir Peter from Clyro can also go. His eldest boy is young, but there is little chance that any of Louis's men will try to take a place so far west."

"Two of my castellans have sons old enough to come with us," Adam offered, "but my lands are too surrounded by Louis's people to draw any experienced men from the keeps."

"That is true of Geoffrey's lands also," Ian agreed.

"Joanna, go and ask Father Francis for parchment, pen, and ink," Alinor directed. "Let us write down what we have and what we need, lest we be lost in a maze of half-remembered matters." When her daughter was well away, Alinor looked at Geoffrey, who was still biting his lip between fury and worry. "Do not fret yourself or be so mad as to forbid her," Alinor said softly to him. "I am no believer that a woman must be a weak reed and I do not doubt Joanna's strength or ability, but I agree that Hemel is too dangerous for a woman alone. It is too close to Louis and not strong enough. Moreover, to leave a woman as castellan invites attack from men who think such a one must be witless. I will keep Joanna here at Roselynde, if only you do not put your foot in your mouth and say something to raise that stubborn bitch's hackles."

Adam had been frowning in puzzlement over Geoffrey's obvious distress. He loved his sister dearly, but he did not tremble with fear for her because he never doubted her ability to do anything. Of course, he realized that certain things were beyond her physical strength, but he thought no less of Joanna for being unable to do those things than he thought less of Geoffrey because Geoffrey could not lift as heavy a weight as he could. Adam acknowledged that Joanna could not don armor and lead men in the field nor join the physical battle on the walls to defend a keep. Nonetheless, he knew that his mother was perfectly capable of directing the defense of Roselynde and assumed Joanna would be just as able to defend Hemel.

Now, however, he saw the reason behind Geoffrey's concern. It was true that most women were idiots, good only for tumbling in bed. He, too, would think a castle held by a woman easy prey. And a man who had not a sister and mother like his own, but women of the lesser sort, would never believe a woman could hold the men-at-arms to their work. Such a man would try more ardently to take the keep the more he was repulsed, thus doing greater damage and creating more losses among the defenders. Furthermore, this would be more true for a keep like Hemel, which was less strong in itself, than for Roselynde, which discouraged attack by its position and size. It was something, Adam told himself, that he would need to remember when he had a wife.

The thought made him frown. It was not for lack of being asked that Adam was still unmarried. Men had been proposing their sisters and daughters to him since he was fourteen, when he had reached the legal age of consent. And it was not owing to a distaste for the married state that had made Adam insist his mother and stepfather refuse all offers thus far. In fact, Adam desired very much to be married. He had been born into a family where love reigned and the deep, unremembered memories of early childhood urged him to find for himself that warm, safe haven of the heart and soul that he had sensed surrounded his mother and father. Even after Simon had died, there had been love. Ian had come to protect them all from the king's wrath—so he said—but his match with Alinor had been for love, and after more than ten years that love still leapt between them as lightning leaps between two hills.

In Leicester's household, where Adam had served as page and squire, there also was love, but it was in that household that he had learned that there are women and women and women. The Earl of Leicester was fond of his wife and she of him, and they lived in peace together. However, Lady Leicester was uninterested and helpless in all things that did not pertain to the immediate concern of women. In addition, Adam had not yet grown the first black down between his legs when the more sluttish of the maidservants were at him. It was all pleasure, and he gave them what they desired, but he knew that more than one who spread her legs for him had a man of her own—and that troubled him. Nor was he much older before he discovered that sluttishness was not confined to the lower classes.

Lady Leicester watched over the maidens in her care and they had no opportunity to try Adam's paces, but their eyes said plainly that they would be happy to ride him. Moreover, there were those who were not under

Lady Leicester's control, visitors or older relatives who came to stay for some time. Adam had learned a great deal from them, both about the fine art of giving a woman pleasure and that the need and desire for that pleasure did not necessarily make a woman a slut. Some who sighed and cried under him were coarse in mind and filthy in spirit, but others were only light and silly, playing at love because they had nothing better to occupy them.

It was the silliness, really, that had kept Adam unwed. He was well found in lands and allied through marriage to the high nobility. Thus, the ladies offered to him were of high estate and their education had fitted them for that estate—that is, it had fitted them to do nothing except bear children. Oh, they could sing and play, talk most amusingly, embroider exquisitely. Adam approved of all these skills most heartily; his mother and sister were both excellent conversationalists and notable needlewomen. However, that was by the way, a lace trimming, as it were, upon the solid cloth of their real abilities. Alinor and Joanna could also manage a keep without the intervention of stewards, run a farm as well as any bailiff, cure a sick or wounded man better than a physician, trade as keenly and keep accounts as well as any merchant and, he suspected from the heavy-eyed look of their husbands on many mornings, play the wanton as skillfully as a high-priced whore.

Adam watched Joanna return from the wall chamber in which Father Francis lived, carrying what her mother had asked for in a small writing desk. It occurred to him that Geoffrey was right to be concerned for his wife's safety. Such a woman as his sister was a pearl without price. In four years of more offers than Adam could remember, he had not found a single girl with whom he would be willing to share his life. Each one, no matter how beautiful or sweet-tempered, would have been no more than a burden to him—worse yet, would have

bored him to madness in a few weeks. Adam shrugged
mentally. He wanted to be married and was aware that
he should breed an heir to his property and his name
as soon as possible. He was the last male of the Lemagne line, his half-brother Simon being Ian's son, a
de Vipont. Nonetheless, Adam was not yet prepared to
take second best. Somewhere there must be a girl who
would fulfill his expectations of what a woman should
be.

On the same day in Tarring keep, Gilliane sat alone
before the fire and dutifully employed her needle in
embroidering a collar for one of Saer's gowns. Her
resentment over such a duty was not nearly so strong
now as it had been in the past. She would rather have
been working on a gown for her husband or herself,
but she was sufficiently content with her current condition to give her service to her guardian without bitter
anger. She had so serious a puzzle about Saer to work
out that she had little room for anger; also, she had
begun to realize that Saer was all that stood between
her and Osbert.

That name made her shudder with a mixture of fear
and revulsion. The cruelty and cowardice of that creature repelled and sickened Gilliane far more than poor
Gilbert, but Osbert's cowardice was her bulwark and
her protection. He would not touch her or harm Gilbert as long as Saer lived. For that reason, Gilliane
prayed for Saer's well-doing in the enterprise he had em-
barked upon. Besides, Saer was much changed. He had
not beaten Gilliane once since her marriage, and one
time, when he came in unexpectedly and found her trying to shield Gilbert from Osbert's cruelty, he had
knocked his son to the ground and threatened to take
him apart piece by piece if he hurt or frightened Gilbert
again.

Gilliane had been stunned. She could not believe there
had been a sudden reform of Saer's character; yet he was

plainly as delighted as she at the effect marriage had had on Gilbert. The first sign of the change was Gilbert's attempt to comfort Gilliane on their wedding night. The second sign—Gilliane blushed faintly—was the coupling itself. When she had kissed him at the wedding ceremony, his lunge toward her had been entirely animal, a mindless, instinctive movement. In the bed, however, a different set of memories—if the confused maelstrom in Gilbert's mind could be called memories—had come to the fore.

Gilbert had responded to Gilliane's kiss, but gently. He had kissed her in return, stroked her body softly. The blush died out of Gilliane's cheeks and anxiety came into her eyes. She was guilty of the sin of lust; she knew that. It was lust, pure lust, that made her writhe and whimper with pleasure in Gilbert's embrace. Not that first time, of course. That had hurt, although less than Gilliane had expected. The salve Catrin had given her had been quite effective. In a few days, however, there was no need for it. As soon as Gilbert began to caress her, a tingling, aching pleasure centered in Gilliane's breasts and loins pervaded her body. Her thighs would part of themselves, her own moisture would fill the passage, making Gilbert's entry easy, and she would lift herself eagerly to meet the thrusts that brought delight with impalement.

That was lust. Gilliane did not pretend she loved her husband. If Gilbert was no longer completely an idiot, he was not a man either. She had a pitying sort of affection for him, but that was not love. Thus, her pleasure was owing to her own lust. Yet there was really no way to curb herself. It was her duty to accept her husband; it was her duty to conceive a child by him if she could.

That brought Gilliane's mind back to Saer and the anxiety deepened on her face. It was not reasonable, not natural, that Saer should be pleased by Gilbert's improvement. True, it was not much—the ability to say

a few stammering words, to recognize Gilliane, to learn
to use a crutch so that he could walk about the keep
rather than crawl. Still, so much advance might mean
that the wound in his head was healing. And if Gilbert
should regain his ability to reason, would not Saer lose
his hold on Tarring and on Gilbert's men?

What was more, it was perfectly plain that Saer
greatly desired that Gilliane conceive a child. He had
asked regularly whether she was breeding and had been
disappointed when she told him her flux had started at
its usual time. Gilliane thought he would strike her
then, but after a moment he had lowered the hand he
raised and had said only that she had better try harder
to get with child. She was to urge Gilbert to coupling
and never to refuse him. Nor was she any longer permitted to close the door to her bedchamber. A maid sat
in the antechamber to listen and be sure that Gilliane
and Gilbert performed their marital duty at least once
every night. Gilliane began to blush again. Even that
could not abate her lust. She bit her lips to keep herself
as silent as possible, but the red, pulsing pleasure came
anyway.

There had to be a reason for the change in Saer. She
worried at it, but twist and turn the matter as she
would, she could see no possible profit for Saer in
Gilbert's recovery or in her conception of Gilbert's
child. The puzzle was insoluble to Gilliane because she
did not understand the attitude of Neville's men. Saer
had always been sure he could get them to accept the
terms of the wedding contract. It was the next step that
worried him. After he killed Gilbert, how could he
make Neville's men agree to Gilliane's marriage to
Osbert?

First of all, it must be plain to them (as it was to
Osbert's father) that Osbert was no prize. That, however,
might work as much in Saer's favor as against him because the men would believe they could rid themselves
of Osbert easily enough once his powerful father was

out of the way. Saer did not care about that. He loathed Osbert almost as much as Gilliane did. All Saer cared about was that Tarring and its rents should be his own for the span of his life. Saer desired his own aggrandizement, not the foundation of a dynastic line, and for this only a creature like Osbert would serve.

The solution to Saer's problem had occurred to him soon after he mentioned to Sir Richard Gilbert's brief periods of semirationality. It was not true that Gilbert had tried to throw himself from a window—that had only been Saer's excuse for keeping the poor creature locked up—but even as the words came out of Saer's mouth, he realized they gave him the answer to part of his problem: that of explaining Gilbert's murder. Then the second part of the problem solved itself.

Just before dawn on Gilliane's wedding night, Saer had crept quietly from the bed of the maid he was currently using to make sure that there was blood on the sheets of the wedding bed, evidence that Gilbert had consummated the marriage. Gilliane had started awake when Saer pulled the bed curtains aside to let the candlelight fall upon the bed, but she had spoken soothingly to Gilbert. For a wonder, the idiot had not soiled himself with terror or curled up into a fetal position. He had reached for Gilliane—half seeking protection and half desiring to protect her. The girl was obviously having a very strong, stabilizing effect.

Saer's first instinct was to beat and torture Gilbert into idiocy again, but he restrained himself because there would be no way to hide the marks and Gilbert's screams might rouse the guests. Cursing, he withdrew. By the time he reached his own bed, however, he was smiling broadly. All his troubles were over. Gilbert's recovery would fix Saer's good intentions firmly in the minds of Neville's men. Then, as soon as Gilliane conceived and it seemed likely she would hold the child and carry it to term, Gilbert would die.

Saer knew just how he would explain the death:

Knowing his wife was bearing his bloodline, the poor cripple had felt he had the right to end his miserable existence. Then Saer could demand that Osbert be permitted to marry Gilliane to guarantee that Saer would not be ousted from his position as protector and guardian. After all, if the young widow were seized by someone else and married, that person would have the legal right to control Tarring. Saer was perfectly willing to sweeten his demand by promising to send Osbert away, even back to France, so that there would be no danger that he would hurt the Neville heir. It was the perfect solution. Neville's vassals and castellans would probably accept so reasonable a compromise, and Saer could go on being the great man of the area.

All went according to plan until King John unexpectedly died on October eighteenth. Saer had the news from a friend in Louis's force a week after the event. At first, he was delighted. It seemed to make more certain Louis's grasp on England and thus ensure Saer's own position. However, by the end of the next week, the situation began to look less hopeful. Word of the defection of men from Louis to swear their faith at Henry III's coronation began to drift through the country, and the tale of the stubborn defense of Dover and other places held for the boy king gave credence to these tales.

When Louis raised the siege at Dover, it occurred to Saer that he had better do something to impress Neville's men with his personal power. He did not think there would be a generalized rebellion among them unless Louis yielded and fled England—which was very unlikely. However, if there was a period of protracted fighting and King Henry's party approached this area, one or more of Neville's men might think that if he killed Saer he could gain control of the idiot and reaffirm his faith to the king.

What Saer must do to keep such an idea from even

entering the men's heads was obviously to clean out
the one spot of loyalty to King Henry in the immediate
vicinity. That action would serve two additional purposes—it would remove a center from which adherents
of the king could attack the surrounding French bas-
tions, and it would bring Saer himself most favorably
to Louis's notice.

The trouble was that the loyal lands belonged to that
accursed loudmouth, Adam Lemagne. A huge sense
of unease rose in Saer. Moments later, rage replaced
the unease. Before meeting Adam, he had never in his
life feared any man. He was cautious not to arouse the
animosity of men who had greater power than he, like
the Comte de la Marche, but the closest he had come
to abject terror had been the moment when he realized
he was caught in a pincer between Adam's forces.
Shame at the memory of the indecent haste with which
he had fled the field, and rage that he should have been
so shamed, overwhelmed the unease. Rage took the
place of caution, and deceived his mind by urging into
it the notion that Adam would not be on his lands. He
would have gone to swear his loyalty to King Henry.

The next day Saer's mercenaries were summoned
from their billets in the surrounding area, supplies were
wrested from the long-suffering people and, by the end
of the week, Saer was on the march. Gilliane never
thought she would regret Saer's absence, but this time
his departure frightened her. Osbert would be without
restraint. However, Saer had not been unaware of the
situation. Before he left, he took the precaution of explaining his plans again, very carefully, to Osbert—
except the part about sending him back to France—
stressing why Gilbert must be left in peace. He also
warned Osbert that he must permit any of Neville's men
to visit the keep; Saer was sure that one or more of the
men would come as soon as the news of the political
situation trickled down to them.

Saer had been perfectly correct in that assumption. As soon as they heard of King John's death and Louis's retreat from Dover, Neville's men began to wonder whether they had chosen correctly. Perhaps now was the time to shift their allegiance back to the English king. Still, Louis's men held most of the shire. Discretion seemed the better part of valor. Sir Richard decided to visit Tarring and see whether Saer seemed uncertain of the future, whether perhaps he had some knowledge of what Louis planned to do.

Most of Sir Richard's questions were answered by Saer's actions. It seemed plain that Saer did not take Louis's abandonment of the siege of Dover as a sign of retreat. If he believed that, he would have strengthened his defenses at Tarring rather than take his men out to attack. Such an action implied that Saer expected Louis to begin a new offensive directly against the young king rather than yield his position. It would not be safe, Sir Richard decided, to try to shake off Saer's influence at this time.

The decision was made easier, as Saer had hoped, by the clear evidence of Gilbert's improved condition. Although the young man did not yet recognize his father's old friend, he was obviously much stronger physically, not nearly so terrified of any male, and completely devoted to Gilliane. She, for her part, was consistently gentle and patient in dealing with her pathetic husband. To Sir Richard, it seemed that it would be a serious mistake to destroy so careful and considerate a guardian as Saer was proving himself—although Sir Richard could not manage to like the man, no matter how hard he tried.

The only mistake Saer had made was in expecting to curb Osbert's vicious tendencies by reason. Osbert had not quite broken free of his fear of his father, but he had begun to devise in his mind ways to circumvent the restrictions placed on him. Thus, the only thing that disturbed Sir Richard was Osbert. He did not like the way Gilbert whimpered whenever Osbert approached him or the way Gilliane rushed to interpose herself physically between Osbert and her husband. It was clear that Osbert enjoyed terrorizing the poor cripple and might even try slyly to hurt him. Sir Richard also did not like the way Osbert looked at Gilliane or the fact that she was alone with Osbert in the keep and had no protection from what was obviously a completely dishonorable man. Moreover, Sir Richard did not like the way Osbert spoke to him.

The rudeness was the last straw. Sir Richard chose a moment when Gilliane was alone and approached her. The widening of her lovely dark eyes and the way she braced her body were significant. Sir Richard was a firm husband and father; he had lessoned his wife and his daughter when it was necessary. However, he did not mistreat his womenfolk and they did not fear him unless they were conscious of some fault. Nonetheless, Sir Richard had seen enough women beaten for sport to recognize the signs.

"I beg you not to fear me, Lady Gilliane," Sir Richard began. "I mean you only good. I am most grateful to you for your kindness to my poor overlord."

Gilliane's face brightened. "He is much better, is he not, Sir Richard? I think the hurt to his head is healing itself slowly. Do you think, perhaps, he will recover altogether?"

"I do not know, my lady. That is in the hands of God. At first I would not have believed it possible, but now I have some hope of it—so long as no man deliberately thrusts him backward."

"I do my best," Gilliane said faintly. "And the servants help as they can. They give me warning if . . . if . . ."

"Believe me, I have seen that you do. In fact, you do more than many women would for such a husband.

I also know that in these times it is unwise to leave a keep without a man to defend it. However, I could wish Sir Saer had not chosen to leave his son."

Tears magnified and increased the brilliance of Gilliane's eyes. "I wish it, too," she whispered. "I fear . . ." She dared not finish that. "We are safe while someone is in the keep." Her face became thoughtful. "Sir Richard, if we were to have frequent and unexpected visitors, perhaps Gilbert would be left in peace, particularly if it were made clear that the visitors expected to see progress in Gilbert's health. Truly, fear does him much harm. When he is alone with me, he speaks much better and does not forget so easily."

Sir Richard looked troubled. "I will do my best to arrange it," he said, "but I am promised to take my wife to my daughter, who is near to her lying-in. I can come next week again, but after that I will be away. However, my son will be at Glynde. If you have real need of help, you can send to him and he will try to come."

"Thank you," Gilliane breathed. For two weeks, at least, she would be safe. There was no hope of escape while Osbert was in the keep, and, now that King John was dead, the value of escape was greatly diminished. Gilliane knew nothing of the men who were ruling for the boy king; she was not even certain of their names. However, Sir Richard seemed to like her and certainly he cared for poor Gilbert. Gilliane was just considering whether she dared voice her suspicion of Saer's motives when Sir Richard stopped her tongue on that subject.

"I sincerely hope that Sir Saer finishes his business swiftly and returns," he said. "You will be safe while he is here."

Gilliane bit her lip. Perhaps Sir Richard was right. All evidence pointed to the correctness of his estimate. Only Gilliane's long experience with Saer made her heart flutter with fear. She had not the thinnest, smallest shred of proof, yet she knew that Saer was planning something that boded ill for her and Gilbert.

"I hope we will be safe," she sighed. "I hope so."

CHAPTER FOUR

Saer de Cercy had good reason to congratulate himself on his accurate perception of the situation and on the speed with which he had acted. He did not waste time attacking Telsey again. He had a far larger goal in mind. He intended to take Kemp while its master was gone. The start of this project was unusually propitious. Not only was there no resistance to Saer's passage across Adam's land, but he had the good fortune to come across and capture a patrol of Adam's men who were ranging out from Telsey keep to give warning of just such an invasion as was taking place.

The capture was not without cost. The few men fought fiercely and seven of the eleven were left dead, or good as dead, on the field before the leader of the group could be captured. It seemed to Saer, when he saw who his prisoner was, that fate had decided to repay him for the indignities Adam had inflicted on him. Sir Robert de Remy's face looked out after the helmet had been removed. Saer chortled with pleasure as he thought of the revenge he would have to salve the unpleasant memories. Nonetheless, his voice was cordial when he spoke to Sir Robert.

"So we meet again."

"That is how it seems," Sir Robert replied neutrally.

He had not had an opportunity to take personal measure of this man. There was nothing in the attack upon Telsey to indicate whether or not Saer was an honorable man. The shooting of arrows at Adam during a parley hinted that there was something rotten at the core, but it could have been an accident. In any case, Adam had called the parley. Saer had given no promise to observe a truce. As far as the attack itself went, it was not dishonorable for an avowed enemy (and Saer was Louis's man) to make a surprise attack, nor for that enemy to choose the best tactical time for his attack. And it was nothing but common sense to capture a patrol that might destroy the surprise. Thus, Sir Robert could see no reason to be defiant or offensive. If Saer was an honorable man, he would imprison Sir Robert until the campaign was over, and then set a ransom for him so that he could be freed.

Sir Robert was bleeding from several small wounds. Saer eyed the red trickles for a moment and then bellowed for servants to remove Sir Robert's armor and for a leech to treat the hurts. Sir Robert was still too furious with himself for being caught to feel much relief, but Saer did seem an honorable adversary. He felt somewhat surprised when Saer began to tell him of the power he already had and of his intention of widening his sphere of influence, but some perfectly good men could not resist boasting, especially to an enemy. Since it would be impolitic to laugh in a captor's face, and stupid to increase an enemy's wariness by giving him warning, Sir Robert did not tell Saer that not only Adam but his whole powerful family would rush out to crush this invasion. He bit his tongue and kept his eyes on the ground.

Saer had no way of judging Sir Robert, either. True, he had closed Telsey and fought back, but that did not prove anything. It was entirely possible that Sir Robert hated, envied, and feared his overlord as Saer hated, envied, and feared the Comte de la Marche. Under those circumstances, especially if he knew Lemagne was close by, Sir Robert would not dare yield the property entrusted to him. However, if the man were offered protection and reward, he might be the key that opened the gates of Kemp without bloodshed, Of course, having got the gates open, the lock would be changed and the key thrown away—but Sir Robert would know nothing of that part of the plan until it was too late.

"How would you like to be a vassal instead of a castellan?" Saer asked, after a recital of his possessions and future plans had, he was sure, made Sir Robert aware of his ability to fulfill such a promise. "A vassal with far better lands than that little nothing at Telsey—a vassal holding Kemp, let us say?"

Fortunately, just at that moment the leech did something very painful to Sir Robert. His howl of outrage had enough physical pain in it, and the pain made him sufficiently breathless, to prevent him from speaking. He was able to conceal his reaction, but he could not trust himself to say what he knew must be said.

"What?" he gasped, as if pain had made him uncertain of what he had heard.

Obligingly, Saer repeated and elaborated his offer. "It will be easy and safe enough," he urged. "All you need do is ride up to the keep with fifty of my men. Doubtless they will close it when they see you because I have reason to believe Lemagne is absent, having gone to the coronation of this babe the fools intend to set up as king. That will make it easier. You have only to say that you have been summoned to bring the men to him. Or, if he is there, you can say you have come to support him because you have news that I am on the way to attack Kemp. In either case, you will be welcomed in. It will be little work then to fall upon the men-at-arms who will be unprepared and kill those who resist. Or, if you cannot take the whole keep, at least you will be able to take the towers that guard the portcullis and drawbridge. Then I can come in with the remainder of my men and we will make short work of the castle."

Sir Robert's eyes bulged. Instinctively, before reason and guile could control him, he shook his head.

"There are worse things than death that can happen to a man," Saer suggested. "I am rich now. Your ransom is nothing to me."

The personal threat was a blessing. It enabled Sir Robert to feel rage instead of revulsion. He shook his head again. "I did not mean that I refused your offer," he got out, knowing that his choked, unnatural voice would be taken for a sign of fear. After all, Sir Robert thought contemptuously, fear was what Saer would have felt, so how could he attribute any other emotion to another man? "What I meant was that it would not work."

"Oh?" Saer said suspiciously. "In what is the plan lacking?"

Truly it was not lacking in much. Sir Robert knew that it would work because he was a trusted friend. In fact, he would need no excuse for whatever tail of men he brought. On his word, Saer's whole army might have marched into Kemp keep. A weird and painful pleasure seized Sir Robert. He did not delude himself as to the final outcome. He would die. Possibly he would die in agony. He knew, however, that he would die in any case. Saer was not the man to keep a promise, particularly to someone he already knew to be untrustworthy. Thus, there was a kind of delight in tricking the trickster that made bearable the fearful sinking of his heart, a bitter satisfaction in knowing he would taste his revenge for his own agony before it overtook him.

To gain that revenge and make his own trickery successful, Sir Robert needed to make Saer believe he was unprincipled and a coward, and thus completely willing to fall in with Saer's plans. What if he were not a trusted friend but a new castellan in whom Adam did not yet have full confidence? How would Adam have reacted to such a man arriving with fifty supporters? How would Alberic, the master-at-arms, react to such a situation if Adam were absent? Sir Robert began to voice his objections to Saer's plan. They were sound objections, and Saer recognized them as such. Then Sir Robert began to make suggestions that would get around the difficulties he had fabricated.

Saer questioned and probed, but the answers he got were all obviously true. By the time Sir Robert was done, Saer was reconsidering his decision to kill the man after Kemp was taken. Sir Robert was clever in military matters. Perhaps he would be useful. There was a shadow of a smile on his lips from time to time that hinted he was enjoying the planning of his overlord's downfall.

"I see there is no love lost between you and that young upstart that rules here," Saer remarked when the plans were set and he and Sir Robert were sharing a flagon of wine.

Sir Robert's face set hard. "My feelings for Adam Lemagne are my own business," he said stiffly. "Let it be enough said that I welcome this chance to do what I am about to do."

Saer laughed. "Very well, I am content. Now I will arrange for your comfort, Sir Robert. You are wounded and will no doubt be glad of some rest before we begin our march again."

To that Sir Robert agreed gratefully. He did not know how much longer he could have maintained his pretense, particularly if Saer continued to speak ill of Adam, to whom Sir Robert had become most sincerely attached in the year he had served directly under him. Saer went out. There was no guard at the open flap of the tent nor could anyone be seen who seemed to be watching. Sir Robert grinned wryly. He was not likely to fall into so obvious a trap. He was sure there was no chance at all that he could escape. A man so given to treachery as Saer trusted no one, probably not even long-time "friends." Certainly he would not leave a prisoner unguarded, except in an attempt to trick him into some action that would betray his true intentions.

Quietly, Sir Robert finished his wine, praying that he would be able to die with dignity. Then his eyes brightened and he reached for the flagon again, poured a little more, and drank it off. There was a chance after all—not a chance to live, but a chance to die as a man should rather than screaming as he was torn apart by hot pincers or flayed alive. When Saer returned, Sir Robert wiped away the smile that had been on his lips, but he was not much concerned whether Saer had seen it. That treacherous rat would only think he was contemplating the reward he would reap for his betrayal.

In fact, Saer *was* thinking along those lines, and Sir Robert's behavior on the march confirmed his opinion that de Remy hated Adam. Temptation after temptation was offered Sir Robert. He was given a tent to himself and allowed to keep his eating knife. Instead of slitting open the wall of the tent and attempting to escape, Sir Robert went quietly to bed and, seemingly, slept through the night. The next day his own horse was brought. No one led it; no bonds were placed upon him to tie him to the saddle. When he rode out of the center of the group to the very front of the force, no one blocked his way or warned him back. But Sir Robert did not set spurs to his horse and try to escape. He rode up to Saer and pointed out the most uninhabited areas through which to travel so that there would be the least chance of warning Kemp of their coming.

Saer was delighted. It did not occur to him that keeping his army on the uninhabited grazing lands also protected the people and the small hamlets and outlying farmsteads from being harmed. Saer would never have considered the safety of such people. That night Sir Robert did not sit drinking with Saer. He said his wounds hurt and went to bed as soon as he had eaten. Saer frowned and warned those who were secretly watching to be especially alert. They were now near enough to Kemp that a man could hope to steal a horse and, if he had even a short start, outdistance pursuit to the keep. Sir Robert, however, did not stir, except twice to drink and once to piss.

The next morning the army itself did not break camp at dawn. Sir Robert, Saer, and the fifty men detailed to follow them made ready. The most trusted of Saer's captains was instructed to move the main body of the army to Kemp in as close to half an hour's time as he could judge. As they mounted, Sir Robert looked at Saer, then down at his own body, and shrugged.

"What is that for?" he was asked sharply.

"There is one thing I did not mention before, but I fear it will tell the tale. What knight in these times rides abroad without shield or weapons?"

Saer snorted. "Are you telling me I must arm a prisoner?"

"I am telling you only that the meanest man-at-arms will see that there is no shield on my shoulder, no sword by my side, no mace or ax on my saddle. Moreover, they will see me traveling in the company of a full-armed knight."

"How does it come about you never mentioned this before?"

"Because it never came into my head that you would not see that to keep me unarmed would give away the entire scheme. And what you say is true, of course. It is not a prisoner's place to ask for arms. You must decide which chance to take. I can only swear I will do my part, but I do not wish to be blamed if I am not believed."

Saer grumbled a little, but in his heart he was convinced that what Sir Robert said was true. Moreover, as he judged all men by his own nature (which is a common fault), he was greatly inclined to believe that Sir Robert lusted after the prize of vassalage he had been offered and, in addition, would be glad to do his overlord an injury if he could. There was also the evidence of Sir Robert's actions. He had had, seemingly, enough chances to escape and had not tried to do so. Finally, he was one against fifty-one. What could he do? Having warned his prisoner not to make any suspicious moves, Saer ordered that Sir Robert's shield and weapons be returned.

Sir Robert's behavior could not have been more docile on the short ride to the keep. He rode exactly where Saer told him to and kept exactly to the pace prescribed. Only at the start he kept fidgeting the strap of his shield, moving it forward and then back until Saer asked impatiently what ailed him. It rubbed on a wound, Sir Robert replied shortly, and he was seeking a position where it would not hurt him so much.

"Oh, take it on your arm," Saer growled impatiently. He was keyed up beyond belief. In fact, he could not remember being so eager and excited since he was a little boy. Revenge was indeed a very sweet and heady draught.

Sir Robert glanced at his captor and then hastily averted his eyes lest the joy in them give him away. He had not hoped for such a piece of good luck, only to accustom Saer to the movement of his shield so that he would not instantly realize what Sir Robert was doing when he finally shifted it from his shoulder to his arm. Now what he hoped for had become more possible. Not only that; now there was a small chance—very small, but real—that he would escape with his life. Trembling with eagerness, he concentrated desperately on not arousing Saer's suspicions, on doing exactly what Saer expected of him.

In normal times, visitors were very welcome to any keep. They brought news and variety of conversation to people who were too accustomed to the company they had. Even in normal times, however, the unexpected arrival of fifty armed men would have been greeted with caution. In the midst of a civil war, the draw-

bridge went up and the portcullis down, as soon as the
sentries on the walls made out the dark line moving
toward them. More men were summoned, crossbows
were wound, longbows strung. There was a slight relaxation when two knights separated themselves from the
troop and rode a little ahead. That was usually the sign
of a friendly visitor who wished to identify himself.

One knight rose in his stirrups as if to give his voice
more carrying power. "I am Robert de Remy," he
shouted, but before relief and pleasure could greet that
announcement, he had twisted his body and struck
ferociously at the man beside him with his shield. "I
am prisoner!" he shrieked. "There is an army on its
way. Shoot! In God's name, shoot!"

A good overlord breeds loyal and devoted retainers.
The people on Adam's land were not as fanatically
devoted as those of Roselynde, where the same family
had held sway for more than one hundred and fifty
years. To the serfs and villeins of Roselynde, the lord
or lady who ruled was near a god. One died and another took power, it was true, but, to the common people, they were almost indistinguishable. Male or female,
the ruler of Roselynde was the fountain of all help in
times of trouble, all punishment when evil was done,
all joy when celebration was decreed.

On Adam's land the faith was not so absolute. Simon
had conquered or purchased each of the holdings only
some fifteen years past. Before that, each had had a
varied history. Some had had many holders, good and
bad; some had fallen into decay and become subject
for sale or conquest either because the holder was de-
praved or because the holder was too mild or too im-
provident. All the people were aware, however, that
their overlords were not immutable; they came and
went. This made them less likely to rush to the defense
of any particular overlord because they knew he could
be overthrown and another take his place.

On the other hand, the people were also aware of the difference in their lives since Lemagne had come to rule them. Lemagne, father and son, and the dark man who had ruled them while the son grew from boy to man, were hard but just, and mercy and good humor tempered both hardness and justice. Thus, if the people on Adam's land could help their overlord without endangering themselves, they were glad enough to do so. When an army passed through the lands of Telsey, they did not run to give warning, as those of Roselynde would have; they fled and hid. However, after the army was gone, some brave souls crept out to see whether the keep was besieged or taken. They were greatly relieved to see all quiet there. The fields of the serfs where the army had passed had been trampled, of course, but that had done no harm because it was November and the harvest was already in. Perhaps it was their own lord's army?

That notion was eliminated when one of the men came upon the bodies of the men-at-arms who had been with de Remy. Greed warred with fear. Could the bodies be stripped and the accouterments hidden until it was safe to sell them? If such an act was discovered, torture and death would be the punishment. A faint sigh of a groan tipped the balance to caution. Hastily, the serf searched out the man still living, brought him water. Caution was soon reinforced by a safer greed. If the serf would go to the keep and tell them there to come and fetch him, the man-at-arms promised there would be a reward.

By midmorning, three messengers from Telsey were galloping toward Roselynde. Sir Robert's master-at-arms, John of Kendal, had already been disturbed when his lord had not returned to the keep for the night. It was most unusual for Sir Robert to be away without saying where he might be found in case of emergency. When he had seen what the serf had to show, John waited no longer but sent for help. Since he knew it was useless to send to Kemp, being aware that Adam had ridden west to the new king's coronation, John addressed his plea and warning to the place that was likeliest to know Adam's whereabouts.

The messengers took different routes but the first man to arrive in Roselynde was the one who had taken the most direct land route. He had valuable additional information also, because he had been fortunate enough to spot and avoid Saer's army. Thus, when he was brought into Adam's presence, he was able to tell his master that it was Kemp that was the target of the attack, as well as the fact that Sir Robert was taken—dead or alive he did not know.

Adam rose to his feet, his eyes glittering with hard gold and green sparks. Ian and Geoffrey rose with him. Alinor's face went white as whey, and Joanna bit her lip.

"Ian . . ." Alinor cried softly.

"Robert is my friend and the son of my friend. I have known him since a child. It was by my word that he was given the governance of Telsey keep," Ian said quietly, but the steel could be heard very clearly under the gentle voice.

Alinor made no further protest. She knew that nothing she could say or do would stop her husband from going to Kemp. Geoffrey limped over to place his hand on his wife's shoulder, but his eyes were on his mother-by-marriage.

"This cannot be Louis," he remarked, offering subtle comfort by assuring Alinor that Ian was not about to fling himself against a greatly superior force. "A really large army would not have passed Telsey by when it could be swallowed in a day or two and its stores taken. Nor would Louis have been in such great haste to pass without hindrance that he would leave the dead unburied."

"I think I know who it is," Adam said, and reminded

them of Saer's attack on Telsey. "He seeks revenge on me and knows that Kemp is the heart of my lands."

"How strong do you judge him to be?" Ian asked.

"He attacked Telsey in the summer and, had I not come, he had men enough to take that place. We beat him soundly, but he fled so fast when Sir Hugh and Sir William arrived that his losses were not great. If he has been planning this since then and hiring and training men, using the resources of Neville's lands for that purpose, he will surely be strong enough to take Kemp."

"But not strong enough to withstand our combined forces. However, they will take time to gather," Geoffrey put in thoughtfully. "Say it is Saer and he has half again or double the force he brought against Telsey. How long do you think Kemp can withstand him?"

"It is well supplied and full-manned. I do not fear force so much," Adam replied. "Unless a real army comes against it with real mangonels and siege towers and tools for tunneling, Kemp will hold. It is not as strong as Roselynde, but it is not an easy nut to crack, either. What I fear is that Alberic will be tricked in some way. He is a good man, loyal to me to his last breath and not stupid—but all his life he has obeyed orders. It has not been his part to watch for tricks or reason out what men will do."

Ian nodded. He had besieged Kemp himself once, when it was held by a rebellious castellan, and he knew that what Adam said of its strength was true. "It is for you to decide, Adam. Shall we call what men we can reach at once and start as soon as they arrive, or should we dare a week's delay? Even so, the men from Ealand, Clyro, and my people from the north will need to follow later."

"A week certainly cannot matter," Adam said between his teeth. "Kemp will not fall from weakness or starvation in ten times that time, and, as for falling to trickery, that would be tried first, I think, so that the damage would have been done already, even if we started today." All the good-natured laughter was gone from his face, leaving it a hard, handsome mask. "If this is Saer, he must die. I warned him to leave me and mine alone. He is the kind, it seems, that does not learn."

"I agree heartily," Ian responded. "I will go further and tell you we must take Tarring after we drive him off Kemp. I have heard that Neville's son is alive, but an idiot. Thus, anyone who takes Tarring can rule all the Neville lands in his name. That would be a very nice profit to us, and it would greatly further the purpose we spoke of the other day. Well, Alinor, what do you say?"

Relieved by the knowledge that her husband would have another week to gain strength, Alinor nodded briskly. "Yes, to take Tarring is wise, if it can be done without great loss. To kill this Saer and leave an idiot prey to any man who desires to seize him would be to leap from the pot to the coals. It is too likely that the poor creature would be taken by someone both greedy and ambitious who would only make more trouble for Adam. Besides, Simon knew old Neville. He was not a bad man. It would be a kindness to see that the son was well cared for and that Neville's vassals were well led."

Adam need not have worried about Kemp falling victim to trickery. Sir Robert's action had not only given the castle warning but had resulted in his own escape. When he roared orders to shoot, the men on the walls had obeyed instinctively. A hail of arrows flew out toward Saer's fifty men-at-arms. Several were struck, as were several horses, which reared and screamed and lashed out, spreading disorder and confusion.

Meanwhile, the stroke of Sir Robert's shield had knocked Saer half out of his saddle. More than anything in the world, Sir Robert would have liked to draw his sword and try to kill the man who had insulted him by thinking he would betray his oath of homage. However, duty was more important than the immediate satisfaction of his pride. Sir Robert knew for certain that Adam was not in Kemp, although he had neither confirmed nor denied what Saer had said, hoping that would be further evidence he was not in his overlord's confidence. It was thus Robert's plain duty to get himself into Kemp if it was humanly possible, and defend it.

Although killing Saer would have solved the problem even more effectively, there was really very little chance of succeeding in that because Saer's men-at-arms would come to his defense as soon as the first shock of surprise was over. Sir Robert struck once more with his shield, this time at the horse. The animal promptly shied and began to run so that Sir Robert was able to spur his own horse into a gallop in the opposite direction. He rode toward the wall and then along it, praying that someone would notice what he was doing and open the small postern gate that let men out to go directly to the dock down a winding road. Even a few minutes' delay in opening would seal Sir Robert's fate. Saer already had his horse under control and was shouting furious orders at his men.

It was just the opposite situation that saved Sir Robert. When the main gates were closed, no orders had been given to the men at the small gate, and the sound of Sir Robert's warning to the men in the watchtowers had not carried around the wall. The postern gate was still open as Sir Robert thundered around toward it. Hearing the horse, the men ran in and began to shut the heavy door. Desperately Sir Robert spurred his horse, pulled his feet from the stirrups, leapt off and charged right through, shouting his name so that the guards would not spit him as he came in.

The maneuver was successful at the small cost of two men bowled over and a sprained ankle sustained by Sir Robert when he flung himself out of the saddle. He did not even notice it as he rushed to help the men close the gate. They were only just in time. Barely had the bars been shot home when Saer and his party came galloping in pursuit. As the riders tore by, not even noticing the postern in their haste, Sir Robert staggered and fell, aware for the first time of the exquisite pain in his ankle, and the guards groped for the pikes they had thrown down to attend to the door.

"De Remy," Robert gasped, pushing back his helmet so the men could see his face. "Where is Alberic? One of you run for him at once."

There was another frantic half-hour, while messengers were readied to ride to Roselynde and men were sent to warn Kemp town. Sir Robert told Alberic everything he had been able to glean about Saer's force. Then he had his ankle bound and all settled down to watch and wait. They were outnumbered, of course, but, with the advantage of the protection the keep afforded, their chances of holding out until Adam came were excellent—if the messengers were able to get through. Unfortunately, that hope was denied them. The next morning five gibbets were erected just out of arrowshot of the front gates. On them were hung the pitiful remains of what had been men before they were tortured to death.

When it was sure that all the castlefolk had seen or at least heard of what had befallen their late comrades, Saer sent a herald to blare out his terms. If the castle yielded at once, all except Sir Robert de Remy would be given quarter and would be free to leave with their possessions, their families, and anything else they desired. No questions would be asked about what was taken from the keep. If, on the other hand, they resisted, all would meet the same end as the messengers, not excepting the women and children—after those had been used by Saer's army. They did not need to answer at once, the herald added. The terms would stand until the assault began.

Alberic came down from the wall where he had

listened to the terms to speak to Sir Robert. There could be no question of his loyalty, nor of the loyalty of any of Adam's men, because they were well treated and knew it. However, the capture of all the messengers was a deep psychological blow.

No one wished to yield; all were angry at the mistreatment of the men who had been captured. Nonetheless, a seed of hopelessness had been planted in the defenders and that would grow over the following days as they watched the construction of rams, scaling towers and ladders, catapults, and other machines designed to destroy or surmount the walls.

"It would have been better for us had they flung themselves upon us at once," Alberic said to Sir Robert.

"Of course, but the man is no fool, no matter how foul," Sir Robert replied. "He knows as well as you the effect of what he does. There is one thing he has overlooked, however, and this you can tell the men. Our lord will come—in no long time, either—and with an army. De Cercy has forgotten that he took me while I was on patrol. When I do not return at my appointed time, John of Kendal will send men out to seek for me. Doubtless they will find those who were killed or the signs of the passing of Saer's troops. Perhaps they will wait a day, or even two, but after that John will send direct to Roselynde. He knows Adam is not here."

Alberic's face brightened. "I had forgot that myself. I will spread the word." His eyes narrowed in thought. "I will tell them we cannot expect our lord for two weeks or a little over so that they do not grow discouraged with looking for him too soon."

"That is a good thought. Whether he comes in that time or not does not matter, because we will be engaged before then, and once the fighting starts de Cercy's offer will be void and the men will be steadied anyway. But we do not need to fear those poor devils' fates. I know Lord Ian is in Roselynde now, and Lord Geoffrey, too, most likely, because he went with Adam to the new king's crowning. I think Lord Ian and Lord Geoffrey will come with Adam when they have the news from Telsey that I am missing."

"Lord Ian and Lord Geoffrey, too?" Alberic began to laugh. "They will squash this cur like a bug if they all come together."

"Yes," Sir Robert agreed, "that will be Adam's intention. He warned de Cercy when he attacked Telsey never again to trouble him or his."

"Then de Cercy will die," Alberic said. "I will tell the archers to take care not to shoot him if he should happen to come close to the keep. My lord will be fit to eat alive any man who harms a hair on de Cercy's head until he can meet him and finish him himself."

Sir Robert nodded. "The whole shire will be a healthier place when de Cercy is gone."

Later that day Sir Robert's words were shown to be all too true. Kemp town was overwhelmed and put to the torch. The men in the keep cursed and fumed, but there was nothing they could do. To attempt to help the townspeople would merely hand the castle, as well as the town, over to Saer. More gibbets appeared, bearing ugly, noisome fruit—but that was a mistake on Saer's part. To take and loot a town was a reasonable act for a besieging army. Wantonly to kill and torture its citizens after burning and looting inspired more rage than fear in the defenders of Kemp.

Once word had been passed that their master would not remain ignorant of their need and would come, probably accompanied by his powerful stepfather and brother-by-marriage, the men-at-arms regained confidence. Over the next days they watched the construction of the machines of war almost eagerly. They wanted to lock horns with the man who had burned their haunts of pleasure and probably killed their friends and relatives in the town.

Saer pressed ahead with the construction of assault weapons in earnest, but he had depended too much on cleverness. Although the catapults had begun to fling their stones against the walls, they had done little damage by the time a patrolling guard came running to report that the dawn's light had revealed a small army of men resting in their arms to the southwest. Saer rode out at once to assay the force opposed to him. He was relieved to see that it was not very large. Even if the men of the keep came out to help their supporters, he would still have the stronger army.

His relief was not long-lasting. Before the sun had actually risen, Saer knew that he had been trapped. Other forces lay to the north and to the southeast. The besiegers were besieged, surrounded by their enemies. There was no escape. Saer gave orders to make ready to fight with a sinking heart. No heralds had been sent out from the encircling army to parley. No terms were suggested or offered. Saer at last understood Adam Lemagne's warning—too late.

CHAPTER FIVE

A little more than a week after Saer had found himself surrounded by Adam, Ian, and Geoffrey and had foreseen his death, Gilliane looked out from the walls of Tarring at the same force. Her face was perfectly calm, her voice when she spoke was low and steady. There was now no man or woman in Tarring keep who knew Gilliane well enough to realize that her large, beautiful eyes were quite empty. Gilliane had passed through the ultimate of fear and horror. She had no hope and no expectation. All that remained was a little desire to do something for the castlefolk who had always been respectful and obedient to her, sometimes even kind.

Two days after Adam Lemagne's mighty arm clove Saer from neck to breastbone, the bloody, disheveled remnant of the force he had led made its way back into Tarring keep. They came at night; they were in such terror of the monster that might be pursuing them that they had traveled only at night, hiding through the day, even after it was plain that Adam and his men were no longer at their heels. Their tale was told to Osbert—there was no one else to tell. At first his one interest was to be sure, absolutely sure, Lemagne was not close behind them. When he was certain of that, he dismissed the men who had brought him the news of his father's death with a self-satisfied smile.

As soon as they were out the door, Osbert rose and beckoned to the two men who slept in his room and truly were his own. Osbert had tried many before he found these two, and he had perfect confidence in them, in which feeling he was not far wrong at that time. The three were soul mates. It was not only the generous wage Osbert paid that made Pierre and Jean faithful but also the fact that they shared and really enjoyed Osbert's perverted pleasures. They admired him, too, although they knew him to be a physical coward, which neither of them was. Osbert had what they lacked—an active imagination. It was he who devised the "little games" that brought them delight. Neither of them, for example, would have thought of coupling with a woman tied hand and foot so that she could not struggle while her fingernails were torn out. The convulsions of her inner body added a real thrill to the process. What Osbert ordered now would not be so high a treat as that, but there was always some pleasure to be had in the terror of a helpless victim, and, since this terror would culminate in murder, the satisfaction would be enriched.

On that night Gilliane had slept quietly. Her plea to Sir Richard had not been in vain. He had remained in the keep for several days and had made clear to Osbert what he would think, and what Neville's other men would think, of any relapse in Gilbert's condition. That had been enough to keep Osbert from more than sly pinpricks for a few days, and, before he had gathered enough courage to "forget" Sir Richard's implied threat, another vassal had arrived on a visit, saying he had heard of his lord's improvement and had come to be sure nothing had set back his progress. He had also made clear to Osbert that if anything happened to Gilbert—anything at all—Osbert would be considered at fault. Gilliane needed only to keep herself and Gilbert out of Osbert's way while he was actually in Tarring to be relatively safe from persecution. Thus, she slept soundly, unaware that the life she knew had come to an end.

She was not wakened by the closure of the door to the chamber. Now that Saer was gone, the maids set to watch her often did her the courtesy of closing her door. If anything, the click of the latch sent Gilliane deeper asleep because of the sense of security and privacy it imparted. She was brought awake by a double terror—by Gilbert's shriek of fear and by the sensation of being held down and gagged by cruel hands.

Only the night candle was lit, but the room was not dark to Gilliane's eyes. She did not miss a single move of her crippled husband's struggle against Osbert and Pierre, who dragged Gilbert from the bed and thrust him, writhing and weeping, out of the window. After his first cry, his mouth had been gagged—as hers had been—but Gilliane heard the thin wail as he fell and the ugly sucking thud when he struck the hard-packed earth and died. Her horror was so great, she did not then feel afraid. In that moment of pity and grief, she would almost have welcomed being thrown out after Gilbert. Fortunately, she was given little time to dwell on what had happened.

"You are a widow now," Osbert murmured, grinning, "but not for long. Tomorrow you will be a new-wed wife again."

The hand clamped across her mouth held her so hard that Gilliane was not only gagged but also incapable of moving. Still, Osbert must have seen her answer in her eyes. She had passed beyond fear. He could beat her to death, but he could never bring her to agree. It was borne in upon him that Gilliane preferred even the crippled idiot to himself. Because of her position and the way his man was holding her, Osbert could not strike her or kick her. He drew his knife, but even as he did, he remembered that her death would also kill his expectation of succeeding to Neville's estates through marriage. Instead of bringing the blade down on her throat, he brought the hilt down on her head with all the force of his rage and his hate.

Of the next five days, Gilliane had no real memory. She had swum dizzily up toward consciousness a few times, but before she was actually able to move or speak, a bitter potion had been tipped down her throat by a hard-faced woman she did not recognize, and the world drifted away again. She had a dim awareness of being fed and once of being dressed and held upright, of her hand being taken, of something being thrust into it, her fingers held closed over that thing and moved, of her head being tipped up and down in a sign of affirmation, but all that was meaningless. There was also a recurrent nightmare of being mounted by a man and used cruelly. She had tried to fight off that nightmare, but her arms and legs would not move and her drugged tongue could not form anything but blurred, incoherent sounds.

When at last the world came into focus again, Gilliane found herself bound and gagged on her own bed, with Osbert looking down at her. Sense restored, her eyes widened and blazed with hate. Osbert laughed.

"I have a few things to tell you, my beloved wife— for you are my wife. Here is our wedding contract." He displayed a roll of parchment and flung it on the bed beside her, laughing again at the way her eyes followed it. "It is your copy. You may destroy it if you like—that will do you no good. I have a copy, too, and copies have been placed in safekeeping with the Bishop of London and in the church in the town. We were well and truly wed, and your mark, duly witnessed, has been placed on every copy. There are also unimpeachable witnesses to the fact that you were well bedded as well as wedded, so do not think you can free yourself by claiming that I have not done my marital duty."

Tears of impotent rage filled Gilliane's eyes and, for a few minutes, she struggled against the bonds that held her. Then, realizing she was merely giving Osbert pleasure, she swallowed the tears and lay still, schooling her face into a blank mask.

"I would suggest that you have that contract read to you before you destroy it. You will find that you love me so much you have been unusually generous. You have given over your property to my control during your life and, of course, made me your heir."

That information did not affect Gilliane at all. She had never considered the property to be in her control, even when she had hoped to be able to yield it up to King John. In fact, she felt a little flicker of satisfaction. Osbert was stupid. Had he behaved properly toward Sir Richard and Neville's other men, perhaps his plan would have succeeded. Instead, he had been fool enough to make those men hate him. Whether she lived or died, Gilliane knew that Osbert would get no good out of the Neville lands. Perhaps the satisfaction showed in her face, because Osbert laughed again.

"You think your Sir Richard will keep me from my own, but you are wrong. I will bring him to heel, to crawl and beg for my favor. Nor do not think to cry murder upon me and thus free yourself," Osbert continued. "No person but you saw me or my men up here before the idiot fell from the window. I was found in my bed by the guard who came to report that Neville had been discovered dead in the courtyard. So far, all believe that he, of a sudden, went mad and decided to do away with himself. His crutch was by the window, and you nearby, with your head bruised, as if he had struck you with the crutch. If you hold your tongue, it will be assumed that you were trying to save him from himself. If you begin to cry aloud of murder . . . well, who could have thrust him from the window but you? There was no one here but you. He could have struck you while trying to defend himself."

Gilliane continued to stare stonily into the distance, but her heartbeat quickened. Cry murder? One must be alive to cry murder. If Osbert was warning her against speaking out, then he did not plan her death—at least, not immediately. She did not permit her eyes to flicker toward him, she hardly dared blink lest she betray the sudden flare of hope that rose in her. If she could hold to life, then somehow, someday, she might find a way to revenge poor Gilbert and herself.

"And do not think that my father will school me for this," Osbert snarled, having again perceived something in Gilliane's expression despite her struggle to hide what she felt. "My father is dead at the hands of the monster who defeated him at Telsey cliff. The men say he is eight feet tall and cleaves a full-armed man in half as easily as one would slice a cheese. He gives no quarter. Every man except those who fled incontinent was slain."

There was such pleasure in Osbert's voice that Gilliane could not prevent herself from stealing a glance at him. She was not surprised at Osbert's pleasure in his father's death, but she was amazed at the relish with which he was describing Saer's slayer. She would have thought Osbert would be terrified because such a man as he described would very likely pursue his advantage and attack Saer's holdings after he had killed the master.

Catching her eye before she could withdraw her glance, Osbert nodded, grinning maliciously. "Oh, you hope the monster will not stop at my father but will rid you of me also—I know that. However, I am too clever to try to stem the tide. I am taking the proof that these lands are mine to Prince Louis. He will doubtless crush this Lemagne, who brays aloud like an ass that he is King Henry's man. Meanwhile, my *dear* wife will hold the keep for me."

Unable to command herself, Gilliane began to shake her head. Osbert nodded at her again, his eyes gleaming with malice.

"Oh, yes, you will hold it—or try to. I told you

Lemagne will give no quarter. If you yield, he will kill you. Once you are dead, he can rule here—or he will think he can, so you will have to die. However, if you do not yield, you will have a chance to live. Tarring castle is strong. It will withstand a heavy assault with little defense. The men-at-arms will fight because they have heard what Lemagne is from those few who escaped him. You only need hold out for a few weeks. By then, I will return. Louis will relieve the siege, and you and I, my love, will live happily ever after."

Perhaps if he had not said that, Gilliane would have considered trying to save her own life. However, Osbert's words made clear to her that either she would die anyway, as soon as he returned with Prince Louis, or, worse yet, she would live as Osbert's wife. In the past, when he had been proposed as her husband, Gilliane had occasionally thought lovingly of death. Now, when all hope was gone because he had made her his wife, she certainly would not shrink from the thought of dying. It would be far better to die than to be Osbert's wife, and if her death came at Lemagne's hands, she would, when she had expiated her sins, come to joy and peace everlasting in God's presence.

For some time the night candle had been growing paler and paler as dawn lit the sky. Osbert glanced at the window and Gilliane became aware that the room was much brighter. Fearing that Osbert would see her determination in them, Gilliane closed her eyes. Almost at once, a huge pain burst in her head and total blackness engulfed her again. The first sensation Gilliane was aware of after that was a renewal of the pain in her head, although it was more a dull ache than an explosion of agony. Then she heard a woman sobbing. At first she wondered whether the sobs could be her own. There had been many times when her own sobbing had wakened her from her dreams. But it was soon clear the sobbing came from someone else. Waveringly, Gilliane lifted a hand to her aching head.

It was that gesture that recalled Osbert's presence and what he had said because her hands were now free. Painfully, Gilliane opened her eyes and looked at the sobbing woman. It was not the stranger who had forced the evil-tasting potion down her throat but her own maid, Catrin. Gilliane looked cautiously around the room as far as she could without moving her head. It was morning now, she realized, and Catrin was the only person she could see. Ignoring the pain, Gilliane raised her head to see more fully. She was alone, except for the maid. Osbert was gone. Before she could feel relief, Gilliane remembered everything he had said.

"Are our enemies upon us already?" Gilliane asked Catrin.

The woman's breath caught and she lifted her head from her hands to stare at her mistress. "Lady?" she breathed. "Lady? Are you better?"

"My head hurts," Gilliane sighed. Then she asked, "What do you mean, better? Have I been ill?"

"Very ill. From when the late lord went mad and struck you and . . . and . . ." Her voice faltered as Gilliane's eyes widened, and she began to cry again.

"Hush, Catrin," Gilliane whispered. "I was not ill. I was drugged. Where is that woman who was 'caring' for me?"

"Dead. Lord Osbert grew angry with her yesterday and cried out that she had not kept her promise to make you well, that you were worse, and he signaled his man who, of a sudden, drew his sword and struck her down."

Gilliane shuddered. What Catrin said confirmed that Osbert had let her live only to hold the keep. In the same way he had destroyed the tool he had used to force Gilliane into marriage, he would destroy Gilliane herself when she had served her purpose. Osbert had implied that Louis would support him whether or not Tarring held out. Gilliane was not certain whether that was true, but she knew that any force trapped between a hostile castle and a hostile army would have far less chance than a force that held Tarring keep. Lemagne might indeed be a monster, another Osbert with Saer's strength and courage, but he had done nothing to her. Whatever could be done to make Osbert's life harder and increase his danger, Gilliane would do.

"Osbert's men," Gilliane asked, "where are they?"

"Gone with him and also about thirty of the men-at-arms."

"Who remains with us?"

"The wounded from Lord Saer's force and those who would not go with Lord Osbert."

"You mean he gave the men a choice and some would not go?" Gilliane asked in surprise.

The maid shrugged, cast a glance at her mistress, and then said, "Cuthbert said he would rather take his chance with Lemagne than be in Lord Osbert's service. He said also it was a shame that any man would leave so gentle a lady in her sickness and that while he could he would defend you."

Tears rose to Gilliane's eyes and flowed down her cheeks. She could not simply order the men to open to their enemies and perhaps be slaughtered like sheep. She must try to do something to save them. She was, however, still too sick and dizzy to think of anything practical. Perhaps if she washed and ate, she would feel better. With Catrin's help, this was accomplished, but Gilliane found herself so exhausted that she staggered back to bed and slept away the rest of the day. She woke to eat again, only to be so overwhelmed by panic and grief that she sent her women away for fear of infecting them with her hysteria and despair. She wept and prayed and then, again exhausted, slept.

The next morning when Gilliane woke, she was calm. She had finally found resignation. She rose and dressed and came down to break her fast in the great hall. The joy with which she was received almost broke her serenity. Life could be a sweet thing, indeed, if Osbert did not exist. Having eaten, she sent a manservant to summon Cuthbert, and she discussed with him the various choices open to them if they should be attacked by Adam Lemagne. The master-at-arms was not much help. He assured Gilliane that the men would stand by her and defend her as best they could, but he admitted that he was not fit to order the defense of a castle. He could not judge from where an attack would come, or whether it was better to ride out and assault the besiegers or wait behind the walls. Also, they were somewhat thin of men. The best he could say was that he thought they could hold out for several weeks if the army that came against them was not very large. If Lord Osbert returned with help soon, they might be safe.

Gilliane caught and held the mercenary's eyes. "I will tell you plain," she said, "that I would rather—far rather—this keep fall into Lemagne's hands than that it be given back to that . . ." She stopped herself. What Osbert had said about her accusing him of murder was true. It was safer not to plant the thought of murder in anyone's mind. She could not say that, but she could and would make her hatred plain. "He married me by force, for I was never willing. He was cruel to poor Gilbert. No matter what befalls me, if I can prevent it, Osbert will not have the use of me nor the profit of Gilbert's lands."

Cuthbert nodded. If any expression showed on his face, it was a flicker of relief. "We will as gladly defend you against him as against Lemagne, but without help, we cannot hold the keep forever."

"Not forever, not even for long," Gilliane said. "It is my thought that, however fierce Lemagne is, he would rather take Tarring at little cost than shed much blood over it. If they come, I will try to make terms with him for you and the other men to go in peace with your arms."

"And you, my lady?"

"He can do me no harm," Gilliane said quietly.

It was true, as far as she was concerned. She could only die, and that would be a happy release from a life that seemed only to heap horror upon horror. Cuthbert misunderstood his lady's despairing calm. He assumed she would be safe because she was the holder of the land and worth a high ransom. They discussed the way the terms should be made to reduce the chance of treachery and then the master-at-arms took his leave with a light heart. He had, with great misgivings, chosen to obey his conscience, and now it seemed he would save his life as well as his honor, and make a profit, too. Freed from his contract to Saer, he and the other men could take service with a new master, who would pay them again.

The next morning Gilliane was wakened to hear that the keep was encircled. This, then, was the end. She rose and dressed and even ate without haste. She felt no fear; in truth, she felt nothing at all. When a man came to tell her that a herald from the besieging force was at the walls, she rose readily and followed him to the tower. There she listened to the message she had expected to hear. The keep must be yielded; Lord Gilbert de Neville must be given over into the besiegers' hands.

"Tell him," Gilliane said to Cuthbert, "that Lord Gilbert is dead and that Lady Gilliane, Lord Gilbert's wife and heir, now holds the keep."

This message was shouted down. The herald sat for a few minutes, as if puzzled for a reply, and then, without answering, set spurs to his horse and rode hastily back to the camp from which he had come. From the wall, Gilliane saw three men converge upon him. Even at that distance, it was plain that two of the men were very large. The third, who limped, was slighter. After some talk, three horses were brought and the three men came themselves to stare up at the tower in which Gilliane stood.

It had not taken Adam, Ian, and Geoffrey long to decide that it would be as unsafe to leave a woman to be captured and used by one of Louis's men as the helpless idiot they thought they had come to take in charge. Also, there were women and women. It was a suspicious thing that Neville should have died so conveniently and so soon after Saer. Whether Neville's widow was helpless and innocent, or guilty of his murder and in need of punishment, Tarring must be taken. Now, however, they were slightly at a loss. None of them really felt comfortable threatening a woman.

"Tell your lady," Adam shouted, having been chosen as spokesman because his voice would carry best, "that for her own safety and protection she must yield to us. If there is someone in the keep who knows the ways of war, let him look out upon our numbers and our machines of war and he will see that we must conquer. We do not come for looting nor for revenge, but to ensure the future safety of our own lands by making these clean of our enemies. Thus, we cannot be bribed with tribute. The keep must be yielded."

The deep bellow, softened by distance, made Gilliane's breath catch. What had she done, she wondered, to be accursed of God? Why was the last sweet thing in her whole life, her memory of her father's voice, to be taken from her? Why should the man who would kill her speak to her in her father's voice? She could not see well through the narrow, arrow-slit windows of the tower, so she went out the door and onto the wall, Cuthbert following anxiously. From between the crenellations, Gilliane looked down. Because of the distance and the nosepiece of the helmet, she could not make out the face of the man who spoke, only that he was clean-shaven and very large.

"I am no enemy to any man," she called down. "If you leave me in peace, I will not trouble you."

The words were meaningless. Gilliane knew words would never change these men's minds. She spoke because the urge to hear that voice again was irresistible. Adam's head tilted back and he raised a hand to shield his eyes from the brightness of the morning sky. He could see little beyond the soft rose color and the flutter of a woman's garments.

"Lady Gilliane?" he asked.

"It is I. You come and say 'Yield.' Why should I? If we must die, then we will die defending ourselves. You offer me nothing that could make me wish to make your conquest easier."

"If you yield, no man will die," Adam answered promptly, "and you will be treated with honor, as befits your station."

"Those are easy words to say," Gilliane responded bitterly, "and promises made of air are cheap to give. I—"

"Not to me!" Adam bellowed indignantly. "I do not promise what I cannot perform."

Gilliane saw the other big man hastily put a hand on the speaker's arm, and the smaller man said something eagerly, his voice too soft for Gilliane to hear. Her heart sank into deadness again. They were planning some trickery. She must take care that they agreed to and did exactly what Cuthbert had outlined. She watched the men talk for a few moments more and then saw the speaker shrug and fling back his head.

"What guarantee do you desire?" he asked, and the deep voice was hard and angry.

The little core of warmth that Gilliane had carried all her life, that had sustained her through fear and loneliness and physical hurt, began to freeze and shrivel into nothingness. Calm with complete desperation and hopelessness, Gilliane began to outline the plan for saving the men-at-arms. When she had wrung agreement on that from them, she began to bargain for the safety of the castle servants. There was not much she could do for them except bind Lemagne, who had identified himself, with oaths to treat them kindly. If she could, Gilliane would have sent them out with the men-at-arms, but there was no place for them to go. No one would take them in. They would starve to death once they were cut loose from the place and people to whom they were bound.

For herself, she made no bargain. She knew that any agreement concerning her safety would be violated—Osbert had made her fate clear to her—and the coldness in the deep voice that had once signified love and safety to her confirmed the end of all things to Gilliane. She hoped, however, that the fact that she had extracted no promise concerning herself, and thus that no oath would be violated whatever they decided about her, would be an inducement to these men to honor the oaths they *had* made, which would cost them little.

To give Cuthbert and his men the greatest advantage, Gilliane dragged out the negotiations for two days. She dared wait no longer, partly because she sensed the suspicion and impatience in the besiegers and partly because she had no idea how quickly Louis would respond to Osbert's plea. Whatever happened to her, Gilliane wanted the strangers well entrenched and familiar with the offensive and defensive abilities of Tarring before Osbert and his supporters returned.

After mass on the third day, Cuthbert and his men being well and safely away, Gilliane gave orders that the drawbridge be let down and the portcullis raised. Then she went to the great hall and seated herself in the lord of the manor's great high-backed chair. She did not feel afraid, except for a hollow trembling sensation just under her breasts. In her hand, Gilliane held her marriage contract to Osbert. She did not believe that could save her, but she wished to be sure that, if she died so that Lemagne could rule Neville's lands, Osbert would be Lemagne's next target.

Adam, Ian, and Geoffrey watched the opening of the keep with wary eyes. The whole thing had been suspiciously easy. In a way, it was reasonable. If Neville was dead, it was very doubtful that his vassals and castellans would extend themselves to protect his widow, particularly if they suspected her of murdering him. Thus, the woman must know she had no chance of holding the keep for very long. On the other hand, they were accustomed to Alinor and Joanna, who would never yield an inch of land, much less a keep, no matter what the threat. Also, sending forth the small troop of men-at-arms was a very odd thing. That might have been done to lull their minds. It was not impossible that a much larger force was concealed in the keep, ready to fall upon them as they rode in, and that the troop that had ridden out had gone to get help. If their entire force came through the gates, they could be trapped in the bailey and courtyards between the keep itself and the walls while a force of rescuers, fetched by the men-at-arms who had ridden out, fell on them from behind.

"But where is the problem?" Adam asked Ian, who was expounding these ideas. "I and my men will ride in. You and Geoffrey will wait outside. The first thing I will do is make certain that we control the drawbridge and—"

"No!" Geoffrey and Ian exclaimed simultaneously.

Adam looked from one to the other, irritation mingling with affection on his face. He was Ian's "little son" and Geoffrey's "little brother." Neither could bear the thought of him springing a trap that either would gladly spring himself without a second thought.

"God give me patience," Adam sighed, grinning at them. "I am not a babe, and I will be the least loss. You both have wives . . ."

"But I will have one no longer if Joanna hears that I let you ride alone into a trap," Geoffrey protested.

"And your mother will be a widow in any case," Ian pointed out, "because she will kill me for this."

"Oh no." Adam laughed. "You cannot make headway by that path. Neither of you is going to leave *me* to face my mother and sister with the news that you were hurt or slain winning a prize for me. If you are mad enough to put all our necks in a noose at once, you can come with me, but I intend to go in and, to speak the truth, I will be safer without your company. If it is seen that we are aware of the trap and the larger part of our force is safe and free to avenge me, likely the trap will not be sprung at all."

Although they fretted and fumed and argued, it was so obvious that Adam's reasoning was correct that Ian and Geoffrey yielded at last. They made a great show of massing their men and readying them for assault, displaying the scaling ladders and devices for crossing the moat as a warning. However, nothing moved on the walls that they could see. The drawbridge lay quiet, the portcullis did not quiver as if it were being held aloft to be dropped suddenly. Adam rode in at the head of his men. Their shields were ready on their arms, their swords bare in their hands.

All that met them was an unearthly quiet. No servants scurried about in the bailey and yards. No voice called to them. As soon as they were within, men leapt from their horses and rushed into the towers where the winches were that controlled the drawbridge and portcullis. The doors opened at their touch. The towers were empty. They raced up the stairs and out upon the walls. Those were empty also.

When the party from the left tower met the party from the right, a man rushed back to call down to Adam that all was clear. He, meanwhile, had charged the forebuilding with another group. Here, too, the door yielded to a touch. All was empty. Adam returned to the bailey, swallowing an ugly feeling of discomfort. It was like a place of the dead, or rather, a place under an evil enchantment. Cattle lowed gently in pens somewhere in the background. In the kitchen courtyard, one could hear the crackle of the cooking fires, but no single human voice or footstep aside from their own came to them. He sent a man out to summon Ian and Geoffrey. Whatever there was in this keep to fear, it was not a surprise attack.

After Adam's messenger had recounted what he had seen, Ian and Geoffrey left their men outside and rode in alone. If Adam's troop held the towers and walls, their men could come in any time. By the time Ian and Geoffrey entered the bailey, the eerie emptiness had had its effect on everyone within. Adam's men held their arms ready and watched warily on all sides for they knew not what; their voices had fallen into silence.

Ian and Geoffrey dismounted and, with Adam and a few men-at-arms at their backs, they entered the forebuilding, climbed the outer stair, and walked into the great hall. There they stopped and stared. The hall was as empty as the rest of the keep. All alone in a great chair by the hearth sat one young girl. So surprised that they forgot to sheathe their weapons, the three men advanced upon her. Slowly, she rose to greet them, one hand gracefully on the arm of the chair and the other clutching tight a roll of parchment.

"What the devil are you doing all alone in this place?" Adam roared, hurrying forward.

He could not remember being so uneasy in his life as he had been that half-hour he waited in the silent bailey. It was clear to him that the power that had engendered the silence was in this woman, and he was furious at being frightened half out of his wits by a slip of a girl.

"Adam, be still," Ian said sharply. "The poor child has enough to bear without you shouting at her."

Then Adam saw that the hand resting on the chair held so hard to it that the knuckles were white and the parchment was fluttering against the girl's skirt with her trembling. That she was frightened made Adam a little remorseful, but no less wary.

"I beg pardon, Lady Gilliane," Adam said more softly, and then doubtfully, "You *are* Lady Gilliane?"

"I am." The voice was low but only a little tremulous.

"Perhaps I should not have spoken so sharply," Adam continued, "but I still desire to have my question answered. Where are the castlefolk? Why are you all alone?"

"I am here alone so that you may do what you will with me and not need to . . . to stop the servants' mouths to keep your secret. You may tell them I was taken for ransom or any tale you will, and so they will serve you willingly and be safe."

"What the devil did you think we were going to do?" Adam bellowed, losing his temper again.

"My poor child," Ian said softly, moving toward her. Then he stopped, realizing he was still carrying his naked sword in his hand. He sheathed it hurriedly. "You are perfectly safe, both your person and your honor, I assure you."

But Gilliane's eyes did not move to examine the man who offered her that kind assurance. She stared at the owner of the voice that had lived in her memory as a symbol of love and now roared threats.

"Do sit down again, Lady Gilliane," Geoffrey urged, also sheathing his sword and tapping the hand in which Adam held his weapon to bring it to his attention. Geoffrey was ready to be polite, but he was less soft-hearted than Ian and wished to be sure he was not confronting a clever murderess before he offered promises of safety and support.

Adam also put up his sword and then cleared his throat uneasily. He was suddenly aware of Gilliane's beauty and of her youth. "I beg pardon again," he rumbled, "but I do not like to be thought a liar. I passed my word you would be treated with honor. Why should you think we planned your hurt?"

Naturally, Gilliane could not say that she had been given good reason through most of her life never to trust anyone. There was thus no answer she could make, so she merely stared. Uncomfortable under the steady gaze, Adam pushed off his helmet and unlaced his hood. Gilliane's eyes widened when she saw how young he was—and how handsome. This was no monster, she realized; this was the knight of her dreams, deep-voiced, giant-big—and he was forever beyond her reach. He believed her to be an enemy. It was the monster to whom she had been in thrall most of her life who made Adam Lemagne her enemy. It was the monster to whom she was married who told her Adam Lemagne would harm her.

Until that moment Gilliane had been totally unself-conscious. When one fights to keep abject terror under control, little things like the fit of one's gown or a smudge on one's nose are of no importance. Manners become insignificant when one faces death. It is suffi-cient if there is strength enough to maintain dignity. All at once Gilliane took in the fact that she was *not* going to die—at least, not immediately. With that understanding, the freezing despair that had blocked all lesser things melted. Then came a huge roiling mix-ture of all the thoughts that she had subconsciously suppressed, most of them utterly silly. Gilliane remem-bered with a horrible sinking feeling that she had not combed her hair that morning and, worse yet, she had not ordered any dinner to be prepared.

CHAPTER SIX

No dinner! The ultimate sin in a woman's household lexicon—and three noble guests to feed. When fear of death is conquered, lesser fears take hold. Gilliane uttered a faint squeak of dismay and looked wildly around for the servants. As she remembered that she had told them all to hide, her hand was taken and held gently.

"We mean you no harm. Truly, we do not," a mellow voice comforted.

Gilliane looked up and gasped. Never in her life had she seen so beautiful a face on a man—and kind! The eyes were luminous with warmth, the mouth tender in spite of a stubble of beard.

"We know that to de Cercy we were enemies, but we do not make war on innocent women. If you have done no wrong, you will be safe."

That voice was lighter, a pleasant tenor. Gilliane turned her head to examine the third man. He was smaller and slighter and not as handsome as Adam Lemagne, but the light-brown eyes that stared somberly at her were very keen. There was a faint stress on the words *innocent* and *no wrong* that had some dangerous meaning, Gilliane guessed, but her overriding concern was still the lack of dinner.

"And I *still* want to know where the castlefolk are," Adam insisted, a bare tinge of anger in his voice.

As a magnet is drawn to a lodestone, Gilliane's eyes came to Adam as soon as he spoke. Geoffrey raised his brows. Adam must be warned. The girl was a real beauty, yet different enough from both Alinor and Joanna that she might be especially attractive to Adam. If she was an innocent victim of circumstance, that might be a good thing, especially if she really was the heiress of Neville's property. However, if she was a clever murderess, it would be a disaster for Adam to be entrapped by her. Adam was as passionate and headstrong as his mother, and Geoffrey feared that once his affections became fixed, he would be as tenacious.

"They are below—the men—and the women are in their quarters above. And I must fetch them at once," Gilliane said breathlessly, finally answering Adam's question.

Adam blinked. "At once? Why the sudden need for servants in haste? You were bold enough to meet us all alone. There are other things more important . . ."

Suddenly in the wake of the enormous relief of knowing she would live, Gilliane was swept with irritation. There were always things more important to a man than the preparation of dinner, but if the meal was not perfect and served exactly when that same man desired it, it was the woman, who had been told there were more important things to do, who was beaten. At that moment it did not seem significant to Gilliane whether she was beaten now for insolence or later for inefficiency. At least she would have the satisfaction of speaking her mind, since either way she would be beaten.

"There may be more important things to you, my lord," Gilliane said, "but for me, who is responsible for dinner, setting the servants back to work—"

"You must be mad!" Adam exclaimed. "First you accuse me—without the slightest cause—of desiring to murder first you and then a whole castle full of people to conceal my crime, and now you begin in the middle of yielding a keep to babble of dinner. Is this a time to be thinking of dinner?"

"If you wish to eat it before it is totally dark, it certainly is," Gilliane retorted smartly.

Ian burst out laughing and even Geoffrey smiled, although his eyes were still wary. Gilliane, who had tensed with fright a moment after the sharp retort passed her lips, stared with amazement at the three faces that confronted her. Adam looked bewildered, Ian and Geoffrey amused. Certainly none of them were angry at her sauciness. The breath she had held trickled out slowly.

"Both of you are so very right," Ian said, "that I scarcely know with which to agree. I cannot deny that I would very much like a decent meal at a rational hour. Your household at Kemp, Adam, leaves a great deal to be desired, and I am tired of food little better than that of a camp served any which way at any time someone remembers to ask for it."

Adam shrugged his shoulders. "Oh, very well. I bow to the immediate needs of your bellies, or the next thing I will be accused of is starving my father and brother apurpose. By all means, Lady Gilliane, summon and set the servants to work—but do not forget to return to us here."

She did no more than curtsy before she hurried away to start the life of the castle again. She now realized Osbert had lied about Adam's desiring her death. Had he also lied about Adam's desire to swallow the lands? But if Adam did not desire the lands, what *did* he desire? When he found that Osbert and Saer between them had stripped the castle of everything of value, every jewel, every mill of money, even every decent horse and piece of cloth, would he simply go away, leaving her at the mercy of her husband?

Gilliane never noticed that she had begun to think of the "monster Lemagne" as "Adam." It was impossible to think of that very young, mobile face with any sense of formality. Contorted by rage, Adam's face might be fearful; softened by love . . . Gilliane wrenched her mind away from that. She was married, and besides, he must have his choice of any woman he desired. He would never look at her. Still, it was not possible for her to feel a sense of distance. Adam's expression, when he was not angry, was very open and . . . and . . . friendly.

In fact, Gilliane was so far wrong about the fact that Adam would never look at her that Ian and Geoffrey were watching his eyes follow her to the stairwell with feelings of considerable trepidation.

"Adam," Ian said sharply when Gilliane had disappeared, "you have promised to treat the girl with honor."

"What?" Adam murmured, pulling his eyes away and looking at Ian in a slightly bemused way.

"Lady Gilliane is your captive. I am no longer your master, my son, but I hope you do not intend to shame my teaching or Robert of Leicester's by forcing your attentions on her."

"Force!" Color rushed into Adam's face. "No! How can you—"

"Adam," Ian repeated reprovingly, "you know I do not mean you would knock her down and rape her, but . . . for God's sake, you are a most desirable man, you know that. The girl is under your hand. You must *not* set yourself to win her into your bed."

"Ian," Geoffrey remarked, "has it entered your mind that Adam might not be the seducer?"

"Oh, come now," Ian began to protest.

"Listen to me," Geoffrey insisted. "Lady Gilliane had every reason to believe Adam was the leader among us. He parlayed with her from the wall. He spoke first when we came upon her in the hall. Although Adam did say we were his father and brother, that was afterward. Did you not notice that she looked nowhere but at Adam at first?"

"Well, if I were a young woman, I would look at Adam also," Ian pointed out merrily.

"Nonetheless, we must not forget the other possibility, either," said Geoffrey, "—that Lady Gilliane *murdered* her crippled idiot husband the moment his protector was dead, and that, having been forced to yield to our superior force, she intends to win her freedom from us by trickery."

Adam flushed bright red, but his angry protest was drowned in Ian's explosive "Nonsense!"

Geoffrey shrugged. "I hope it is nonsense, but I beg you to consider what this girl has already accomplished. She has sent out from this keep a complete troop of men-at-arms, fully armed and horsed, scot free. She has saved every one of her servants even one bruise—for doubtless some of our men would have been carried away by excitement and struck at the servants if they were about the keep when Adam entered. On top of that, she has made us all feel—I also, I freely admit—that we are brutes and monsters to threaten and frighten one poor, helpless, defenseless girl."

"But you cannot fault her for wishing to save her servants hurt," Adam said quickly.

"I cannot fault her for *anything* she has done," Geoffrey replied impatiently. "If Lady Gilliane's only desire is to protect herself and her servants, she has acted with great wisdom. I only ask you to consider how many women would dare meet a whole army all alone, without even a few women servants to be thrown to the invaders if needful? Such resolution argues a very strong spirit."

Ian shook his head. "I do not believe it. That the girl has courage and wisdom is plain from her actions, but that she is a murderess and plans some betrayal . . . it was not in her face."

Adam thought of Gilliane's face and experienced a most peculiar sinking sensation. It was such a lovely face, heart-shaped and dominated by huge dark eyes

framed in long, curling lashes. Could that tender mouth
with its soft, rosy lips have spoken nothing but lies?
Adam loved Ian deeply and had an enormous respect
for his military abilities and perceptions, but he knew
that Ian was not always the best judge of people. He
was so soft of heart that he saw only the best in everyone. On the other hand, Geoffrey had the keenest mind
Adam knew. He was almost never at fault in his estimation of character or purpose.

"Do you really believe Lady Gilliane murdered her
husband?" Adam asked rather harshly.

Geoffrey frowned at him in a worried way. "To
speak the truth, I find it most hard to believe that. If
she were not a woman, I would say that eyes, voice,
and manner spoke of a brave soul facing the inevitable
with great courage and honesty."

"There, you see," Ian said with satisfaction.

"Wait," Geoffrey interrupted. "Ian, think how often
you have been cozened by Alinor into doing what you
had no intention of doing. The ability to mask the
truth is a woman's best weapon. Remember that our
good and Lady Gilliane's good are *not*—to her mind,
at least—the same."

"Does that make her a murderess?" Adam asked.

"No! I am not really accusing the poor girl of anything. I am only trying to warn you that a sweet face, a
soft voice and manner, do not really spell compliance
or innocence in a woman. I only wish to say that she
must be watched. For God's sake, Adam, you have
laughed at me often enough for being, as you say, enchained like a slave by Joanna's thinnest hair. At least
I know that Joanna and I have the same end purpose,
even if we might go about achieving it in different ways.
Do not permit yourself to be similarly enchained by a
woman who seeks a different end from yours."

"I have no intention of being enslaved by any woman," Adam replied indignantly.

"One never does," Ian remarked dryly. "Often one

does not *intend* to love at all. Geoffrey is right there. Lady Gilliane is a very beautiful woman. I warned you not to take advantage of her helplessness. Be careful, also, that you do not permit her to use her helplessness as a weapon against you."

As Ian spoke, they became aware that the keep was no longer empty and silent. Sounds from the stairwell indicated that servants were coming up to cross over to the stairs that would take them down and outside. Geoffrey started hurriedly to go out also and make sure that the waiting men-at-arms holding the walls and courtyards did not think this was the start of an attack. Ian and Adam saw him stop and exchange a few words with Gilliane, who then came across toward them. She was still holding the roll of parchment that had been in her hand when they came into the hall. This she offered to Adam. She was trembling again and looked little less frightened than when they first discovered her.

"I have yielded the keep," she said rather breathlessly, "and you hold it now, but I am not sure that it was in my right to yield it."

Adam smiled grimly. "It is a little late to think of that now. We are within, and, unless this is a far stranger place than any I have ever seen, or you have discovered how to make armed men invisible, you have no way to put us out."

Gilliane looked at him, then dropped her eyes. "I have no desire to put you out," she said softly.

Color stained Adam's face. He lifted his hand, as if to touch her, but the roll of parchment she had given him frustrated that intention. There was a brief silence as Adam recognized what he had been about to do and reminded himself that perhaps Ian's and Geoffrey's warnings were not very wide of the mark.

"What is this you have given me?" he asked, avoiding any comment on what Gilliane had said.

"It is my marriage contract," Gilliane replied, her distaste plain in her face and voice.

Of course it was not surprising that she had taken no pleasure in being the wife of a feeble-minded cripple, but Adam wished that her repugnance had not been tinged with hatred. He had heard from common friends that young Neville had been a pleasant, decent man before the wounds that reduced him to helplessness had been inflicted. To Adam, it seemed Neville was more deserving of pity than hate; however, for a woman faced with a whole life bound to such a wreck . . .

"There is no need to prove your right," Ian remarked, interrupting Adam's thought. "It is not a sensible thing to lie about because the truth would very soon come to light."

"Not my marriage contract with poor Gilbert," Gilliane said, her voice shaking and her eyes suddenly full of tears. She made an effort and steadied herself. "Saer never gave me or showed me that. Perhaps it is among the other documents. That which I gave you"— she choked and again there was hatred in her voice— "is the contract of my marriage with Osbert de Cercy."

"You were not a widow long," Ian said, and he looked cold and hard for the first time.

"No," Gilliane agreed, very low, but then she looked up again—only her eyes sought Adam's, not Ian's. "But it was not by my will. I was forced. I hate Osbert de Cercy."

A whole series of emotions of increasing intensity passed through Adam. First there had been a mild pleasure and relief when Gilliane spoke so gently of "poor Gilbert." Then came shock and, for some reason Adam did not wish to consider, rage at the realization that Gilliane was not a widow. The rage was colored by an immense disgust when Ian's remark made the situation all too clear. Gilliane's last statement, that she was forced into her second marriage and hated her husband, brought an even more inexplicable burst of joy. That feeling was so strong that Adam recoiled from it. It should not matter to him whether Gilliane was married or not. He had taken Tarring to preserve the peace on his own lands and to forward the cause of King Henry, not to play games with a pretty girl.

"It makes no difference," Adam said harshly. "We are here, and here we will stay. Possession," he sneered, "is nine points out of ten in any court of law—and in these times, the man with the strongest arm *is* the law."

Gilliane had heard the change in Ian's voice, had seen the emotions flickering on Adam's expressive face. An enormous bitterness flooded her. Without even being there, Osbert had again inflicted hurt. Gilliane was very clever at reading expressions and inflections. She knew what the men were thinking—Osbert had not lied about that. They were wondering whether she had done away with her useless hulk of a husband and grabbed the first male available to take his place. Or, even worse, whether Osbert had been her lover all along and they had waited only to be free of Saer so that they could murder Gilbert and make their union official. She did not care what the man called Ian thought, but the look on Adam's face was unbearable.

"You need fight no point of law with me," Gilliane said bitterly. "From what I was told, the lands were yielded to Osbert in that contract anyway. As to your possession, Satan himself would be more welcome to me in this place than Osbert."

It was a great sin, Gilliane knew, for a woman to criticize or show repugnance for the most monstrous of husbands. It was a woman's place to marry whom she was told to marry and to accept any treatment meted out by the man to whom she had been given. Therefore, she expected the anger and disapproval on the faces of the men to deepen. Perhaps she had gone too far this time and would be beaten. It did not matter. Nothing mattered but the look of revulsion on the face of the man whose voice had been the foundation of all her dreams. Amazingly, however, his expression did not darken. If anything, it cleared somewhat. The eyes were wary, but the sick disgust was gone.

To Adam, who had grown up in a household where a woman possessed and ruled her own lands, whose mother was violently tenacious of her right and her possessions, Gilliane had virtually proved the truth of her statement that her marriage was forced by her bitterness. Her remark about yielding the lands in the contract was, to Adam, clear evidence that Gilliane could not have been willing. Of course, the desire to possess the land did not exonerate her from suspicion of having murdered the man who originally owned it. If anything, the possessiveness rather increased the possibility that Gilliane was a murderess. However, for some reason, that did not trouble Adam much—not nearly so much as the idea that she had rushed from her husband's bier into the arms of a waiting lover.

Instead of being relieved by the relaxation of suspicion she perceived, Gilliane was further distressed. These were men such as she had never met before. Though she was utterly in their power, they had neither threatened nor struck her. From their expressions, they even seemed to believe that she had not welcomed the marriage with Osbert. Now she must renew their distrust by seeming to threaten them. Clasping her hands nervously, she said, "I must tell you something more. You will be angry, but I cannot help it. When Osbert left here four days ago, he said he would go to Prince Louis and that the prince would come here or send a force to destroy you and take back the keep."

Again the reaction she got was totally foreign to Gilliane's experience. Adam burst out laughing. "God should so favor us," he exclaimed, and when he was finished laughing, he looked hopefully at Ian.

Ian smiled also, but before he could speak, Gilliane heard the third man, the one called Geoffrey, approaching with his odd, uneven gait. "Geoffrey," Ian called, beckoning, "Lady Gilliane tells us that Osbert de Cercy has gone to bring Louis down upon us."

The keen golden eyes flashed to Gilliane. "How did he know we were coming?"

"Those who fled away from Saer's army returned here. What they told him, I do not know. I was . . ." Gilliane hesitated. She was afraid to bring up Gilbert's death. Whenever she mentioned it, the expressions of the men broadcast danger. "I was not myself for near a week. All I know is what I have told you."

"And why have you told us?" Geoffrey asked pleasantly.

"It does not matter why Lady Gilliane has told us," Adam put in impatiently. "What is important is whether or not it can be true."

There was a silence while the men looked speculatively at Gilliane. The warning might merely be a device to frighten them away or it was intended to keep them in Tarring. The last was the likeliest reason, but the purpose behind Gilliane's desire to have them stay was not so clear. It was possible that keeping them in Tarring would forward some purpose of Osbert's or Louis's elsewhere in the country. Their eyes moved from Gilliane to one another, but what they wanted to say could not be said in her presence.

"One thing I can assure you," Geoffrey remarked, "is that there is no present danger to us in the keep. The only men acquainted with the use of arms are too few and too badly wounded to do anything."

"And as for your question, Adam," Ian added, "whether or not it is true that Louis will come, he will certainly not come today. So, since we are safe here, we might as well take our ease." He turned and bowed to Gilliane. "I do not wish to be offensive, Lady Gilliane, but we are now resident in this keep. We would, of course, prefer that you regard us as guests. Might I ask you, then, for refreshment and to see that chambers are readied for us? We would enjoy your company, if you will be so good as to favor us with it. However, I do not wish you to feel that we demand your service. If our presence is offensive to you, you may withdraw to the women's quarters."

Color flooded up Gilliane's throat and into her face. Her hand fluttered to her lips. "Oh, do pardon me," she gasped, realizing that although she had made arrangements for dinner, she had neglected every other duty of a hostess. "Indeed, I will see to your comforts at once. I am a little overset by what has happened today."

"As well you might be," Ian agreed kindly. "There is no blame to you, but the worst is over now, so let us see if we cannot come to a more ordinary way of life."

Hardly able to believe her good fortune, Gilliane hurried away to give directions to the maids to strip and air Saer's and Osbert's beds and to set up again the one Sir Richard had used. Although she did not really expect that this pleasant situation would last, she was accustomed to snatching at brief joys and pushing future fears into the background. Perhaps the kindness with which she was being treated was only some type of pitfall. If it was, Gilliane did not wish to think about it. She had spoken and acted nothing but the truth in every matter except Gilbert's death, so there was no trap into which she could fall. It was senseless to worry about problems completely beyond her knowledge and experience. For as long as circumstances permitted, Gilliane would be happy.

"Do you think she knew we wished to be rid of her?" Ian asked.

Adam could feel himself flushing with indignation on Gilliane's behalf, and he bit his tongue to restrain a hot denial. Each time he spoke to her it seemed more certain to him that she was as guiltless and guileless as she was beautiful. The very strength of his feeling made him uneasy, so it was with considerable relief that he heard Geoffrey make the denial for him.

"I doubt Lady Gilliane has been treated with much subtlety by de Cercy—father or son." Geoffrey's expression became thoughtful. "In fact, I doubt she has been treated with much courtesy. It seems to me that it might be no hard thing to win her to our cause."

"Win her?" Adam questioned. "You heard what she said about de Cercy—he forced her and she hates him. She must be ours already. It needs only—"

"Women—" Ian and Geoffrey began together. Both stopped and Ian went on alone, being the better authority on the subject. "Women believe that only the end of the matter they desire is of import. The means a woman will use to gain her ends would turn a man's hair white. There is *no* honor in them, and right and wrong are what will best or least forward their purpose."

"It is true, Adam," Geoffrey emphasized. "You must remember it. Not that they are to be blamed for it," Geoffrey added fairly. "What can a woman do? Can she challenge you to meet her body to body . . ."

Adam and Ian began to laugh. "That, yes," Ian said, grinning. "It is a challenge few men can resist or come away from victorious."

"Very well, you may laugh," Geoffrey said defensively, "but that, too, is something to be guarded against. As you say, it is very hard to deny a woman what she asks at such a time."

"You manage to do so," Adam remarked, knowing that what Joanna wanted was for her husband not to ride to battle.

Geoffrey shook his head. "I wish I could take such credit, but I cannot. I can only thank God that Joanna loves me enough not to wring from me promises that would break my heart in the keeping."

"That is the very point," Ian urged. "Love is all to a woman. She will tear out her own heart, sacrifice her body, lie, see a whole country go up in flames, all to serve her love. If Lady Gilliane does love this Osbert, she would think nothing of saying she hated him, of blackening his name and betraying his honor by coupling with you, me, Geoffrey, the whole troop—if she thought it would serve him."

Adam said nothing. His eyes were all dark, the green and golden light that normally brightened them quenched.

"But I see no proof of the matter one way or the other," Geoffrey said. "From what we know of the older de Cercy, he was a crude, treacherous brute. A man grows the way he is trained and led. It is not unlikely that the son is no better than the father was. Thus, Lady Gilliane might well have spoken the truth. Unfortunately, women are peculiar. I have known some who seemed only able to love those who abused them shamefully. Still, I tend not to think that of Lady Gilliane. She fired up finely over that matter of ordering dinner, and there is a spark in her eyes that leads me to believe she does not enjoy being ill-used."

To his own irritation, Adam's heart leapt at Geoffrey's speech. It was ridiculous that he should not be able to control his own feelings. It was even more ridiculous that such feelings should be centered on a girl he had seen for the first time—aside from that glimpse on the wall—only an hour or so before, and who was already tied in marriage. His father and brother had been quite right to direct their strictures at him. Probably they had seen in his expression the effect Gilliane had had upon him. Probably she had seen it, too! Damn her! Well, he was warned now. No matter how his unruly heart sank or leapt, he would guard against falling into any trap she might lay.

CHAPTER SEVEN

Adam turned his globet of wine and watched the torch-light play on the dark surface. Alberic had fallen respectfully silent when he saw his young master lost in thought. That was something new about Adam that Alberic had noticed only since they had come to Tarring and Lord Ian and Lord Geoffrey had left. It was common enough for Adam to join his men-at-arms in the evening when he had no noble company. He was no reader, and, unless minstrels or players came to the keep, there was nothing for a man to do if he had no lady with whom he could talk, play chess, and then bed. Adam was a convivial soul who took no pleasure in isolating himself in order to appear remote and godlike to his men. They were quite sufficiently impressed with his power and ability without that. If nothing more important drew his attention, Adam gambled with them, listened to their tales, and told a few warm stories of his own.

In Tarring, he had followed his usual custom, only waiting until Lady Gilliane had retired to the women's quarters, but Alberic noticed that his master laughed less and often slipped into thoughtful silence. Another thing Alberic noted with surprise was that Adam had not taken any woman to his bed since they had entered Tarring. For the first few nights this abstinence had not surprised the master-at-arms. Adam never forced an unwilling woman and he always waited, when they had taken a place by force, until he could tempt a girl to come to him eagerly and without fear. Then, too, Lord Ian and Lord Geoffrey had been in the keep. Alberic had heard that neither of them ever meddled with women. He thought that might have exerted a restraining influence on his master. But Lord Ian and Lord Geoffrey had been gone for near a week, and still Adam was sleeping alone.

The thoughts of master and man were not far divided. Although Adam was not thinking about his unusual state of continence, he was thinking about Ian's and Geoffrey's departure and about one woman in particular. Gilliane remained a puzzle, and a puzzle that needed urgently to be solved. Everything had run smoothly in her favor at first. When Gilliane had returned from seeing rooms made ready for them, she had lost much of her nervousness and appeared more like an eager hostess, ready and willing to enjoy pleasant company, than a victim of conquest. She began to show a charming, playful wit, a delicate, mischievous sense of fun; her eyes were bright and a soft rose warmed her dark skin so that she seemed to glow from within. Adam found it increasingly difficult to look at anyone or anything else while Gilliane was within his view.

By the fourth day there, the question of why she was glad to have them had become more doubtful. Soon after vespers, a tired messenger had come pounding in from Roselynde bearing news and a warning. On the day after St. Martins, Louis had finally begun to move. He had besieged Hertford. Ian and Geoffrey promptly made plans to go north to Hemel, which was only about twenty miles from the scene of the action. Because it was the habit of the French, who considered themselves to be in a hostile country, to live off the land, the immediate area of Hertford would soon be stripped of supplies. Then raiding parties would move further and further afield, and finally, they might easily begin to raid Geoffrey's land.

When Gilliane had heard the news and saw the preparations for departure, the light had died out of her eyes and the color had faded from her face, leaving the skin sallow. Adam remembered the scene that had followed vividly. It replayed itself now in his mind.

"Will you leave me defenseless here to be taken by any passing force?" Gilliane had cried. "Will that ensure the peace of your lands? Even if I were a man and knew how to defend this place, there is hardly a man trained to arms in it. How——"

"You need not fear for that," Adam remembered interrupting her. He also remembered how furious he had been that the appeal had been made to Ian. "I am quite capable of defending this place without my father's overseeing."

"You mean you will stay here, my lord?"

As vividly as if she were standing before him at the moment, Adam recalled the emotions that had sped across Gilliane's face when she spoke. First her eyes had lit and her color had come back. Then she had grown pale again and her expression was frightened. Hard on the heels of that, blood had flooded into her face once more until she was blushing so hard that she did, indeed, look like a dusky rose. At that point Gilliane had mumbled something about being content so long as she was safe, had excused herself and fled. Adam turned the goblet in his hands again and tilted it so that the torchlight glowed on the ripples he created.

Wondering again what Gilliane's reactions had meant sent Adam's mind further back to the day they had arrived when they had been discussing whether her declaration that she had been forced into marriage and hated her husband was true. Adam found himself very reluctant to think about that, but it was all mixed up together. He remembered himself protesting at the time, "What we need to know now is whether or not Louis will give de Cercy the help he asks for, or even come himself—if she spoke the truth and that is where he has gone."

"Where else could he go?" Geoffrey asked.

"To Neville's vassals," Ian responded promptly.

Geoffrey smote his forehead in exasperation at his own stupidity and Adam nodded, although he felt a little sick. If Osbert had gone to gather Neville's men to defend or take back Tarring, Gilliane might have said he had gone to Louis to throw them off their guard. Louis would be much slower of response than the local vassals and castellans. To warn them of a future threat might result in present carelessness. Swallowing his reluctance, Adam voiced these thoughts.

"It is not impossible," Ian agreed, "but would the girl understand such matters?"

"There is no way to judge that except by the result," Geoffrey had remarked. "If within the next week or two Neville's men come, we will know."

"We will know that de Cercy went to them, but will that prove anything?" Adam could not help asking.

There was a brief silence. "Nothing proves anything with a woman," Geoffrey had replied at last, "but that is partly because a man will believe what he desires to believe about her, despite any facts."

Adam uttered an exclamation of irritation and swallowed the wine he had been toying with in three long gulps, gestured to Alberic to stay comfortably where he was, and went off to bed. He did not think he was lying to himself about the facts, but he was by no means sure. There was nothing for it but to question Gilliane directly and see whether he could startle or confuse her into exposing her true purpose.

Adam undressed slowly. He had refused Gilliane's service and that of her maids, even though the eyes of some of the younger ones had promised as complete a service as any man could wish. Gilliane would know if one of her women was taken into Adam's bed—the thought appalled him—and to have Gilliane herself in attendance would only confuse him further, Adam knew. In fact, he had been avoiding her as completely as possible during the five days since Ian and Geoffrey had left.

Exasperated, Adam tossed the shoe he was holding in his hand at the wall with such force that it bounced back and hit him. Gilliane's reaction to his avoidance was something else he could not understand. At first she had seemed in total agreement—that is, she had been as assiduous to avoid him as he to avoid her. When they met unexpectedly she had blushed furiously and withdrawn without a word; when they were forced into company by convention as at mealtimes, she had been pale and silent, sad, very unlike the girl who had blossomed in Ian's and Geoffrey's company. For two days they had dined together in nearly absolute silence. Then, this afternoon, Gilliane had come to dinner with a high color. She had initiated a conversation that had seemed innocent enough, mostly concerning Adam's family, but in the end, it had come around to his oath to King Henry.

At the time it had seemed perfectly natural. Adam had explained the political situation, waxing enthusiastic over the hope for a permanent peace between the barons and the king provided by Magna Carta. Gilliane listened in a rather puzzled way, asking whether it was not better to have a strong king who could protect his vassals than a boy constrained by rules that might not fit every case. Adam had pulled out the stops in a discourse on unrestrained power and to what it could lead, which Gilliane countered by raising questions about anarchy and its abuses. She did not use any of the technical words; indeed, when Adam used them, she had to ask him to explain what they meant, which lent a pretty air of childish innocence to her argument and drew Adam deeper and deeper into the discussion.

Doubt had come to Adam quite suddenly when he

found himself talking facts and figures—numbers of men, marching time, necessary supplies—instead of vague theories. He had stopped what he was saying and stared at Gilliane, quite bemused between her beauty and the horrible suspicion that he had betrayed information better kept to himself. Another realization came to him in that moment: Gilliane was far more becomingly dressed than usual and looked quite enchanting. Under his stare, Gilliane had dropped her eyes guiltily and then blushed hotly. Adam looked away. He should have been enraged—at himself for being so easily tricked and at Gilliane for her slyness. Instead, he felt a most unreasonable pride in her cleverness, which was nearly overridden by his desire to take her in his arms and kiss her into silliness.

A short, awkward silence had followed, ended by Gilliane, who, with a face still rosy with blushes, had excused herself in a choked voice and fled. Adam had remained at the table finishing his meal. When he could think with clarity, he reviewed the conversation and determined with some relief that he had disclosed nothing dangerous. However, it was painfully clear that his discretion had been completely accidental.

The girl had bewitched him—and, Adam guessed, that was *not* accidental. She had set him up cleverly by her coldness and the restraint that coldness placed upon his natural exuberance and conviviality. Then she had dressed herself—not brilliantly—which he would have noticed and suspected—but with such subtle good taste as to ravish his eyes, and had showed him the warmth and eager attention to which he was accustomed and had sorely missed. No doubt she expected he would be so eager to take advantage of this change in her manner that he would talk on any subject to which she led him without thinking of what he was saying. And she had been exactly right! It was only by the favor of Christ and all the saints, Adam thought, that he had not told her everything of importance he knew.

Adam threw his other shoe at the wall with equal force. So much for subtletv and not permitting Gilliane to know that they suspected her of being other than a simple, submissive woman. The pretense had done no more than leave her free to set a trap, which he had tumbled into like a blind babe. The horrible truth, Adam admitted—too absorbed in his thoughts to get into bed although he was shivering with cold—was that even now, warned as he was, he did not trust himself to see another trap if she set one. The safest thing was to question her and tell her outright that he knew she was his enemy.

While Adam lay quiet, frozen in his cold decision, seeking oblivion in sleep. Gilliane tossed in her bed in a hot restlessness of indecision. She knew her desires were wrong and sinful. If she yielded to them, she would go to hell. It seemed very unreasonable to her that she must be faithful to a marriage vow that she had not been conscious of making. not even known was being forced from her, but she also knew that it was not the place of a mere mortal to question the workings of the Divine Will. However it was done, the marriage was made, and it was a sin to violate it with her mind or her body.

The trouble was that she could not prevent her mind from sinning. From the moment she had heard Adam's voice, she had been drawn to him. And day by day, the longer they were together. the greater her desire grew. If she was already steeped in sin and damned, was there any sense in tormenting her body? Could worse befall her for yielding? Gilliane knew the answer to that. The penance for evil thoughts was light compared to the penance for the performance of evil deeds.

Unfortunately, that knowledge did nothing to bring Gilliane closer to the decision that she knew she should make—to resist Adam. A harsher penance could be performed and absolution would be given. Thus, one was no more likely to be damned for the greater evil

than for the lesser. Gilliane sighed and turned again.
Then why had she not yielded when, of a sudden, the
words had dried in Adam's mouth and he had begun
to look at her with doubt and desire? Why had she run
away? Gilliane sighed again. It was not her purity that
had sent her scurrying. It was the shadow mingled with
Adam's desire. Gilliane's sighs changed to soft sobs.
If she yielded, he would account her a whore.

That was really why she had to resist. Gilliane did
not fear hell. She had lived so long in misery that a little happiness seemed an adequate return for much suffering. What she could not decide, had not been able
to decide from the beginning, was whether there could
be any happiness for her in yielding to Adam. It seemed
more a question of whether the misery of resisting
would be less or greater than the misery of enduring
Adam's contempt while he deigned to use her.

Gilliane had not faced this problem at first. Her fear
of rape by her conquerors had disappeared at about
the same time as her fear of being killed. Within the day
that Tarring had been yielded, Gilliane recognized that
these conquerors would be far gentler than her so-
called protectors had ever been. She saw, too, that
Adam thought her desirable but Lord Ian and Lord
Geoffrey looked at her differently. To one, she was a
child; to the other, an enemy, or, if not an enemy, one
to be warily watched. Also, she had learned that afternoon at dinner that Lord Ian and Lord Geoffrey were
so fast bound in love to their wives that they did not
look elsewhere.

For a little while Gilliane found ease, thinking about
what Adam had told her of his mother and sister. She
had not known there could be such women or that men
could accept them. Yet it was plain that Adam loved
and respected them; in fact, Gilliane came to understand, although Adam did not say it in plain words,
that he regarded women of any other nature with a
kindly contempt. They were rather like dogs and horses,

to be used and fondled according to their deserving, even valuable in a way, but not creatures of thought or feeling. She had understood, too, that part of the admiration in Adam's eyes was for what he had mistakenly thought her cleverness and courage in the manner of yielding Tarring so that the servants and even the mercenary troops had been saved hurt.

Although she found this hard to believe at first, Gilliane was now convinced it was true. The whole discussion about the duty of a king to his barons and barons to their king had proved the point to her. Saer would have hit her in the mouth at her very first murmur of agreement. It was not, to Saer's mind, a woman's place to listen to such things, and to dare to speak on such a subject, even to agree, was to ask for a beating. Adam, to the contrary, had taken her murmur as a sign of laudable interest and when, greatly daring, she had ventured to disagree, she had not been told to hold her tongue. Without any sign of anger, Adam had merely set about trying to convince her of the rightness of his views.

It was a waste of time. Gilliane was ready to believe that pigs could fly or that snow was hot if Adam said so. However, she was sharp enough to realize that he did not want that. He wanted her to understand what he said, to question if she did not understand, and to offer suggestions if she had any. It was after she had made a remark about how to arrange provisioning for a troop on the march that Adam's conversation had faltered and he had looked at her with such a mingling of doubt and desire. Gilliane's breath caught on a new sob. She was back to the heart of her problem again—to offer herself or not to offer herself.

When Adam had said he would remain at Tarring after Lord Ian and Lord Geoffrey left, her first delighted relief had given way to a brief fear of what he would do once the restraining presences of his stepfather and brother-by-marriage were withdrawn. Almost

as the fear had touched Gilliane, a rush of eager pleasure had displaced it. The thought of being embraced
by Adam, she realized, was far from fearful. Such a
flood of desire had rushed over her that she had felt
dizzy, and then shame at her lust had made her red as
fire and she had run away.

For the next few days Gilliane had suffered the
strangest dichotomy of feeling. Her body desired Adam,
ached for him, but she could not bear the thought that
he was less than perfect. Gilliane had at last seen in
real life the men described in the fanciful romances re-
cited by minstrels—men who spoke softly, bowed over
her hand, cut the best pieces from the roast to place
upon her trencher. They requested instead of ordering;
they did not assault or insult her, even though they had
no reason to be respectful of her. Was she not nothing,
a helpless captive?

On the one hand, Gilliane could not bear to see
Adam fall away from this ideal. If he forced himself
upon her, he would be little better than Saer, only
covering male foulness with a veneer of sweet, false
words. Fearing to see clay feet under her god, Gilliane
hid away from him, barely replied when he spoke to
her. But a day passed, then another, then still another,
and Adam remained courteous even though Gilliane
could see he was hurt and angry when she refused to
talk to him. When he withdrew into offended silence
and still offered her no insult, Gilliane was appalled at
what she had done because—not to wrap a foul thing
in clean linen—she *wanted* Adam to "rape" her.

She had not quite understood her own motives until
she had seen the look in Adam's eyes at dinnertime.
Until then, she had thought a million thoughts about
him, but she had not permitted herself to wonder why,
if she did not wish him to insult her, she had spent
nearly all her time frantically sewing new and more becoming gowns. It was unkind and rude, she had told
herself, not to talk to a guest. Then something she

said—or perhaps she had touched his hand—had set off his desire and he had stared at her face and at her new, close-fitting gown.

Gilliane did not doubt that Adam found her attractive and desired her, but there was more than desire in that look. There was a startled comprehension that betrayed Gilliane to herself. She had dressed herself and started the conversation to tempt a man, not to do honor to a guest—and Adam knew it. He had been blindly treading the path she had almost as blindly laid out for him when something had made him aware. He found her lovely and desirable, but he found the temptation foul. Gilliane knew that if she stayed in the room and continued to entice him, Adam would have satisfied her body's need—but she would have lost him forever. One thing that had come clear under all the jesting when Adam spoke of the faithfulness of Lord Ian and Lord Geoffrey to their wives was that the wives deserved such sacrifice. Gilliane, too, was married. If she openly tried to seduce Adam, would she not be a whore in his eyes?

The result of their musings, which ran on parallel but widely separated tracks, was an increased awkwardness when Adam and Gilliane met in the morning. Adam was already seated, chewing bread and cheese, a black scowl on his face, when Gilliane entered the hall. When she saw Adam, she stopped in her tracks. The frozen moment stretched. Then Adam got slowly to his feet.

"Come here, Lady Gilliane," he said.

Panic seized Gilliane. The deep voice was Adam's, but the tone was Saer's. Long experience had taught Gilliane it was useless to run; there was no place to hide. Ashen pale, she came forward. No blow struck her down, however. The bench was pulled out with the same courtesy as ever and gently pushed in behind her.

She knows already that I have seen what she tried to

do, Adam thought. For a moment, his resolution faltered. Gilliane's pallid face and frightened eyes wrung his heart. It was only for a moment, however. If she was so intent upon the matter that discovery could cause this fear and pallor, she would try again if he did not make clear that he would not endure it.

"It is time for us to understand each other," he said. "I have Tarring and I mean to hold it. I am King Henry's man, and nothing will make me break my oath of homage."

Gilliane stared at him, utterly uncomprehending. It was the dearest wish of her heart that Adam should hold Tarring, and what his oath of homage had to do with anything at all was beyond her.

"Do you understand me?" he growled.

"I understand your words, my lord," Gilliane faltered, "but I do not understand why you address them to me. I yielded Tarring to you in good faith, although you know it may not be mine to yield. As to your oath of homage—what has that to do with me?"

Adam's lips thinned with frustration even while his admiration for Gilliane grew. Clever witch that she was, she had denied nothing, told no lies, nor yet had she acknowledged anything.

"What has it to do with you? I think you would rather see me Louis's man than Henry's. Did you not tell us that de Cercy"—Adam found he could not say "your husband"—"had gone to bring Louis down upon us? Yet Louis has moved in the exact opposite direction, toward my brother Geoffrey's lands. I wonder if your warning was not a device to fix us here to favor Louis's action."

Gilliane's eyes had been growing wider and wider with surprise. "I told you exactly what Osbert said to me," she protested, but her voice was faint. It was dawning upon her that the doubt in Adam's expression the previous day might have had nothing to do with her virtue or lack of virtue.

"What he said to you?" Adam snarled. "You mean, I suppose, what he told you to tell us."

"I do not know," Gilliane gasped, shocked at a possibility that had never occurred to her. "I mean, he did not *say* to tell you what he said, but it is not impossible that he intended that I should tell you. He knows I hate him. I made no secret of it. He knows I would do what I could to spite him. He is so sly, so slimy in his mind, that he might well tell me a lie, guessing I would repeat it."

Suddenly Adam was feeling much better. It was the word *slimy*. He could imagine a woman saying she hated a man that she loved to forward his purposes, but he could not imagine calling a beloved person "slimy" for any reason at all. Gilliane might have said "cruel" or "brutal"; such words had power in them. But to think of a man as "slimy" precluded affection.

As he watched her, color flooded into Gilliane's face, and her lips drew back in as near a snarl as a gentlewoman could achieve. "Filth," she whispered, more to herself than to Adam. "It was all lies." Her eyes lifted to Adam. "He said you were a monster and that you would kill me. That was a lie. He said you would slay the men-at-arms and menservants without mercy and throw the women to your troops. That was a lie. It might well be that his saying he would go to Louis was a lie also. He must have known you would not hurt me without cause. He intended I should tell you, and, when it became plain I had misled you, then you would kill me and leave him, my heir, lord of Tarring."

With every fiber of his being, Adam desired to believe her. Had he wanted it less, it would have been impossible to doubt Gilliane's sincerity. It was himself he doubted. Having been once caught, as he believed, Adam was too wary for his own good.

"If that is true," he said stiffly, "why did he not kill you himself? You cannot befool me a second time, Lady Gilliane. If de Cercy did not intend to appeal to Louis for help, where did he go? And why? Is it not possible he went to summon Neville's men to try to take back Tarring?"

Gilliane completely missed the sarcasm in Adam's question. Her angry flush receded; an expression of hope crossed her face. "Oh, do you think he could have been so stupid as that?" she breathed.

The question confused Adam almost as much as his first remark had confused Gilliane. "What do you mean, *stupid?*" he snapped. "Where would a man go for help but to his vassals and castellans?"

"But they hate Osbert," Gilliane replied. "He was rude and contemptuous of them when they came to visit Gilbert."

"Oh, was he?" Adam asked suspiciously. "And if they endured it then, why should they now find him unendurable?"

"But Saer was alive then," Gilliane said. "They never swore to Osbert."

Her mind, however, was not really on her answer. The expression on Adam's face was now very nearly exactly the same as it had been the previous day. It was, she realized, political infidelity of which Adam suspected her, not marital infidelity. She very nearly smiled with relief, but had sense enough to restrain the impulse. For all Gilliane cared, the Grand Turk could become King of England. So long as it suited Adam, she would find it an excellent arrangement—only, she realized, Adam must not be allowed to see that she did not care. That would not fit right with his idea of a "proper" woman. Nor could she let him think she had shifted her loyalty from Louis to Henry. But he would never believe her if she said she had always been of Henry's party—

"Neville's men accepted Saer's rule? Why?"

Adam's voice cut across Gilliane's thoughts. She brought her mind to his questions with an effort. Her first impulse was to cry, *I am a woman. How should I know such a thing?* But an answer like that would either make Adam despise her or simply convince him she was lying and therefore had been lying about everything else. Gilliane racked her brains for scraps of conversation she had heard, for the implications of the little Saer and Osbert had said in her presence.

"Saer was strong and the men thought he had the ear of Louis. I cannot be sure, of course, but it seems to me they feared that their lands would be taken from them because their lord was dead and poor Gilbert helpless."

"They are firm, then, you believe, in their allegiance to Louis?" Adam asked.

This question was quiet, almost indifferent. It might be that Adam did not care or it might be another test. Neither case was important to Gilliane. Sir Richard had been kind to her. Gilliane had no intention of saying anything that could hurt him. She knew one thing for which no man could be blamed that would make Sir Richard's action acceptable.

"I do not think that at all," Gilliane denied. "I do not know whom they favor or even if they favor one or the other. Gilbert's vassals and castellans are good men. They were loyal to their overlord and followed his will."

As she said it, Gilliane's own path became clear. Her father had been John's vassal. She had the perfect reason to be of Henry's party, even though she did not know England. It did not even matter if Adam did not believe her at first. In fact, it would be better if he did not. That would make him watch her closely—and the closer Adam watched Gilliane, the better she would like it. In the end, he would have to believe she was loyal to his party, for, in truth, whatever party he held to she would support heart and soul.

"So," Adam snapped, "you know Neville's men." She was laying some kind of snare for him, Adam was sure. Her eyes were sparkling bright, and he could see she was restraining a smile with effort.

"Of course I know them—although not all of them. Four came when I was married to Gilbert."

"But not when you were married to de Cercy?"

The incipient smile and sparkle died. "I do not know," Gilliane whispered. "I told you I was not myself. Someone held my hand to make my mark on the contracts and, perhaps . . . I do not really remember, but it seems to me someone pushed my head so that I nodded when it was needful for me to give consent. Oh, I do not *think* Sir Richard was here. I spoke to him of my fear of Osbert and he saw that Osbert was cruel to poor Gilbert. I cannot believe he would be a party to what he must have seen was a forced marriage."

"Was that how you were married?" Adam asked in a strangled voice.

"I *think* so," Gilliane replied, trying not to sob. "I do not remember, I tell you."

That was real. Doubts or no doubts, Adam could not believe the emotions Gilliane had displayed in the last half-hour were a pretense. She did hate de Cercy and she had been very ill for nearly a week after her first husband's death. The serving women had been discreetly questioned by Jamie, Tostig, and Alberic so that Adam knew some of the facts surrounding Neville's death. Gilliane was now looking down at her tightly clasped hands. Without thinking, Adam laid his hand over hers.

"You need fear de Cercy no longer," he said softly. "He will never come near you again—that I promise you."

Gilliane looked up, her eyes magnified by the tears in them. Her lips trembled. Irresistibly drawn, Adam leaned forward. Gilliane's lips parted; she lifted her face to him. Then, realizing where they were and what they were about to do, she gasped and turned away.

"How can you promise that?" she asked, her voice

shaking. "You are here now, but I am not such a fool that I do not know you have other lands and other duties . . . to King Henry, for example. Sooner or later, even if no private matter arises, the king will summon you and you will go. Perhaps you will try to leave me in safe hands, but so long as I am Osbert's wife . . ."

"I do not make idle promises," Adam said, but his voice was very cold.

"Why are you angry?" Gilliane cried, too startled by the change in tone and manner to be careful.

"It must be plain to you that I am a fool," Adam snarled, "for you have twice tricked me into wagging my tongue when I should have been still, but do you think I am so much a fool that I do not know when I have been caught in a clever trap? Do not be too quick to rejoice. You will not get the good you expect of this. You will not bind me by my promise to you to violate my oath of fealty."

Gilliane had been staring at him with frightened bewilderment. "I would never think of such a thing," she protested when she understood what Adam thought she had done. "It is *you* who keep saying I am of Louis's party. Why do you not ask me? I care nothing for Louis. I have done him no homage. I owe him nothing."

"Saer de Cercy was his man."

"Saer killed my father, and I was given to him as ward. Do you think I have any reason to love Saer?" Gilliane spat, the bitter rage of years taking hold of her. "He kept me unwed to wring dry what had been my father's lands. Then he brought me here and married me to a witless cripple." Her anger faltered; her eyes filled with tears again. "Poor Gilbert. He, at least, was gentle to me." The tears did not fall. Renewed rage drew them back to their source. "But Saer did not know that. He would not have cared if Gilbert had been a raving madman and had torn the flesh from my bones.

What should I feel about Saer, except glad that he is dead? What should I care for his oaths or loyalties?"

Adam was staring at her. The heat of her rage glowed through her. There was a red light in her dark eyes, and Adam had the feeling that if he touched her flesh his fingers would be burnt. He had considerable experience of angry women, his mother having a quick and violent temper, but Gilliane's anger was different from Alinor's. It was not all flash and sparkle, like dry twigs that would burn themselves out in a little time. This was like the heart of the fire in the hearth, deep and glowing, long-burning, almost impossible to quench. Gilliane did not shriek and wave her arms. Her voice was low but hot, like the hate in her eyes.

"I know nothing of Louis and less of Henry," she continued, less passionately, "but my father was vassal to King John."

"John?" Adam repeated. "Where were your father's lands?"

"Near Chaunay. I do not know exactly. Saer was careful I should not know what was mine."

That was very likely true, but what was more significant was how Gilliane had spoken of the lands. Saer "kept her unwed to wring them dry"; Saer was "careful she should not know what was hers." Then, if she did not care for Osbert—and Adam was almost certain that was true—and she had no bond to Louis—that was more doubtful, but possible—clearly she had set trap after trap for him because of the lands. Adam was delighted! He had no quarrel with a woman's love of property. It seemed right and reasonable to him, because of the attitude of his mother and sister.

All that puzzled Adam was why Gilliane felt the need to lay traps for him. He could not own her property except by killing her and de Cercy, and plainly she did not suspect him of any intention of harming *her*. He would take from Tarring enough to pay the costs of the damage Saer had done to his town and people and to pay the cost of this expedition, but he was in no immediate need of funds and that indemnity could be arranged so that it did no injury to Gilliane's property.

Suddenly, light dawned on him. Gilliane wanted him to make sure Neville's men would obey her. Adam had not thought of it at first because neither his mother nor Joanna needed help in obtaning obedience from their vassals, but Gilliane's situation was different. The estates were not hers by blood. She was a stranger married to the rightful heir, and without even a child of the true bloodline to bind loyalty. To add to her difficulties, small holders in these times wanted the assurance of a strong overlord who could bring an army to protect them among the changing fortunes of civil war. Gilliane understood that. She had pointed it out to him when she explained why Neville's men had accepted Saer's management.

The glare Adam turned on Gilliane was extinguished almost immediately by amusement and admiration. A few smiles and sweet words, a kiss or two, perhaps even more—but that was a cheap price for the use of his men and his strength to cow her vassals and castellans. After all, she was a wife already and had nothing to lose. Adam choked trying to restrain his laughter. His mother would have approved highly of Gilliane's maneuver. He could not even fault Gilliane for being a miser. Poor girl, between the elder de Cercy's hiring of men for an army to attack Kemp and the younger stripping away what was left, she had not a mill in money nor even a cheap ring to sell to offer payment.

"Enough of this fencing," Adam said briskly. "I will believe that you had and have no love for the de Cercys, father or son. I tell you, too, that nothing will make me go into France to try to reclaim those lands for you, and also that if I am summoned by the king I will go—no matter what you say or do. However, I will keep the promise I made to you. Moreover, I am perfectly willing to make sure that Neville's men acknowledge you as their liege lady."

"Acknowledge me?" Gilliane gasped, her eyes as wide as they could get. "But——"

"I tell you that you need not act the innocent with me on this matter," Adam exclaimed, a trifle irritably. "I think it perfectly reasonable that, since the lands were left to you and there is no other heir, you should wish to rule them. We will get along much better if you say outright what you desire of me rather than leading me to believe . . . well, never mind that."

If Adam thought it reasonable that she should rule the lands, Gilliane resolved that she would rule them if it killed her. But there were a few practical difficulties that he had not touched upon. "There is a little problem," Gilliane suggested as steadily as she could. "The men desire a strong leader. Tarring is stripped clean, as you know. I cannot buy a good captain. You do not think I can don armor and lead the men, do you?"

The last question was perfectly serious, and Gilliane's voice trembled a little as she asked it. It was quite mad that Adam should think such a thing, but no more mad to Gilliane than that he believed she had expected to own and rule Gilbert's estates. In fact, she had not so far thought about a future for herself. She thought only of each day, hoping Adam would stay at Tarring, unable even to guess what would be done with her when he must go.

"There is no need to be sarcastic," Adam snapped. "I know my mother once led an army into Wales, but even she did not think of donning armor and engaging in battle. I understand that if I demand the men swear to you, I must offer them my protection and that of my family."

It was possible, Gilliane realized suddenly, really possible, that there would be a future, not just these few days. If Adam bound Gilbert's men to protect her and obey her and they did not, he would come to punish them. They would understand that. Also, if anyone came and threatened her, Adam would come to drive the attacker away. In any case, the central fact remained: Adam would come!

"How can I thank you?" Gilliane faltered. "I have nothing . . . nothing."

"I do not do it for you," Adam said severely—and most untruthfully. "I do it for a reason you may not like but must accept. If I offer to lead and to protect Neville's men, they must return to their allegiance to King Henry. I will require that you swear homage to me and, through me, to the king for the keeping of your lands, and acknowledge that Henry, not Louis, gives and confirms your charter to these lands. If Louis marches into this area, your vassals and castellans must resist him—but they will not stand alone. They will have good and sufficient help."

Gilliane would have sworn homage to the devil on Adam's order. "For myself I accept," she said eagerly, her eyes bright, her cheeks delicately flushed with hope and enthusiasm. Then her color began to fade and apprehension showed in her eyes. "But is it my right?" she asked anxiously. "In the marriage contract, my rights are ceded to Osbert."

"I have told you already that possession is nine-tenths of the law," Adam assured her.

There was, however, no relief in her expression. "Possession of me as well as of Tarring," Gilliane pointed out. "If by some ruse Osbert should seize me when you are gone—he is sly as a snake—would not the men be constrained to obey him, either by my forced consent, as I was forced to consent to marriage, or even for fear that hurt would be done me and they would thus violate their oaths?" She looked blankly out into space. There was no future, not really. "Not so long as Osbert lives," Gilliane whispered. "I can never be safe while Osbert lives."

Adam stared at her, his mouth going dry, his hands

cold. Because he had decided Gilliane was a strong woman and she, striving desperately to be what he desired, had acted the part, Adam did not realize Gilliane was only frightened. It seemed to him that she was inciting him to kill her husband. He swallowed. If Osbert had treated her as she said, he deserved killing. Still, if hate led Gilliane to scheme the death of this second husband, had greed led her to scheme the death of the first? Careful, Adam warned himself. With this woman it is needful to go most carefully.

CHAPTER EIGHT

Had Gilliane known of Osbert's experiences since he left her, she would have been considerably less frightened of him. In truth, Osbert was stupid as well as sly. He had misunderstood the courtesy with which his father was treated for fear and obligation. Louis had granted readily all that Saer asked because what Saer asked of him cost him nothing—his name and seal on parchments giving away rights that were not his to give. Because Osbert wanted more, he found Louis equally polite but far less accommodating. Although Louis did not deny Osbert's plea outright he offered no more than vague promises for the future.

Not knowing what else to do, Osbert joined Louis's party. After his first disappointment, however, Osbert became rather pleased with his choice. He left his men to forage for themselves by theft or violence so that they were no charge upon him. For himself, he found it quite easy to borrow money on his expectations as overlord of Tarring. Also, for Saer's sake, he was welcome as a guest in many a French lord's lodging. No one seemed to think it odd that he had been driven from his land. It was too common a happening in a time of civil war. Indeed, it seemed to bring him into a circle of similarly disappointed gentlemen, some of whom he found remarkably sympathetic.

However, Osbert soon discovered that his new situa-

tion was not all pleasure. On the third day an assault
was made upon Hertford and Osbert found, to his horror, that he was supposed to lead his men in person.
He could not refuse outright. To refuse to fight for the
prince might induce Louis to go back on his promise
and refuse to help Osbert regain his own keep. Sweating
and trembling, Osbert agreed. In fact, Osbert never did
mount any ladder. Just as he approached the foot—
somewhat later than most of the other scaling parties—
a nearby ladder was thrust outward from the wall by
the defenders. Slowly, almost gracefully, it rose upright and then arced backward, spilling men who
screamed in terror as they fell. Osbert, struck unconscious by fear more effectively than by a missile, pitched
forward on his face and lay still.

Fortunately for Osbert the assault was unsuccessful,
and he did not need to explain his absence in the fighting on the walls. Luck continued to favor him. Within
the week, Walter de Godardville asked for a truce to
consult his overlord. If Faulk de Breauté could not
bring him help, he must yield soon on terms or be defeated. Louis was very happy to grant the truce. He
knew that Sir Walter's appeal to his overlord for help
must be denied. If Faulk could have brought help to
Hertford, he would have done so long before. Louis's
estimate of the situation was perfectly correct; the expected answer—Breauté's permission for his vassal to
yield the keep—soon arrived. If Sir Walter and his men
were allowed to leave in safety with their arms, their
families, and their horses, Hertford could be given up.
Faulk was a realist. It was senseless to lose the men
as well as the castle. This way, he would have the use
of Sir Walter and his troops and not be obligated to pay
ransom for them. He hoped, too, that Louis would stop
to enjoy his victory for a month or two.

This latter hope was not to be fulfilled. Louis was
wise enough to strike again while the iron was hot and
one success might lead to another. Another motive

spurred him to continue his attacks on the king's strongholds. On the eve of their securing Hertford, Robert FitzWalter Lord of Dunmow and chief of the rebel barons, presented his claim to the keep and town, saying that the charge of it belonged to him by ancient right and had been reft from him by King John. Louis was furious; however, he was not Philip of France's son for nothing. No spark of temper showed in his placid face. It would be necessary, he said, to consult his council of French knights on so serious a matter.

He did raise the subject, confident of the advice he would receive, and he was not disappointed. In fact, he got rather more of a good thing than he desired. FitzWalter did not deserve to have so valuable and important a stronghold in his hands, the council decreed, because he was a traitor to his own king already and could not be relied on to keep faith with any man. Naturally, Louis did not repeat this decision to Fitz-Walter in the words in which it was given. What he said was that he could not spare so valuable a supporter when he was in the middle of a campaign. As soon as the kingdom was subdued and FitzWalter's military acumen and ability were no longer so necessary to him, he would give FitzWalter every one of his rights and more besides. This diplomacy did little to satisfy Fitz-Walter, who guessed all too easily that Louis did not trust him enough to let him out of his sight. But he had to accept the decision. As one of the initiators of the rebellion against King John, he could not expect a welcome among King Henry's supporters, even though many men who had changed sides were being accepted back into the king's fold. Two days later, Prince Louis started his army toward Berkhamsted, carefully skirting Geoffrey's territory where reports warned him a substantial army would contest any attack. Louis had no intention of fighting so strong a force if they did not move against him. When the force at Hemel was surrounded, they might well yield without battle.

Geoffrey and Ian were not indifferent to the plight of Hertford and whomever else Louis was moving to attack, but they dared not attempt a battle against what they knew to be a superior force without any hope of support or reinforcement. They had inquired more than once of Faulk de Breauté whether, if they harassed Louis and thus managed to prolong the siege, he would be able to come to their assistance and had been told it was impossible. They would best serve the king's purpose, Pembroke wrote, through Faulk, by holding their own land secure.

The king's party was not yet ready to fight. In fact, they were winning without fighting a single battle even while keeps fell into Louis's hands. Every time Louis let his men loose to live off the land, he made enemies; every time he took a keep and refused to return it to its English overlord (when that man was of his party), giving it instead into the hands of one of his French adherents, he lost support. No one believed that Louis could be driven out completely without a battle, but his own actions were weakening his hold on England.

Another group of men-at-arms was on the move. When Cuthbert and his troop left Tarring, they marched directly north, intending to go to London where the concentration of noblemen promised the best chance for employment. By the time they arrived, however, the major portion of Louis's army was settled in around Hertford, and those French knights who remained had no need for more men-at-arms. What was worse, Cuthbert found that he and his English-speaking troop were regarded with contempt and distaste. One gentleman to whom he applied told him to seek employment with the English turncoats who could understand his men's pig-grunting.

Disheartened and somewhat frightened because he was a Sussex man and had served in that shire most of his life, and even those who spoke English in the

London area spoke it with a different accent, Cuthbert took council with the oldest and steadiest members of the troop. It did not occur to him that those men were also the least adventurous and had the strongest ties to Sussex. Some suggested an immediate return to their native place; others, incensed at the attitude of the French, wished to strike westward and find an adherent of the king who would hire them.

A compromise was reached. They would travel both south and west, hoping to find a patron before they were too far from the border of their native shire. They found no employment, but they soon came across information of great interest. Adam Lemagne, his stepfather, Lord Ian de Vipont, and his brother-by-marriage, Lord Geoffrey FitzWilliam, had most excellent reputations. A man-at-arms could not be better situated than in one of their retinues. They were told this more than once, and each time Cuthbert's unease grew. He had always felt it was wrong to leave Lady Gilliane, but he had his men to consider and it had seemed the best and safest move. Now it appeared he had been wrong. He should have known better than to listen to the ravings of wounded and defeated men. They would have done much better to yield and put themselves at Lemagne's mercy.

By the end of the second week, when they still had found no one who wished to hire a whole troop of unknown men, Cuthbert proposed that they return to Tarring. Lemagne might refuse to hire them and might order them to leave the area, but he would not order them imprisoned or killed if they did no harm. Cuthbert's suggestion was accepted with great relief by the majority of the men. Even the younger, more daring members of the troop were growing homesick. The few who were not native Sussexmen objected, but they were told they could cut loose and seek employment as individuals if they did not wish to return to Tarring. It was always easier for a single man to find a position than a whole troop, but the troop had stuck together because that advantage was offset by the fact that a single man was much more at the mercy of his employer and of the older, established men in the troop.

Thus, just as Adam was explaining to Gilliane that her next move must be to send Neville's men formal notice of Neville's death and her accession to the honors, Cuthbert and his men were no more than an hour's march away from Tarring. Gilliane had no idea what such a formal notice should be like, but she had absorbed so many shocking ideas since she had come down to breakfast that she simply nodded. There had been a clerk in the castle before Saer came—Gilliane had heard the servants speak of a Father Paul. Perhaps he had taken refuge with the priest in the town. She would send one of the serving men to find him, if possible. Likely he would know the forms.

"And what do you think would be best to do? You know the men. Would it be best to send a summons at the same time as the notice, or do you think the notice will bring the men without a summons?" Adam asked.

"Some might come of themselves," Gilliane answered slowly. "But . . . it would not be wise to trick them into coming and force them to swear. I must also tell them that Saer is dead and that you have conquered Tarring."

Adam smiled down, his eyes warm. She might be greedy to own the lands and she might well try to wheedle him into killing her present husband (she would not have to wheedle very hard), but he did not think she had had any part in killing Neville. She was too clever to want to end Neville's life. If she understood so easily that forced oaths were worthless, she was not likely to have overlooked the advantage of keeping her witless husband alive. As long as the poor creature lived, Gilliane would be as much mistress of the estate as she would be when a widow. More, in fact, because the men owed obedience to Neville and there would be excuses enough for them to break their ties with her if they wished to do so.

"Then you must send a summons to them also."

"Very well," Gilliane agreed, "but what am I to say to them, my lord? It is unreasonable to tell men to walk defenseless into the arms of their enemy. They would say I was a witless woman and break their bonds if I bid them come and yield themselves with no warranty for their safety. You say you will help me rule these lands, but if I am to do so, the men must trust both my wisdom and my honesty."

"Tell them the truth," Adam suggested, grinning wickedly, "that your father was John's man, that you had no love for Louis. Thus, when I, King Henry's man, came, you yielded gladly upon terms."

"What terms?" Gilliane asked, looking up. "I asked for nothing beyond the safety of my people."

Her eyes were soft, her lips a little parted; she did not look as if she really knew what she was asking. With an enormous effort Adam looked away. He did not know whether the expression was genuine or whether the half-dazed invitation in her eyes was an invitation only to agree to *her* terms. He cursed himself impatiently. So many women had looked at him with the same invitation in their faces, and he knew they desired only him, not their own advantage. Why had those other swooning looks left him indifferent beyond the eagerness to exchange a little easy pleasure? The answer was not far to seek. He was indifferent because he was bored, because he did know exactly what those women thought and desired. Gilliane was a challenge.

"They will be easy enough terms," Adam muttered, intensely relieved that it had always been his intention—to which Ian and Geoffrey had agreed—to ask no more than to have their costs repaid and make Tarring a vassal state to Lemagne. He tried not to wonder whether, had he desired harder terms, he would have had the strength to demand them. "Tarring must pay for the hurt done my people and for the costs of the men and supplies we expended in coming here."

Gilliane was already shaking her head, and Adam was torn between delighted amusement at her boldness and chagrin to think she had read him so clearly that she believed he was ready to do as she desired in everything. The chagrin made it possible for him to speak sharply.

"What do you mean, no?"

"Only that there is nothing with which to pay," Gilliane replied. "You have examined the keep from base to top and the outbuildings also. You know there is no coin, no piece of jewelry—unless you count the seashell cross. You may have that, if you think it of sufficient value to take. With what can Tarring pay?"

"I would not take your only ornament, no matter what it was worth," Adam said indignantly, and then burst into laughter at how neatly she had almost caught him again. By filling him with guilt over the idea of robbing a poor, defenseless widow of a trinket more fit for a villein's woman, she had nearly tricked him into saying the costs would be little or nothing.

Delighted that she had pleased him, and completely ignorant of how, Gilliane continued in the same vein. "Indeed, you might have it with my good will. I only wish it was worth taking, for I do not think it will be possible to wring anything from the demesne serfs nor, I would guess, from the people in the village. Saer did not permit me to know, but he was not a good master in France and I cannot believe he was much changed by a passage over the narrow sea."

"You are quite correct," Adam agreed dryly. "I have been in the town and over the estate and a more wretched—"

"Then how can Tarring pay?" Gilliane interrupted anxiously.

"Not today, but over the years," Adam responded

firmly, determined not to let Gilliane push him into
accepting a loss.

In truth, he was less concerned with the money
than with retaining his pride. Gilliane could not help
but feel scorn for him—no matter how pleased she was
at her victory—if he yielded all to her.

"Which brings me to my next condition," Adam
continued. "Neville, if I remember correctly, held
directly from the king. Now that I have taken this
place, you will hold of me—that is, I will be overlord
of Tarring and you will pay tribute to me. It will be
necessary to gain permission from the crown—but that
is my affair and will be easy enough to accomplish." He
said it quick and hard, expecting protest. The king was
a far-off overlord, which allowed vassals much greater
freedom than an overlord who was a near neighbor.
Instead of protest, a faint blush rose into Gilliane's
cheeks, and her eyes were raised adoringly.

"Does that not mean, my lord, that you will be
pledged to protect me always?"

Adam's mouth opened, then closed. He thought of
overlordship in terms of being able to draw upon his
vassals for men or money when he was called to do
some service for the king or when he needed to discipline a rebellious vassal or castellan of his own. It
had not occurred to him before, but the contract
worked the other way also. If a vassal was in trouble,
he had the right to call on his overlord for aid. Suddenly it became clear to Adam that, in this case, Gilliane was getting the better of the bargain by far.

She knew, Adam assumed quite wrongly, that it
would be useless to call upon Neville's overlord—the
king—for help. The king's guardians could barely
protect the king's property. It was obviously impossible
to obtain help from that source. But here he was, with
an army all ready, which, if not large, was certainly
sufficient to bring Neville's men to heel. And all for
nothing! It would not cost Gilliane a penny because

she had not a penny to pay. He must carry the cost in the expectation that it would be repaid in the future. Meanwhile, she doubtless hoped she would find a way to squirm out of paying anything—perhaps thinking if she had time enough she would be able to work her will on him.

Naturally, she wanted to do him homage. She had nothing to lose, everything to gain. Helplessly, Adam began to laugh again. Worst of all, swearing homage would probably mean nothing to her. A woman had no honor to sustain. When it suited her, she would go back on her swearing as lightly as she had sworn in the first place. Witch that she was! With all his care, she had trapped him. He had already agreed that Neville's men should be induced to swear fealty directly to her.

"Dear lord," Gilliane breathed, "how glad I am that you do not mind being burdened with me. I have been greatly afraid that, seeing there was nothing but ruin here, you would abandon me. I will be a faithful liegewoman, so far as it is in my power to be."

Lightly, lightly, all thought of cost and pride flew out of Adam's head. "And I will be a good liege lord to you and faithfully protect you against all harm," Adam murmured, and bent forward and gave his new vassal what was not quite a kiss of peace.

CHAPTER NINE

What would have happened after Adam's lips touched Gilliane's was a puzzle neither was sure it was desirable to solve. The sound of running feet jerked Adam upright. Gilliane dropped her head, red as fire, unable and quite unwilling to move.

"There is a troop of men approaching the keep, lord," Alberic reported.

"What colors?" Adam asked.

"No banner that I can see."

"Perhaps mercenaries looking for employment," Adam said, a pleased smile replacing the slightly stiff expression of embarrasment he had been wearing.

One of Adam's problems had been to find men he could train into an adequate fighting troop so that he could leave some of his own men in Tarring to keep it safe while he went out to coerce or replace Gilliane's vassals and castellans. Usually this was not a serious problem in the relatively populous south for a man with as good a reputation as a master as Adam. Unfortunately, Saer's grandiose ideas of conquest had stripped every likely candidate for an army from the surrounding countryside. What was worse, the men had been so harshly treated that the few who had escaped Saer hid from Adam's recruiters.

Since they were instructed not to draw in unwilling men—Adam had been taught that such men never

150

made adequate fighters and deserted at the first opportunity—the best the recruiters could do was to spread the word that Adam was hiring and hope that the news would bring in any footloose men in the area. The hope seemed to have blossomed into a fuller-than-expected reality. From the wall, Adam watched the men. Obviously, they had come a long way; they were very travel-stained. Still, they were in good order and clearly eager by the quickness of their marching.

At a respectful distance, the troop stopped and one man came forward. When Adam heard the name, he nearly fell off the wall in surprise and then wondered for one wild moment if Gilliane really was a witch. How else could she have arranged everything so neatly, just in time for Cuthbert's return? Then he smiled grimly. She was no witch. She had miscalculated just a little. He still had wits enough left to remember that, whatever was said, these were Gilliane's men. Doubtless they would be brave and loyal—so long as his interests and Gilliane's were identical.

"Come in," Adam ordered. "There is no need for us to shout at each other across the moat." And when he was face to face with Cuthbert, he asked mischievously, "What brings you back to Tarring?" for he wished to hear the tale Gilliane had devised for her man-at-arms to tell.

"It troubled me always that we left my lady," Cuthbert responded immediately.

This was rather surprising to Adam, who did not expect that Gilliane would permit her name to come into the excuse at all. Then he reproached himself for underestimating her again. Surely she would have guessed he would be suspicious. What better way to disarm suspicion and prevent questions than to admit from the beginning that the men were attached to her? Since he would never have believed otherwise anyway, it was best to make a virtue of a necessity. He listened to the rest of Cuthbert's story, however, with considerable interest, marking the real bitterness with which the man related his experiences in London.

Had he done Gilliane an injustice, Adam wondered. Was Cuthbert's tale true? Could Gilliane have been so long-sighted that she had sent Cuthbert to London, guessing what his reception would be and thus ensuring an even greater devotion to her? If so, then she surely did not care which party triumphed and only desired security for herself.

Without more ado, Adam told Cuthbert to bring his men in. He would not pay them again, he said, even though their last contract had been with Saer. He considered that they owed the full time of service to whoever held Tarring keep. However, he would not put any penalty upon them for leaving their post, either, since they had done so with the permission of the present holder, Lady Gilliane. They could simply resume their duties exactly as before, except that orders would come from Alberic or himself.

"And the lady?" Cuthbert asked anxiously, after agreeing to Adam's terms with relief. "She is well?"

Wherever the orders came from, Adam thought, it was certain where Cuthbert's loyalty lay. "Perfectly well," Adam responded dryly. "Go inside and ask for her. She is not a prisoner and is free to speak with anyone she chooses. Lady Gilliane has agreed to take me as her overlord. At present, we are as one on the need to bring Neville's vassals to obedience. Do you know the men? Have you aught to say on this subject?"

"I can tell you what their own men say of them, my lord," Cuthbert responded readily. "What that is worth, only you can judge."

"Good. Tell me."

"Sir Richard is a good master. His men are devoted servants who will not hear a word against him. Sir Philip is also well liked, although I have heard a complaint now and again that he is too changeable of purpose. Sir Edmund is young and said to be hot-headed. That may not be a fair judgment on the men's parts because he has only recently come into the estate and the men were accustomed to his father's ways."

"They stayed with him, his father's men?" Adam asked. That was usually a good sign.

"Yes, and it might be only fondness, the older men fearing his hurt if he thrusts himself forward."

Adam shrugged. He had suffered considerably from that kind of protective complaint before his own men realized just how strong and skillful he was.

"Sir Andrew is also a good master, but, to speak the truth, he is not too clever. I have heard his men boast that they were able to get away with mischief by wrapping it up in many words. Sir Godfrey is not stupid, but he is so stubborn, it has been said, that he will strive forward to his own hurt when he is urged to go another way. Left alone, sometimes he will change, but threats or explanations serve only to fix his purpose. Of Sir Matthew the tale is different. His men are sullen and say little, which I have never thought a good thing. A soldier who does not complain is a man afraid."

That was a shrewd remark and gave Adam a good opinion of Cuthbert's judgment. It remained only to be determined whether the man had some private reason for lauding Sir Richard and damning Sir Matthew. Adam hoped that would not prove to be the case because he rather liked Cuthbert. If the man had spoken the truth, he would make a good, responsible henchman—always keeping in mind his basic loyalty to Gilliane. Adam thanked the man and dismissed him. It was interesting and revealing that he went into the keep—presumably to speak to Gilliane—before he went out to call his men in. Amused, Adam busied himself discussing with Alberic whether it would be best to break up Cuthbert's troop or keep them as a unit.

After his discussion with Alberic, Adam had gone up

into the hall quickly, wondering whether he would surprise Gilliane and Cuthbert in some guilty glance or word. Instead, when he was noticed, it gave apparent pleasure to both. Naturally, Cuthbert said nothing, but merely bowed and smiled and pulled his forelock before retreating. Gilliane came forward with a hand outstretched and glowing eyes.

"How kind you are, how very kind to take Cuthbert and his men in. He told me how he was turned away by Louis's people. You will not be sorry you have given him back his employment. He is very honest and loyal."

"I did not do it to please you," Adam said harshly. "I did it because he owes near half a year of service and that will save me the cost of paying new men for that half-year."

Gilliane withdrew the hand Adam had not taken and blushed hotly. She was not certain what had angered him, but she guessed it had nothing to do with Cuthbert. Perhaps he was ashamed of having kissed her. Gilliane threw a flickering glance at Adam, saw that his color was also high, and was better pleased with his bad temper than she would have been with a smile of complacency. Certainly he was not contemptuous, so he did not blame her for immodesty. She dropped a curtsy.

"Whatever your reasons, my lord, what you have done is greatly to Cuthbert's benefit, and so I thank you, for he stood by me when many others fled," she murmured. "I will go now and see to the maids' work and be out of your way."

"Not so fast," Adam ordered. "Cuthbert's return has solved a problem for me. I do not need to take the time to train fighting men. Instead of sending your vassals and castellans notice that your husband is dead, we will go and tell them."

"Yes, my lord," Gilliane responded without an instant's hesitation and without a shadow on her face. It was a matter of complete indifference to her whether they stayed at Tarring until they grew roots, or whether they traveled the length and breadth of the world, so long as they did it together.

"It is my men who will stay in Tarring, however. Cuthbert and his troop will come with us."

"As you will, my lord. I am sure you will find Cuthbert most eager to please you."

"You mean you have agreed that he should obey me?" Adam asked sardonically.

"Well, of course," Gilliane said in a surprised tone. "What a fool I should be to do otherwise."

She meant she had no power to contest Adam's will. He took her remark to mean that she would be a fool to obstruct a purpose she desired. Adam was pleased because he felt she was being more open with him, although he warned himself that the openness might disappear at their first disagreement.

"How long will it take you to provision the men?" Adam asked.

Gilliane blinked. "How many men, for how long?" she asked instinctively, more to delay the admission that she had never done such a thing and had no idea what to do than because she realized she had to know.

"Cuthbert's fifty and one hundred or so of mine," Adam replied, watching her narrowly, but there was no change in her slightly blank look.

Adam was not at all surprised. He had not seriously thought Gilliane would believe him so much a fool as to put himself in her power by taking no men of his own. The blankness he assumed to be a result of mental calculation concerning supplies. It was, indeed, owing to mental activity, but the frantic scurrying of Gilliane's brain could scarcely be called *calculation,* and it produced no result. She would have to confess her ignorance, Gilliane thought, and Adam would scorn her.

Desperate to delay her diminishment in Adam's eyes, Gilliane said, "You will have to give me a little time to see what is in the storage sheds." Then a glimmer of hope came to her and she raised her eyes. "That is, if I have your leave to look therein, my lord."

"What do you mean, my leave? We are agreed, are we not, that you are now subject to me—but not my prisoner. You do not need my leave to look into your own storerooms."

That avenue of escape blocked, Gilliane curtsied. "Then I will go and look. I hope what you need is there," she remarked.

"Go and look," he said curtly, "and come to me with word as soon as may be. I will be in the stables." They would need horses, and those, too, had been taken by Saer and Osbert. Adam had those Saer had taken now, but they were at Kemp and were scarcely useful for his present purpose.

They began to walk toward the stair together, but a manservant stopped Gilliane to tell her the priest was there. Adam did not bother to inquire what need there was for a priest. Doubtless, he thought caustically, Gilliane wished to confess all the lies she had told. Gilliane herself did not remember summoning a priest, at first, but it was unwise to turn away a man of God and she waited with what patience she could, thinking all the while of how she could conceal her ignorance from Adam. Then, just as the priest said, "I am Father Paul. Blessings on you, madam, for recalling me to my place," light dawned on her. Cuthbert would know what a man needed on a march, and, since Gilliane knew how to plan food for the castlefolk, she should be able to tell what the whole troop would need.

Gilliane smiled at the priest, whose blessing seemed to have brought with it a minor miracle, and then, his words having penetrated her brain, she remembered that she had summoned him to write the notices to the vassals. That, of course, no longer needed to be done, but, if Father Paul had been driven out by Saer and had nowhere else to go, of course he must be received back again. She looked at him keenly, a small, once-rotund man with a high complexion that came from good living. His robe was dirty and worn now and hung loosely upon him—a sign that the times had been hard for him—but the cloth was of as fine a quality as any nobleman wore.

"You are very welcome to me, Father," Gilliane said, "for I am new in this place and land and there is much you can tell me and teach me if you were chaplain to Lord Gilbert."

"I held the place for fifteen years—before Sir Saer turned me out."

There was in Father Paul's voice a harsh bitterness that was not consonant with the resignation to the will of God a priest should have, but Gilliane had no quarrel with his sentiment. "It was not by my will, I assure you, Father," Gilliane said, "but we are in better hands now. My new overlord, Sir Adam Lemagne, is of a different character. I must warn you, however, that he is master here and is fast tied to King Henry's cause."

"I, too," Father Paul said happily. "That was why I was thrust out to starve. I said the pope had forbidden us to defy King John."

"Then we are all agreed," Gilliane sighed, relieved at not being faced with the dreadful dilemma of either telling a priest to go and being cursed, or confessing to Adam that she had brought an adherent of Louis into the household. "I must leave you now," she continued briskly, realizing the priest had done her a double favor by separating her from Adam because she could now send for Cuthbert without betraying herself. "Do you, meanwhile, see if your old quarters are decent. If anything is lacking, I will see to it when I return. Now I must attend to something else by my lord's order."

Gilliane then hurried to the sheds in the bailey, having dispatched a servant to send Cuthbert to her. From him, she obtained the information she needed, but it was useless to her. There was meat and fish preserved in brine, turnips and apples, barrels of wine, and sacks of wheat—provisions for those who lived in the keep—although Gilliane realized with alarm that they were not sufficient to feed the number of folk now resident until the new vegetables began to grow. Possibly there was not even enough meat to last until the ewes dropped their lambs in the spring. It would be necessary to be less generous, far less generous, with meals in the future.

Worse than that, because she knew it would bring Adam's immediate wrath on her head, there was virtually nothing of what Cuthbert said was needed for marching troops. Nearly all the dried and smoked meat and fish were gone; only a few bushels of lentils and beans lay in the huge bins reserved for them. Even barley and oats were almost completely lacking. With a heavy heart, Gilliane turned to dismiss Cuthbert and found Adam staring at her from the doorway, his expression bleak and hard. "I am sorry," she faltered.

"Oh, no, it is I who must apologize," Adam snapped caustically, looking from her to Cuthbert. "Doubtless I interrupted you before you were able to complete your planning."

"There is nothing to plan about, my lord," Gilliane confessed anxiously, gesturing toward the near-empty storage bins. "Cuthbert says that there are not enough provisions to sustain a troop on the march for even two days."

Adam looked from one to the other. Both met his eyes with obvious anxiety but no sign of guilt. He turned his attention to the storeroom and cursed fluently. Gilliane paled and stiffened. She would be well beaten for this, she knew. If only she had admitted her ignorance, she might have escaped, but now . . .

"It is my own fault," Adam growled furiously. "I should have thought of it when we came. If I had told you to look then, Ian and Geoffrey could have left most of what they carried with them. We were well supplied, thinking there might be a siege of some weeks. Curse me and rot me—"

"No, my lord!" Gilliane cried.

"No, what?" Adam asked blankly.

"Do not curse yourself—do not," Gilliane begged, her eyes full of tears. "If you are angry, beat me. I should have looked without your telling me. It is a woman's part to know what provender a keep holds. I . . ."

There were air spaces under the eaves of the outbuilding in which the supplies were kept that let in a little light as well as air. Adam moved closer and stared down at the lovely face turned up to his. "I do not wish to beat you," he murmured. "I would not wish it even if you were to blame—which you are not."

"But you will wish it," Gilliane said desperately, determined to get the complete confession of her sins over with, "when I tell you that there is not enough food stored to last us all through the winter."

She was pale and trembling, but she did not shrink back when Adam lifted his hand. Nor was there any need for shrinking. He only cupped her chin in his palm, so she could not lower her head. Diplomatically, Cuthbert stepped backward until he could sidle from the building. It was plain enough to him that his presence was not necessary, and he was quite sure that the lord and lady would be less annoyed that he had left them without permission than they would be if he interrupted them now to obtain permission.

"That is the first silly thing I have ever heard you say," Adam remarked softly, teasing her. "Naturally, if near three hundred mouths are added to the usual number, there cannot be enough . . ."

Adam's voice drifted away. The rapt adoration on Gilliane's face silenced him. Moved more by tenderness than by the passion her beauty could stir in him, Adam touched her lips with his. Had there been the slightest quiver of fear or withdrawal, he would have let her go without thought or effort. His impulse had been to comfort, because she was so distressed at having failed and because she was so grateful to him for not punishing her. There was, however, no shadow of resistance, not even that which came from surprise. Gilliane was not surprised. The way Adam had held her face, the softness of his voice, were warning enough to her. Nonetheless, the moment their lips touched, her nimble wits were completely paralyzed by a flood of desire so violent that she could have cast herself down on the cold earth floor and played the greensleeves.

Enough awareness remained to stop Gilliane from such coarse and blatant behavior, but her lips parted, her eyes closed, her breath caught. Although she gave no more overt sign of her response, Adam caught fire. He let go of her chin and brought both arms around her, crushing her urgently against him. It was not a very satisfactory embrace. Both wore heavy woolen under and outer clothing, topped by cloaks, for the weather was cold and raw. Nothing could be felt beyond the simple pressure, but heat flashed from their joined mouths and ran down, pulsing, through their loins.

Gilliane could not lift her arms, which were imprisoned by Adam's. Crushed almost breathless as she was, still she desired to be closer. She bent her elbows and tried to seize Adam's hips, but the heavy folds of his fur-lined cloak slid under her grip, frustrating the attempt. Both their mouths were open now, Adam's tongue seeking solace in a substitute penetration. Naturally enough, far from calming them, this activity merely inflamed them further. Blind to the fact that no closeness could remove the impediments to the union she needed, Gilliane began to struggle to free her arms. She wanted only to hold Adam closer, to seek through his clothing to touch his flesh, but he felt her movement as an effort to escape.

"Dear heart," Adam whispered, releasing her lips but not his hold upon her, "do not be frightened. I will not hurt you."

With the removal of Adam's lips, some sense returned to Gilliane. She could not yet think what was best to do, but she could fear. At this moment, of course, Adam felt nothing beyond the desire she also felt, but later, when he was sated, he would know her for what she was—lustful, unchaste. A sob shook her.

"Sweet beloved, do not weep," Adam begged, interspersing his words with soft kisses. "I will not force you."

"Oh, Mary help me," Gilliane wailed, "I do not fear you will force me. You will not need to force me. Have mercy. Do not let me make a whore of myself! Do not ask me what I desire. What I desire is foul. Help me!"

"Love is not foul," Adam soothed, kissing the tears that were running down her cheeks and then her lips. "Love is sweet and holy."

"Not for us," Gilliane wept, finally finding the will to push him away. She might as well have pushed against the eighteen-foot-thick wall of the keep. "I am another man's wife. It is matrimony that is holy."

"You said you were not willing," Adam said, stopping his efforts to capture her lips again. There was a hint of sharpness in his voice.

"Does it matter?" Gilliane asked wildly. "Does it matter that I would prefer to be bound to a venomous serpent? That poor, crippled, feeble-witted Gilbert was far more welcome to me? The priests say it is God's law that a woman must keep her vows—no matter what her husband is." Sobs choked her again. "Oh, let me go," she begged desperately. "I do not fear damnation. I fear only you."

"Of all men in the world, you have the least to fear from me," Adam protested.

"No," Gilliane sighed, letting herself go limp against him, her head falling back. "Any man can beat me or rape me or kill me, but only you can destroy me because—God help me—I love you."

CHAPTER TEN

The three small words acted on Adam like a pail of cold water emptied over his head. He stared down at Gilliane's passive face and knew that if he took her now she would not resist him, that she would probably respond with great passion. He wanted her so much his body hurt. There was a drawing in his thighs and in his groin—but she had said she loved him. If that was true, then the other thing was also true: he could destroy her.

It was plain to Adam that Gilliane had been used and abused by men who thought her nothing, and she had withstood that because she hated them. The very fact that she had felt hatred, that she had not meekly accepted what was done, had helped her to survive. Now, however, she would accept—willingly, joyously, she would come to him, even though she knew she was sinning against the laws of both God and man. That would not matter to her—just so long as it did not matter to him.

One part of Adam's mind protested indignantly that, of course, it would not matter to him. Gilliane's marriage vows were a farce. She had never knowingly sworn to "love, honor, and obey." One cannot be unfaithful to what one has not sworn. Thus, she was clean of breach of faith. Why, then, should he think ill of her? He never would, never could, think ill of

Gilliane. The little weight of her resting in his arms, the sweet, hurried breath he could feel, drew him to taste her lips again.

They were offered willingly, parting readily under his, but Adam did not kiss them long. Her eyes haunted him; wide open, fearful and trustful at the same time. He knew he *had* thought ill of Gilliane, as little as a few minutes ago when he found her with Cuthbert. He did not, could not believe this was a game she was playing for profit, but . . . but . . . But what if after he took her, some other thing roused his suspicion? What if his quick temper brought to his lips words he did not mean—or, worse, did mean? Knowing herself guiltless, Gilliane might weep and be hurt—if she loved him as she said—but, after she was cheapened in her own eyes, what once might have been a little prick could become a wide and gaping fatal wound.

Gilliane trusted him. Before Adam could let her yield herself, he must be more sure of her and of himself. He closed his eyes, swallowed, and lifted his lips to kiss Gilliane's brow. "You are a cruel taskmistress," he murmured, "to lay upon me the burden of your soul."

"I am too weak to bear it myself," she sighed. "It is yours. All of me is yours. You must do with me what you think best. I am lost to myself."

Adam sighed also, then shook her gently, his hands on her shoulders to steady her. "That is not a good thing, Gilliane," he said soberly. "I am only a man. Do not ask of me more than I can do. I, too, can fail."

"Not to me," Gilliane replied passionately. "Never to me. But I will try, my lord, to carry my own burden if you say I must."

"Say *Adam*," he suggested, smiling. "You have made me your servant and lightly bound a load upon me. Is it not more fitting to call me by my name?"

"Adam," Gilliane repeated obediently. It was so very appropriate—Adam, the first and only man. "But it is the lord who carries the heaviest load, not the servant."

"You are quite right about that," Adam agreed, and his smile changed to a wry grin. "And, lest the devil find some mischief for this lord's idle hands, I had better set about mending the breach my carelessness has made in your storerooms."

"*My* carelessness," Gilliane said firmly.

"*Our* carelessness." Adam laughed. "Although why you should believe you are to blame for telling a conqueror no more than he asked—"

"I told you I never felt that. I feared you. You were always welcome to me, though, because you drove Osbert away. Only how . . . Forgive me, dear lord, if I seem to speak against your will, but the serfs are starving already. Many will die before spring. If you take any more from them, there will be none left to work the land."

Impulsively, Adam kissed Gilliane again, but it was swift and light, a mark of approval. He ended before it led to anything more. She was so wise, and so sweet in offering her wisdom, not rapping it out as an exasperated order—a habit too common to Alinor with her son.

"Poor things. No, of course I will not take from them. If I am successful, perhaps there will even be a little excess we can use to relieve their misery." Adam grinned with mischievous pleasure. "I will go raid the rich demesne farms around Lewes. Louis's men have grown too accustomed to having their own way in these parts."

The light in the storeroom was dim. Adam did not see how pale Gilliane became. All her life Gilliane had feared on her own account. Even that morning, when she thought Adam would leave her, it was her safety for which she feared. She had not projected her mind into what he would be doing. However, it was no longer a question of guessing. Adam had told her: he was going to fight to get supplies.

"No!" she cried faintly, catching at his arm.

"No? Why no?"

There was cold suspicion in the question, but Gilliane did not hear it. She was entirely taken up with the long-buried knowledge that her father had died in battle. She had barely known his love and comfort and he had been taken away. Now she had found love and comfort again, and again it would be snatched away.

"You will be hurt. You will be killed," she panted, clinging to his arm as to a lifeline.

"*I?* Raiding a demesne farm?"

Adam did not know whether to be furious because she was using the device of love to protect Louis's man or because she had denigrated his fighting ability, whether to laugh at her sweet ignorance or be melted with tenderness because love could make his wise Gilliane so silly. It was frustrating not to be able to see her clearly. Adam slid his free arm around Gilliane's waist and led her out into the bailey. Her blanched face made clear to him that, whatever the true reason, there was a desperate importance to her in the matter. He held her close for a moment, struggling with himself, realizing that he did not want to know. Why should it matter? If he never allowed her to influence his decisions . . . Adam swallowed. How long would he know his own mind if these few minutes had already changed him so much?

"Well, then," he said, forcing what he hoped was an indifferent tone while he watched her face, "if you do not like me to raid Lewes, I might try Dover."

The effort was not a complete success. Even though Gilliane was absorbed in her vision of a lover dead before he had even become a lover, she was aware of the strain in Adam's voice and manner. She realized something was very wrong, but she did not know that Dover was King Henry's castle and she did not know a trap had been set for her. She only knew that Dover was farther from Tarring than Lewes. Gilliane could only interpret Adam's reaction as indignation over a woman's interference. Yet, with his customary kindness, he had not hit her or even angrily told her to mind her needle. He had offered to change his plan. Common sense told Gilliane that the best and easiest would be the nearest place and the place first suggested.

"No, do not go farther," she cried. "Oh, pray, my lord, do not heed me at all. In my fear for you, I will say something stupid that will drive you into greater danger. See what I have already done amiss by pleading for the serfs. Better they should starve than you should be hurt—"

Enormously relieved, and more than willing to believe it was fear and not a desire to aid Louis's cause that drove Gilliane, Adam hugged her tightly, interrupting her. "Gilliane," he said softly, torn between tenderness and laughter, "do not be so silly. Do you not realize that you are insulting me? How could I be hurt raiding a few farms?"

"Can you not?" Her eyes were raised to his trustfully, searching his face. "Truly?"

This, Adam guessed, was a subject with which Gilliane was totally unfamiliar. Because she had never cared what happened to any of the de Cercy men, she had learned nothing about raids, war, or fighting in general. Easy reassurance rose to his lips, but he could not say the words—not with her innocent, trustful eyes fixed upon him. It occurred to Adam that this was a danger he had not foreseen. He could not lie to Gilliane. He shrugged.

"Be reasonable, Gilliane. God may smite a man any place, any time. I cannot say it is impossible. I can say that if I should be hurt, it would be near a miracle." A tremulous smile made her lips irresistible. Adam tasted them again, but very swiftly. He was aware they were visible from the walls. The guards should be looking outward, but men's eyes do wander, especially when attracted by voices. "Now do not argue with me," he added firmly. "I will do what I must do. Go in. You are shivering with cold."

By the evening, his plans were set. Alberic and the majority of his troop and some of Cuthbert's would stay at Tarring, closing it against all. Adam would take Cuthbert with about an even number of the Tarring people and his own. Alberic was not too happy with this arrangement. He did not like even the small chance that Cuthbert would turn on his master, although he admitted that the men seemed uniformly happy and grateful to be taken back into service. There had been nothing suspicious in their behavior.

Nor did they fail in any way when Adam rode out with them the next day. Cuthbert knew the area well and was most assiduous in guiding them through uninhabited territory so that no warning of their attack would precede them. It was fortunate Cuthbert was an honest man for, in truth, Adam was not as alert as he should have been against treachery. His eyes looked where Cuthbert directed, but half his mind was back in Tarring.

For Adam, the hours before he had left had been piercingly bittersweet. They were sweet because the companionship he was sharing with Gilliane was exactly what he expected marriage to be. The bitterness was engendered by his doubts. Had Gilliane's absolute trust in what he had told her cured her fear, or had the fear been only a pretense? Did she truly feel love for him, or did she merely desire to be free of the hated Osbert? And if it was love, how was he to lay hands upon Osbert? What if he never found him? What if Louis was defeated and Osbert fled with him to France?

Sweet was the moment of parting. Adam, his eyes full of the exquisite face and form in the chair opposite him, had become uncomfortably aware that Gilliane was *not* his wife. He had silenced Father Paul, whom Gilliane had invited to read to them, with a gesture and risen to his feet.

"I must be abed betimes, Father," he had apologized, "for I must be early away."

Gilliane stood up also, and in response to that movement the priest had folded up his book and gone away. "Adam . . ." she said.

It was more than his name. It was an offering of herself. But even as she spoke and held out her hand to him, fear flickered in her eyes. Adam understood. Gilliane was afraid that if she let him go she would never have him. A surge of desire froze his expression and brought him closer. He caught her hand and lifted it to his lips. Feeling it tremble, he realized that to take her would be to fix her growing fear that he had lied to her and there was danger. Before he returned, she would have convinced herself that harm had befallen him and she would have suffered agonies of terror. It was not worth it. Adam licked his lips. He needed easing, but he could take a girl on the road the next day.

"I will be gone before you wake tomorrow," he said.

Gilliane's eyes filled with tears. That meant he would not share her bed. Otherwise, how could she fail to wake when he did? Still she shook her head. "Whenever you leave, I—"

"No," Adam ordered, "do not come down, even if you should happen to wake. I will return soon enough —perhaps in three days or four. There is no need for you to lose sleep—"

"Please, my lord! Please!"

"No!" Adam snapped.

"I will not weep or trouble you. I . . ."

"No. Go up now to your chamber and obey me."

But she had not obeyed him—and that was sweetest of all. The devil of doubt within Adam had already put forth the idea that Gilliane had wanted him to come to her bed so that she could dissuade him from attacking her friends in the most forceful fashion a woman can persuade. However, even that devil could not make up a bad reason for a woman to kneel shivering, hidden by the curve of the stairwell, without a sound, only to catch a glimpse of him as he went down. Adam just happened to turn his head to glance rather longingly at the women's quarters as Gilliane peeped around the curve of the wall. She uttered a squeak of dismay and fled.

The comical aspect had hit Adam first, and he began to laugh, which prevented him from calling out to her. Then, even before his laughter had completely died, it was clear that his only safe path was to ignore the encounter. To condone openly such an act of direct disobedience was to make any order he gave in the future into a jest. Yet what could he do? Adam could not bear to think of scolding Gilliane for disobeying him on this occasion. As they rode out, Adam even berated himself for unkindness, wondering if the poor girl would fear he would punish her upon his return. He almost turned back, telling himself it was better she should be disobedient than unhappy. What held him on his path was a nervous conviction that if he now got near enough to Gilliane to comfort her, he would not stop at that.

The desire for Gilliane soon grew so powerful that Adam signaled Cuthbert to him with the intention of asking about the nearest village lightskirt. As soon as he formulated the idea, an intense sensation of distaste cooled him into complete indifference. Surprised by his own reaction, Adam asked instead about the holders of the land they would need to traverse. Doubtless he would have learned more from Cuthbert's answer if he had listened more closely, but his attention was too often diverted by little things—by a pair of chestnuts the master-at-arms took from his saddlebag to munch that had just the rich sheen of Gilliane's hair, or by the gurgle of a stream that had something of the sweet liquidity of her laugh.

Fortunately, Adam was well enough trained to absorb details of terrain and manpower half dead, so the fact that part of his mind was fixed on personal matters had no effect on his efficiency in arranging the plan of attack. His new technique worked well and they had a rich take, gained without a single scratch. Grinning cheerfully, Adam dispatched the fruits of his cleverness down an open road toward Tarring where the tracks of carts and cattle would be meaningless. A guard of fifteen experienced men would protect against any chance encounter. When the loot was well away, Adam dispatched another twenty men under Cuthbert to muddy their trail. The remainder of the men watched the farm from various vantage points until daybreak. After that it was only a matter of time until the raid was discovered. Adam withdrew his men to a safe distance along the back trail, set guards to warn them if a troop should approach, and told the men to eat and get what sleep they could.

At midday the watches were changed and, shortly thereafter, a scout rode in to tell Adam, amid much laughter, that his ruse had been successful. The raid had been discovered in the morning and a messenger had rushed to Lewes keep; later a party of armed men had ridden off north along the false trail Cuthbert had laid. Adam stretched and yawned and nodded. Then a thoughtful look came into his eyes and he sent the man to wake and summon Cuthbert.

"Do you know who holds the nearest keep to the north?" Adam asked the master-at-arms.

Cuthbert mused, scratching his head and yawning. "There is none so very near, my lord. Tonbridge is the nearest, and I do not know who holds that place now."

Adam racked his brains, but he could not remember whether the keep at Tonbridge had been yielded to one of Louis's French adherents or was still in the hands of an English baron who was supporting Louis's cause. In fact, if an English baron held the place, it was no longer sure from day to day whether he was still Louis's man or had returned to his original allegiance to the Plantagenet house. It would not be safe, Adam realized, to involve any of the rebellious barons because, if they had recently reestablished their ties to Henry, he would not wish to bring an attack upon them and shake that resolution.

It was a shame, Adam thought, that he did not know the badges and colors of any of the Frenchmen. He would dearly love to make mischief by raising bad feelings and distrust among Louis's adherents while feathering his own nest. Suddenly, Adam's eyes lit with unholy joy. Not far away, less than ten miles, there was Halfand. Adam was not sure what the holder's loyalties were, but he knew the man had borrowed money from FitzWalter in the not-so-distant past. Thus, there was some connection for FitzWalter in this area. FitzWalter and Arundel—a very shaky and uncertain ally of Louis —did not love each other anyway. If men who left evidence that they were bound to FitzWalter attacked Arundel's property, there might well be mischief made. Grinning broadly, Adam issued instructions. FitzWalter's shield was *or,* a fess between two chevrons *gules* —that is, gold with a bar set between two red chevrons; red and gold. Red and yellow cloths were found and tied around arms and bridles and their battle cry was to be only "Dunmow! Dunmow!"

Just before nightfall Adam scribbled a note to Gilliane and dispatched it with a man-at-arms to warn her that he might be longer away than he had first thought. "It has come to me that I might make double and triple profit from a bare two or three days more in the field. Do not fear for me. This new business is no more dangerous than what I thought first to do."

Adam found it was no trouble at all to lie to Gilliane when he did not need to look into her eyes, at least not when the lie was for her own peace of mind and comfort. If he could have seen her face when Father Paul read her the brief message, he would have realized that with ease of lying came ease of disbelief. She did her best to hide her terror from the priest and castlefolk and

was successful, largely because they had no particular
reason to be afraid. It was only in Gilliane's mind that
guilt for disobedience, for lust, for other unrecognized
sins, which added up to being happy, produced a conviction that Adam would be killed, or that he was so
disgusted by her behavior that he had decided to throw
away any profit he could receive from Tarring only to
be free of her.

The arrival of the loot from Adam's first successful
adventure made nonsense of her fears, but did not reduce them. Love knows only its own strange logic.
Adam was lost to her, and all she would ever have was
his letter. This being so, she must know the meaning
with her eyes as well as her ears. Gilliane went to Father Paul and demanded to learn to read. He looked
at her as if she were mad, but something in the set of
the jaw and the firmness of the usually soft lips told
him that argument could produce no more than his
expulsion from recently recovered comforts. It was
peculiar, very peculiar, for a woman to desire such a
skill. Father Paul did not really like the idea of any
layman knowing the mystery of reading and writing.
What would become of men like himself, who had
spent their lives in study, if everyone could read and
write and keep accounts?

Nonetheless, he wrote out the letters and combinations of letters and showed Gilliane how the black
marks were equivalent to the sounds of speech. Although he mumbled often that this mystery was not for
women, not even for men who did not dedicate themselves to God, being too deep for their shallow minds,
Gilliane struggled on. Deep need coupled with a keen
mind made learning, even in the face of steady dis-
couragement, possible. By the end of the day, Gilliane
had the alphabet and the combinations of vowels and
consonants firmly fixed in her memory. In her bedchamber that night, she drew Adam's letter from her
breast and pored over it.

At first Gilliane could see no connection between what she had learned and the markings Adam had made. Then she found one familiar word—her own name. Never before had such a feeling of success, of conquest, enriched her. *Gilliane.* That was she, herself! The letter was hers because the name was hers. No one could take away what had her name written on it.

Then it occurred to her that there were other things with her name—the marriage contract with Gilbert that made her his heir had her name written in it. For the first time Gilliane felt, *knew,* the lands were hers. She remembered, too, that the men swearing homage had said her name, sworn to her name. Her eyes gleaming, her lips tight with determination, Gilliane told herself that the very next day she would look through all the parchments concerning the lands and pick out those that bore her name. When she could, she would read them and understand what they said.

Success breeds success. She studied the letter again. It could not be said that she read it, but she made out enough letters, and here and there even a word, to be convinced that the priest had lied. The mysteries of reading and writing were not too deep for her brain. She had learned so much in one day that it was quite clear it would not take her many years. Hugging her victory to herself, Gilliane tucked her letter under her pillow and went to bed.

Just as her eyes closed, the man who filled both her waking thoughts and her dreams realized he had got himself and his men into a very tight situation indeed. The previous evening Adam had led his men around the north of Lewes, carefully keeping to the south of the farm they had raided. That was a tricky march because there might have been small troops of men out, watching for the raiders; however, they had successfully achieved their objective and had concealed themselves in a wood north of Horsham to sleep and rest during the day. Soon after dusk, they had ridden south a few miles and raided a demesne farm on the north side of Knepp castle.

There had been no attempt at secrecy this time. They shouted and burned and took only such dried and smoked provender as could be loaded quickly on horses and carried away swiftly. Without pause, leaving fire and ruin behind them and shouting "Dunmow! Dunmow!" to keep in touch with one another, they had continued riding south and east, risking disaster to ride twelve more miles in the dark, skirting Amberly castle, to fall on the town of Arundel just before dawn. Here, where they had really only intended to cause confusion and insult, they had a piece of luck—whether good or bad was still unknown and would depend upon the outcome. They came by accident on a merchant's warehouse that was chock full of just the supplies needed for war or siege. Doubtless the supplies had just arrived and were meant for Arundel's keep.

Adam knew the danger but could not resist. Parties of men were sent out to scour every available horse from the area. As they came in, the horses were loaded and sent galloping eastward with a few men. They were to meet in the hilly and wooded area north of Bramber castle, each group to find and take the best concealment they could and to stay quiet through the next two days until either Adam or Cuthbert could gather them together. If neither came by the end of the second day, they were to make their way as best they could back to Tarring. Adam, with Cuthbert and ten of the fighting men who had been trained to use the longbow, remained until, after the sun was up, armed men rushed out of the castle in response to terrified messages from the town.

The calculated risk had paid off. The castle was already thin of men because Arundel was with Louis and the castellan did not dare take the chance that the attack on the town was a feint to make him weaken the force holding the keep. No more than thirty men galloped down the hill toward Adam. When the party was seen, Adam abandoned the near-empty warehouse and rode madly northwest toward the hills that separated Arundel from Farnham and Guildford, leading the remaining packhorses and taking great care that their calls of "Dunmow" should be heard.

Because they were a small party, they found places enough for concealment from which a fusillade of arrows could be launched, driving the larger force to retreat and giving Adam's party time to ride away and find another suitable ambush. Retreating and retreating, they escaped, but that was not the end of their troubles. Warnings went out from Knepp and Arundel to arouse the whole neighborhood. There was not much danger while they were in the forest north of Bramber, but Adam dared not continue east because his own properties of Trueleigh and Devil's Dyke lay there. The very last thing he desired was to arouse even the smallest suspicion in his neighbors that it was he who had attacked them.

Until now, despite their conflicting allegiances, Adam and his neighbors had managed to keep the peace. Arundel certainly wanted no trouble with Adam Lemagne. He had known and liked Adam's father, and he liked and respected Adam's stepfather. King John's excesses had driven Arundel into Louis's arms, but he was uncertain and uneasy in his new allegiance. He was not a clever man, but even he had noticed the lack of trust with which Louis's English allies were treated. Had he not feared the contempt and rejection of men like Pembroke and Lord Ian, who had never wavered in their allegiance, he would have forsworn himself a second time and returned to King Henry's party. Instinctively, he shrank from offending such men even further, and was happy to leave Adam, deeply beloved by both, strictly alone.

Adam knew this. He also knew that Arundel was a

courageous blockhead. If he believed himself to be insulted by Adam, he would cast all other considerations
aside to avenge his honor. Thus, it was not possible for
Adam to seek safety in the keeps of his castellans. No
matter what the risk, he must seem to avoid his own
lands as if those held greater danger to him than any
pursuit. It took another day to gather his scattered troop
and their booty from the hills around Bramber, but
they eventually found all but five men. That night they
set out northward, as if to return to London. This
might add conviction to the idea that they were Fitz-
Walter's men, for Dunmow, his main seat, lay northeast
of London. It was a dangerous move because it was
the path they would be expected to ride.

In fact, they had not been on the move for more
than an hour and a half when a troop bearing the colors
of Knepp castle came blundering out of a side road
nearly into their arms. With a shout, Adam sent the
laden pack animals off, protected by a small group who
had been instructed to keep them together and get to
Tarring if they could. He and Cuthbert, with most of the
men, turned to confront their pursuers. Had he had the
full troop with which he had started, there would have
been no doubt of the outcome, but their numbers were
considerably reduced and they were only a few more
than the thirty men they faced. That troubled Adam far
less than the fact that their exact whereabouts were now
known. Nonetheless, a fight was a fight.

"Dunmow!" Adam roared. "Spit the French dogs."

They did not, of course, take the Knepp castle men
by surprise. Each party had seen the other at the same
time. However, Adam's reaction was swift enough to
prevent most of his opponents from fewtering the
lances they carried. His party had none. Spears are not
handy things to carry along on a raid meant specifically
to collect loot.

Fortunately, most of the men in the front ranks
simply threw down their lances when they saw Adam's

party so close and bearing down on them with drawn swords. Behind them, however, a smaller group had time to get the lances steadied and spur their horses forward. Their own group parted before them, and they rode full tilt toward Adam and his oncoming men. There were only about ten of them, but four of the ten lances were directed toward the trumpet voice of the giant leading the charge.

CHAPTER ELEVEN

Gilliane was abed but not asleep. She berated herself for this foolishness. Alberic was not in the least worried about his master, and Gilliane did not confuse his lack of concern with indifference. Over these six days she had become well acquainted with Alberic. Their relationship had begun the day after Gilliane's first reading lesson. True to her resolve, she was in the chamber given over to accounts, looking through the documents under the frowning and disapproving eyes of Father Paul. This impressed Alberic most favorably. There were very few women who either could or would trouble with the accounts of their estates or defy the opinion of their priest.

He decided to present to Gilliane a minor problem of discipline among the men. She listened to him with an expression of amazement and, he suspected, distress. He was somewhat disappointed, for, like any subordinate, he wanted his opinion to be supported by someone in authority. His expression was as plain to Gilliane as hers was to him. He will tell Adam, she thought, and Adam will think me unable to rule the men and unworthy of his notice.

"But, Alberic," she protested, making her voice steady with some effort, "I do not think it is my place to order the punishment of Sir Adam's men. I . . ."

"They are not my men, my lady," Alberic pointed

out. "I know what my lord would order in such a case. They are the men who returned with Cuthbert."

"Oh!" Gilliane's face cleared. She had seen the solution to the problem of not having the faintest idea of the appropriate punishment. "Well, their lessoning must be the same as that given to your own men. It would be most unwise to treat them differently. Do you tell me what Sir Adam would order, and I will order the same."

Alberic sighed with pleasure and relief. The lady was as wise as she was beautiful and had a proper feeling for the management of men-at-arms. He was equally pleased with her manner when, having told her his lord would order ten strokes of the lash, she came down with him, heard the case, reprimanded the men with great dignity, ordered the punishment, and stood by, totally unmoved, while it was being administered. In fact, Gilliane *was* unmoved. She was astonished at Adam's leniency, having seen far worse things done to men in Saer's keep for far less cause. Her last act, however, sealed Alberic's good opinion and made the men-at-arms her devoted servants. Having watched the whippings with perfect calm, Gilliane sent a man-servant for water, old cloth, and her box of unguents and with her own hands dressed the torn flesh of the groaning culprits.

From then on, Alberic brought all his doubts to Gilliane. A child was lost in the village. Should he send men to help seek for it? On the one hand, Adam had told Alberic to seal the keep against attack. On the other, Alberic was sure Adam would have sent the men out to look for the child. Gilliane ran down at once to question the weeping woman. The child was young; it could not have wandered very far. Let the men go at once, Gilliane ordered, but let them go full armed and let one or two stand guard to cry warning if an enemy should come. Since this was exactly what Alberic thought should be done—though he was afraid to accept the responsibility for the decision—Gilliane became his penultimate source of authority.

By a fortunate circumstance, the child was found alive and unhurt. More significant for the life of Tarring, the disciplined behavior of the men Alberic sent to help in the search woke a hope in the townspeople that their sojourn in hell was ended. Neville might not have been a perfect master, but his demands were ordinary, and, if once in a while a woman was raped or the men of the keep made free with what was not theirs, the keep could usually be counted on for assistance in times of emergency. With the advent of Saer, every appearance of men-at-arms was a catastrophe. Only Saer's French troops were used among the townspeople because they had no ties of friendship or family there. They enforced Saer's outrageous demands, and committed robbery and rape while they did so, adding injury to injury, and knowing there would be no punishment.

Gilliane began to enjoy her power. Having so long been a victim, she now found it a great pleasure to give orders. Her combination of fairness and generosity was a miracle that could not be kept secret. Word spread from the town and soon others crept to the keep, weeping for help or redress. Gilliane's days became so full that she had no time to fear for Adam, and she was so weary at night that she seemed to have no energy to dream. Nonetheless, when five days had passed, Gilliane did ask Alberic whether she should have a suitable dinner prepared for Adam's return. The master-at-arms looked surprised and then smiled. "Do not count the days, my lady. You will see the lord when you see him. If he learns of a chance to bedevil Louis's people, he will seize it."

Gilliane turned pale. "Sir Adam said nothing of that. He said he would raid a farm or two . . ."

"Now, do not fret yourself about the lord's fits and starts, my lady," Alberic soothed, very well pleased to see so strong a sign of concern. "For all he is very young, he knows what is possible in matters of war."

"War . . ." Gilliane breathed, turning even paler.

"No, no," Alberic hastened to say, "there is no war in these parts. I only meant that he would not lead the men into unnecessary danger."

This quite false assurance comforted Gillane regarding Adam's safety, but Alberic's manner, which indicated amusement that she should have expected Adam to return so soon, started a new anxiety in her. For Adam, was a woman out of sight also out of mind? That night she dreamed—not of fear, but of love—and woke sobbing with frustration. Fortunately, the day was very busy. A French ship, unaware of the changes that had taken place, anchored in the harbor south of Tarring. Gilliane's good reputation as an overlady had spread and a messenger rushed up from the port to warn the keep of this development. Alberic was again torn between two needs. Adam would not have let such a prize slip from his hands, but to denude the keep of men was dangerous.

Take the ship, Gilliane ordered when Alberic came to her, if it can be done quickly. Even a few men could keep Tarring sealed against foes for the few hours Alberic must be away. The venture was successful and the prize far beyond Gilliane's expectations. There was wine and bales of fine silks and brocades meant for the Lord of Lewes. There was even a casket of necklets and arm and finger rings. That was all good, but there was much to be decided. What should be done with the crew? With the ship itself? When the shipment expected did not arrive in a reasonable time, would the Lord of Lewes send to inquire about it? If he learned the truth, would he mount an attack on Tarring?

By the time the cargo was unloaded, those who had warned the castle rewarded with a suitable share, and the remainder carried up to Tarring, the captain and crew of the vessel were disposed of in a cell in the lowest level of the keep. Then a new captain and crew had to be found for the ship so that it could be sailed away to Roselynde harbor, where it could be concealed or refitted for use. The townspeople had to be warned what to say if inquiries were made. When all this was accomplished, Gilliane found she had missed dinner and was so tired that she did not care. She crept into bed, sure she would be asleep as soon as her eyes closed. Instead, she remembered it was the end of the seventh day and Adam had still not returned.

In that instant, she was wide awake. Fear pricked her, but not harshly. Alberic was not worried and Gilliane knew her ignorant terrors were senseless in the face of his informed experience. But where could Adam be? What could he be doing? Alberic said he would take whatever advantage he could to harass Louis's men. Did that mean Adam would try to take a keep? No, that was silly. Gilliane knew better than that now. A man did not attack a castle with less than one hundred men. But that was the only thing Gilliane could think of that would take many days, except . . . Adam must have a woman—many women. Gilliane knew from her maids that he had slept strictly alone all the time he had been at Tarring. Perhaps he had taken a whore on the days he had ridden out, but a man like Adam would not be content with those filthy creatures.

That must be it! No wonder Alberic was amused at her anxiety and not at all worried himself. Adam must have gone to his woman. Naturally, he would not be satisfied with a hasty few hours. Doubtless he would spend some days making up for his past abstinence. Gilliane ground her pretty teeth and wished every disfiguring and loathsome disease that existed would strike whatever woman Adam was holding in his arms. She passed from rage to envy, imagining his big, clean-limbed body stretched in her bed, thinking of how he could be wakened with kisses, of his response. She wept with remorse at having let him go out of Tarring unsatisfied and ripe for any woman. Since she would never be able to marry him anyway, why had she been such a fool as to deny him? Now he would return sated and indifferent, his mind and his eyes full of another woman.

How could she have been such a fool! Surely there was something she could do. Somehow she must make him come back. More important was how to hold Adam once he came, fresh from the arms of some exquisite whore skilled in the ways of love and gowned and jeweled in the latest fashion. It was obvious that Adam found her attractive, Gilliane thought, but he was hungry for any woman then. Now she would need to compete with his memory of an elegant lady. How could she compete with two or three simple gowns of common cloth without any adornment beyond her seashell cross? Even as the question entered her mind, Gilliane remembered the cargo of the French ship. A short struggle with her conscience—Gilliane had assumed that the cargo would go to defray part of Tarring's debt to Adam—ended when she suddenly thought that Adam might use the beautiful fabrics as a gift for his mistress. It was soothing to imagine his irritation when he heard of the usage of the cloth melting into appreciation after he saw Gilliane in the pretty gowns she would devise.

Imagination is often a far stretch from reality, but it was seldom further afield from the truth than on that night. Had the men holding the lances been belted knights, Adam would have been dead. The men-at-arms, however, were not trained with the same care and intensity and did not use that weapon with much nicety. In addition, the short distance between the parties when they became aware of each other and Adam's immediate charge toward his opponents prevented the men from developing any real speed. He was thus able to catch two of the spears on his shield and thrust them away. Another he beat aside with his sword. That defensive gesture, however, opened his right side, and the fourth lance struck him midway between armpit and waist. A twist and wince sideways saved Adam from being spitted, and his armor, the very best double-linked mail, held, except for one ring that burst and another that spread sideways. The tip of the lance caught his skin. Adam leaned away further and brought his sword down in a backstroke that beat the spear aside.

Behind him he heard a shriek and knew one of his men had not been as fortunate as he. Wrenching his horse around, he pursued the closest of the lance-wielders, struck him down from behind, started after another. Meanwhile, the main body of the men from Knepp castle had come up. Adam bellowed his false battle cry, urging his men to greater effort.

The ground on which the parties had first come together was open, a grazed-over field near a track leading down to a farm. Striking and thrusting, Adam drew his troop after him across the field to a darker darkness that indicated a wooded area. When they reached this, Adam remained on the periphery, permitting his men to pass between himself and two or three other superior fighters, holding back the Knepp castle men. To speak the truth, the labor was less hard than it could have been. Few of them were anxious to come within reach of Adam's long arm or his gray Fury's flashing hooves. When Cuthbert finally came abreast of his master and the six who had been charging back and forth along the periphery of the wood to prevent pursuit, all of them melted back between the trees as swiftly as possible.

They were not followed immediately. Each man hesitated to plunge into the greater darkness ahead, which might hold the bellowing giant leader of that pack of thieves. Adam's men, naturally, had no such reservations and rode ahead as quickly as they could.

Haste was more important than silence. There was no doubt in any man's mind that the troop they had fought would not give up the chase this easily. There had been wounded on both sides, but the men from Knepp castle could send their wounded back to give news of what they had found and to ask for advice and reinforcements. They might or might not choose to engage again; they could simply follow until reinforcements came from the castle. Sooner or later Adam and his men would be overtaken by a far superior force. However, the farther they were from Knepp, the less would be the advantage held by their pursuers.

In the wood, Adam turned the men hard south. For as far as the trees stretched, they could hope that their change of direction would shake the men who followed them. It was not easy to hold direction because the branches of the trees broke and obscured the outlines of the constellations by which they guided themselves. There was a narrow band of wasteland, swampy with a blocked stream, and Adam waited there while the men went forward. For a time it seemed that they had lost the men from Knepp, but just as Adam re-entered the eastern portion of the trees, he heard them—well to the north but still following. Emerging at last, Adam recognized the outlines of several landmarks. They were now almost due north of Kemp, about four miles from Lewes. He looked across the relatively open hills and frowned. Then he strained his eyes to the east and began to curse luridly. Another troop was riding toward them from the direction of Lewes—at full speed.

But that was ridiculous! Adam realized in the instant that, against the background of the woods, his men could not be seen. Thus, whoever was galloping toward them could not be riding so fast to attack them. In that case, the speed must be an effort to elude pursuers. Adam signaled his men back into somewhat better concealment and watched the oncoming force. They must be either a troop of raiders trying to escape with their loot or a defeated war party, he guessed. Then he smote himself on the forehead. Dunce that he was! That was *his* loot and the men he had sent with it, fleeing from some armed party they had met accidentally. Now they had had it! They were caught between two fires.

Even as he thought "two fires" Adam knew the answer. It was a common device to set a second fire to block the progress of one raging out of control. It might not work, but it was the only chance they had. Bidding his men stay still as mice in the wood, Adam rode out toward the fleeing party, crying, "Dunmow! Dunmow!" The men recognized the trumpet voice as well as the battle cry and slackened their pace a little, veering southward toward their master. Hard behind them came a troop of men from Lewes who had been guarding the demesne farms against another raid. Adam gauged the distance and nearly wept with joy. They should just make it.

"Dunmow!" he bellowed, signaling the men to cry out the same after him, and plunged back in between the trees.

Once in the shadows, he checked his horse as suddenly as possible. Obediently, the men pulled in their beasts and the train of pack animals also came to a halt. One by one, Adam sent the men off southward. If his trick did not work, this was as good a place as any to stand and fight. If it did work . . . The last group of packhorses he held back, cutting the rein that held them to each other so that they were free. Northward could be heard the sounds of the men of Knepp coming through the wood. To the east, the troop from Lewes was about one hundred yards from the trees. Choking with laughter, Adam pointed his ten packhorses north and east out of the treed area.

"Dunmow!" he bellowed. "Dunmow!" bringing the flat of his sword down good and hard on each rump.

With startled neighs, the horses bolted out of the

wood, dashing straight ahead in the direction they had been pointed.

"Dunmow!" Adam cried, encouraging them. "Dunmow!"

The sound of his voice was caught by the trees behind him and flung outward. To those coming out of the wood, the battle cry seemed to come from the open area ahead. To those riding west on the heels of a pack train of loot, it seemed to come from inside the wood. The packhorses ran straight ahead, clearly emerging from between the trees until they heard and saw the mounted troop from Lewes thundering toward them. Then, following the instinct of their kind, they turned to join the herd. Adam knew perfectly well that he should ride off at once and join his men, but he could not resist staying to watch.

Perhaps the gods of chance enjoy an appreciative audience. What followed was as perfect as if both troops of men were engaging in maneuvers at Adam's direction instead of being out for his blood. The men from Knepp crashed out of the woods with the infuriating cry of "Dunmow" ringing out—apparently from the oncoming troop, which they assumed to be reinforcements for the raiders. The packhorses racing from the wood south of them seemed to be the tail end of Adam's troop joining their fellows. Contrariwise, from the point of view of the men of Lewes, the pack train had entered the woods, met friends there, and was now reemerging to engage them.

Without more ado, the two parties fell upon each other, cursing and swinging their swords. Adam nearly fell off his horse laughing at the mess of pottage he had stirred together. The only thing that saved him from choking to death on his own muffled guffaws was his regret that he could not wait to see the end of the matter. He hoped both groups would be so infuriated that they would fight each other until one was beaten and fled or until both were at a standstill. Unfortunately, there was another possibility. Both groups might come to notice that neither used the battle cry "Dunmow," and might realize that they had been tricked. If so, it behooved Adam and his men to be as far as possible from the scene of the crime when that realization came.

Whatever the outcome of the battle, one real good had come of it. Adam could quite safely flee southward now. It would not arouse any suspicion because any fugitive group, seeing its path blocked north, east, and west, would naturally fly south. Then, another mischievous thought struck Adam and he began to laugh again. They would soon be on the outskirts of Kemp land. There, Adam would tell the serfs to load anything of value into carts and take it to Kemp. His men would then fire the village and he, as much a victim as the lords of Lewes, Knepp, and Arundel, would complain bitterly of his loss.

He could even have stopped at Kemp to have his wound treated, but he did not wish to do that. He sent Sir Robert a message explaining what he had done and rode on to Tarring. Adam was thinking of Gilliane and how much nicer it would be to be treated by her than by the castle leech. Since he was not in the least concerned about the wound itself, although he was a little puzzled as to why it had bled so much, he could see no reason why he should not get some pleasure out of it.

CHAPTER TWELVE

In fact, rather more happened than Adam had bargained for. They had no more trouble with pursuit and arrived safe at Tarring with about three-quarters of their ill-gotten gains just after Gilliane had broken her fast. She was actually busy turning over the cargo of the French ship to choose cloth for a gown and muttering maledictions on the head of the woman who held Adam in thrall when a servant came running to tell her that he was a few minutes away. For one moment Gilliane was paralyzed by joy and relief. Then she ran to change her dress. Never again would she permit Adam to see her in garments more fitting for a maidservant than a lady. Gilliane was not only jealous, she was fast becoming aware of her own worth.

However, love was far stronger in Gilliane than pride. Although she told herself that she should wait for Adam in dignity in the hall, her effort at self-discipline failed. Drawn as if by some physical force, she went step by step across the hall and down into the forebuilding, arriving in the bailey just as Adam was dismounting from his horse. The sight of him effectively wiped everything else from her mind and she ran forward to embrace him, only to be spun around and pushed away with such force that she did not even fall, being propelled forward about five feet into the arms of an oncoming groom.

Gilliane uttered a single cry, tore herself free, and fled without daring to look behind her. She heard a confused noise and nearly died of shame. Adam was laughing!

She could not have been more wrong. Adam would have been cursing, could he have spared the breath. The inarticulate grunts being forced out of him were of effort. He was clinging to his stallion's reins, trying to prevent the enraged creature from killing everyone in sight. The unhappy coincidence of Adam sliding from the saddle just as Gilliane rushed toward him with outstretched arms had keyed all the animal's defensive mechanisms. Adam had barely been able to push Gilliane out of the way before the war horse savaged her.

He was at a grave disadvantage because he had been holding the reins rather loosely in his left hand while he dismounted. The stallion was tired and the men knew the fierce temper of the big gray horse well enough to approach it only on signal from Adam. Thus, he had been unprepared for its sudden lunge. Now he was in danger himself—not because the horse, who knew his scent, would intentionally attack him but because the wildly flailing hooves might strike him by accident. He could, of course, have let go completely, but then the stallion would have charged through the bailey and certainly injured a number of people before he could be captured and quieted.

A wild fifteen minutes ensued while Adam clung to the rein, twisting it round and round his hand in an effort to shorten it and draw the stallion's head toward him. He grabbed repeatedly for the bridle with his right hand, grunting with pain as a sensation of tearing and then of warmth told him he had reopened the wound on his right side. Finally, as much by luck as by good management, his hand caught the leather just above the bit and he was able to bring the horse's head down so that it could not rear. The grooms, who had been watching, horrified and helpless, rushed forward to add their weight. Having caught his breath, Adam began to stroke his destrier and speak soothingly until, at last, the animal quieted enough to have the girth loosened and the saddle removed.

That ended the crisis. Fury, the horse, was appeased, but fury was aroused in Adam. "Idiot woman!" he snarled, striding off into the keep. He was by no means pacified to find Gilliane nowhere on the main floor and no one assigned to help him out of his armor. Gilliane had told the maids she would undertake that task, and none of them realized what had happened.

"Gilliane!" Adam bellowed, pulling off his furred cloak and flinging it ill-temperedly toward a chair. "Where is your mistress?" he roared at a shrinking maidservant.

Naturally enough, he received no reply beyond a terrified shake of the head. None of the servants had seen Adam in a temper before, and the hall was emptying as if magic were making its normal population invisible.

"Someone fetch her to me," he snarled. "If I need to wait for my comfort, I will have satisfaction for every minute out of the hides of every one of you."

The maid fled. Everyone else, even the few bolder spirits who had been lingering tentatively, hoping the storm would blow over, also disappeared. Turning about to ask a man to bring him wine, Adam found himself completely alone. Never had such a thing happened to him before. His own and his mother's servants were well accustomed to outbursts of temper, and, although they might slink along close to the walls and perform their tasks as silently and unobtrusively as possible, they would not run away. They knew that no worse would befall them than a sharp slap or a harsh word.

Whatever the state of the servants had been under Neville, half a year of Saer's management had put real fear into them. Men and women had been maimed, tortured and killed for no better reason than the master's bad mood. Now all believed the horror would begin again. Some must suffer, but each hoped that someone else would be caught and the lord would be appeased before he or she was found.

When the pallid and shaking maidservant flew into her chamber, stammering out Adam's order and threat, Gilliane rose from the chair in which she had been sitting and went with a sleepwalker's face and gait to the stairwell and down to the hall.

"What ails you and the servants in this miserable place?" Adam shouted as soon as she appeared.

"They are afraid," Gilliane replied with the quiet of despair.

"Afraid of what?" Adam roared. "I will teach them to be afraid if I come again from a week in the field and find no welcome. Is there no one to unarm me? By Christ's holy bones, am I to go hungry and thirsty?"

"Which do you desire first, my lord, to be unarmed or fed?" Gilliane asked, wondering if he would beat her to death when she came near enough to be struck.

"Oh, get this damned armor off me," Adam said, still irritably but in a normal voice. "I have not been out of it for a week and I am galled to death by my own sweat."

No matter how indifferent the spirit feels toward a bitter fate, the body shrinks instinctively from hurt. Gilliane had been approaching Adam with somewhat lagging steps, and when he spoke of food and drink, an unbidden hope rose in her. If she was sent to procure refreshment, she might yet escape injury. The demand to be unarmed killed that hope, and as it died Gilliane did not understand what else was said, although she heard. Hope gone, Gilliane now only desired to get her agony over with. She came forward more quickly and Adam swung around to face her. As he did, the bright wet smear of fresh blood caught her eye.

"My lord," she gasped, "you bleed."

All Adam's rage came flooding back. "It is a miracle I am not dead and half the castlefolk with me," he snapped, his face crimsoning. "If ever I saw a more idiotic woman than you, I cannot remember when. Do you not know enough not to run at a destrier's head?"

Neither words nor tone made the slightest impression on Gilliane. She forgot rejection and pain. Everything was swallowed up in fear for Adam.

"Let me see," she cried.

Appeased by Gilliane's reaction, Adam said, "It is nothing. A prick. I cannot think why it is bleeding so much."

She had undone the strap of his helmet and dropped it to the floor. Adam winced. "Have a care," he began, but Gilliane pulled out the lacings of his hood and then bent to lift the skirt of his mail shirt.

"Sit," she ordered, hooking a stool forward with her foot.

Adam did as he was told. As his rage dissipated, his energy went with it and he felt tired, ordinary fatigue being increased by loss of blood. Gilliane pulled the hauberk over his head and dropped it unceremoniously on the floor.

"Gilliane!" Adam protested.

"Did I hurt you?" she cried.

"No, but first you drop my helmet, and now my hauberk. For a man like me, mail shirts do not come cheap. Besides, it was my father's and . . ." But she was not listening. She was unfastening his tunic. He caught her frantic hands. "Gilliane," he laughed, "are you going to undress me here? It is cold, and . . . and it is not polite to be naked in the hall."

She struggled to get her hands free, repeating, "Let me see your hurt. Let me see."

It was plain enough that Gilliane's love was magni-

fying the importance of his injury, and Adam was filled
with tenderness at the idea that her fondness could wipe
out all her experience and turn her silly. He transferred
both her hands to one of his, pulled her down close
to him, laughed at her foolish fears and kissed her.
Gilliane froze into immobility. The laughter, coupled
with the kiss, pierced her like a knife. The strength of
Adam's hands and of his grip upon her told its own
tale. He was hurt, yes, but not seriously. Sick with
shame, Gilliane wrenched her mouth free.

"Let me go," she begged.

Adam thought he understood. It was quite true that
this was not the time or place. "Very well," he conceded, "but only if you will be more sensible. If you
are going to be so silly, I might as well be silly, too.
I would much rather kiss you than have you use me
for a sewing sampler, even if it is a foolish thing to do
right now."

He had been so angry, but now the voice was again
the voice of Gilliane's dreams, a deep, warm rumble,
soft with amusement and affection. For the first time
since he had returned, Gilliane dared look into Adam's
eyes. The expression in them confused her utterly, for
there was no contempt or indifference. Surely the glow
in them was lit by desire. Yet when she had run to
greet him, he had thrown her aside and laughed at her.
Why? The men! Gilliane shuddered and pulled away,
and Adam let her go. She covered her face for a
moment, swallowed, and raised her head.

"You were not expected, my lord," she said. "There
is no chamber warmed and ready for you. Will you
come above to my room where there is a fire? Can you
walk so far?"

Adam chuckled. "If you will let me lean on you,
I will make shift to crawl up the stairs."

He was delighted. To him the invitation into the
women's quarters was significant. It did not occur to
Adam that the de Cercys had not accorded their women-

folk the courtesy of privacy. In his mother's home, no man except Ian came abovestairs, except for a special reason. Thus, to Adam's way of thinking, Gilliane's invitation could only mean that her desire had triumphed over her fear. It was a common enough reaction to a man who had returned wounded. Still chuckling that Gilliane should one moment carelessly set him to wrestling with his maniac destrier and the next ask him if he were strong enough to walk up a flight of stairs, he slipped his arm around her waist. She did the same to him, taking a firm grip on his hip and sliding her shoulder under his armpit to afford him support. Adam bent his head to drop a kiss on her headdress. He had no idea that Gilliane had taken his jest about needing help seriously, and since he could not see her face he assumed she was returning his affectionate embrace, cuddling as close to his body as possible.

To Gilliane, the offer of her chamber had no meaning beyond the fact that it provided the greatest comfort. Should Saer or Osbert have demanded warmth and discovered there was a fire in her room that she had not mentioned, she would have been beaten for it. Gilliane did not give the matter another thought. Her mind was completely taken up by the fact that all Adam did was laugh at her. Gilliane could hardly breathe for her misery. She would far rather he had beaten her than shown his contempt so openly. Yet he did not look contemptuous or say cruel things. He only kissed her and laughed.

The maidservants, hearing steps, had clustered together, clinging and shivering with fright. However, the sight of their mistress in the lord's embrace and of the good-humored smile on his face did much to restore them so that when Gilliane told one to bring water, another to fetch her chest of healing stuffs and a third to seek out clean garments, the group broke up easily

to spread the word that the lord was now contented.
Gilliane continued on into her own chamber, releasing
her grip on Adam as they approached the chair set
beside the fireplace. He was not so willing to let go,
however, and swung her around in front of him.

"No!" Gilliane cried softly, bending her head so that
Adam could not catch her lips.

"Why?" he pleaded, but he knew why.

She wished to treat his hurt and the maids would be
in upon them any moment. Gilliane was wiser than he,
Adam acknowledged with a sigh, and let himself sink
down into the chair. Before he had got farther in his
thoughts, Gilliane was beside him, carrying a wooden
goblet. Adam sighed again with content as she handed
him the warm spiced wine in silence. For a moment,
he dared not look at her. No woman had ever been so
perfect. She was perfectly beautiful; she did not scold
and rage like his mother; she showed her love more
openly than his reserved sister; she was as clever as
either of those loving, shrewd women; and she also
understood when a man needed to be served in silence.

When he looked up to thank her she had already
turned away to take the casket of salves and powders
from her maid. Adam grimaced and closed his eyes.
He did not look forward to what came next, but it
must be endured, and the sooner started, the sooner
ended. He felt Gilliane standing near him and said, "Do
what is needful."

Then there were hands on his tunic. It was lifted, but
the shirt came up with it and Adam grunted with pain.
Both were firmly stuck with clotted blood to the torn
place beneath. The pull relaxed at once.

"Pull it loose," he said. "I understand it must be so.
I will not be angry." The assurance was not unnecessary. It was common enough for a man to strike those
who treated him because they caused him pain.

"I am afraid that would do more harm," Gilliane

said. "From what I can see, the skin is torn away from the flesh beneath, and to pull it would tear it further."

"So that is why it bled so much," Adam remarked in a rather satisfied voice, as he opened his eyes. "I knew the lance had barely touched me, and I could not for my life understand wherefrom came all that blood."

"Are you still cold?" Gilliane asked. "If you could endure to soak in a tub, it would soon come free."

It was strange to talk so easily about such ordinary things, she thought. Who could believe that this was the same man who had thrust her away contemptuously because she dared approach him in the presence of his men-at-arms? Why should he bother to be so cheerful and patient when she was not worth his enduring a grin from some common soldiers? She heard Adam agree with pleasure to a bath, laugh about the fact that he needed one sorely. She made some conventional reply and then hurried away to order that bath and water be brought up. Adam watched her go and smiled. She was a damned clever girl, far quicker of wit than he. She would accomplish all her purposes in one stroke— clean his wound, get him naked, and make him a sweeter-smelling lover—and all without a single hint of immodesty.

When Gilliane returned with a train of menservants lugging the bath and buckets of hot and cold water, Adam winked at her. When she knelt to undo his shoes and cross garters, he chuckled. When she took down his chausses, she looked aside, and Adam began to laugh aloud, which he continued to do—between gasps of pain—while Gilliane washed him, eased the clotted cloth free of his side, and sewed the ragged triangular flap of skin that had been pulled free back into position. Gilliane hardly spoke at all, even when Adam asked mischievous questions, and would not look at him, but her cheeks were flaming red. That made Adam laugh all the harder. Little witch that she was, she knew she had been found out. The whole sweet device delighted and amused him.

Right on cue, after having finished stitching him up, Gilliane asked, "Will you lie down and rest for a while on the bed, my lord? It is warmed and ready for you."

Adam nearly choked. Gilliane certainly knew what she wanted and the most direct route to obtain it. He had wondered how, in the middle of the day, she would get him from the bath to the bed, but he had not thought of the very simple expedient of asking him outright if he wanted to rest.

"I will rest awhile," he said huskily and very deliberately, and, not to be outdone in circumspection and cleverness, "if you will give me your support so far as the bed."

Gilliane came forward at once, although she was quite sure that when Adam leaned on her she would fall to the ground. She was so hurt and embarrassed that her body was beginning to fail under her spirit's perturbation. It was plain that she had betrayed herself, betrayed the fact that her lust outstripped both her pride and her shame. From the moment Adam had agreed to bathe, the fever of desire had raged so strong that her flesh tingled and her breasts were swollen, as if Adam had been handling them.

When she first spoke of soaking his wound free, there had been nothing in her mind beyond the wish to spare Adam as much hurt and pain as possible. However, when she went to order the bath, she had realized she could not set him into water with the shirt and tunic on him. They would soak up the wet and turn cold. It would be necessary to cut both off his body, except for the patches that were stuck. That had done it. The notion of Adam's nakedness had set her afire. She had crushed the desire down, denied it—but Adam had known at once. His wink had acknowledged the lewdness of her lust, and he had been aware of every increase in her heat, aware that every time she touched him—to unlace his shoes, undo his cross garters—the touches had sent pulses of desire through her. How he had laughed when she turned aside from his engorged manhood, but even with that laughter ringing in her ears she had nearly fallen upon him then and there.

How could he be so cruel as to laugh? It was plain that he did not care for her, but he did have a desire for her. He must know it was not a thing that the will could command. As soon as Gilliane had sewn up Adam's wound, she fled to the opposite side of the room. She had intended to go away altogether, but found she could not force herself out of the chamber. Pretending to choose clothing, she struggled to control herself but realized she could not bear to touch his naked body again. Thus, she said the first thing that came into her head that would delay the need for her to dress him. If Adam would only lie down and sleep for an hour or two, perhaps she could master the need that was consuming her. Two minutes, she told herself, as she came near to support him to the bed. If she could hold steady for two minutes, he would be abed and she could be free of him.

The arm Adam slid around Gilliane gave far more support than he received. As soon as he touched her, he became aware of her violent trembling and the laughter died in him. He would have comforted her, but his throat was suddenly constricted between desire and tenderness, and he led her into the bedchamber without a word, pausing to kick the door shut with his foot before turning to take Gilliane in his arms. The sound of the slamming door woke her to the enormity of what she had done, and she tried to pull away, to cry out a protest. It was too late for that.

In the brief time it had taken them to walk from the antechamber into the bedchamber, Adam had come to the decision that he would bed Gilliane now and marry her as soon as he could find and kill Osbert de Cercy. He was aware that Gilliane's shaking might indicate as much fear as passion, but he assumed that the fear was the same as that which had caused her to beg him to save her from herself a week past. Adam had, however, no longer any reason to doubt *himself*. He knew quite well that Gilliane and he might have different ideas and purposes, and he knew that he might have painful doubts as to whether she loved him or merely wanted to use him. He knew also that it did not matter. He had to have her—not physically, although he wanted that, too—he had to have this woman for a life companion.

Adam knew that the devices that delighted him now might break his heart in the future. He was aware that it might turn out that Gilliane had never cared for him but only used her body to try to bend him to her will. The difference was that Adam had come to understand this could hurt only him. It could not change the way he felt about Gilliane. As to his hurt—he had a right to risk his own future pain for his own present joy.

Although he felt the stiffening, the attempt to pull away, Adam did not heed it. Holding Gilliane with one arm, he pushed her face up with his free hand and kissed her. She struggled against him, one last convulsive effort to save herself, but it was hard to guess whether he even felt the pathetic attempt to salve her pride. His grip was inexorable, and the molding together of their lips and bodies was not affected in the least by Gilliane's abortive struggle. He held her until he felt her melt against him, until her lips parted to welcome his tongue and hers followed his when he withdrew it, until the arms that had pushed at him came up around his neck to draw him closer.

Then was the time to break the first long embrace for little kisses on the eyes and nose, for nuzzling along Gilliane's throat—an attempt impeded by her wimple which, naturally, was unceremoniously removed. The break in love play produced a sobbing, "Please . . ." from Gilliane, but Adam paid no mind, pulling the pins from her hair so that it cascaded down to her hips in shining chestnut waves, kissing the lobes of her ears when she turned her head and her nape when she tried to bury her face in his breast.

Fire coursed from his lips over Gilliane's body. Dimly into her mind came the assurance that she had nothing more to lose. Adam already thought the worst of her. Nothing she did could lower her in his estimation. Why, then, should she struggle so with herself, trying to force herself to struggle against him? Why should she not take her pleasure, since she had already paid the price for it? She raised her head to meet his lips without needing urging from his hand, which was busy undoing her dress.

Adam was pleased that Gilliane's token resistance ended so quickly. He was accustomed to overcoming coquettish protests, which often continued much longer, but he had never thought of Gilliane playing that game. She had placed herself in his keeping, and it would be silly and affected to pretend reluctance when, in his mind, he had accepted the responsibility for her honor and her happiness. Adam had never found reluctance—even patently pretended reluctance—a stimulating form of love play. He wanted his woman to display the overt hunger that burned in his mother's eyes when she looked upon her husband.

He got what he wanted, full measure and overflowing. It was Gilliane who tore off her garments, dropping them in a trail as they kissed and fondled on their way to the bed. At the last step, Adam lifted her in his arms and fastened his lips to her breast as he laid her down. Gilliane whimpered and clutched at his head, let it go to run her hands feverishly over his back and shoulders, pulling him urgently onto the bed to cover her with his body.

Now it was Adam who resisted. Subconsciously, he

knew he was too tired to begin again once he was finished. Gilliane must be contented beyond desiring another coupling—at least until he had slept for a while. He did come into the bed, but beside her. His hands played over her belly, found their way between her parted thighs. She sought him blindly with her mouth but, to Adam's delight, she did not seem to know how to handle a man to increase his passion. Obviously, in spite of being married and having coupled, Gilliane knew very little about the art of love.

"Slowly, beloved, slowly," Adam whispered. "So we will find greater joy."

Quick at everything, Gilliane was an apt pupil. She had opened her eyes when Adam spoke to her. She was afraid to look at his face, afraid what she saw there would contradict the shaking tenderness of his voice. Her eyes were drawn to his body, and she caught her breath at its magnificence—at the hard curve of the muscles that banded arms, chest, belly, and thighs, at the glint of white skin under the curling mat of black hair. Here and there a line of dull white marked a healed wound, but there was no sense of horror about those scars as there had been about Gilbert's mutilations.

"You are so beautiful," Gilliane sighed. "I have never seen a man so beautiful."

It was not the first compliment Adam had ever received, but it was the first he believed. The other women who praised him he knew had praised men before him and would praise men after him. He had never loved and had never, until this moment, bedded a woman who really loved him.

He did not reply in words, but with his mouth and his hands he worshipped her who worshipped him— and had the response he desired. Fascination drew Gilliane's fingers and lips to Adam's body. Her first touches were tentative, but her lover's gasps and sighs, the way he strained toward her, soon taught her the value of such touching. Soon she was near weeping, again crying brokenly, "Please . . . please . . ." but with a far different meaning.

CHAPTER THIRTEEN

The cataclysm of pleasure that struck Gilliane when Adam finally consummated their love play left her nearly senseless. She was only dimly aware of Adam's weight lifting off her, of his hands gently smoothing the hair she had tossed wildly. Her senses returned slowly as the fierce palpitations of pure sensation faded, and she realized that Adam was now lying beside her, breathing deeply in sleep. Gilliane had no idea what she should do. She was afraid to move lest she wake Adam. She was also afraid to remain in the bed and expose herself to the likelihood that, when Adam woke, he would dismiss her as he would any slut who whored for him. In addition, she could not bear to move because to lie thus beside the man she loved was, she feared, the last taste of joy she would have.

Between fear and longing, she lay so still that she slipped into sleep herself, to be awakened some hours later when Adam turned and landed half atop her. A shock of terror changed at once to a thrill of pleasure when she saw Adam, but this was followed by a dreadful sinking of despair. How angry he would be if he woke and saw her lying there as if she had the right of a wife. Blinking back tears, Gilliane began to inch herself out from under Adam's weight, but the arm he had thrown across her tightened, holding her firmly.

"Lord, what fools we were to fall asleep," he said

muzzily. "I am sorry, Gilliane. The thing is we were riding and fighting every night and during the day we all slept with one eye open lest we be taken by surprise. I was tired." He grinned, looking much wider awake. "Especially after this last bit of riding. I have never bestrode a more mettlesome mare."

Gilliane stared at him, wide-eyed. Voice and face were one, tender as the hand with which he was stroking her hair. Could she have misunderstood the laughter? No, because no one could misunderstand the anger with which he had thrust her away in the bailey.

The grin faded from Adam's face, and he raised himself on an elbow. "Come, love, do not be wroth with me. I could not help it, I swear. I am sorry to spoil your clever plan to conceal our doings from the maidservants. Indeed, it was well thought of and very wise, but if you whip well the first who looks askance or speaks amiss, you will have no further trouble with them."

It was fortunate that Gilliane was so surprised that Adam thought she had wanted to conceal their relationship that she was unable to say anything. Then, suddenly, she believed she might have the explanation for his rejection when she ran to meet him. Adam could have been trying to protect her from her own folly. How stupid she was! Why should Adam care that his men knew he was bedding a married woman? It was no blame and no shame to him. It was the woman who would be considered foul. A little flicker of fear that Adam's circumspection might come from a determination to keep clear of any claim she might make on him passed through Gilliane's mind, but she put it aside and reached up to touch his face.

"I am not angry," she murmured. "How could I be, when the fault is mine? It was I who should not have fallen asleep." She was about to add that she did not care a whit what the maids said or thought, but that flicker of fear touched her again. Perhaps it was Adam who wished to avoid gossip. He was not married, Gilliane knew, but he might be betrothed or negotiating for a betrothal, in which case he would not want his relationship with her spread abroad. "The maids will not gossip," she assured him. "I will see to that."

Adam lay down again, completely content. He was convinced that Gilliane had the sweetest temper of any woman born. "You must not blame yourself for my faults," he remarked, grinning again. "My mother tells me I am little enough wont to believe I am other than perfect. You will make me unbearable if you constantly agree with me."

Not to me, Gilliane thought, but she was aware that Adam was joking and she made a light rejoinder, moving to sit up and slide out of the bed. Adam caught at her.

"We have already overset the fat into the fire," he murmured, rubbing his lips suggestively over her breast, "stay with me a little longer."

Already Gilliane could feel her body responding, but she tried to pull away, saying in a shaking voice, "Oh, my lord, do not."

"Why?" Adam urged, stretching his neck to kiss the cleft between her breasts.

"It is very late," Gilliane quavered. "Oh, dear, there will be no dinner."

But the arms Gilliane had placed against Adam's chest to keep him at a distance felt all boneless and exerted no pressure at all. And then, as Adam's lips wandered from the center over toward the nipple, her hands slid downward along his body quite of their own volition. Soon her mouth was too busy to utter any further protest. In any case, all thoughts except those concerning what she was doing had flown out of her head. Therefore, when the climax had been passed and she was drifting up out of the daze it induced, she was surprised to hear Adam laughing again. Her breath caught and her eyes widened in panic, but the fear did not last long, for Adam was bending above her, kissing her nose and eyes.

"What a woman," he chuckled. "It is a wonder to me that you are not fatter than a styed hog. All you think about is food. Was that a time to talk of dinner? And I remember when we had just taken the keep and any other woman would have been prostrate with terror, you were very angry because we interfered with your preparation of dinner."

"It is not *my* dinner I care about," Gilliane protested indignantly. "It is yours."

"Oh, I am well satisfied with the feeding I have had," Adam assured her.

"Now you are," Gilliane replied, half joking and half serious, "but when you sit down at table and nothing is brought to you but a mess of pottage, you will feel otherwise, and I am the one who will feel the weight of your hand to measure your disappointment."

Adam turned his head, and his eyes were cold and bright with anger. Before Gilliane could shrink away, his arms were around her. "You will never feel the weight of any hand again, Gilliane. One of those who hurt you, I have paid already. Had I known, I would not have killed him so cleanly. When I find the other, believe me, he will suffer a thousand torments for each blow he dealt you."

"No!" Gilliane cried, shuddering.

"No?" Adam asked very softly, his arms stiffening. "Why no?"

"I am afraid for you," Gilliane whispered. "He is sly and evil. Oh, I know he is no match for you in any honest way," she added breathlessly, sensing Adam's hurt and anger and remembering how he had said she insulted him when she feared for his safety before. "But Osbert is not honest. He will seek some dishonorable ruse to hurt you that you would not even think of, being an honorable man."

"Do you not desire him dead?"

"God knows I do," Gilliane answered fervently. "I pray for it—and I do not care if it is a sin to pray for another's hurt. Let him only die of the pox, or by hanging, or by any cause—but not by your hand, beloved. I fear—I fear that if you kill him for me, my sin will come upon you. Adam, if any hurt should befall you through me . . . I could not bear that."

In her earnestness, Gilliane had pulled free of Adam's embrace and sat up. Her eyes met his without the smallest hint of evasion. Adam sighed. He believed her. He had to believe her because she was all, everything he had ever wanted. Not to believe could only tear him apart. Besides, he had every intention of killing Osbert no matter what Gilliane said. If Osbert had hurt her and been cruel to her, he had to die. If Gilliane rejected him after Osbert's death . . . no, he would not even consider that, but to be on the safe side, he would say nothing to Gilliane about marriage until her husband was dead and she was free. His attention was diverted by the fact that Gilliane was sliding from the bed.

"Where do you go?" Adam asked harshly.

Gilliane began to giggle. "I am afraid to answer you, my lord."

Adam sat up, too. "What do you mean?" he began, and then, realizing why she was laughing, he began to laugh himself. "Will nothing divert you from the delights of the table? Go then, but return here as soon as your precious dinner is planned. There are a few more pressing questions—even if I will never convince you that there *are* more important things than dinner—that we need to consider."

Having pushed her head through her shift, Gilliane looked at her lover and her heart smote her. Under the week's growth of beard, his skin was pale and his eyes were heavy. There was also a red stain on the bandage she had wrapped around his ribs. She should never have permitted him to make love to her.

"Do you hear me?" Adam asked more sharply.

The quick irritability was another sign of an over-tired man. Gilliane dared not go back to the bed and kiss him and beg him to lie down and sleep. She was sure to approach Adam would end in their coupling yet again. There was something in the way his eyes followed her fingers doing up her bodice that was sufficient warning. To tell him he was exhausted, Gilliane was sure, would only result in his denial and insistence on getting up altogether. Perhaps if she made a jest of it, he would stay abed and sleep.

"Yes, I hear you," she said saucily, "but since you have been so unwise as to promise me I would not feel your hand nor any other's—I think I shall be disobedient."

"What?" Adam exclaimed, sitting more upright.

Gilliane laughed at him. "Lie down, my lord, do. I was only teasing about dinner. Truly, there are more important things, and I have been greatly at fault in allowing my pleasure"—her voice faltered a little and her eyes caressed Adam's big body, but she picked up her cotte and pulled it on as she continued—"to draw me from my duty. I must look to the wounded men and also see to the proper storage of what was on the pack train. Do you permit, my lord?"

"Good God, yes!" Adam exclaimed remorsefully. "Poor devils. See what you can do to make them easier at once. It was cruelly hard on the worst hurt to ride so far, but I dared not leave any behind lest our pursuers take them. When you are free, though, come back. We must decide what to do about your vassals, whether we should tell them—"

"Yes, my lord," Gilliane interrupted. "Do you wait here, where we can be sure no one will overhear. I will return as soon as the men are bandaged and dosed."

Actually, Gilliane attended to everything—dinner first, because it was most important to her that Adam have a proper meal, then the men and then the storage of supplies. When all was done, Gilliane stopped by the cooking sheds again to see how far forward things were. "Not before dusk," the cook Gilliane questioned said despairingly. "Could the lord be pacified with some pottage until the meats are ready?"

Laughing, Gilliane took a large bowl, a ladle, and a small pot of the thick soup and went back to her chamber. Adam was fast asleep, sprawled across the bed in exhausted abandon. Gilliane set the pot on the hob to keep warm and sat down near the door where the light was best. She worked for a time at a simple dress she was embroidering in an attempt to make it more elegant, but when she had used up her supply of silk she did not wish to leave the room again in case Adam should wake. He had been moving restlessly. She sat for a while with idle hands but found that her eyes kept wandering to him, which made him even more restless. Finally, she laid a small writing desk she had adopted on her embroidery frame and began to practice writing.

"To whom do you write?"

Gilliane jumped and nearly spilled the ink. "Oh, my lord," she gasped, "how you startled me. I . . . I do not write to anyone."

"That is no account book," Adam said harshly. "I do not know what else can be written that is not written to someone." Gilliane's face became flooded with color and Adam stared at her, his heart sinking. "Let me see," he said, stretching out his hand.

"It is not written to anyone," Gilliane insisted, blushing even more. "I was only practicing my writing."

"Practicing?" Adam repeated. "I saw you write as easily as my mother or sister, who have been writing since childhood." He got out of bed and came toward her.

"Only because I have written these words so often," Gilliane explained breathlessly, "but . . . but . . ."

She was put aside by a hand gentle enough but hard

as steel. Adam looked down at the desk, stared dumfound.

"It is a dreadful waste of parchment," Gilliane said in a very small voice, "but I will scrape it clean and it will be good enough——"

She did not get to say any more. Adam had caught her to him and kissed her. Then he released her lips to laugh, and then he kissed her again. Written over and over on the parchment was his name, coupled with a selection of the most tender endearments.

"I told you not to look," Gilliane protested when her lips were freed.

"You did not," Adam contradicted, still laughing. "All you said was that it was not written to anyone, but that is clearly not true—or do you dare to call me no one, you little witch?"

There could be no answer to that. Gilliane pushed futilely at Adam's chest, and he laughed and kissed her yet again. She did not push very hard while their lips met, but when Adam lifted his head she said, "Let me go. I must get clothes for you. Adam, let me go. You will take a chill."

"Not *beloved Adam,*" he teased, "nor even *dear Adam?* Why should an old piece of sheepskin be given sweeter words than I?"

"You are cruel always to laugh at me," Gilliane complained, although she was smiling, too. Slyly, she relaxed completely against Adam so that, after a moment, his grip slackened. Instantly, she had twisted free and fled to the antechamber. She returned with an armful of clothes, which she insisted Adam should put on. While he dressed, she removed the pot from the hob and ladled its contents into the bowl. Turning to present the soup, she shook her head over the patched garments and apologized.

"You are so big," she said in extenuation, putting the soup on a small table so she could tie Adam's cross garters, "and I have had no cloth fitting to make new clothes for you until yesterday when . . . oh, I have so much to tell you, my lord. A French ship came into the harbor and we captured it—I hope we did right?"

"*We* captured it? Do not tell me that you—"

"No," Gilliane laughed, "Alberic went down to the port, and . . . I think it will be better if he tells you himself what exactly he did because I do not well understand it, although he did explain. But, Adam, the ship was for the Lord of Lewes, and the cargo was very rich. Now I will be able to make you some clothes that will be fitting for you, and—"

"For Lewes?" Adam pursed his lips and whistled. "He has been twice stung in only a few days. I had better look to the walls and our weapons. When he hears—"

"Oh, I hope he will not hear of it. We took the captain and crew prisoner. They are below waiting your pleasure, my lord. And the ship we sent to Roselynde— that was where Alberic thought it could be most easily hidden."

Alberic, Adam thought. Alberic never thought of anything in his life. Not that the master-at-arms was stupid or ignorant. He had a fund of knowledge and experience, but would never use it on his own. It was Gilliane who had thought—not of Roselynde but of the need to hide the ship. Once she had pointed out the necessity, Alberic would be likely to suggest Roselynde harbor. Adam wondered briefly why Gilliane was so reluctant to take credit for her own successes, but she had exclaimed again and run back to the bedchamber from which she returned a moment later carrying a small casket.

"And see what else was aboard. Now there is something with which to pay your costs." Gilliane opened the casket to display the jewels looted from the French ship.

Adam looked from them to Gilliane's face. "What is their value?" he asked, firmly subduing the impulse to tell her that he would not take them—which was what he feared she expected.

"How can I guess, my lord?" Gilliane replied, looking puzzled. "I have never owned such things and, to speak the truth, neither did Saer's wife or daughters. Sometimes, if he wished to make a brave show of them, he decked them out in jewels, but he took them away again. Is there enough to pay the cost you have sustained in saving me?"

Saving her! If that was truly how Gilliane felt, there could never be a question of debt between them. Adam opened his mouth to say that she had already paid him back a thousand times over by her sweet love—and clamped it shut again. There was too much chance that was exactly what she expected of him. Nonetheless, he could not take the things from her. He cleared his throat awkwardly.

"It is too soon yet to decide exactly how the costs must be paid—or even how much will need to be paid. We are only in the beginning of our attempt to obtain your lands. For now, let us say the jewels are mine but lent to you so that you will not look a pauper to your vassals and castellans."

Gilliane had a clear memory of the first time the vassals had seen her, in a dirty, patched dress with her hair tied up in an old cloth. She nearly told Adam that, but felt shy about mentioning her marriage. Also, she was troubled by Adam's answer. She had thought he would take the jewelry at once. It was valuable, and she did not really want the responsibility of caring for it.

"Whatever you say, my lord," she replied doubtfully, "but will you not keep it? I have no strongbox nor any way to ensure its safety. This one day I hid it, but that could not answer for long. And, although I have the list of what should be there, made by the ship's captain or a scribe for him, I have no desire to be counting these things over every day and worrying about them."

Was that meant to be a slap at him for lack of generosity, Adam wondered. There was nothing in Gilliane's face to indicate disappointment or irritation. Did she want him to say *I will not hold you responsible* so that she could hold out a few pieces? Nonsense, why should she tell him there was a list? She could have kept half what was in the chest if she had destroyed the captain's list. And I am going to destroy myself if I do not stop seeing three meanings in every word she says, Adam warned himself.

"Very well, give them here."

Adam took the chest and tucked it under his arm. Gilliane smiled, which was the expression most fitting to the feelings she had described. Adam was no better off because his too-fervent desire to believe her left him—in spite of having just warned himself about the dangers of doubt—unwilling to accept the simple truth. He was aware of an odd hollowness in his belly, which was making him very cross, but he would not yield to it and snap at Gilliane just because she had behaved as properly as a pattern piece. He turned to walk away, knowing he would not be able to hold his tongue much longer—and nearly tripped over the small table on which Gilliane had set the bowl of pottage. As soon as the odor assailed his nostrils, Adam began to grin. No wonder he was cross and felt hollow. He had had nothing to eat since the afternoon of the previous day.

"You are a very wise woman, Gilliane," Adam said, setting the chest down and seizing the bowl. "How did you know I would be starving? Did you forget a spoon? Never mind. I will use the ladle." He grabbed that from the pot and sat down in the nearest chair.

After a few mouthfuls, he looked up at Gilliane, who was watching him. "Sorry," he said, swallowing what he was chewing, "you must be hungry, too. It is long past dinnertime. Come here." He patted his knee. "I will share the ladle with you."

Laughing, Gilliane denied that she was hungry

enough to steal food from a starving man, but she went to sit on his lap and, for the pleasure of eating from the same implement Adam was using, took a few mouthfuls. No one was in the antechamber, but the maids' voices could be heard in the large room outside.

"We are not being very discreet," Adam sighed as he became aware of the sounds after the bowl had been emptied.

"I think it is a little late for that, my lord," Gilliane said cheerfully.

Somewhere deep inside she knew she would someday pay for this exquisite joy with equally exquisite pain, but she would not think of that. Not one single spark of happiness would be dulled by foreboding. Until disaster overtook her, Gilliane was going to milk every drop of pleasure from each moment.

"So? Well, if you are content," Adam remarked, "I have no complaint." He settled her more comfortably in the hollow of his legs. "Now it is time for business. Have you given any thought to how we should go about convincing your vassals to obey you?"

"I have not had time to think of anything," Gilliane protested, and gave Adam a précis of the events of the past week. "Between all the people asking me what to do when Joseph's sheep fouled Mary's well, or when John fell into Henry's ditch and squashed a hen and broke a leg—did John need to pay for the dead hen or Henry for the broken leg?—I have not had time properly to oversee the maid's spinning and weaving, much less *think*."

Adam's shoulders shook. "If you *will* be a good mistress and a wise one, the people will come to you. Your mistake was doubtless to give a fair judgment the first time. If you had ordered both complainants to be beheaded, you would have heard no more complaints."

"Likely you are right. It is quite remarkable how quiet people are after their heads are removed, but they are also very slow about planting and reaping," Gilliane replied tartly, which made Adam laugh harder.

"Let us hope you have good crops to pay for your trouble." Adam rather expected a sharp *There had better be,* but Gilliane only smiled, and he was pleased that she was softer of manner than his mother, although he did not doubt Gilliane, too, expected to be paid in an indirect manner for her efforts. "But you had better think of the larger matter now," he pointed out.

"One thing comes to me," Gilliane said slowly. "After Saer left, Sir Richard of Glynde was here and I spoke to him of my fear of Osbert. I begged him to come again or to ask some other of Gilbert's men to come. He told me he was going away—to a daughter's lying-in—but he must have written to the others of my plea because Sir Philip came from Leith Hill. Sir Philip told me before he left that Sir Andrew also intended to make a visit—but Sir Andrew never came."

"It could have been some private matter that prevented him."

"Yes, perhaps, but I do not think so." Gilliane's brow was creased with concentration. She had never thought in this way about such things before, but Adam expected it and she must do it; necessity sharpened her keen wits. "I think either that Sir Richard came home and rode over—Glynde is only five or six miles away—and was told by someone the keep had been taken, or even saw the siege and fled before he was noticed, or that Sir Andrew did come and it happened to him. Either way, I am sure that Neville's men know Tarring is taken, although they may not know by whom."

After considering, Adam nodded. "I think you are probably right and the news is out. There is, then, no use in subtlety. What do you wish to do? Do you think I should just march to Glynde, say you have taken me for overlord, and call Sir Richard to duty since Neville's will makes you his heir? If I do not say anything about—about this forced marriage—"

Gilliane shuddered in Adam's arms, and he tightened his grip reassuringly, pleased at the sign of distaste. He mistook her reaction, however. As strong as Gilliane's hatred was for Osbert, it was nothing in comparison to her dread at the thought of Adam assaulting Sir Richard's keep. She knew nothing of the defenses of Glynde, but thought even a serf's mud hut a fearful obstacle if it was opposed to Adam. However, she had learned that she must not say to Adam that a thing was dangerous. Various conversations with Alberic had made clear to her that the surest way to get Adam to do something was to tell him that it was difficult or dangerous. A warning always affected Adam like a dare.

In addition, Gilliane had been trained all her life to the idea that for a woman to tell a man he should or should not do anything was a sure path to a beating. She did not think of that consciously; she no longer thought that Adam would beat her. Moreover, she would have gladly accepted the beating if it would keep him safe at Tarring. She simply could not answer his question directly and say *I want you to forget the whole subject of Neville's men. Let them rot. Stay here safe with me.* Yet somehow she must keep Adam from fighting.

"You know better than I, I am sure," Gilliane began placatingly, "but, my lord, would it not make you very angry if a man should come with an army and bid you do something—even if it was something that you might have thought it right to do?"

Honesty forbade Adam to say indignantly that he hoped he had more sense than to cut off his nose to spite his face. He admitted that he might, indeed, object to such handling.

"And it is so near, only five miles," Gilliane hinted.

"Are you suggesting that I should ride over by myself and—"

"No!" Gilliane exclaimed immediately, seeing her

lover taken, imprisoned, and tortured, even though she had every reason to believe Sir Richard was a kind and honorable man. She almost said that *she* would go alone, but realized in time that such a suggestion would be a terrible affront to Adam's pride. "We must take enough men to be sure Sir Richard could not attack us with impunity—although I do not believe he would do so without cause—but not enough to be a threat to him. And we—"

"*We?*" Adam repeated.

"But, my lord," Gilliane pleaded desperately, sure that if she was there, she could do something to keep the men from flying at each other in sheer, unreasonable aggressiveness, "he is *my* vassal by law . . . unless he is Osbert's . . ."

"Do you think," Adam began hotly, "that I intend—" But he checked himself, realizing she was right. Whatever he intended, if she did not go with him and take her vassal's homage herself, she would be nothing—or, quite reasonably, the vassal might refuse to do homage at all.

"I know that whatever you intend will be for my good," Gilliane cried. "I only—"

"No, you are quite right," Adam interrupted curtly, and then, seeing there were tears in her eyes, he laughed and kissed her. "You *are* right, and I am a fool. If we do as you say, it may well be that Sir Richard will be willing to honor his oath at your wedding without being forced to it. But the question of de Cercy remains. If we conceal the second contract—"

"No, no," Gilliane insisted. "I think that will be the strongest inducement to Sir Richard to swear to me— or you. He loathed Osbert. Not only must we tell him, but I must bring the contract. We must prove that Gilbert was dead before you ever entered Tarring keep."

"Prove that Gilbert was dead!" Adam roared. "Do you think I would harm a poor, witless cripple?"

"Dear lord," Gilliane cried, taking his face between her hands, "*I* know you would not. No one could be more gentle to the helpless. You have not even chastised me when I well deserved it for stupidity or carelessness. But how could Sir Richard know that?"

"No man of honor would think of such a thing," Adam said, still indignant, but in a much modified voice.

"Perhaps not, but Sir Richard cannot *know* and . . . and you must admit it would be a great temptation, even for a man who was not a monster. Gilbert was not happy or well, poor thing. A man might tell himself it would be a blessed release for Gilbert. I do not know about England, but in France I heard tales enough about the marriage of rich widows to their husband's slayers."

"It is true in England also," Adam replied stiffly, "but *I* have not married you."

Gilliane turned her face aside, almost as if he had slapped her, and Adam wished he had bitten his tongue. His next impulse was to assure her that he fully intended to remedy the condition as soon as she was legally as well as morally a widow—whatever suspicions that might arouse in Sir Richard's mind—but his own suspicion leapt up and seized him by the throat and silenced him. Had she wept, he would have been conquered regardless of suspicion. However, Gilliane had never really had any hope that Adam would marry her, and she recovered quickly from the hurt of hearing him say so.

"You must do as you please, my lord," Gilliane said quietly. "I am very ignorant. I spoke because you asked me to say what I thought, and it is my duty to obey you."

Adam could scarcely believe his ears. Gilliane's voice held no inflection of sarcasm or spite or anger, and when she turned her face back to him, her expression confirmed her tone. She looked a trifle anxious, but not at all angry. Either Gilliane really did have the sweetest temper of any woman born, or she did not care enough about him to be angry. Adam could feel a cold sweat break out on his body. That was ridiculous. She had been so careful of his little hurt, so eager, so passionate abed, she had rushed to greet him when he came—and driven his horse wild. Had Gilliane hoped a chance blow would kill or maim him? Involuntarily, Adam shuddered. Had she disposed of one maimed husband "for his own good," and now planned to dispose of her conqueror in the same manner?

"You are still cold!" Gilliane exclaimed remorsefully. "Let me get a cloak."

The eyes turned up to him were dark, luminous pools of love. Great sweetness dwelt in the soft curve of the lips. "No," Adam murmured, drawing her closer and bending his head to kiss her. "I am not cold. Stay with me."

He was mad to conceive such an idea, not only because Gilliane was sweet and good, but for much more practical reasons. Whatever she felt for him—whether she loved him or only pretended to love him—there could be no doubt that Gilliane was determined to rule her lands. Her activities the week he had been away—giving help and justice to the people, urging Alberic to take safe and suitable aggressive action, which he never would have done on his own—was one proof. A second proof—which also proved that, at this time, Gilliane certainly wished Adam no harm—was her insistence that she go to claim fealty from her vassal and the advice she had given him concerning Sir Richard. It was wise and sound. If anything could bring Sir Richard willingly to acknowledge Gilliane as his overlady and King Henry as the rightful king for whom he must fight, it was Gilliane's suggestions.

"Well," Adam said when he released Gilliane's lips, "you are right all ways. We will go with one hundred men and ask Sir Richard to come out with the same number and parlay with us. After all, he cannot have many more than that in the keep—I hope."

"I would not count upon that," Gilliane warned. "If he knew Tarring to be besieged and yielded three weeks ago, he had time to call up and hire more."

"It does not matter," Adam assured her, smiling. The caution certainly indicated that Gilliane was concerned for his safety, not her own. The worst that could happen to her if Sir Richard attacked them and captured her was that Sir Richard would rule the lands in her name. The vassal could not wish to do Gilliane any physical harm. "I will look over the ground tomorrow and choose a place for the parlay where we can see if Sir Richard brings out more men. If he does, we will simply ride away. He cannot have enough to overpower us completely, no matter how many he has hired, and—"

The light in Adam's eyes and the cheerful good humor of his voice told a clear tale. Adam would not mind a bit if Sir Richard decided to fight. He would enjoy the engagement far more than a peaceful yielding. Gilliane looked at him in despair. Men were very peculiar. Even Adam, who was so gentle to her, *liked* to fight. If she was not careful, Adam might deliberately misunderstand something Sir Richard said or some move he made just for the joy of combat.

"But, my lord," Gilliane interrupted hastily, before Adam could talk himself into believing that treachery was intended, "I only said that because . . . because I am silly and I fear even what I know will not happen, for your sake. Truly, Sir Richard seemed to me a most kindly, honest man. I cannot think he would do so dishonorable a thing."

Checked in his flight of fancy, Adam was a little annoyed, but in a moment he laughed at himself. Cuthbert had also given Sir Richard a clean name as a good master and an honest one. Really, it would be far, far better to come to terms with such a man than to beat him in battle. If he could be brought to swear to Gilliane willingly, he would be a strong influence on the other vassals and castellans. And if they would not come to terms, Sir Richard, who knew their keeps and natures, would be of help in bringing them into subjection.

"Good enough," Adam agreed. "We will try for peace with soft words and reason. You will have your way in all things. Now, do you reward me for my compliance—"

"Oh, I will," Gilliane cried, springing off Adam's lap. "I will provide you with a feast worthy of a great overlord of many rich properties. See how the light has faded, my lord. Dinner must be ready."

"Dinner was not what was in my mind," Adam protested, but he was laughing. He really was hungry, and it was plain that Gilliane was deliberately teasing him with talk of food. There would be time enough for love.

CHAPTER FOURTEEN

In Louis's camp around Berkhampsted, love was an emotion conspicuous by its absence. The feeling between English and French grew more strained by the day. Tension had been gravely increased when they had first arrived by an attack from the keep upon the forces of Sir William de Mandeville. Great damage had been done to his men and supplies, and his battle banner itself had been seized and carried away. Sir William complained bitterly that the French contingent nearest him had looked on without the smallest attempt to come to his aid.

Instead of pacifying Sir William by saying that the leader of the French group was absent and the men did not want to act on their own, the Count of Perche—who was a high official of Louis's court and should have known better—implied that the fault was Sir William's for not guarding himself better and not resisting the attack more firmly. There might have been a shred of truth in the first criticism, but the second was completely unfair. Sir William's men had been attacked while they were in the process of pitching and setting their tents in order, arranging the pickets for the horses, and performing other tasks necessary to making a suitable camp. The men were in confusion, running hither and thither. In fact, considering the disadvantage at which they had been taken, they had defended themselves with fortitude if not with success.

Unfortunately for the harmony among Louis's supporters, it soon seemed as if the Count of Perche's nasty implication had much truth in it. Later in the day, while the French knights were sitting at dinner, a large party bearing Sir William de Mandeville's battle standard fell upon them without warning. Less physical harm came of this second attack than the garrison of Berkhampsted hoped. Far from regarding Sir William's men as allies and thus remaining quietly at their meal, the French knights had leapt to arms as soon as the banner came in sight and had thus saved themselves from any serious loss.

They could not openly accuse de Mandeville of attacking them because he had already complained of the loss of his banner, but there was a strong suspicion among the French contingent that he might well have lied about that. If he had not, one said to another, why did he not send them warning as soon as he saw men carrying his standard? That he might not have seen the men come out of the castle, that they might have concealed the banner at first, or that, justifiably annoyed, Sir William might have wanted the French to taste the pie they had baked for him—none of these possibilities was mentioned. Another man, irritated by the scattering of a troop of horses, remarked bitterly that he would not be surprised to discover that Sir William had connived in the attack on them. Or even, Osbert offered, the whole thing could have been a conspiracy to add to Sir William's supplies at French cost by staging a raid on his own camp.

No one responded very heartily to this statement at the time, since Osbert's reaction in the face of the threatened raid had given most of the other men a hearty distaste for his company. He was jaunty enough, believing that no one had noticed his cowardice in the confusion, but rumors of his behavior at the assault on Hertford had begun to creep upward from the men-at-arms to their masters, and his recent action had confirmed the truth of those tales. Osbert was not desired as a neighbor or supporter in the coming battle for Berkhampsted. Nonetheless, his remark was repeated with a sly snicker here and there, and the seeds of suspicion planted between English and French contingents were well watered.

Needless to say, the situation was in no way improved when news came from Lewes and from Knepp about the raiding party that had used "Dunmow" as its battle cry. The French lords who held the keeps flew to Louis to complain.

"It is ridiculous," Louis said. "FitzWalter is here and no large party of his men is missing. Moreover, he has no interest in that part of the country."

It was ridiculous. If FitzWalter's men had business in Sussex, why should they not present themselves and demand hospitality? They were allies and would be received. No, that was silly. If FitzWalter wished to keep his interest in the area secret, he would forbid his men to announce themselves at any keep. But then, surely, the men would not use "Dunmow" as a battle cry. Even Englishmen could not be that stupid! Unless—it might not be stupid at all, especially if FitzWalter expected men to think, as Louis himself had first thought, that no one could be that stupid. FitzWalter, Louis told himself, would bear watching—most careful watching.

Louis was beginning to be concerned at the rapidly increasing bitterness of the English barons. He was not ready to change his policy of keeping power out of their hands, but he believed it would be most unwise to increase their animosity by any further slights. He had spoken quite sharply to the Count of Perche about the incident involving de Mandeville and had gone to the trouble of calling that gentleman into his presence to sympathize publicly with his loss. Thus, Louis had no intention of permitting FitzWalter to be annoyed by a complaint that he could claim was so farfetched and ridiculous that bringing it against him was a harassment.

Louis dismissed the men, but the situation did not pass so readily from his mind. Something would have to be done both to pacify FitzWalter and to discover whether he really was involved in the trouble in Sussex. No immediate solution presented itself to Louis, until another complaint was brought before him, this one concerning the depredations of Osbert de Cercy's men. At first Louis could not recall who Osbert was, but the de Cercy name finally made connection in his mind with Tarring, which was only a few miles from Lewes. Since Osbert's cowardice was already a standing joke in the camp, Louis knew he was useless in battle. He could employ him in another duty and be rid of his men who only disrupted the camp. Since Osbert knew the lands around Lewes, he could go there and determine who was raiding the farms and trying to blame FitzWalter for it.

Louis was quite pleased with this plan and felt he had extracted considerable good from the misfortune of the attack on Lewes and Knepp. The prince did not know, however, that the mischief Adam had done had already spread beyond his control. News of the raiders who had cried "Dunmow" had come not only to the holders of Lewes and Knepp but also to the Earl of Arundel. This gentleman was not overbright, but he had become aware of the miasma of contempt for the English barons that floated around Louis. Thus, he would not go to the prince for satisfaction but took his complaint directly to FitzWalter.

Perhaps the complaint could have been phrased more diplomatically. A clever man would have—as Louis intended—raised the point in terms of warning FitzWalter that someone was using his battle cry to get him into trouble. Such subtleties were beyond Arundel, who took everything at its exact face value and berated FitzWalter for permitting his men to raid the territory of an ally.

"I do not blame you for sending them to take what they could get from the accursed French," Arundel concluded indignantly. "The way they act, you would think they were masters of this land instead of invited guests in it. But I am no French reaver. If we do not respect each other, no one will respect us."

FitzWalter was not in the best possible temper, and besides he did not like Arundel, who spoke often of honor and duty, saw things in black and white, and had truly believed when he deserted John and joined Louis that he was doing it for the sake of the country. Arundel was blustering about how his people would have been glad to supply FitzWalter's men if they had asked in a civil way—and FitzWalter's temper snapped.

"Only you could be fool enough to believe that my men would raid your lands crying aloud my battle cry," FitzWalter snarled. "Do you think I am an idiot?"

"What do you mean—only I?" Arundel asked stiffly.

"By the eyes and nose of Christ, a man who steals something does not scream his name into the ears of those he is robbing," FitzWalter stormed. "They were not my men! What the hell would my men be doing down by Arundel anyway? Think, man, try to think."

Arundel rose to his feet, his face set and angry. He was dull, but not an idiot. When a thing was pointed out to him, he could see and grasp it. He merely did not see side paths to a situation on his own. Now that FitzWalter had made a denial and pointed out the evidence, Arundel saw the logic. It was true enough that if FitzWalter had sent the men, he would have told them to use a different battle cry. Arundel even understood that there was some cause for FitzWalter to be annoyed. No man likes to be accused of something he has not done. Still, he did not like the tone of voice

FitzWalter used, nor did he like being called a fool. That was neither polite nor necessary. In addition, he did not like FitzWalter. He had strong suspicions that FitzWalter had become involved with Louis for personal profit and not for the good of the realm.

Only long training in matters of courtesy kept Arundel from dragging FitzWalter to his feet and forcing a quarrel on him. He had come as close to that as good manners permitted him to come in a man's own house. He needed some outlet for his spleen, but he would not think of complaining of a fellow countryman's behavior to the French, whom he was coming to hate, and he was even reluctant to complain of Fitz-Walter to the other English barons in Louis's camp. One other form of pacification was possible and was completely harmless. Arundel stamped back to his own part of the camp, signaled a small troop of men to accompany him, and went to exercise off his bad temper in a long ride.

He was not going anywhere in particular and paid no attention to the direction in which he rode. After a few miles he noticed a small village ahead that was obviously defended. A rough wall of trees, roots forward with their lopped branches interwoven to provide a barrier, surrounded the place. Then Arundel remembered that this was Geoffrey FitzWilliam's land. He stared for a moment indecisively and then, still furious at the slights he had received, sent a man down to ask whether Lord Geoffrey would receive him.

Half an hour later a small troop rode into the village and Arundel saw his man coming back, followed by a single mailed knight. At the sight of the shield he bore, Arundel rode forward eagerly.

"De Vipont!" he exclaimed. "What are you doing here?"

"I am helping my son-by-marriage guard his lands against the French," Lord Ian answered—as if there were no Englishmen involved in the action against

Berkhampsted and Arundel was not himself a member of the force. "Geoffrey was not in the keep when your message came, but I am sure he will receive you with great pleasure."

"I will need safe conduct to leave again," Arundel said cautiously. "Er . . . uh . . . you know I am . . . er . . . Louis's man."

"Of course," Ian replied genially. "Upon my honor, you will be free to leave as soon as you desire—free of the keep and the lands also—without let or hindrance. Come and dine with us. You must be tired of camp fare after that siege at Hertford and now another."

"Thank you, I will." ·

Arundel already felt much better. The obvious pleasure Lord Ian displayed at meeting him was soothing. They were not friends in the sense of seeking each other out, but they had known each other for many years and each had a hearty respect for the other as an opponent and as a man. Arundel did not feel even the smallest flicker of doubt concerning his safety as he rode with ten men toward a castle holding several hundred who were technically his enemies. Lord Ian's word was a perfect guarantee that Arundel would be as safe in Hemel as in his own camp—safer, actually, because in Hemel there was no chance that he would be attacked by a raiding party from Berkhampsted.

Tactfully Ian began talking of a tourney fought ten years previously, long before the kingdom had been openly split and drawn into civil war. Arundel eagerly followed this lead and, in pleasant reminiscence, they came into Hemel, where Geoffrey came forward with hands outstretched in welcome saying Arundel's visit did him much honor as he placed his guest in the best chair by the fire. He called for wine, moved away to set a small table more conveniently near Arundel's elbow—and his eyes met Ian's. In answer to his unspoken question, Ian raised his brows and shrugged infinitesimally. He did not know why Arundel had come. The wine arrived and was poured. As the warmth of the fire penetrated, Arundel shed his cloak and gloves, and agreed to be relieved of his mail, although he refused a bath. They talked pleasantly of their womenfolk, which brought Arundel back to the ten-year-past tourney.

"I did not understand that jousting," he remarked, shaking his head. "Nor for that matter did I understand why John should have chosen you king's champion. It seems to me—"

Ian burst out laughing and interrupted him, but neither he nor Geoffrey missed the hurt and anger that came into Arundel's face. That gave them to understand that someone had been making jest of Arundel's slow mind.

"I beg your pardon," Ian said hastily. "I was not laughing at you, Arundel, but at my own stupidity in falling into John's trap. Great care was taken that you should not guess anything of what was planned because you are known to all as a man of honor and you would never have countenanced the king's doings."

"I do not see that you were so stupid, Ian," Geoffrey put in, skillfully picking up his cue. Although he had been only a young squire at the time, Geoffrey knew that Ian had not fallen into John's trap but had accepted the danger to achieve a purpose of his own. For some reason, Ian wanted now to emphasize his personal problems with John. "Who could have guessed that the king would take so violent a spite at you for having married Lady Alinor that he would plot to have you killed?"

"Was *that* what it was?" Arundel gasped.

"Yes, and it was not the only time," Ian answered wryly. "When John took a spite, he never forgot it."

"Yet you were faithful to him," Arundel said, with a tinge of bitterness in his voice.

Ian made a gesture of negation. "Not out of love.

To speak the truth, I do not know how to explain that to you, William, only . . . All I can say is that I hated the king so hard that I could not part from him. You will think me mad, but when John died, I was heart-broken. My hatred was so much a part of my whole life . . . Well, that does not matter now. What was more important in a practical way was that I liked the men opposed to John even less than I liked the king. You will pardon me, I hope, for speaking ill of your friends, but—"

"They are no friends of mine," Arundel snapped angrily.

Geoffrey's eyes glowed golden for a moment as the firelight caught them raised to his guest, and then he looked down again. So this was where Ian had been aiming to get. Ian had seen more clearly than he had. Most likely because he and Arundel—except that Ian was certainly not stupid—were truly birds of a feather. Basically, they were simple men who wished that all things were plain black and white. Ian had seen that Arundel had been hurt and angered by something or someone among Louis's men, and had set himself to showing Arundel where his true friends and sympathizers were.

There was a moment of silence while Ian and Geoffrey tried to think of something to say. Arundel saved them the trouble.

"Men make mistakes," he remarked heavily.

"God knows that is true, and I have made many," Ian agreed quickly. "It is all too easy to make a mistake on matters of state."

"That is often a hard choice," Geoffrey added, "and, to my shame, one I feared to make. My lord, even if you now feel you chose wrong, at least you had the courage to choose. All men must honor you for that. Like a coward, I locked myself into my keep, afraid to follow either my heart or my head."

Ian cast a glance of warm admiration at his son-by-

marriage. Geoffrey had said in plain words but with
the utmost delicacy exactly what had to be said. In a
few brief sentences, he had flattered Arundel, while
agreeing with him that he had made a bad choice, and,
in addition, had made it very plain that if Arundel
wished to change sides again he would be received with
honor rather than scorn. From the lift of Arundel's head
and the squaring of his shoulders, it was clear that
Geoffrey's points had not been missed.

"Now, now, Lord Geoffrey," Arundel comforted,
"your case was harder than mine. You were tied in
blood to John. It is one thing to see a man is a bad
king and that no remedy can mend him—and I will
tell you outright I still believe that to be true."

"I also," Geoffrey agreed.

"So you can understand why I felt there was no
other path but to choose a new king. However, it is
quite another matter to take up arms against one's own
blood kin. Do not blame yourself."

"You are very kind, my lord," Geoffrey sighed.
"Still, it remains that I had not the courage . . ."

"Perhaps, but see where my courage has placed me,"
Arundel exclaimed bitterly. "I would have done better
to follow your way, Lord Geoffrey, and to sit on my
own land and trust in God. We were given warning
enough. Again and again, the pope bade us be obedient and trust in God. I did not listen, and so I am
smitten, while to you, who were patient, God has given
an answer. John is dead, and you have a king and
comrades who honor you."

There was a brief silence. Arundel had been brought
to say aloud exactly what Ian and Geoffrey wished to
hear. Geoffrey began to signal urgently to the servants
and the noise of setting up the trestle tables for dinner
broke the silence and permitted another tactful change
of subject.

They talked long and pleasantly over the meal. As
Arundel's tongue was oiled by the good food and wine,

all the news of Louis's camp was related, including the raid by the group that had used FitzWalter's battle cry. Ian and Geoffrey laughed heartily over that, apologizing if they were offending Arundel but well pleased that FitzWalter should be annoyed. Even though he had been a sufferer, Arundel laughed with them. In this genial company, he accounted the loss of farm produce far less important than FitzWalter's rage. The light of the short winter day was already fading by the time dinner was over, and Arundel regretfully took his leave.

"I cannot break my given word," Arundel said, clasping Ian's and Geoffrey's hands in turn, "but if God sees fit to save me from my own foolishness, I will not err in such a way again. And you can tell your friend Pembroke, Lord Ian, that I wish I had listened to him— and there are many others among us who wish the same."

"You may be sure I will tell him, and that he will understand perfectly why you must act as you do. You may also be sure that if you should be freed from your present bondage, you will be most honorably received by King Henry, who is a sweet child and has had no false tales poured into his ears."

"Is that so?" Arundel said thoughtfully. "I will remember."

He rode away, and Ian and Geoffrey watched him. "That was a good day's work we did for the king," Geoffrey remarked. "Lord, what a dunderhead."

"Perhaps," Ian agreed a little absently, "but he is at least an honest dunderhead. He rebelled because he could not bear John and his ways, not for the sake of breaking all authority so that he could raid and pillage—and, speaking of raids, who do you think is yelling 'Dunmow' while stealing from the French?"

"I cannot even guess," Geoffrey replied as they turned their horses back toward Hemel, "but I think we had better write to Adam. If this is another Willikin of the Weald rising—someone with a personal spite against FitzWalter—then Adam should try to contact him. It may be that Adam could give him some help, but also he should be warned not to raid Kemp or Tarring. And it can do no harm to encourage him in his good work."

"You do that," Ian agreed, "and I will write to Pembroke. Perhaps there is some way he can show Arundel that he would not be spat upon or otherwise slighted if he abandons Louis."

CHAPTER FIFTEEN

Geoffrey's letter did not find Adam at Tarring. It had taken the messenger several days to come from Hemel because he had needed to duck and dodge off the roads a number of times, lie hidden for several hours to avoid a party of armed men, and he had ended by losing himself. By the time he found his way to Tarring, Adam and Gilliane had left for Rother.

They had gone with Cuthbert and a hundred men, fifty of whom had been left in a wooded area about a mile from Glynde. From the brow of a small rise about a half-mile from the keep, Adam had sent a messenger to say that Lady Gilliane desired speech with Sir Richard in a place neutral and safe for both. The lady would bring to the exact place of meeting any number of men Sir Richard specified up to one hundred, but she wished Sir Richard to know that one hundred were within call. To their surprise, Sir Richard himself returned with the messenger. Adam dismounted and went forward alone, ignoring Gilliane's gasp of fear.

"I am Sir Adam Lemagne," he said. "Do I have the honor of addressing Sir Richard of Glynde?"

"You address Sir Richard, but whether it is an honor . . . Is my lady your prisoner, Sir Adam?"

"She is my vassal."

"*She* is your vassal?" Sir Richard asked, his face

suddenly darkening. His destrier danced, indicating the sudden tightening of his hand upon the rein.

"Sir Gilbert de Neville is dead," Adam said quietly, "but not by my hand, I assure you, nor by any contrivance of mine." He was deeply grateful to Gilliane for having prepared him for this. Had they not discussed the matter previously, Adam knew he would have flown into a rage at the suspicion implicit in Sir Richard's expression and manner. "Sir Richard," he went on, "you came here alone, knowing Tarring was taken. You must then have had some reason to believe you would be treated with honor."

"My son is waiting with every man in the keep armed and ready. If I do not return in a very short time, he will come seeking me."

"I believe you," Adam replied, "but nonetheless you came alone. Thus, you must have known or guessed that the conqueror of Tarring did not desire your hurt. Why, then, should you believe I would harm a poor, helpless creature whose living would have been greatly to my benefit?"

Gilliane had prodded her mare forward. "It is true, Sir Richard. Indeed, poor Gilbert was dead over a week before Sir Adam and his companions arrived. And I do not speak through force or fear." She paused a moment and then said bitterly, "I told you what I feared, and it came to pass. No sooner was Gilbert dead than Osbert forced me into marriage. I have with me the signed contract."

"What?" Sir Richard gasped, and then, "How came Lord Gilbert to die?"

"He fell from the window of our apartment, but how that came about I do not know," Gilliane replied, her voice trembling just a little. "I had a blow to my head, and knew nothing. For that matter, I do not know how my mark came upon this contract, for I would have died sooner—I swear it. But this I can tell you. If I made that mark at all, someone held my hand to do it. I do not need to mark an X. I can write my name."

"Lady Gilliane!" Adam exclaimed, remembering despite his shock at the bold-faced lie to address her formally. Even Adam the heedless realized that to display his relationship with Gilliane at this moment would merely make it harder to convince Sir Richard that he had had nothing to do with Gilbert de Neville's death.

"Do you not believe that I can write?" Gilliane asked with a touch of plaintive indignation that made Adam's eyes widen.

He knew that most women were capable of displaying emotions they did not feel, but he did not like to be reminded of it with respect to Gilliane. Even less did he like being made a party to the lie, yet he was trapped. To show any doubt of Gilliane's truthfulness could only start a whole series of suspicions in Sir Richard's mind that might end in his conviction that the marriage contract was a forgery. Adam stiffened. He had never thought of that. It was conceivable that Gilliane would employ such a device to keep herself free of a real forced marriage. She had had time enough while she kept them outside the castle ostensibly bargaining for Cuthbert's safety. She could have . . . No! He would *not* think about it. He would end a madman.

"I know you write, Lady Gilliane," he said stiffly.

"It does not matter," Sir Richard said bitterly. "I need no proof that Lady Gilliane would not willingly accept de Cercy. I saw his behavior to her, and to poor Lord Gilbert, also."

"Yes, and so when I came to my senses—for I was ill a long time after Gilbert died—Osbert was just leaving the keep. He told me to hold it while he went for help, but I did *not* hold it. I yielded Tarring and all else in my hands to Sir Adam. I had rather be prisoner or dead than wife to Osbert de Cercy."

"But . . . God in heaven, what does that contract say?"

"That Lady Gilliane was Gilbert de Neville's heir and that all the honors and powers of her inheritance are to be held by her husband during her life and inherited by him after her death," Adam replied deliberately.

"No!" Sir Richard exclaimed.

"Just so," Adam agreed. "When I, with my stepfather, Lord Ian de Vipont, and my brother-by-marriage, Lord Geoffrey FitzWilliam, came into Tarring, Lady Gilliane took terms, accepting me as her overlord. She complained to me of the forced marriage, and I agreed that it must be repudiated."

"Yes, although I do not see how. . . . But I will not have Osbert de Cercy as overlord, not even if I must gainsay my oath of homage."

"There is no need for that," Adam pointed out. "You swore to Lady Gilliane, and there is no reason to violate that oath. De Cercy, after all, has made no claim on you."

"But what if he does?"

"Sir Richard, we need time and comfort to discuss this matter. It is cold here for Lady Gilliane. Is there some place that you would consider safe for you—and safe for Lady Gilliane—where we could be at ease to talk?"

The older man looked down at the younger for a long, considering moment. "I knew your father very well, Sir Adam, when he was sheriff in these parts. He was the most honest man I have ever dealt with. I know your stepfather by reputation. Let me ride back to Glynde to tell my son that all is well, and then I will return with you to Tarring."

"I thank you, sir, for your courtesy," Adam said. "I swear, upon my life, you will not regret what you now do."

Neither man regretted it. The talk was most satisfactory on both sides. Trust was established, and it was agreed that, as Sir Richard had had no part in old Gilbert de Neville's switch in loyalties, he was not responsible for Lady Gilliane's change back to King Henry's party. He had been loyal always to his overlord and would continue in that path. Sir Richard was not completely happy at the thought of Louis's strength in the area, the great keeps of Pevensey, Lewes, Bramber, Hastings, Amberly, and Arundel all being in the hands of Louis's men. However, he had heard rumors of the favoritism shown to the French. With Saer dead, his choice was between taking Osbert as overlord for his French connections and accepting Adam with his affiliation to the king's party.

The lesser of the two evils was plainly Adam. Sir Richard had always felt a sneaking uneasiness about repudiating John. He had comforted himself with the thought that his oath was to Neville and he had no way of controlling his overlord. After John died, his uneasiness had increased. It seemed dreadful to be part of a group that was attempting to deprive a child of his heritage. Only the knowledge that his own wife and children would be the immediate victims of any attempt to unseat Saer had convinced Sir Richard to keep the status quo.

He felt an enormous sense of righteousness and relief in returning to his original loyalties, and this was bolstered by his knowledge of Adam's connections. Adam pledged Lord Ian's and Lord Geoffrey's support in the face of any attack by the prince's forces. Sir Richard renewed his oath to Gilliane with considerable enthusiasm, and then sat down to plan bringing Gilliane's other vassals into line.

"I am sure you will have no trouble with Sir Andrew and Sir Edmund. In fact, I had much ado to keep Edmund from repudiating Saer as soon as John died. He was all for the little king. I held him only by pointing out that there was no contest in these parts and he could only lose his land by declaring against Louis with no support."

"Sir Edmund is where?" Adam asked.

"Alresford—some ten miles from Winchester," Sir Richard replied. Adam whistled between his teeth, and Sir Richard nodded. "Yes," he continued with a wry smile, "Edmund is a nice young man, but a little hot in the head. Ten miles from the stronghold of Saer de Quincy, the second greatest rebel next to FitzWalter, and he wishes to declare openly for the king."

His tone invited Adam to agree that the young were foolhardy, as if Adam were a man of his own age instead of younger than Sir Edmund, but his eyes were watchful. However, he was not disappointed. Adam had not been trained by Robert of Leicester—the most famous fence-sitter of the age—for nothing.

"There is no need to blazon abroad the answer to a question no one has asked," Adam replied promptly. "We will need to write to Sir Edmund—something soothing that will induce him to hold his tongue and keep the peace until we can come to him. There is no need to waste time on someone whose sympathies are already with us. Believe me, I have no desire to start a war single-handed. However," Adam added firmly, "when it is time, I will expect you all to do your parts to thrust Louis out."

"If there is a reasonable hope of it, we will not fail you," Sir Richard agreed. "Of the other men, Sir Andrew . . . well, I do not mean to speak ill of him. He is a good man of his hands, but . . . if I tell him it is right, he will swear to Lady Gilliane. I am not sure he understood that Neville *had* gone over to Louis. It would be unwise to discuss the matter with him, if I may offer a word of advice."

"Please do not hesitate to do so. You know these men, and I do not wish to fight Lady Gilliane's men if it can be avoided."

"Yes, well, I am afraid it may be necessary if we are to hold Bexhill. Sir Godfrey was one of the first to urge old Lord Gilbert to swear to Louis. One cannot blame him, really, caught as he is between Pevensey and Hastings. Also, he is a man most set in his opinions, argument or threat only making him more stubborn."

"Then Bexhill had better be left to its own devices until we are all of one mind," Gilliane said.

Both men turned to stare at her. She had said very little, beyond the usual feminine offerings of food and wine, since Adam and Sir Richard had begun their talk. Sir Richard had been a little surprised when Adam set a chair for her, because he could not see that a woman would have any interest in such a discussion. That she was technically his overlady was a thing apart from any practical reality. He knew summons would be sent in Gilliane's name, for example, but he assumed Adam would be the real sender and have complete control. After Sir Richard's initial surprise that Adam expected Gilliane to listen to them, however, he was pleased; it was a kind and courteous gesture on Adam's part to seem to include his direct vassal in the planning. The interruption surprised Sir Richard even more, but not nearly so much as what followed.

"It is my land, after all," Gilliane said gently, "and I suppose I must be allowed to decide."

"Within reason, my lady," Adam agreed, "and so long as I believe that your decision does not harm my interests or the interests of the king. What is your reason for abandoning Bexhill?"

Gilliane's reason was that she did not want Adam to fight anyone, anywhere, ever, but she had sense enough not to say that. "From what you said earlier about Sir Edmund, and from what I understand to be Bexhill's position, to take it from Sir Godfrey by war, perhaps after a long siege and many assaults, would be the same as stirring an anthill with a stick. That is, surely all the activity would draw undesirable attention from Hastings and Pevensey. If it were possible to come in such force that Sir Godfrey would yield at once, there would be much less likelihood that the suspicions of Louis's people would be wakened or their interest aroused."

Sir Richard said nothing. His mouth hung a little open and he stared at the big soft-brown eyes, the delicate heart-shaped face with its fine nose and sweet, full lips. He had never heard such talk from a woman. His instinct was to tell her to mind her own business—which was the needle and the cooking pot—only what she said made remarkably good sense. When the second shock that realization gave him passed, he looked apprehensively at Adam. Young men did not love advice, least of all from a conquered woman. But Adam was smiling at Gilliane with the proud look of a hen with one precocious chick. All of a sudden a brilliant idea came to Sir Richard. One worry in the back of his mind had been that if Adam found the costs of defending Lady Gilliane's lands higher than the profits to be taken from them, he might abandon his new vassal and her men to their own devices after setting them at odds with Louis. Sir Richard did not really believe this; he was sure Adam was too honorable. However, the danger did exist. Now he saw a certain way to avoid it. Adam must marry Lady Gilliane—as soon as they were rid of de Cercy.

"That is reasonable enough," Adam said, controlling an urgent desire to take his grave counselor into his arms and kiss her soundly. "Let us leave the question of Bexhill stand aside until we have seen what else lies before us."

Fortunately, Sir Richard had recovered enough from his surprise to respond naturally. "If you are asking me what I think best, my lord, I would say we should go first to Sir Andrew at Rother. That need not take much time, but he is . . . er . . . not quick of understanding, and his feelings would be hurt if we only sent a letter and did not . . . er . . . ask courteously for his loyalty and assistance. Then . . . then I think we should take the chance of riding to Sir Edmund. It is a fair journey, but if Andrew and Edmund are with us, Philip will agree to swear to Lady Gilliane without protest. I . . . er . . . Sir Philip is not a bad man, and he is very clever, but . . . er . . ."

"But he wishes to be sure his interests will not be overlooked?"

"Yes."

Gilliane's eyes had been moving anxiously from Sir Richard to Adam. She realized that Sir Richard was trying to avoid the suspicion of bad-mouthing his fellow vassals to increase his own value and importance. There was danger in that. Adam, sweet-natured and trusting as he was, might take the words as said instead of as meant. In this, Gilliane badly underestimated Adam, who, though good-natured enough, was far from trusting. Sir Richard's meaning was relatively clear to him. Before Sir Richard could reply to Adam's bland comment, Gilliane spoke.

"And if he thinks his interests are not cared for, he will care for them himself. Is that what you mean to say, Sir Richard?"

"Well . . ." the vassal hesitated.

Adam's lips twitched. "It is a characteristic of women, I have noticed, to be most nice and delicate about spitting and pissing but to say those things that had better be wrapped up in white linen in the most bald and uncompromising manner."

"I beg your pardon, my lord," Gilliane offered meekly. "I only wished that there should not be any misunderstanding. Sir Richard is too generous to speak his true suspicions, I fear, but here, in private, the worst should be said so that it may be considered along with the best."

Again both men stared at Gilliane. She had made an important point. Sir Richard cleared his throat. Adam shrugged. "She is right, you know," he said.

"Very well, then I will speak as plain as I can and

beg you to remember that I do not speak for spite.
Sir Philip is no coward and is a valuable man to have
as an ally. Nor do I believe him to have treacherous
intent. He will not fail you on the field of battle. However, he thinks too much. If he has overmuch time for
consideration before a battle, for example, it is not
unknown for him to grow to believe he is ill-used, put
too much in the forefront. Then, he will withdraw. Or,
if he should be besieged and you do not come swiftly
enough to his aid, he will believe *he* is betrayed, and
you may find yourself with two enemies instead of one
when you do come."

"I will make sure to speak to him often, soothe
his care, and assure him of my good will." Adam
nodded, dismissing Sir Philip. One could never really
predict the behavior of such men, but Gilliane had
been right. The plain speaking was necessary. Now he
would know better what to watch for in Sir Philip's
behavior. "The last, then, is Sir Matthew of Wick."

The struggle on Sir Richard's face was interesting.
He was an honest man and did not wish to lie, but
plainly he hated Sir Matthew and was finding it hard
to resist the temptation to say what he felt.

"I am not the right man to speak of Sir Matthew,"
he got out at last. "I have a personal reason to know
him as a treacherous dog—but I have no proof of it,
nor of the fact that the thing was done on purpose.
Probably, if we all come together with an army, he will
yield. That he will be faithful—I do not believe it, but
you must judge for yourself."

"That is something to think about also," Adam said,
shooting a meaningful glance at Sir Richard. "But our
first moves are clear. I cannot see any plan better than
what you have offered. We will ride to Rother as soon
as is convenient for you, Sir Richard."

"The sooner the better for me, but will it be safe
to leave Lady Gilliane alone in Tarring? I hope—"

"I ride with you," Gilliane said firmly. "To whom will Sir Andrew swear if I do not?"

Adam grinned as Sir Richard's mouth gaped again. It was a reaction with which Adam was quite familiar. Men who did not know his mother always looked that way from time to time while holding conversations with her. It was a considerable delight to Adam that his woman should have the same effect.

"But, my lady," Sir Richard expostulated, "this is not the time of year nor is the land in a state of peace proper for ladies to travel. The baggage wains will be mired—"

A trill of laughter cut him off. "My dear Sir Richard, you are so very kind to be concerned for my comfort, but truly I am a hardy creature. One pack-horse can carry all things needed for my ease." Her eyes darkened and the laughter died. "I assure you there were no baggage wains when Osbert de Cercy brought me hither from France, and I wore a knife strapped to my thigh for my own protection."

"Now that," Adam remarked, "is an excellent idea. I have thought more than once that an eating knife is no more than a toy. I remember when my sister had need to go alone into a keep where we were not sure of a friendly reception that I bid her carry a real knife, but I was concerned that it would be hard for her to hide it. You must show me—"

He cut that off and blushed. Gilliane also colored. Adam was appalled at his slip, but it was really most fortunate. By and large, Sir Richard had been taken up with the practical concerns of changing political sides and his shock at Gilliane's unwomanly perspicacity. He had not noticed any sign of love.

In any case, that thought was the least compelling in Sir Richard's mind. The hardness that had changed Gilliane's normally sweet expression when she spoke of Osbert, and Adam's casual acceptance of the notion of a woman defending herself with a knife and his comment about sending his sister into an enemy's stronghold alone, worked so powerfully on Sir Richard's mind that he had little attention to give to the subject of the relationship between Adam and Gilliane. Although Glynde was a substantial holding with an extensive demesne and several freehold farms attached to it, Sir Richard knew that he and Adam were not really of the same class. Adam had no title; technically, Sir Richard and his overlord were both simple barons. Nonetheless, Adam's connections were wide and powerful. He was overlord to a number of men very like Sir Richard. Most probably, Sir Richard thought, the women of Adam's class were different.

It was a comforting thought and Sir Richard clung to it as plans were finalized and Gilliane somehow induced him to offer his son as guardian of Tarring during the time they would be away. Adam was a trifle annoyed because he did trust Sir Richard and did not want any shadow of the notion that the young man would be hostage for the father's behavior. Gilliane, however, was even willing to endure Adam's displeasure to ensure their safety and blandly ignored his frown as she maneuvered Sir Richard into leaving his eldest boy to "manage" Tarring keep.

A day earlier Osbert de Cercy had bowed low before the Prince of France. Louis knew Osbert was a coward and a coxcomb, but he did not know the man was also a fool. Thus, he thought he might gain doubly by dispatching him to the places that had been raided by men using FitzWalter's battle cry. He would be rid of a tale-bearer, and he might get some information about who had done the raiding. The prince did not bother to wrap the matter up in clean cloth.

"I have heard, Sir Osbert," he began abruptly, "that you are not fond of scaling walls or thrusting yourself into breaches."

"My lord," Osbert protested, his voice high with shock.

"Do not bother to explain to me," Louis interrupted. "As it happens, your distaste for battle and my need fall in very well together. Doubtless you have heard the tale of the raiders who cried 'Dunmow.' I know they were not FitzWalter's men, but I do not know who they were nor why they used this device. Since you are more like to turn all awry in an assault than to help it forward, you will be of more aid to me if you ride south to Knepp castle, Arundel keep, and Lewes keep. You are to do two things in each place—assure them they were the victims of a treacherous trick, for Robert FitzWalter had no part in their loss, and try to discover any hint as to who played this trick."

"I will do your bidding, of course," Osbert replied, ignoring Louis's all-too-frank reasons for the assignment, "but I am not rich, my lord, and to support my men away from the camp will be difficult."

Grudgingly, Louis gave Osbert a little money and a letter instructing all men to give Sir Osbert de Cercy all aid and comfort possible while he was about the business of Louis, Prince of France. With this, Osbert had to be content. He had every intention of extending his researches into the raiders for some time—at least until Louis concluded his campaign and came to rest in winter quarters in London. The thing that displeased Osbert most was Louis's warning that he not dally along the way and most particularly not stop in London.

There was something in Louis that pierced Osbert's stupidity and self-satisfaction enough so that the warning took hold. Feeling spiteful because he could not enjoy himself as he had intended, Osbert spent three days ostentatiously "making ready." It was only when an assault on Berkhampsted was being planned that, grumbling, Osbert set out. However, he had taken Louis's warning to heart. Instead of traveling southeast to London, he went due south, turning a little east at Uxbridge. He planned to stop at Leith Hill and demand hospitality from Sir Philip. His demand, however, was thrown back in his face. Sir Philip knew Saer was dead; he did not know what else had happened, but he wanted no part of Osbert de Cercy, with or without a letter from Prince Louis.

Osbert was livid with rage. It was already time for dinner and he was cold and hungry. However, after uttering some ill-advised threats that he had no power to carry out, he was forced to ride on. He feared at first that he would need to ride back to Guildford or to Reigate, which would take him out of his way, but then he remembered that the Abbey of St. Leonard was little more than eight miles away and in the right direction. Abbeys did not offer the kind of entertainment Osbert liked, but in this case, austere hospitality was better than freezing and starving.

The letter Geoffrey had written from Hemel caught up with Adam in Sir Andrew's keep at Rother. It had been sent on from Tarring by Sir Richard's son, and Sir Richard and Sir Andrew were highly impressed when a message bearing the double seal of Lord Ian de Vipont and Lord Geoffrey FitzWilliam was delivered to Adam just before they sat down to dinner. He excused himself for opening the missive immediately, but when he had done so, the worried frown smoothed away and he was shaken by laughter. Gilliane, who had whitened at Adam's initial exclamation of surprise, regained her color.

"Is it good news, my lord?" she asked. Her voice was still somewhat tremulous. After several days of listening to conversations among the men, Gilliane had come to realize that what she might regard with horror, Adam considered great fun.

"It is amusing news and may well lead to good news," Adam replied.

However, he had no intention of really telling them at what he had been laughing. He did not think it safe to mention his raiding exploits in front of Sir Richard and Sir Andrew. If Arundel did come back to King Henry, it would be most unfortunate if he should discover that Adam, rather than a Frenchman, had been the raider who had started his quarrel with Fitz-Walter. Sir Andrew was exactly like his mother's vassal, Sir Henry of Kingsclere, and could never be trusted with the smallest subtlety or secret. He was loyal, honest and well intentioned, but anyone could extract information from him without his having the faintest notion he had spoken amiss. Later, Adam thought, he would tell Gilliane and they could enjoy the joke together. For the others, he had a safer story.

"Prince Louis," Adam continued, grinning broadly, "is doing as much for King Henry's cause, I am happy to tell you, as any of Henry's most devoted subjects."

He went on to describe in detail the incident concerning de Mandeville, omitting only the fact that Louis had apologized for the Count of Perche's behavior. Also, without mentioning what had caused Arundel's dissatisfaction, Adam told them of the earl's visit to Hemel, reading bits of Geoffrey's letter aloud to them. He had cause, seeing the expressions on Sir Richard's and Sir Andrew's faces, to bless his mother for forcing him—much against his will—to learn to read and write. Had he needed to withdraw to have a clerk read the message to him, it would never have had the same effect. Although the men might tell themselves that it was only reasonable to listen to a family communication in private, a faint unease would have been created, possibly even a feeling that Adam had had time to make up or embellish the tale he told.

As it was, the impact of Geoffrey's news was most convincing. True, Sir Andrew's reaction was at first largely indignation at the French attitude, but Sir Rich-

ard soon pointed out that had they not come under
Sir Adam's protection, the defection of the Earl of
Arundel from Louis's party would have left them open
to attack and confiscation as rebels. This notion, once
inserted into Sir Andrew's head, took strong hold. It
was he who suggested that they go as soon as possible
to explain these matters to Sir Edmund.

Accordingly, they set out the next day. Sir Andrew
had been somewhat surprised to see Gilliane, but the
conditions under which she was traveling did not really
sink into his head until they were out on the road. He
was then so loud in his wonder at her ability and
endurance that she was hard put not to laugh in his
face. In fact, except for one thing, Gilliane had never
been so happy in her life. The respect with which she
was treated by everyone, the fact that Sir Andrew and
his wife had given up their own bed to her—which she
would have refused had Adam not frowned at her
severely so that she realized she was obliged to accept
the courtesy—the bows and shy approaches of the
daughters of the house, who sent Catrin away and
offered their own service as maids just to speak to a
great lady, were all wine to Gilliane's soul.

Everything smiled at her. The weather was cold, but
clear and dry. Her mare was strong and beautiful and
of a docile disposition so that her limited experience
with riding was not obvious. Also, she grew more confident and experienced with each mile traveled so that
she no longer needed to concentrate on staying in the
saddle and controlling her mount. Then it became a
great pleasure to look around at the countryside, which
was all new to her.

Gilliane told herself not to be a fool. Men never
paid any attention to women when they had other
men for company. In addition, she and Adam had
agreed that there must be no sign of intimacy between
them, and she knew Adam had refused the company
of a woman in Sir Andrew's keep. How could he look

at her, anyway? He rode ahead with Sir Richard and Sir Andrew. To look at her, he would have had to turn around in the saddle. It was ridiculous to keep hoping he would do so, but the fact that he did not cast a faint pall over Gilliane's joy.

It did not occur to Gilliane that Adam was suffering more than she was. To her, everything was new and exciting and distracting. Adam, on the other hand, knew the countryside, and although Sir Richard was an intelligent man, his conversation was no substitute for Gilliane's, which Adam found far more interesting. Moreover, whenever Gilliane was not looking at the scenery through which they passed, she looked at Adam. It was safe enough to do so. He rode with the other two men a few horse lengths ahead. No one could see on which man her eyes were fixed and, in any case, it was natural to look ahead. Adam, however, could feel her attention—one can sense being stared at—and he reacted almost as strongly as if Gilliane had been stroking his naked back with her hand.

Frustrated desire worked upon Adam in the same way that enforced inactivity would. He had a growing need to exert himself physically. If he could not make love or fight, he needed to ride hard rather than dawdle along at a pace suited to foot soldiers. At first, it seemed that this desire, too, must be subdued, but soon after they had stopped to rest the horses and eat a bite themselves, Sir Richard remarked that they would be entering St. Leonard's forest in a mile or so. Adam's eyes lit.

"Do you think the abbot would give us leave to hunt?" he asked.

Sir Richard was surprised. It was a little odd to think of stopping to hunt in the middle of a purposeful journey, but in a moment he smiled indulgently. Adam had been so serious and so sensible all the time they were making their plans that Sir Richard had almost forgotten how young he was. Poor boy, to carry such a weight on his shoulders. No wonder he longed for a little respite.

"I doubt he would think of denying us," Sir Richard replied with a glance at the tail of men stretching down the road.

Adam laughed shortly. "No, but I do not wish to imply any threat. I know the Church officially supports King Henry, and I would not like to act as if I thought we could therefore make free with Church property."

"I will ask, then," Sir Richard offered. "I have hunted here with my late lord once or twice. Besides, we can crave hospice for Lady Gilliane. She makes no complaint, but she must be very tired, and, truly, I do not like to think of her lying on a pallet on the ground."

"Why?" Adam asked, genuinely puzzled and thereby innocently giving Sir Richard the false impression that he hardly thought of Gilliane as a woman. "She is young and strong."

Adam could not understood such coddling. His mother and his sister never made anything of camping out. Then he thought that Sir Richard might feel he was slighting his overlady's honor and he apologized for his casual attitude, saying he meant no insult and explaining that Alinor and Joanna often traveled rough when there was need. Nonetheless, it occurred to him that the hospice was an excellent idea. Gilliane could make the necessary visit of politeness to the abbot and save him trouble.

The men-at-arms, of course, could not be accommodated at the abbey. Cuthbert and the other two masters-at-arms were told to march the troop southwest to some open fields where they could set up a camp while Gilliane, Adam, Sir Richard and Sir Andrew presented themselves to the abbot. They were welcomed graciously and permission to hunt was given readily. A lay brother was told to guide them to the foresters. Without more ado Adam said farewell and

drew his companions out to ride off, regardless of the
fact that the afternoon was not the usual time for a
hunt.

In summer, the beasts went to earth during the day;
in winter, however, sometimes they foraged all day.
In any case, Adam insisted they had not much time.
It would be more sensible to try to catch a stag at his
dusk feeding than to wait until the following dawn.
If they did not kill at once and were caught out at dark,
well, doubtless there was a lodge somewhere. Sir Richard sighed. He had been looking forward to a decent
dinner and a warm bed. The sigh, however, was indulgent, and Sir Andrew saw nothing wrong with
Adam's enthusiasm. He was himself a passionate huntsman. In any case, neither man associated Adam's desire for the chase with a need to escape from Gilliane.

Gilliane was somewhat alarmed at being left in the
august company of an abbot. Adam did not realize
how limited her life and experiences had been. However, the abbot was not of Adam's mind concerning
what made for a good woman. He had no high expectations of Gilliane's mind or abilities. Thus, he addressed
a few kind words to her, which she received in modest
silence. This being most proper, the abbot was pleased
and showed it, considerably relieving Gilliane's mind.
Then he suggested that she must be tired and would like
to rest. The prior who was summoned led her in silence
to a small, neat house, separated from the abbey by
a gate and a wall, which was the area set aside for
female guests. Gilliane retreated to this haven promptly
and thankfully. She was tired and was glad enough to
sleep for a while on the bed Catrin had warmed and
spread with her own sheets.

She woke some hours later, ate the meal sent in by
the monks, who could not have a woman in their refectory, and then became horribly conscious that she had
nothing at all to do. This freedom immediately trapped
her mind into its familiar round of hope and fear. If

Adam loved her, would he not pay her more attention? Then she blamed herself for that doubt, reminding herself that his attentions would brand her a whore to her own men.

Logic is not very satisfactory to a woman who desires kisses and strong arms around her, however. Gilliane knew she did not care for anyone's opinion but Adam's. Had he been willing, she would cheerfully have let down her hair in public. Since he was not willing, perhaps he had other reasons than her honor. Perhaps there was another woman, a woman whose delicate ears he did not wish sullied with the fact that he had a mistress. Yet he had refused a woman in Sir Andrew's keep. Did that mean he was merely still sated by their lovemaking? Did it mean he cared enough for her to wish not to hurt her? Or was it all for the sake of some sweet maid for whom he was negotiating? Surely if it was for her own sake, Gilliane thought, he would have looked at her and spoken to her more these past days.

Having come round to the beginning again, Gilliane gave an impatient exclamation. It was ridiculous to sit in this tiny bare room thinking herself into sadness when she should be happy. God knew, there would probably soon be reason enough for misery. While she could be happy, she would be. Gilliane rose and took her cloak. If it was forbidden for women to walk in the cloister, surely there must be some place set aside for guests to exercise.

In this supposition, Gilliane was quite correct. There was a small garden just behind the house along the abbey wall. It was dead and dry, but Gilliane was able to see how the beds were laid out and how the root stocks of the perennials were mulched. She examined the monks' arrangements with care because they were famous gardeners and Gilliane was aware that the gardens of Tarring were now her responsibility. She was a little surprised at how much that knowledge increased her interest in the subject and continued her examination of the bedding out until it was too dark to see clearly. She might have lingered longer, had she not heard the arrival of horsemen at the gate. Gilliane was too late to see who had arrived, but assumed it was Adam and his companions. She hurried into the chamber assigned to her to make sure everything was neat and welcoming. Surely he would come to her now . . . surely? But no one came.

Osbert de Cercy told his troop to camp about half a mile north of the abbey. They had just passed a village, so the men raised no demur. They had their own methods of making themselves comfortable, and their master, if he did not make any attempt to see to their welfare, did not question what they did when he left them to their own devices. Osbert himself, with Jean and Pierre, rode on and passed through the abbey gates just before they were closed for the night. Dinner was long past and the abbot at his evening devotions, but the prior welcomed Osbert and saw that something was found for him to eat.

Disturbed because the dark and cheerless refectory offered so little comfort, the prior chatted amiably, deploring the lack of company. Few traveled in winter, he remarked, especially in these uneasy times, but they did have other guests. It was a shame Osbert had not come a few hours earlier; then he could have accompanied Sir Adam, Sir Richard, and Sir Andrew when they had gone hunting. The dim light of two candles, which made eating possible, was not sufficient to show the prior that Osbert had turned white as a lily. To begin with, Adam was not a common name for a nobleman, and in conjunction with Richard and Andrew in this area, it could only be Adam Lemagne. Between chewing and swallowing, however, Osbert had time to recover from the shock and recall that the prior had said Adam was away hunting.

He even managed to ask when the prior expected his

other guests to return. The prior did notice that Osbert's voice had changed, but assumed he was a little choked with what he was eating and said, regretfully, that he was afraid they would not come back until midmorning of the next day. He assumed, since they had not come in before dark, that they would sleep in the lodge and hunt again in the dawn. Osbert's sigh of relief was misunderstood by the kindly man as a sign of regret and he cast about in his mind for something to assuage Osbert's disappointment. His eyes brightened.

"The lady is here, in the women's house by the south gate," he offered hopefully. "I am sure Lady Gilliane would be glad to speak with you if you wish for company."

"Lady Gilliane?" Osbert choked. "I . . . I do not wish to impose myself upon . . . You see, it is dark already . . . I am cold and tired and the lady . . . she must be tired also and wish to go early to bed."

Gilliane! Gilliane here! A hundred different notions danced in Osbert's head, but he needed a few minutes alone to think about what to do. The prior was sorry his guest did not like the treat he had offered, but he had nothing else to suggest. He was sorry he had spoken about the lady at all. Osbert was plainly embarrassed and awkward now. It seemed best to excuse himself and go away so that his guest could recover his composure. Osbert nodded indifferently, scarcely noticing the prior's departure, his mind busy with this stroke of luck.

The question was, good luck or bad? And how to use it? Did he want Gilliane back right now? A sultry heat stirred Osbert. The girl was a fine piece of meat, even drugged and flaccid, but that was not important. Would she be useful to him? And could he get away with her without exposing himself to any real danger? The last was most important and, after a little thought, Osbert decided it would be possible. He could not take her tonight, because getting the horses from the stables would arouse too much interest, but Lemagne was not expected back until he had had a morning's hunting. If Osbert left just before dawn, which would be natural enough, there might be a way to take Gilliane along without arousing suspicion.

Leaving the remains of his meal untidily strewn on the table, Osbert took himself off to consult with his henchmen. Jean went out softly to spy out the situation while Osbert considered whether the gain was worth the risk. There would be no risk at all in killing Gilliane, but unfortunately Osbert had given his true name to the monks and he would certainly be accused of her death. This would wipe out his claim to the Neville lands because the Church forbade the inheritance of a victim's property by the murderer. That meant if he took her he would have to produce her in good health, and a reluctant woman was a nuisance to drag along on a journey.

Osbert felt very annoyed with Adam. He had counted on Adam's killing Gilliane to facilitate his seizure of the lands, but that stupid Lemagne had not done it. Doubtless he had forced that ninny to yield everything to him. However, the yielding could be easily contested because the marriage contract Osbert had had written ceded all rights and powers to Gilliane's husband—and he was Gilliane's husband. Maybe Gilliane had not mentioned that fact to Lemagne in an attempt to save her life. Stupid, stubborn bitch, she always managed to make trouble.

The word *stubborn* started another train of thought. Gilliane was stubborn. She might appear to yield, but as soon as she had a chance, she would rebel again. How was it that Sir Richard and Sir Andrew were so friendly with Lemagne that they should go hunting together? Why had the little bitch not gone sniveling to them to protect her? Osbert shrugged and grinned, thinking of the methods Adam would have had to use to convince her to obey him. Apparently he had been so thorough about it that Gilliane was too frightened even to appeal to the monks and he believed it was safe to leave her. Probably Gilliane wished a thousand times that she was back in Cercy keep in France or that . . . Osbert sat up and smiled more broadly. Doubtless Gilliane often wished she was back in his hands. Well! She might even come willingly.

Osbert knew no other way of dealing with women than reducing them to a pulp of terror, but he had noticed that gentleness after severity produced the greatest docility. If he could get her away and into one of Louis's keeps, it would strengthen his claim to Neville's lands greatly. Her presence might even make the Lord of Lewes interested in taking Tarring for him. Once Gilliane was in his power completely, with no servants or vassals to support her and a clear memory of how much worse her state had been under the hand of a brutal conqueror like Lemagne, it would be easy to make her affirm the marriage contract.

Soon after Osbert had concluded this brilliant piece of reasoning, based on utterly false premises, Jean returned with the news that the wall surrounding the women's guest house would not be difficult to scale. In fact, he had been over it already and had found a small door in the wall that the monks used to bring in garden supplies and take out refuse. It had been locked, Jean said, but was not locked any longer. It would be very easy to remove the lady without raising any alarm.

Gilliane had waited for Adam to visit her till the dusk turned to full dark. Then she told Catrin to light her candles, and still waited. It seemed incredible that no one would come a few steps to bid her good night, to ask if she were safe and comfortable. Then it occurred to her that it was not a few steps. Male and female guests in the abbey were lodged in widely separated quarters. How silly to have forgotten. Perhaps the abbot considered it wrong for the men to visit the ladies' house after dark. Would that stop Adam if he desired to come? If he desired it, nothing would stop him. Gilliane sighed and fought back tears.

In her bed robe, while Catrin brushed her hair, Gilliane told herself firmly not to be a fool. She felt odd, she assured herself, only because it was strange to be alone in a house. True, it was a very small house, and it was not isolated, being separated only by a wall and a gate from the abbey proper. Still, in winter, there were few travelers and there was no one in the guest house except herself and Catrin, and . . .

Alone! It was the first time, Gilliane realized, that she had not been surrounded by the servants and families of her men since she and Adam left Tarring. Although she had longed for Adam's embrace, Gilliane had not been silly enough to imagine he could come to her under those circumstances. But here . . . the monks did not guard the wall or the gate. Perhaps Adam had not come because he intended to make it a really good night later, after everyone else was abed. Gilliane promptly sent Catrin off to her own tiny sleeping cell.

When the woman was gone, Gilliane began to cast around in her mind for a suitable subject for conversation. In the few days they had been lovers, Gilliane had discovered that Adam, for all his big body and eager passion, was not in the least animalistic. He did not like to grab her as soon as they were together and set about lovemaking. First he wanted to talk. Almost any subject would do, but it was best if it was something that could soon lead to kisses or touches. Gilliane frowned and then smiled broadly. He had asked to see how she wore her knife. What could be better than to show him her naked thighs? She popped out of bed, gasping a little as her feet touched the cold stone floor, retrieved her weapon from where Catrin had laid it on the chest, and strapped it on.

Comforted and expectant, Gilliane did not fight sleep, but something in her remained dimly aware so that she

knew she would wake at any sound. Little could be
heard through the thick mud-and-wattle walls, however, and Gilliane slept peacefully until the sound of
the bells in the high tower drifted down through the
thatch of the roof. It was shortly after compline that
she had gone to bed; thus, when the mellow tolling
disturbed her, she knew it was the bell for matins. Midnight, and Adam had not come. Fear and reason fought
each other in her head, mixing with dreams when she
dozed intermittently, bringing now hope and now despair. At last, when the night candle began to pale as
the sky grayed with the coming dawn, Gilliane could
bear lying still no longer. She rose and began to dress.
Catrin would be distressed, but Gilliane needed to do
something to fight the black cloud that was enveloping
her spirit.

The movement helped a little, but only a very little.
Desperately, Gilliane searched the room for something
to distract her. The bare monastic cell held nothing of
interest—a bed, a low chest, a stool, a crucifix. Gilliane's eyes lighted on that. She had not dared to confess her sin to the priest, but she could confess it to
the Merciful Mother of God who understood all things
of the heart. She knelt on the floor below the cross and
began to pray. Tears came soon, and the sound of her
own soft sobbing covered the stealthy footsteps in the
corridor that paused and then quickly, very quickly,
entered her doorless cell.

CHAPTER SIXTEEN

When a strong arm seized Gilliane around the breast and an iron hand clamped across her mouth, she felt not fear but joy. Adam did not want her to cry out with surprise, her heart told her. She did not struggle when Pierre pulled her upright and turned her around. Although there were tears on her cheeks, her eyes were alight with love. Her shock at seeing Osbert was so enormous that the expression of delight was frozen on her face for one instant. In the next, before fear could enter her, she realized that Adam had never returned to the abbey the previous night. It was Osbert's horses she had heard at the gate. That revelation held her free from terror just long enough for what Osbert was saying to penetrate her mind.

"So you are glad to see me, are you?" he sneered. "You have learned what it is to be a captive of one of these English barons. Well, well, perhaps you have learned your lesson and now you will be glad to be my wife. I find that you will be useful to me, so, if you will agree to be obedient in the future, I will not punish you for your past misbehavior. Show yourself to be grateful and docile, and I will even forgive you—perhaps."

Glad to see him? Those first words struck Gilliane with almost physical force, making her aware that Osbert had read the expression of joy and misunderstood it completely. Her eyes closed as her senses wavered for a moment when shock and fear dispossessed the gladness. Adam was not in the abbey. He was still hunting in the forest. He did not know she was in danger, could not help her or save her. She was again in Osbert's hands.

Grateful and docile. Those words penetrated also, connected with the first ones, and set up a train of ideas. If she resisted, Gilliane knew what would happen. She would either be killed or rendered unconscious and kept that way by blows or drugs, or bound hand and foot and gagged. In any case, she would be made and kept helpless. By God's grace, perhaps because she was at that very moment praying for help and mercy, she had been given a chance to save herself. All that was needed was the resolution to appear glad, grateful, and docile. Hatred flared up in Gilliane and, for a moment, she thought she would not be able to continue the impression God's mercy had first given Osbert. The thought of the divine help already given steadied her, and then she realized that her pretense need not continue long. Indeed, it would soon be useless. Gilliane knew that Osbert would maintain this softer attitude only while her resistance could cause him inconvenience.

Whether even this knowledge could have made Gilliane act as her intelligence told her she must was not put to the proof. Just as she reopened her eyes, hoping her hatred did not glare out of them like a beacon, Osbert's attention was diverted by Jean, who entered the room softly.

"The maid will warn no one," Jean muttered.

Has he killed poor Catrin, Gilliane wondered, fear replacing hate in her eyes. Her affection for the maid made her raise her hands—not to claw at Pierre's arm but to clasp them prayerfully and extend them as far as she could toward Osbert. He looked at her consideringly and then smiled nastily.

"Let go her mouth," he said softly to Pierre, "but only a little. If she even squeaks, clap her silent again and I will strike her witless."

The moment her lips were freed, Gilliane gasped in a thin whisper, "You have not harmed the maid, have you?"

"Why?" Osbert asked.

To say she was fond of Catrin would sign the poor woman's death warrant, if she was not dead already. *Glad to see Osbert.* Gilliane knew she must prove she was glad to see Osbert. Perhaps she could work on Osbert's cowardice and save Catrin at the same time.

"Sir Adam will be fit to tear you apart if the maid be harmed," Gilliane whispered urgently. "He sets great store by her, and she has been my warden and a spy upon me for each word I say and each blink of my eyes."

Nervously, Osbert glanced at Jean. "Nay," the man responded, "she is only bound and gagged. I thought we might take her as a plaything. She is a little long in the tooth, but not ill favored, and any well will do to stick a ladle in when one is thirsty."

"Leave her here," Osbert snarled. "She can tell her master nothing that the monks will not tell him anyway. I do not wish to be burdened with two double-laden horses." Then his eyes moved to Gilliane. "It was wise you warned me. Come quietly out now. The monks' servants will not come here before it is time to break the night's fast. By then we will be well away, and by the time that loudmouth Lemagne returns, we will be safe behind the walls of Lewes or so close that no pursuit can take us. Even if he comes early, he will rush off to Knepp, which is much closer."

At the words, Pierre released his hold on Gilliane. If the illusory freedom this gave her was meant as a temptation, Gilliane was not stupid enough to succumb to it. She made no move at all while Jean handed Pierre her cloak and the latter put it roughly around her, squeezing her breast and leering as he did so. Even in the corridor, Gilliane's busy brain warned escape would be impossible. If she tried to run toward the gate to cry for help, she would never succeed. There might be a moment when the men were mounting, Gilliane told herself, but she did not really believe it. Even if all three should mount at once, which would be incredible carelessness, what good would it do to run? On horseback the men would overtake her long before she could get to the abbey gate. Bitterness began to rise in Gilliane's throat and hopelessness began to cloud her mind. Still, she was not yet so desperate as to throw away any chance of escape, and she stood quietly while Pierre mounted and did not struggle when Jean lifted her to ride pillion behind him. Osbert was already mounted, but Jean stood close beside Gilliane until Pierre had pulled her arms roughly around his waist and clamped them firmly under his elbows so that she could not pull loose and throw herself off the horse without giving him warning.

"Hold tight," he said, "or you might bounce off and get your pretty ass hurt."

In all her life, no matter how little she had been regarded while Saer was alive, no common servant had dared to speak to Gilliane in such a way. Even Jean and Pierre had kept their distance and kept their tongues still in their heads in the past. Since Saer's death, Osbert had been freed from needing to keep even the appearance of proper behavior, and his servants' license had grown with his depravity. Osbert heard, but made no sign. He was, in fact, growing to fear his men a little, and yet he could not do without them. It was easier to ignore such things. Even if Pierre used Gilliane, what was that to Osbert? Women did not wear out down there. A taste of Pierre as a lover might even make Gilliane more receptive to his own attentions.

Fortunately for Gilliane, shock had held her silent. Emboldened by her apparent passiveness, Pierre bore down on her arms as the horses got under way at a quick trot. Gilliane's hands were forced from Pierre's waist down along his belly. "A little lower, doxy," he muttered, "and you will have a fine handle to cling to."

Still Gilliane was silent, but her shock was past. Hate and rage built in her, stripping away her normal timidity and gentleness. Then the movement of the horse thrust her forward against the saddle so that the knife strapped to her thigh pressed painfully into her flesh. A fierce, bitter joy filled Gilliane. She had forgotten the knife. There was a chance, if not to escape, why then, to avenge herself. Brightly now she looked about her. The horses had spread apart, about a length between them. Osbert led, she and Pierre were in the center, and Jean brought up the rear. The road was paler than the fields on either side, but there was no sign at all of trees. They were moving north at a smart pace and Gilliane realized that they must be going to join Osbert's troop. She would need to act at once.

A little sound finally forced its way past Gilliane's lips. Actually it was a titter, displaying how near she was to total madness, but Pierre thought it was a giggle. He turned his head. Gilliane's face was too close to his for him to see her expression; however, her hands moved, not to pull free but forward and down. Pierre gave a gratified grunt. He was a little surprised, but you could never tell with women, and this one had coupled willingly enough with a crazy cripple. Doubtless she would couple with anything that presented a shaft to her. Still, the idea of futtering a lady was exciting enough to Pierre to produce a visible result.

Pierre relaxed his grip on Gilliane's arms warily, ready to grab if she pulled away. Again came that titter. The sound was strange enough this time to make Pierre a bit uneasy, but, before he could think about it, Gilliane slid her left hand past the slit in his steel-sewn leather armor and gently tickled the shaft that was pressing hard against his chausses. Pierre drew in his breath sharply. Gilliane felt him again, a trifle more firmly. Her other hand moved also, as if unsuccessfully seeking an entry and finding the way crowded. Then it moved up over his thigh. Distracted by the pulses of pleasure that Gilliane's rubbing was generating, Pierre let her right arm slide out from under his. There was no danger of her getting away while her left arm was held, and, besides, she was pressing close, pushing her breasts into his back. He made an obscene remark, not meant to offend but to excite.

The words had no effect on Gilliane whatsoever. She was totally committed to her purpose and nothing could stop her now. As she caressed Pierre's private parts with her left hand, feeling his sighs of pleasure with her body, her right hand groped frantically for the open seam of her cotte and, when through that, for the matching open seam in her tunic. Scrabbling her short shift higher, she at last was able to grip the haft of her knife firmly. It was easy enough to draw it, but she had to increase the speed and pressure of her left-handed caresses while she maneuvered the blade through the openings in her dress.

Now Gilliane could feel Pierre shift in his saddle, pressing back to give more freedom to his swollen shaft. Gripping it firmly between thumb and little and ring fingers, Gilliane extended her index and middle fingers forward to rub round and round on the head, exposed and throbbing. Another choked obscenity burst from Pierre.

"Shhh," Gilliane whispered, thrusting her face over his left shoulder.

Naturally enough, Pierre turned his head in the direction of hers, and Gilliane's right hand rose, flung outward, and came back down with all the strength of her rage and her hate and her terror. The knife was long and very well honed. It cut through the leather hood like butter and sank right to the hilt, cutting the carotid artery under the ear and slitting the jugular.

Indeed, it went so far that the point came through on the other side of Pierre's throat and pricked Gilliane's cheek. She jerked her head back and jerked at the knife, too. A flood of warmth ran over the blade and her icy fingers as the knife came out.

A strange low squawk had come from Pierre's throat as the knife went in, but when the jugular was slit, he was gagged by his own blood and made no other sound. His body heaved in a single violent convulsion. Instinctively, Gilliane clutched at him, quite accidentally driving the knife she still held into his chest. More important, for Pierre was dead already, Gilliane's left hand, equally accidentally, hit the reins, which were just falling from his slackened grip. The blows she had dealt, the squawk and convulsion of death, had purged Gilliane of the madness that threatened to destroy her reason. All at once life was, if not normal, at least rational. She comprehended her situation quite well and saw her only chance for escape lay in retaining the horse.

Perhaps five seconds had passed since Gilliane first stabbed Pierre. Either Jean had not noticed the swift motion of her arm because of the dark or had mistaken it for a gesture by Pierre. However, there was no profit in concealment, Gilliane knew, because each stride of the horse was bringing them closer to Osbert's men. Besides, the jerk of the knife out of Pierre's body had started it moving and it was already sagging against Gilliane's right arm. It would be impossible for her to support that weight. It would be impossible for her to stay on the horse if she could not get into the saddle.

Even as these thoughts ran through her head, Gilliane was pulling her knife free of Pierre's chest. This further unbalanced the body, and, when Gilliane pulled back her right arm, it toppled over in that direction. As it fell, Gilliane kicked the horse's belly and, simultaneously, Jean let out a bellow from behind. The corpse went over and Gilliane grabbed for the saddle pommel with both hands. Unfortunately, although Pierre's left foot came free of the stirrup, the right did not. Walloped by the falling body on the right, prodded by Gilliane's kicks and startled by the shout behind, the horse veered sharply away to the left and broke from a trot into a gallop.

As it turned out, Adam's prediction about the feeding habits of deer in winter had been quite correct. Hardly half a mile into the hunting preserve, he and his companions came upon a stag of considerable size. By the time the hunt was over Adam felt much better. He was tired and sweating, but he had worked off most of his tension. Sir Richard and Sir Andrew were pleased with their sport; everyone was in the best humor. The horses, however, were really exhausted. It was clearly impossible to think of making them go back to the abbey when a hunting lodge was at hand. There was also wood for a fire and pieces of the stag could be roasted over that fire. Then, pleasantly tired, they rolled themselves in their cloaks and slept to wake with the first light of the rising sun, stiff and cold but still pleased with their sport and their companions.

After they were mounted, however, Adam pulled close to Sir Richard to say softly that he was aware he should not have broken the journey for sport. And then he cleared his throat awkwardly, unable to explain why he had been driven to do so.

"It does not matter," Sir Richard assured him. "No more was lost than an hour or two. Lady Gilliane could not ride much farther in any case. It was good for all of us. The lady had some rest, and we had some pleasure, which, after all the worry of these past weeks, was sorely needed."

Adam did not quite see why Sir Richard kept harping on Gilliane's inability to ride. A flicker of concern passed through him. Sir Richard was much older than he and doubtless knew many more women. Perhaps he saw that Gilliane was frailer than most women. Then why did she not say she was tired or . . . Nonsense. Had not he and Geoffrey needed to think of a thousand excuses to stop and rest because Ian, who was not completely recovered from his illness, would have dropped dead from his horse rather than complain? Perhaps Gilliane's spirit was stronger than her body and she, too, needed to be watched for her own good. Without realizing it, Adam picked up the pace. A few minutes more brought them in sight of the abbey and, to their surprise, before they reached the gate, they saw the abbot hurrying out toward them.

"My lords," he cried, "I have most dreadful news. Lady Gilliane has been reft away."

"What?"

"How?"

"By whom?"

It was, of course, impossible to distinguish the questions that were roared at him all at the same time, but the abbot knew well enough what had been asked.

"I beg you to listen and I will tell you at once everything I know. When the lay brother went this morning to bring breakfast to Lady Gilliane's maid, he found the woman gagged and bound. She could tell him nothing, only that it was a man, for it was dark and she was thrown over on her face and bound before she could see who seized her."

"When did this happen?" Sir Richard asked.

One look at Adam's white, stricken face and fixed, unseeing eyes had told Sir Richard that he had better ask whatever questions needed answering. He was very sorry for his young overlord, who had given way to a most harmless impulse of youth and now was so bitterly punished for so small a deviation from strict duty.

"After compline certainly, for the maid did not leave Lady Gilliane until then, but—"

"Have you no idea at all, no guess even, who has taken her?" Adam had recovered his voice, but it did not sound much like his as he forced the words through his constricted throat.

"My lord, let me finish. You will have your answer quicker that way. Although it is not certain, since no one saw what happened, we believe it must have been a guest who came to the abbey after you left, a Sir Osbert de Cercy."

"Sir Osbert!"

"How could he know we were here?"

Sir Andrew's and Sir Richard's voices blended in horrified exclamation. Adam was again stricken mute. His sense of shock was so intense that the world reeled around him and he clung to the pommel of his saddle for fear he would topple from his horse. Adam knew perfectly well that male and female guest houses were separated by the width of the abbey. Therefore, Osbert could not have come upon Gilliane by chance. She must have summoned him. Somehow she must have sent Osbert a message to tell him that she was free of surveillance at last. Why? Why had she cozened him with her eyes, her lips, her body, if she loved her husband? What purpose . . .

"I grieve to say that was our fault," the abbot was replying to Sir Richard's repeated question about where Osbert had obtained the information that Gilliane was in the abbey.

"You mean she asked you to send Sir Osbert a message?" Adam asked harshly.

"No, no. It was an accident. Our prior, believing Sir Osbert and Lady Gilliane both to lack company, since our guest houses were empty except for them, suggested that Sir Osbert pay a visit of courtesy to the lady. It was late, of course, after vespers, so the prior was not surprised when Sir Osbert refused, since he was a stranger to the lady."

"He was no stranger!" Adam exclaimed bitterly.

"Nor a man Lady Gilliane would have wished to see," Sir Richard interposed warningly.

If the abbot discovered that Osbert was Gilliane's husband, his willingness to give them information might be at an end. To a churchman's way of thinking, the bonds imposed by the Church were more important than political purposes and far more important than personal likes and dislikes.

"That is very strange," the abbot exclaimed. "Sir Osbert said nothing of knowing Lady Gilliane. He seemed, from what the prior said, to be embarrassed by the idea of thrusting himself so late upon the notice . . ." His voice checked and a hard expression came into his face. "I see. He did not wish her to reveal what she knew about him. But he would have right of sanctuary here, no matter what he had done, unless . . . Heaven! Is he excommunicate? Is it needful for us to cleanse and resanctify . . ."

Adam had barely heard the abbot's words. Sir Richard's interruption rang through his head like a bell note, clearing the fog of rage and suspicion enough so that he realized that they had to have Gilliane back. Politically, she was necessary to him. It did not matter whether she had lied to him for some purpose he could not even guess at. Certainly Sir Richard and Sir Andrew were no part of any plot—if there had been a plot. Their anger and amazement were sincere. Gilliane could not even have hinted to them that she intended to return to her husband. Perhaps she had not intended it. Perhaps she had resolved to keep her lands any way she could after Osbert had gone for help, even if it meant subduing her revulsion and bedding her conqueror. Only when she saw the man she had murdered her first husband to get, her passion had overcome her greed and, for love of Sir Osbert, she had thrown away what she had worked so hard to obtain. Again Adam clung to his pommel, pain stopping his breath.

"Father," Sir Richard's incisive tones cut across the abbot's worried wondering, "we cannot answer that question, but I must beg you to turn from your own concerns to ours for a little time. Was Lady Gilliane hurt? How was she taken?"

"Alas, I cannot answer your question any more than you can answer mine. There was no blood in her chamber and it was not disarrayed, but it would be easy enough for three men—Sir Osbert had two servants with him—to overpower one small woman. Nothing at all was taken. The lady's combs and brushes and all her clothes except her riding dress lay as the maid left them—so much she told us, but we could get little sense from her, so much did she weep for her lost mistress."

The band that had been cutting so tightly into Adam's chest that it was an agony to breathe loosened a trifle. Everyone assumed Gilliane had been carried away by force. Perhaps she had been. If not, why should she not take Catrin with her? She was fond of the maid. And surely she would have taken her comb and brush, even if she was afraid to pause to pack her clothes. As one agony receded, another crowded forward. If the whole thing was a horrible accident of chance, what was happening to his poor Gilliane?

"Never mind how she was taken," Adam snarled. "What is of note is that we must have her back." He turned on the abbot. "Do you have no help to give us? Did the man say from where he came?"

"My son, be calm. He has been gone since before the sun's rising. A few minutes more or less now cannot—"

"Can they not?" Adam roared. "We are no more than twenty miles from three of Louis's great strongholds. If we catch them before they can enter such a place, we can have Lady Gilliane back safe. But—"

"I will summon the prior," the abbot said hastily. "He is the one—"

"I will go to him. It will be quicker," Adam growled, coming off his horse and throwing his reins to Sir Andrew.

Sir Richard dismounted also, fearing that Adam's
guilt, now that his shock was past, might drive him to
lay violent hands upon the man who had, though unwittingly, revealed Lady Gilliane's presence to Osbert.
He was wrong in thinking Adam was likely to punish
another for what he knew was his own fault, but his
mediation was necessary. Adam was now so frantic,
imagining Gilliane being threatened or beaten, that he
would hardly give the prior a chance to think over what
had been said. Sir Richard could see Adam's big hands
twitching with the desire to shake the words out of the
man.

"He did not say from where he came," Sir Richard
urged, "but think, I beg you. He came late. Did he not
say what places he had passed?"

"Uh . . . not that I . . . oh, yes . . . I believe he said
that Guildford was too far east. . . ."

"North! We should have known," Adam shouted,
turning sharply away and starting for the door. "He
came from the north, most likely from Berkhampsted.
What a fool I am! I knew Louis was there."

"Wait, my lord," Sir Richard cried, following and
seizing Adam's arm. "I do not believe de Cercy was
traveling with only two servants. To speak in plain
language, the man was an arrant coward. If he had only
a small troop of guards, he would have brought them
all with him. That he came with only two men means
that he must have a large troop camped nearby."

"So?" Adam growled, wrenching his arm free and
continuing on out of the abbey.

"I am not afraid to die more than any other man,"
Sir Richard snapped, "but I should like to do so, if I
must, for a good cause. What good could it do Lady
Gilliane if all three of us should be slain?"

"We will not be slain," Adam stated indifferently.
He was too young, too worried, too angry to believe in
death.

"My lord, consider! We are three men. If there be

fifty or a hundred in de Cercy's party—or, what if there be a doubt as to what way they went? How wide can three men spread themselves? Let us summon our own troops. It will take no more than—"

"By all means," Adam replied, stopping for a moment, but the eyes that looked at Sir Richard were not sane. "Ask the reverend father to send someone to tell Cuthbert that he must break camp and follow me north. Do you go yourself, if you think it needful. As for me, I ride north now."

"But will the men believe . . ." Sir Richard began.

He did not bother to complete his question. Adam had already walked away. It was obvious that nothing would deter Adam from riding north along the road to discover Osbert's trail, if he could. Sir Richard paused a few minutes to ask the abbot to send a message to the troops, drawing off his seal ring so that the messenger would have proof that the order did, indeed, come from him. All he could hope was that he would be able, when Adam actually saw evidence that a large troop was involved, to convince his overlord to wait until their own men caught up with them.

Sir Richard was not completely successful in that attempt, but a sight of the size of the deserted camp and the number of campfires did bring Adam to a limited rationality. Even the state of mind he was in, where constant visions of Gilliane being held down and raped alternated with visions of her rushing passionately into Osbert's embrace—and which of the two was more horrible to him was a moot point—could not completely wipe out Adam's long years of training. Half mad though he was, he knew no three men could prevail over so large a force. One other factor contributed to calming him. Sir Andrew pointed out that the horse droppings indicated that most of the men were afoot. That meant either that the whole troop would move slowly enough to accommodate the foot soldiers, or that the few mounted men, ten or fifteen at most, would ride ahead.

Adam would not hesitate to take on ten or fifteen men-at-arms and one knight. He, Sir Richard, and Sir Andrew were better armed and probably considerably more skilled. However, he had sense enough not to say that to Sir Richard. All he said was that he must follow to see which way they had gone. Sir Richard did not protest, although he insisted that they ride the few hundred yards to the village so that someone could tell their troops which way to turn.

What they found in the village made Sir Richard and Sir Andrew growl with anger and disgust. Both of them had loosed their men on helpless villages, but only as an act of war, not one of negligence or indifference. Adam said nothing at first, but he grew white as chalk again when his eyes fell on the crippled women with their bloodstained skirts. Then he spoke softly, calming the fears of the people as well as he could, promising that his men, who were following, would guard those who were serfs of the Church and make sure that the devils that had plagued them would not return. He gave the village headman a piece or two of silver from his purse to buy food and firewood to replace what the troop had consumed. The loss of their slender supplies would have condemned the village to freezing and starvation if the abbot had not chosen to help them. Adam's largesse stilled the worst fears. Bruises and torn flesh would heal. At least no one was dead. The headman took Adam's glove as a token and promised to send a man to set Adam's troops off on the trail of de Cercy and his men.

Without waiting for further assurance or even to see whether Sir Richard and Sir Andrew were following him, Adam rode back to where de Cercy's troop had camped. He was determined to follow, although it seemed certain de Cercy was making for Lewes. It was the nearest stronghold committed to Louis in the direction the troop had headed. Two things drove Adam to follow. It was possible that this trail was a false one to throw pursuers off. Knepp castle was no more than six or seven miles to the southwest. In fact, Adam could not understand why Osbert had not made for Knepp at once. He could have been safe inside that formidable keep before Adam even knew Gilliane was gone. Perhaps he was already there, having sent his men away eastward to draw off those who followed.

Sickness churned in Adam at the thought. There were signs of horses as well as men in the dry earth and broken stubble. Adam pinned his hope on that, trying not to think of Gilliane as a prisoner in Knepp. But he had to know. He had to catch up with de Cercy's men. Among so few horsemen, it would be easy to discover a woman, particularly if she were a bound captive. And if she were a bound captive and if the troop were far along the road to Lewes, the worst of Adam's agony would be ended. The need to bind her would prove she had not gone willingly for love of Osbert; the distance traveled would mean, most likely, that Osbert had not taken time to molest his prize.

All true—if they were not in Knepp. At the spot where the camp had been, Adam pulled in his horse and bit his lip in an agony of indecision. Dare he take such a chance? Would it not be better to ride to Knepp and discover if they had taken in a man and a woman at dawn that morning? If they had, he could bring up the troops they had to make sure that Osbert did not escape and tell the castellan that he would bring a full army to take down the keep if Gilliane and Osbert were not sent out to him. But he had already told the headman of the village to send the men along the track of de Cercy's men. Should he go back and countermand that order?

Suddenly Adam began to shake. "Knepp is so near," he said to Sir Richard. "I see the track to the east plain, but what if de Cercy sent the men east and took

Lady Gilliane to Knepp? Would he not do that, hoping we would pursue the men?"

"That is possible," Sir Richard growled, "but—"

"Well and so, it will not take more than a few minutes for me to ride a wide circle round and look if there be a fresh sign of horses going west or southwest," Sir Andrew interrupted. "There may not be anything, but I have a good eye for such things."

That was very true. During the hunt the previous day, Sir Andrew had twice pointed them in the right direction when the belling of the hounds was confused by intervening woodland. He had seen signs of the stag or the dogs that the others had missed. Sir Andrew might not be sharp-witted, but his eyesight was very keen, and what he knew how to do, he did right well. Sir Richard had been watching Adam's face while Sir Andrew spoke and saw there both relief and a desperate impatience to be doing something himself.

"Go you north, Andrew," he suggested, "at your best speed and then westward and then south, afterward turning east and, if needful, north again. We, in the meanwhile, will follow this track more slowly so that we come together to the east. If you have found nothing, we will be somewhat forward on our way. We also will look for signs of any who might have turned aside."

"The men?" Adam asked as Sir Andrew set spurs to his horse and rode off. He had to wet his fear-dried lips to make them flexible enough to form words.

"There is time for that," Sir Richard replied soothingly. "If we see some sign that Knepp should be our goal, we can return to this place. Then either Sir Andrew or I will wait to turn the men while you ride with the other to Knepp to speak your mind."

Adam had stopped shaking, but the fear that he was not doing the right thing, that he was not acting fast enough, that because of his stupidity and inability Gilliane would suffer, tore at him. They rode in silence,

Adam well to the right of the main trail, watching for
any sign that a party had separated from the force and
ridden south. There were no such indications, but that
was to be expected so close to the starting point. Very
soon—in fact, before they were completely out of sight
of the camp area—they pulled up sharply at the sound
of a voice hallooing and calling Adam's name. When
they turned, they saw a rider coming full tilt who could
only be Sir Andrew. Adam swallowed sickly and the
color drained from his face until even his lips were
white. Gilliane, his Gilliane . . . if she was not lost to
him through her own treachery, what had been done
to her?

He spurred toward the oncoming rider. "They rode
to Knepp?" he called.

"I do not know, my lord," Sir Andrew shouted back,
"but you had better come and see." When they were
galloping back, he continued, his voice still loud with
excitement, "Three horses came off the road, not at
the camp but southward, toward the abbey. There is a
man lying dead, stabbed through the throat, with signs
on the earth that he fell from the saddle and was
dragged. I read other signs also, my lord, but what
they mean I cannot guess. It is best that you see this
for yourself."

CHAPTER SEVENTEEN

Gilliane clung desperately to the pommel and reins with her left hand. She was aware of a sound, a horrible screaming kind of laughter, but she could not pay attention to that and it stopped. Pierre's body, caught by the leg in the right stirrup, was dragging at the saddle and threatening to trip the horse. She was also aware that the haft of her knife was slippery and sticky at the same time. That was funny, that was. For an instant, she shook with laughter, but then she heard Osbert shouting and nothing was funny anymore. She clung tighter than ever to the heaving rump of the horse with her knees and leaned forward to chop at the stirrup leather. The knife caught in it once, twice, then nicked the horse because of the wild jostling.

The poor beast neighed and veered even farther left, increasing its speed to the limit of its ability. Pierre's weight, yanking violently at the slits Gilliane had made in the leather, had its effect and the stirrup tore loose from the saddle. Pierre's body fell free and rolled— right under the hooves of Jean's pursuing mount. With a shout and a terrified neigh, man and horse crashed to the ground. The frightened animal flailed its hooves, the man who had been in the saddle screamed with pain as the horse's weight crushed his leg and its frantic efforts to rise inflicted worse injury. From a safe dis-

tance, Osbert screamed curses at his men mingled with
questions about what had happened.

Clinging precariously to the saddle from which each
jolt threatened to tear her tiring hand, Gilliane was carried blindly southward. The situation could not endure
for long. A more expert horsewoman, who was not in
addition hysterical with terror and revulsion, might
have managed to soothe the horse and bring it to a
stand. Gilliane's body did its best by instinct, but her
mind was black with fear and horror and it did not
help. In a few minutes, the horse set its foot into a
rabbit hole and stumbled. The jolt finished the task that
fatigue had begun. Gilliane's hand was torn from the
pommel, the reins slipped through her fingers, and, as
the horse righted itself and fled onward, she slid to the
ground.

It was cold, so bitterly cold. Gilliane began to whimper and then to sob. So cold. So cold. Feebly, Gilliane
tried to pull her cloak closer around her, but her right
hand was frozen hard around . . . She shuddered violently and choked off her sobs. The knife with which
she had killed Pierre, that was what was in her hand.
She shuddered again, but she wiped the blade carefully on her already bloodstained skirt and, crouching
like a terrified animal closer into the rough brush, she
stared around to be sure no one saw and slid it back
into its sheath.

For a considerable time, Gilliane crouched perfectly
still, keeping herself silent with an effort of will. As the
light grew, she moved enough to find a larger bush to
conceal her. That was the instinct of a hunted thing
and did not require thought, but when the move had
been made, her mind became aware of the cramping of
her limbs and began to consider confusedly why it was
necessary. Shock receded with the brightening morning.
By sunup, everything that had happened was clear in
Gilliane's mind. Far from feeling sorrow or revulsion,
she was aware of a fierce joy and satisfaction in the

memory of Pierre's death and looked with considerable approval at the bloodstains on her hand and riding dress.

Gilliane's only regret was the loss of the horse. She realized that had reduced her chances of extricating herself from this situation alive, but she did not fear death nearly so much as she feared falling into Osbert's hands. That set her heart pounding again, and she peered cautiously out from her inadequate shelter. The low rise of ground on which she found herself seemed to be grazing common, although she could see no signs of animals on it now. Her position afforded very little view, however, and she attempted to rise to her knees. The effort drew a soft exclamation of pain from her, for she was stiff from the cold and from remaining so long in one position.

Hard on the heels of Gilliane's suppressed cry of pain came a somewhat louder gasp of relief. If she had been still so long as to grow stiff, her pursuers must have missed her. Perhaps they had continued on the trail of the bolting horse. If so, they must already know she was no longer on the animal's back. The light had been good enough to see that much for some time, Gilliane thought. It behooved her to get as far from the spoor of the horse as she could—only in what direction? She remembered that she had deduced Osbert was returning to a troop of men he had left camped. It would be a real disaster to stumble into that camp.

The notion did not cause any sense of panic because thinking of encamped men reminded Gilliane of Adam's troops. She knew where they were—a little south of the abbey—but where she was with respect to the abbey, she had no idea. While Gilliane rubbed and flexed her arms and legs to make the blood run quicker in them, she cudgeled her brains. They had gone through the garden of the guest house and out . . . out . . . She could not remember. No matter how often she went back to the freezing moment in which she had seen Osbert standing in the entryway of her chamber, she could remember nothing between the time she had decided that she must seem to go with him willingly and the time she realized Osbert must be riding to join a troop of men. Then Pierre had insulted her. There was a blur in her mind again except for the decision to kill him.

The actual killing was gem-bright in her memory, and she dwelt on it lovingly, gaining strength from the rich satisfaction of vengeance. She wished it had been Osbert. If *only* it had been Osbert! The dissatisfaction reduced her feral delight and brought her mind back to its basic problem. As long as Osbert was alive, he was a danger to her—and to Adam also, if Osbert held her. She must find Cuthbert and Adam's troops. But where? Which way?

Gasping more with fear than with pain, Gilliane levered herself to her knees and then, trembling violently, to her feet. She stared about, her heart thudding in her breast, her mouth dry with fear. Shaking with cold and terror, she looked round and round, but no shouting horseman bore down upon her, and after a moment, she steadied a little and was able to move. Which way? Every instinct in her screamed to crouch again in hiding, to crawl away into the dark. Only there was no dark, no safety on the open hillside, her reason told her. Which way? *"Ave Maria, gratia plena . . ."* Gilliane began to whisper, calling on the source of mercy, the Woman who would understand fear and weakness. Which way? She had only one single fact. Adam's men were south of the abbey. Turning her left shoulder to the newly risen sun, Gilliane began to stagger south.

Gilliane's own fear was the worst enemy she had at that moment. Although she seemed able to think clearly enough on practical matters, she was suffering severely from shock, exposure, and fatigue. Never once did it cross her mind that Osbert must know Adam had only gone hunting and would soon return. In safety, Gilliane might have realized that Osbert would be too frightened of being caught by Adam to search for her for more than a few minutes.

In fact, Osbert had not searched for her at all. Actually, he had very nearly set spurs to his horse to run away as soon as he realized Jean's mount was down and Jean was hurt. The only thing that made him dismount and extricate Jean from his predicament was the knowledge that, if he left the injured man behind, Adam would find him. Not for a single second did Osbert delude himself that Jean would resist questioning for his sake. Jean would tell Adam anything he wanted to know—and a good deal more. If Osbert had the quickness and courage to do it, he would have killed Jean then and there; however, he was not even brave enough to try to stab a hurt man pinned down by a fallen horse. Osbert knew Jean would expect he might try such a trick. He might grab Osbert's hand and then turn the knife against his master.

Cursing and whining, Osbert helped yank Jean's horse to its feet and helped Jean crawl into the saddle. Then he rode swiftly back to camp, leaving his injured man to make his own way as best he could. Osbert was sure Jean would follow. No man wishes to be questioned by an enemy. The camp, Osbert discovered, was a chaos. Only half the men were there, and many of those were drunk. Screaming and laying about him with the flat of his sword, Osbert drove some of the sober to fetch their mates from the village they were terrorizing and others to sober the drunk and strike camp.

Thus, Osbert had never given a thought to the pursuit of Gilliane. He had no room in his mind for anything beyond his steadily rising panic. He could think of nothing except what would befall him if Adam Lemagne should return sooner than expected and catch him. Indeed, no sooner were the men-at-arms who were mounted assembled than he ordered them to accompany him and rode off as fast as he could for Lewes. He knew Knepp was nearer, but Adam would know of that also, and Osbert assumed Adam would go there first. It did not occur to him that the trail his men left would be clear. Besides, Lewes was in the heart of country controlled by Louis, whereas Knepp was only a few miles from Arundel.

Osbert knew, as well as anyone else among Louis's men, that Arundel had been to visit Geoffrey Fitz-William and Ian de Vipont and that he was sulking and glowering. If Arundel should wish to ingratiate himself further with de Vipont by doing him a favor, could he not order Knepp to give Osbert up to de Vipont's stepson? Knepp was not Arundel's stronghold, but they would never defy him. His power in the area was very great.

By sunup, just about the time Adam was stretching and yawning himself awake in the hunting lodge and Gilliane was moving to a better shelter under a larger bush, Osbert's men got under way toward the east. While Adam rode to the abbey, received the news of Gilliane's abduction, and began his desperate hunt for her, the troop moved toward Lewes, making better time than usual because Osbert's panic had communicated itself to his men. Meanwhile, the abbot of St. Leonard, having stared at Sir Richard's seal ring for some moments, moved to help the poor lady entrusted to his care in the most efficacious way he knew. He hurried to the chapel and began to pray.

He told God how a traitor had misused His house for evil purposes and brought shame upon His servants. He prayed for the safety of poor Lady Gilliane and that the intentions of Sir Osbert might be confounded. He prayed also that Sir Adam would not blame him or his innocent monks for the crime that had been committed, that he would recover the lady unhurt and, therefore, not be inclined to vent his wrath on the abbey. Much comforted after confiding his problems and worries to the ultimate source of help, he rose from his knees and went to his chamber. A lay brother was then called into his presence. Slowly and carefully, the abbot related the message he was to carry to Adam's men. When the brother had twice repeated the message correctly, he was given Sir Richard's ring and went to the stables to have a mule saddled.

As the abbot was telling God about Gilliane, she came to the top of another rise. She had been walking for what seemed to her hours. Indeed, the effort she had expended was enormous, for her legs were both stiff and shaky. In the beginning, each step was a torment. Then it became easier for a time, as she grew warmer, but fear is a dreadful eater of energy. A distance that, under normal circumstances, Gilliane would have considered a pleasant walk took twice the time and became an exhausting, overlong journey.

Because it had been so hard to walk in the beginning, Gilliane had kept repeating to herself, "A little further. I must manage to go a little further." The words wove themselves into the staggering rhythm of her walk as she struggled onward. Fatigue and fear and the effort of restraining herself from huddling into a ball and waiting for death dulled her mind until the words she murmured to herself became her only thoughts and she continued to plod, head down, watching herself put one foot ahead of the other.

Gilliane did not realize she had crested a rise; she did not notice that she was coming downhill and that the angle of the slope had been driving her as much east as south. The pull of the down-slope quickened her pace and the low winter sun dazzled her eyes. Tired, hungry, thirsty, she was not watching her path, but only the movement of her own feet. Suddenly, she set her foot unwarily on a stone that tipped, casting her forward. As she fell, Gilliane cried out shrilly. Then, although she was on the ground, it seemed to her dazed mind that she was still falling. And so she was; she was rolling downhill—but she did not understand that and she screamed in earnest, for there is no fear so deep or basic in the human instinct as the fear of falling.

In the neat and well-regulated camp where Adam's, Sir Richard's and Sir Andrew's men were settled, it was relatively quiet. The bustle of wakening, mass, and breakfast was over. Until they received orders to break camp, load the pack animals, and move out, the men were free to do as they liked within the camp. They were talking, doing minor repairs on their weapons and armor, or gambling, but there were no loud voices or rushing about. Such behavior was sure to draw the attention of a master-at-arms, and that always meant trouble.

Thus, when a woman's shrill cry rang out, most of the men heard. If the sound had not been repeated, they would have shrugged their shoulders, thinking it was an animal cry that had been altered by wind or distance. Still, for a moment or two, each man who heard fell silent, listening, and into that silence Gilliane's terrified screams came loud and clear. All rushed toward the sound. In seconds, a keen-eyed youth had spotted the dark bundle rolling down the hillside well beyond the perimeter of the camp.

The dark bundle was moving, struggling to rise. Cuthbert and three of his men set off at a run. Shaken and dazed, Gilliane had not yet struggled to her knees before they were upon her. Actually, she had not even realized that the faint thudding sounds she heard were men running and not her own overdriven heart. The one fear saved her from the far greater terror of seeing herself trapped. Hands had lifted her to her feet and Cuthbert was crying aloud, "Lady! My lady! What do you here? What has befallen you? God save us, look at the blood!"

The hands that had pulled her up so roughly were withdrawn as if Gilliane were made of white-hot metal. She wavered and would have fallen again had not Cuthbert reached out toward her and permitted her to grip his arm.

"The blood is not mine," she said.

Gilliane's voice was thin but perfectly calm. The shock of finding herself safe after so much fear and suffering was so great that Gilliane felt nothing at all. She was responding automatically to what was said to her.

"But you fell!" Cuthbert exclaimed, torn between concern for his mistress and fear that he was somehow to blame for what had happened. "Are you hurt?"

"A little bruised and very tired," Gilliane answered without concern.

"Shall we carry you, my lady? Should I send the men to bring a litter? Where . . . ? The camp—it is not fitting! A horse—could you ride back to the abbey if I led the horse?"

At the word *abbey* a shudder ran through Gilliane and her hands tightened on Cuthbert's arm. "No! Not back to the abbey! I will go to the camp. And you must send a man at once to tell Sir Adam that I am safe with you."

Cuthbert blinked and swallowed. From what Lady Gilliane said, it was plain Sir Adam was not at the abbey. Moreover, her fear at the mention of the abbey could not be mistaken. All Cuthbert knew was that it had been intended she rest there, but his mind boggled at the idea that the monks had had anything to do with her bloodied and disheveled condition. Nonetheless, his first duty was to make her comfortable, and his second, as she suggested, was to let his master know that she was safe. The first was simple enough. Cuthbert had all clothing and gear removed from the

tent he shared with the other masters-at-arms and
brought Gilliane there. He apologized for the crude
and none too clean accommodations, but Gilliane
smiled tremulously.

"I am very glad to be here, and would be were there
only the cold ground to rest upon."

So Cuthbert settled her on his sleeping pallet and
covered her with all the blankets in the tent. Then,
seeing she was still shaking, he offered his cloak. Gilliane refused with another smile.

"The cold is inside me, Cuthbert," she said, "but
I grow warmer already. Now send at once to my lord
that he may know where I am."

Gently as it was said, that was an order. Cuthbert
strode out calling for a horse to be saddled and a man
to serve as messenger. The message the man must carry
was no problem, but where he should be told to go
Cuthbert had not the slightest idea. He was struggling
to think of a way to ask at the abbey where Sir Adam
was without either having the messenger fall into
enemy hands—if the monks were enemies—or betraying that Lady Gilliane was with them. What he could
do if so great a churchman as the abbot came to claim
Lady Gilliane, Cuthbert could not imagine.

Fortunately, these bemused wonderings were all
proved unnecessary in the next few minutes. Cuthbert
was summoned to the northern perimeter of the camp
by Sir Richard's master-at-arms, who pointed at a lay
brother.

"He has brought my master's seal," John of Glynde
reported, "and bids us break camp and march north
along the road where Sir Adam has gone already."

"Break camp!" Cuthbert exclaimed, wondering how
he was going to move his mistress.

Then, suddenly, an idea came to him. As the leader
of a free mercenary group, Cuthbert was far more
accustomed to thinking for himself than a man like

Alberic, who had always had one master he trusted. If Sir Adam was rushing north without summoning the men himself, it had to be because he was in desperate haste. Cuthbert had not forgotten the little scene he had witnessed between Adam and Gilliane in the storage shed, and he promptly connected Lady Gilliane's condition with Sir Adam's haste. He turned to the lay brother.

"Do you know wherefore this message is sent us?" Cuthbert asked.

The whole abbey knew, of course, of the abduction of the lady, for Catrin's screams, once she had been released, had rung through the building. The abbot had not enjoined secrecy, so the lay brother told the tale, delighted to have a piece of news that would keep soldiers enthralled. He related Osbert's abduction of Lady Gilliane with great zest.

Cuthbert clapped a hand to his head. "Let every mounted man make ready and ride north at once," he ordered. Then he turned to John of Glynde. "My lord will follow Sir Osbert with your master and Sir Andrew, having been told that Sir Osbert had with him only two men. But I know that fearful beast would not travel without a party to protect him. Sir Adam and the others will ride into a full troop. Do you go with the mounted men. Meanwhile, I will have the camp struck and we will follow you as fast as we can, carrying the lady in a litter—or, perhaps, leave one extra horse. She said she was not hurt. Perhaps she will wish to ride."

The extra horse was left, but the question of Gilliane's riding never arose. When John of Glynde galloped north at the head of the mounted troops, he saw his master waiting in the road. Sir Richard had decided that it would be best for him to stop the troops rather than let them go to the village and start east. The news, cried aloud by John of Glynde as soon as he knew his voice would carry to Sir Richard, sent

Sir Richard careening off in the direction Adam and Sir Andrew had taken. They were not far out of sight of the road, still examining Pierre's corpse in considerable puzzlement.

Indecision continued to rack Adam, growing worse every moment, so that he now felt completely paralyzed, sure that anything he did would be the wrong thing. "Look here," he called, afraid even to trust his own interpretation of the obvious and totally blind to Sir Richard's haste. "This man has been stabbed—"

"It does not matter," Sir Richard shouted joyously. "Lady Gilliane is safe in camp with our own men. Cuthbert—"

Color flooded Adam's face and his eyes came alive. "Safe?" he gasped. "Safe?"

"She is free and alive, at least," Sir Richard amended carefully, a little concerned that his man's report might be too sanguine, "but—"

Sir Richard had no opportunity to finish what he was saying. It was doubtful if Adam had heard his second statement. He had torn the reins of his great gray horse from Sir Andrew's hand, leapt into the saddle, and was off, flying for the camp at a rate that none of the other mounts could hope to match.

Sir Andrew's mouth dropped open. "What ails him?" he asked. "You said Lady Gilliane was safe—did you not?"

"He is young," Sir Richard replied carefully. "It has weighed greatly on his spirit that he left our lady without protection for so slight a thing as a hunt for pleasure."

Because Sir Andrew was not someone he could confide in on a delicate subject, Sir Richard had not said what he really thought. A rather pleasant idea was stirring in Sir Richard's brain. Had Adam realized, when he thought he had lost Lady Gilliane, that he cared rather more for her than for any common vassal?

It was not impossible. Adam had at first seemed stunned and then furious when they learned of Gilliane's abduction. It was only later, after he had had time to think, that he had become frightened about what could have happened to the lady. Perhaps as the cruelties that might be practiced upon her came into his mind, he understood that she was very precious to him.

For all his looks and his power, Sir Adam was a very innocent young man, Sir Richard thought. In this he was completely mistaken. Sir Richard was confusing the training and advice pounded into Adam by Robert of Leicester and Lord Ian—which forbade Adam to boast of, or even speak of, his relationships with gentlewomen—with lack of experience. This wrong impression had been reinforced by the way Adam blushed when offered a bed partner in Sir Andrew's keep. Because he was already convinced that Adam had no amatory interest in Gilliane, Sir Richard did not understand that Adam's embarrassment was owing to Gilliane's presence when Sir Andrew made the offer. A man of Adam's training did not accept the use of a whore in his mistress's presence.

As it was, Sir Richard decided that Adam should be given a time alone with Lady Gilliane. Having been shaken out of his indifference, Adam might expose his newfound concern. Gilliane was a very beautiful woman, and once the problem of the forced marriage had been settled . . . Sir Richard frowned. It would not be sufficient to have the Church set the marriage aside, he decided, so he would not mention that expedient to Adam; de Cercy would cause endless trouble; he would have to die. The idea caused Sir Richard no discomfort. He was drawn from his thoughts by Sir Andrew gathering the reins of his horse preparatory to mounting.

"Wait," Sir Richard said, coming down from his own horse. He wanted Adam to have more time than five minutes with Gilliane. "Tell me what Sir Adam was going to say about this body."

Had Adam known of Sir Richard's device, he would have blessed him for it. Not that Sir Richard's or Sir Andrew's presence could have affected his behavior. Adam was too far gone to have cared if the whole world stood and watched. He thundered into camp, completely unaware of the confusion of striking tents and loading pack animals.

One of the men set to watch for trouble—Cuthbert knew that setting up and striking camp were the times the men were most vulnerable to attack—did run off to tell the master-at-arms that Adam had arrived. However, Adam did not need his intervention. He had headed directly for the masters-at-arms' tent, knowing that it was the best available and that Gilliane would be there. She had been lying still, fighting the nervous reaction to her ordeal, which became more intense as the shock of relief diminished, when she heard the pounding of hooves. Because Cuthbert had ordered silence in the vicinity of the tent in which Gilliane lay, the sound was clear and the fact that the horse was approaching was apparent. For a second or two, Gilliane refused to believe that this could be a further threat to her.

Soon past terror overwhelmed reason. Gilliane cast off the blankets wrapped around her and jumped to her feet. The low tent, which had been a secure haven, suddenly felt like a trap. She rushed toward the entrance, just as the horse was pulled to a snorting, sliding halt. Too late! Gilliane shrank back, fumbling frantically in her skirt for the opening that would permit her to draw her knife. The tent flap lifted. Gilliane drew breath to scream for help—and Adam stepped in.

That was too much. The alternations of terror with relief at last overpowered Gilliane. She took a single faltering step in Adam's direction, uttered a sound midway between a gasp and a sob, and fainted into his arms.

Adam's bellows of terror brought Cuthbert, Sir Andrew's master-at-arms, and half the men in the camp running with drawn swords. This was of no particular help, except for giving Adam an outlet for the rage fear bred. He cursed poor Cuthbert with every foul word he knew for not attending properly to his mistress, for leaving her, hurt and helpless, without attention, for not bringing her back to the abbey where she might have been cared for properly by the physicians among the monks and her own maid. Had Adam not been holding Gilliane in his arms, Cuthbert might have been dead before he could find words with which to defend himself.

At this point, Gilliane recovered consciousness. "My lord," she whispered, "please do not blame Cuthbert. He wished to take me back to the abbey. I would not go."

"What?" Adam snarled. "Were the monks party—"

"No, no," Gilliane assured him in a stronger voice, pulling herself upright. Fear that in his rage Adam might order his men to attack and even raze the abbey increased her strength. Actually, she had no idea whether the monks were in league with Osbert, but that was far less important to her than keeping Adam from getting into trouble with the Church. "I was only afraid they would have no way to protect me if Osbert returned there. It was silly, but I could not endure . . ." She dropped her head forward and rested it against Adam's breast.

"Gilliane," he exclaimed, "where are you hurt?"

Without waiting for an answer, he lifted her and laid her down on the pallet again, snarling over his shoulder that hot wine should be brought. Poor Cuthbert backed out of the tent fearfully. As soon as they were alone, Gilliane lifted herself and flung her arms around Adam's neck to cling like a limpet, whispering, "Do not leave me. Do not."

"No," Adam assured her. "I will not. Only tell me, beloved, where you are hurt. So much blood . . ." He choked, thinking of the women in the village and their bloody skirts.

"Not mine," Gilliane told him, and her voice was suddenly stronger. "That is Pierre's blood. I killed him."

Adam blinked. The man who had been stabbed in the throat! The frightening pallor was gone from Gilliane's face, and her eyes sparkled with remembered satisfaction.

"Killed . . . how?" Adam asked.

For answer, Gilliane slid one hand through her skirt and drew out her knife. Adam blinked again. There was no doubt about it; that knife had been used recently and not well cleaned. Before he thought, Adam had spoken severely on the subject of not cleaning weapons properly.

"I am sorry, my lord," Gilliane murmured contritely, "it was so dark, and I was so frightened. I could not see to clean it right."

And Adam swept her back into his arms, laughing and crying at the same time because of his relief at having her safe, his joy at knowing surely and certainly she had not gone willingly with Osbert, his gratitude for the docility, the sweetness of disposition that permitted her to apologize when he censured her. Any other woman with the courage and strength to kill her abductor's henchman and escape would have burned the ears off his head for scolding over a trifle like an ill-cleaned knife. Their lips met and, when neither could breathe, parted.

"I have been dying for that," Adam sighed.

"You too? I thought, since you had the company of other gentlemen, you would not long for me."

"Are you accusing me of being a man-lover?" Adam teased.

"Not that!" Gilliane giggled, then continued more soberly, "But I know men find women very dull company and prefer to talk to other men."

"Most women *are* dull," Adam replied, grinning as he added, "but not ladies who stick knives in the throats of those who displease them. That is a sure way of gaining rapt attention—even if it is only to watch your knife hand." He kissed her again. "No, my love, I do not find you dull. In fact, as I feel now, I would give half of all I possess to rid myself of your men and have you to myself for half a day."

"I do not think you should do that," Gilliane remonstrated, brushing her lips across Adam's throat between words. "You would surely regret it—for only half a day. Could we not make the time a little longer?"

"Devil," he groaned, nibbling her cheek and the tip of her nose, "I am suffering the torments of the damned. I want you. And you have been torturing me apurpose." That was said jestingly, but suddenly he kissed her more violently, muttering, "I could feel you looking at me. I was fit to burst all day yesterday. That was why I went to hunt. I could not bear to be near you and not touch you any longer. Beloved, forgive me."

For what he was doing and saying, Gilliane would forgive him anything. Her hands moved frantically over him, but there was no way to reach Adam's body through his mail. Only his face and a small portion of his neck, where his hood was unlaced, were free of the confining armor. Gilliane was just about to voice her frustration when a throat was cleared raucously at the tent opening.

CHAPTER EIGHTEEN

Two flaming faces turned to Sir Richard, who fixed his eyes upon a most fascinating crease in the roof of the tent and hoped blandly that Lady Gilliane had not been severely injured. Since it was evident already from her occupation, her high color and her sparkling eyes that nothing serious was amiss with her, the blandness was scarcely unfeeling.

"No, no," Gilliane stammered, "the blood is not mine." She had said it so often that the words came without thought. "It was Osbert's man, Pierre. When I drew the knife from his neck, there was a great rush of blood."

Sir Richard's eyes, withdrawn hastily from the roof of the tent to fix on Gilliane, bulged with surprise. The change in his expression from rather indulgent approval to amazement bordering on disbelief was very apparent. Adam understood at once that Gilliane's vassal was well pleased with the scene he had come upon. Apparently the flicker of suspicion Sir Richard had felt with regard to Neville's death was gone for good. Adam could only wish he was as sure of Gilliane's innocence as Sir Richard was of his.

The shock of surprise administered by Sir Richard's interruption had temporarily cooled Adam's passion. In place of the heat came a nasty chill. He had suddenly remembered the knife driven into the chest after

297

the man was dead. The lack of significant bleeding from
the second wound betrayed this. It was what Adam
had been about to point out to Sir Richard. But to stab
a corpse was an act of deliberate viciousness that Adam
did not wish to connect with Gilliane's character.

Sir Richard cleared his throat again, swallowed, and
said in a strained voice, "That was a very clever stroke,
my lady."

"Then it must have been God who directed my hand,"
Gilliane replied more composedly. She had recognized
the fact that Sir Richard had no intention of disapproving or asking questions about her relationship with
Adam. "I know no more about where to strike than
you know about embroidery, Sir Richard."

It was Adam's turn to stare as the truth of that
penetrated him. What was wrong with him, he wondered, that he always seemed to burden Gilliane with
evil? How would she have known the man was dead?
He laughed aloud at his own stupidity. Cuthbert, emboldened by the normal conversational tones he heard
and by Adam's laugh, then entered the tent carefully
carrying a leather jack full of hot wine. This he proffered to Gilliane, who looked at the large vessel with
wide eyes.

"Oh, thank you, Cuthbert," she said faintly, struggling to control a rush of giggling.

Gilliane had to suppose either that the men did not
bother to carry drinking cups or that Cuthbert felt
it would contaminate her in some way to drink from
a cup used by a common man. But the smell of the
wine recalled to Gilliane that she had eaten nothing
since the preceding afternoon. Suddenly, she was raven-
ous.

"Thank you," she repeated, reaching for the jack.
"And do you think you could find for me some bread
and cheese, or cold meat, or anything? I am so hungry."

When Cuthbert returned with half a loaf of coarse
black bread and a slab of cheese, Adam began to

instruct him to have a litter prepared for Gilliane. To this she objected strenuously, pointing out that it would slow them down and that her bruises would be more hurt by the jostling of a litter than by sitting in a saddle.

"I can ride," she insisted. "I assure you I can ride."

Sir Richard was again surprised. He was growing more accustomed to Lady Gilliane's hardiness, but still he could not help objecting. "You have suffered great fear and exertion, my lady. Perhaps we should rather stay another day and permit you to rest and recover."

"I will not chance that," Adam replied. "It is most likely that de Cercy has fled to Lewes, but we cannot really be sure. It is also possible that he circled around to obtain reinforcements from Knepp and will come down upon us. We have men enough to drive them off, but I do not want Gilliane in the midst of a battle. What I thought was to carry her to Trueleigh Hill, which is no more than twelve or fourteen miles, and leave her there with Sir Hugh—"

"No!" Gilliane cried, hastily setting down the food and wine and grabbing for Adam's surcoat. "No! Do not leave me behind! I can ride. I swear I can. I will be no trouble to you again, my lord. I—"

"Gilliane," Adam interrupted, catching and holding her hands, "you are never a trouble to me. I am to blame for leaving you unprotected. If only I had not—"

"Let us not waste time and breath on vain regrets," Sir Richard suggested, not realizing he had just prevented Adam from saying that his main regret was not being able to murder Osbert. "You are right that we should move on, although, to speak the truth, I do not believe de Cercy would have courage enough to return. A greater danger is that he will tell braver men that we are traveling in this area and will not tell them that we are so strong a force."

Adam nodded. "It is totally profitless to stir up a hornets' nest here. If we are gone . . . But I expected to arrive at Alresford today, and I do not think Gilliane can go so far as that."

"I can," Gilliane insisted passionately. "I can. Come, let us go now. I am ready."

She stood up at once, stiff with the fear that she would sway or show some other sign of weakness. To her own surprise, she felt quite well, aside from a twinge here and there from the bruises she had sustained when she fell from the horse and down the hill. Sir Richard's mouth gaped in surprise. Adam did not react at all. Once Gilliane had said she did not wish to be left behind, he knew she would behave very much as she was behaving. However, he was troubled by her faint and by Sir Richard's constant amazement that Gilliane was not prostrated by every exertion.

Once before the suspicion had crossed Adam's mind that Gilliane's body might be frailer than her spirit. Her mind and will were very strong, but that was no assurance that her body could keep up with them without harm. If that was true, the matter must be handled with delicacy. As Geoffrey would be hurt if Adam tried too obviously to help with a task that exceeded his slighter strength or that was made difficult by his lameness, Gilliane would be hurt if he seemed aware of her weakness.

"Do you intend to walk all the way?" he asked lightly, as if he were teasing.

Gilliane paused on her way out of the tent. She would gladly have walked if that was the only way she could remain with Adam, but she knew it was a joke. "My mare is at the abbey—and Catrin," she said provocatively. "I could walk there."

"Yes," Adam admitted, chuckling, "but rather than waste time or take a horse from one of our mounted men, which would suit you very ill anyway, I think I will carry you before me."

Instead of looking hurt, Gilliane glowed with pleasure. "Oh, yes," she agreed heartily.

Adam had been thinking only of carrying her as far as the abbey, by which time he hoped he could better assess her strength and ability to ride. Gilliane's delighted acceptance of his suggestion opened his eyes to an aspect of the situation that had not occurred to him. He would be holding her in his arms. If he could find an excuse to drop back for a time, they could at least kiss and talk, even if it was not possible to obtain complete satisfaction.

In the end, Adam carried Gilliane all the way to Sir Edmund's keep. It was a bittersweet joy, for they both knew there could be no culmination to the passion they aroused in each other. The frustration was limited, fortunately, by the fatigue of the long ride and the tension of the initial discussions, which buried the need for sexual release under the more exigent need to present Gilliane's case in the right way to a hotheaded young man. The tale of Gilliane's abduction, easily introduced when she was lifted down from Adam's arms, played a useful role. Since Sir Edumund already felt sympathy for the boy king, it did not take long to convince him to swear to Gilliane and, through her, to Adam.

Actually, it was more difficult to curb Sir Edmund's enthusiasm for his new cause than to convince him to join. He was all for gathering extra men and beginning a campaign to wipe out the rebel forces in the area. Since these were centered in the great keep at Winchester, which Saer de Quincy, the second most influential rebel, now ruled, the notion was, to say the least, not reasonable. It would take thousands of men to reduce Winchester, and long before that happened de Quincy would bring an army to wipe out the attackers. If Pembroke and the king could be brought to support such an attack, it might have some point. Otherwise, it was suicide.

Although Adam was a few years younger than Sir Edmund, his training under Robert of Leicester had been far different. He knew in broad military and political terms what was and was not possible. Nonetheless, he *was* young. His heart responded to Sir Edmund's proposal even though his head told him the idea was wild and foolish. The dichotomy permitted Adam to handle Sir Edmund more wisely than an older, more experienced overlord. Instead of dryly pointing out the irrationality of what Sir Edmund desired, Adam's own eyes lit with enthusiasm. Before a horrified Sir Richard could raise objections, however, Adam sighed.

"I have not the strength," he said regretfully. "Even if I emptied my keeps and Lady Gilliane agreed—and see, she is already shaking her head in disapproval—"

"A woman," Sir Edmund began.

"Your overlady, and do not forget it," Adam replied, frowning.

"Nor are my reasons womanish," Gilliane said firmly. She had listened to Adam's talk with Sir Richard to good purpose. "Let us clean our own house before we look into another's. You and Sir Richard and Sir Andrew are agreed, but that is only half our strength. We must convince Sir Philip, Sir Matthew, and Sir Godfrey. How will it look to the king's guardians if you come swearing fealty and your fellow castellans are rebels?"

"It is true," Adam remarked, "but listen to this. If we can bring Sir Philip and Sir Matthew—"

"Not Sir Matthew," Sir Edmund interrupted sharply. "He is growing rich on French shipping and he is close to Arundel. He will thumb his nose at you and look to change overlords."

Sir Edmund looked offended when Adam and the others burst out laughing, but when he heard why they laughed—the news that had come from Geoffrey—he was delighted. "And I think," Adam went on, his eyes suddenly dancing, "that I will add a little fuel to the fire. I think I am going to write Arundel a most sad and most proper letter about a poor girl whose first husband died, who was forced into marriage by a dastardly coward who fled when I approached to avenge an incursion onto my lands, and—"

"Yes, but I do not see what Arundel has to do with—"

"The Earl of Arundel," Adam interrupted Sir Edmund, "is . . ." There he hesitated. He had been about to say that Arundel was a blockhead, but another blockhead of the same type was looking at him. "Arundel is a very . . . er . . . chivalrous gentleman," Adam continued, grinning broadly. "He would never rob a poor, helpless widow by subverting her castellan. I will tell him how I have taken pity upon Lady Gilliane's sad state and offered to bring her rebellious man to obedience. I will explain that we mean no harm and no offense to him, although to reach Wick we must cross his lands, and I will promise to do no hurt to his people and make restitution if damage is done by accident."

"Why will you cross his lands?" Gilliane asked, paling a trifle as she saw where this talk was leading.

"To bring Sir Matthew to obedience," Adam replied, and his face set like stone when he saw her lips part to object. "This is a matter of the king's need and of my duty, Lady Gilliane," he went on pointedly, "although it will also benefit you. Wick oversees a fine port. Sir Edmund tells me it is being used by the French. It must not be left to their use. It must be in trustworthy hands."

A quick glance at Sir Richard's face sank Gilliane's heart right into the slippers she had put on when she finally changed out of her bloodstained riding dress. Sir Richard plainly approved heartily of Adam's idea. Thus, Gilliane would have no support—for Sir Andrew followed Sir Richard's lead in all things—if she dared oppose the attack on Wick. And what could she say, Gilliane wondered desperately. She knew nothing of the real needs and objectives of Louis or Henry. If she said, in the presence of other men, that she did not want Adam to fight for fear he would be hurt, he would kill her—or, at least, never forgive her for the shame she brought upon him.

So Gilliane sat quietly, keeping her face as expressionless as possible. Still, Adam was quick enough to feel her disapproval. He could not understand it. If Gilliane wanted the lands, they had to be wrested from the grip of men who would not be obedient. Yet she was not willing for him to do that. Why? Sir Andrew was approving of warning Arundel in portentous tones, but Adam heard nothing of it. The only times Gilliane had ever opposed what he wished were when he planned to raid Lewes—a stronghold that supported Louis—and when he planned to oust and replace Sir Godfrey of Bexhill and Sir Matthew of Wick—both of whom were firm adherents to Louis's cause. It certainly seemed as if Gilliane had lied about her willingness to accept Henry.

"But I do not see that there is any need to apprise Arundel of what we plan to do," Sir Edmund said suddenly. "If we do no harm to his people or his property, he has no right to interfere between a castellan and his overlord—I mean, overlady. If you write to him, he may refuse permission to cross his lands. Then . . ."

Adam's train of thought had been broken by the change from Sir Andrew's plodding baritone to Sir Edmund's quick tenor so that, fortunately, he heard what the young man said. "Arundel will not refuse," Adam stated. "In any case, I do not intend to wait upon his permission. Likely, we will be past his lands before he receives my letter. My stepfather, Lord Ian, will mediate if necessary, making the very point you have just suggested."

"But then, why—"

"My reasons have little to do with Arundel's attitude toward our taking of Wick—except that such a letter will prevent him from conceiving of our actions as an insult, which he might take it into his head to do otherwise. More important is that sooner or later word will come to Louis that we are attacking or have conquered Sir Matthew's stronghold. I am quite sure that someone among those idiot French, if not Louis himself, will either complain that he did not prevent me from moving against Wick or even, God willing, accuse him of treachery."

"But that is not fair," Sir Andrew protested. "It is not Arundel's part to support a castellan against his true overlord—overlady. It has nothing to do with Prince Louis."

Sir Edmund's mouth opened, but nothing came out. He looked from Adam, who was trying hard not to grin at Sir Andrew's inability to see below the surface of a thing, to Sir Richard, whose lips were twitching but who was nodding agreement with what Sir Andrew said. Sir Edmund knew that Sir Andrew saw only one thing at a time, but it was inconceivable to him that anyone could overlook the fact that, once in Adam's power, the port below Wick would be closed to the French. Thus, the matter *was* of importance to Louis and Arundel's indifference might imply treachery. In spite of Gilliane's anxiety at the idea that Adam planned to fight, she could see everyone struggling not to laugh at Sir Andrew. That would be unkind and might cause trouble.

"That is very true, Sir Andrew,'" she said quickly, "and from what I have heard of Lord Arundel, he will feel just as you do. Thus, he will be very ill pleased that Louis or his friends should say his motives are dishonorable when they are not. And, if Lord Arundel is insulted and angered, it is not likely that he will agree to attack us himself or permit anyone else to use his forces and his keep to attack us."

All the men now stared at Gilliane. Sir Edmund was much surprised that a woman should speak at all about such matters in the company of men. What was more, he had the sneaking suspicion that she knew as much or more about it than he did and had said exactly as much as was suited to Sir Andrew's understanding and feelings—without telling a lie and without concealing from the rest of them the most important aspect of the matter. If Lord Arundel was insulted and infuriated enough, he might repudiate his oath to Louis—and this, of course, was what Adam intended. Even if this incident did not precipitate the break, it would certainly add to Arundel's dissatisfaction with his French allies and increase his feeling that Englishmen, even enemies, treated him with more courtesy and consideration.

The notion that Gilliane's intervention had been deliberate—to say what was necessary without saying too much—and was inspired by her doubt that any of her male companions would be adroit enough to do so, made Sir Edmund even more uncomfortable. What was more, a glance at Sir Richard's nodding head and barely suppressed smile confirmed the notion, as did Sir Adam's tight-lipped, intent stare. Sir Edmund assumed that a male overlord would not be pleased to discover too much quickness of mind in a female vassal he expected to parrot his own opinions.

In his reading of Sir Richard, Sir Edmund was quite correct. However, he could not have been more wrong about Adam's response. Adam was simply bewildered. He had been very disappointed when he came to the belief that Gilliane had prevaricated about her willingness to abandon Louis's cause. However, he had always accepted that as a possibility. What was more, he had gained confidence because the knowledge of Gilliane's disapproval had not in the least inclined him to change his mind. Adam had not had time to begin to worry about what he would feel if Gilliane started to exert emotional pressure on him because Sir Edmund had distracted him before that idea entered his head. And now, what Gilliane said to Sir Andrew and her manner of saying it certainly implied she understood Adam's purpose in writing to Arundel and approved it.

The situation was not destined to become any clearer because at that point Gilliane became aware of Adam's expression. The smile froze on her lips. Sir Andrew was paying her a long-winded compliment on her cleverness, which permitted her to turn toward him so that her stricken look was not visible to those who could have read it. When Sir Andrew was finished, she thanked him courteously for his good opinion and then added that, as she was very tired, she would leave the gentlemen to their discussion and go to her bed. Sir Edmund immediately summoned a maid to take her to the principal chamber in the women's quarters. Gilliane curtsied to Adam, wished all the gentlemen a good night and sound sleep, and went away.

If Gilliane could have thought of any way to stop Adam from attacking Wick, she would have endured his displeasure, even his rejection, to ensure his safety. A sleepless night of concentrated thought failed to show her a path toward that end. Since Adam had stated so clearly that it was primarily the king's purpose he was forwarding rather than hers, it would do no good to renounce her claim upon Sir Matthew and his keep. Perhaps if she had been alone with Adam, Gilliane would have tried emotional blackmail. Fortunately, the opportunity did not arise.

Adam had also spent a sleepless night going over what Gilliane had said, what she could have meant, how her behavior from the time he had met her fit together. He could draw no satisfactory conclusion. The evidence was too contradictory and, worse, Adam could not trust himself to interpret it fairly. He was too anxious to obtain one particular answer, too aware of that anxiety to trust any meaning he found. To top his problems, he was suffering from a delayed realization of how close he had come to losing Gilliane altogether.

Suddenly, Adam felt overwhelmed. Usually he was, if anything, overconfident of his ability to handle anything, and charged blithely into situations where, as it was said, angels feared to tread. Now new horrors popped up on every side. What if Sir Philip should turn traitor and seize Gilliane? What if an attack should be made upon them for the express purpose of abducting Gilliane? What if Gilliane should subtly work on her men so that they withdrew from the attack on Wick at a crucial moment? In any case, what was he thinking of, carrying a woman into a war? Even if none of his previous fears were fulfilled—and Adam was still rational enough to recognize that they were not very logical—what was he to do with Gilliane after they had dealt with Sir Philip?

There could be no question of leaving Gilliane at Leith Hill. That would be an open invitation to treachery by a man who could adjust his honor to his purposes. Nor could Adam consider sending her back to Tarring. Aside from the danger of the trip itself and the danger that Osbert might attack Tarring from Lewes, there was Sir Richard's son. Adam had not missed the way Sir Edmund's eyes had rested on Gilliane. There was nothing offensive in his admiration, and Gilliane had offered not even so much as a look of encouragement; however, Adam was reminded that he was not the only man who could see Gilliane was beautiful. To leave her alone for an extended period with a young, unmarried man was an open invitation to a different kind of disaster than political treachery.

Adam turned over and groaned. She said she loved him. He had no reason by look or word or deed to doubt that—unless her passion was assumed for some purpose that had nothing to do with love. If she loved him, it should not matter who was in Tarring keep. Still, it would be mad to thrust Gilliane into propinquity with a young man—with any man—without any other person of her own class. If only there was some woman . . . Abruptly, Adam flopped over again on his back and began to laugh. Of all the cod's heads in the world, he was the greatest. Not more than twenty-five miles away lay Roselynde and all the help that any man could need in love or war. He sat up in bed, wrapped his arms around his knees, and began to plan.

When the gentlemen came to breakfast the next day, they found a pale, silent Gilliane and a flushed, tight-lipped Adam just emerging from a window embrasure. The lady did not pause at the breakfast table but swept into the stairwell and disappeared. Adam came forward, his eyes leaping with gold and green light so that, had they not been men of courage, the others would have slunk out of the hall. As it was, they made themselves very busy with eating and drinking because then it would not be necessary to address any words to Adam. He cut cheese, broke bread, and then looked down at what was in his hands as if he could not imagine what it was.

The violence of Gilliane's objections when Adam told her he would leave her in his mother's keeping had produced the bitterest suspicions to torment him since he had almost convinced himself that Gilliane had gone willingly with Osbert. She had begged and pleaded not to be left behind, but refused to give any reason for her desire to remain with them. All she had said, over and over, was that she was afraid, that she loved him, that she would be no trouble, would never oppose his will again in anything.

When Adam asked of what she was afraid, he received no response beyond an offering of Gilliane's lips. That had turned him sick, hinting that she was using her beauty, her body, to tame him to her will. He had tried to push that out of his mind and had remonstrated that there could be nothing to fear in Roselynde. The keep was nearly as strong as the Tower of London; no man could reach her or harm her in Roselynde; and his mother, who was near as strong as the keep itself, would protect her.

What could Gilliane say? Neither of her fears could be confessed. If she told Adam she feared he would be hurt or killed in an attack on Wick, he would be angry because she made so little of his skill as a warrior. Also, he would laugh at her and want to know, quite logically, what good her presence could do. To that, there was no sensible answer. Even Gilliane knew she would, at the least, be useless and might even present a danger to the men. Men-at-arms would have to be drawn from the fighting to guard her constantly, and, if a counterattack should be launched, she might be taken prisoner. Could Gilliane say she feared Adam's mother even more than the danger of being captured by an enemy? If she cried that Lady Alinor would call her a whore, Adam would laugh. You *are* a whore, he would reply—and it was true.

Thus, she had given no answer, only tried to cling to Adam, and he had pushed her away, reminding her harshly of the terms she had accepted. He would win back her men for her, but those men—and she herself—would be pledged to expel Louis from England and set young Henry firmly on the throne. If she wanted to be anything more than a prisoner, watched and guarded constantly, she had better resign herself to keeping her oath. Gilliane stared up at her lover's flushed, angry face and stammered that she did not care about that, and he had snarled, "What, then, do you care about?"

"You, only you," she whispered.

"Then why do you refuse to do what will be best for me?" Adam asked cruelly. "Do you wish me to go into battle with a divided mind, wondering whether you are safe? Lonely? With another man? If you care about me, obey me."

"Another man!" Gilliane had gasped. He really *did* believe she was a whore! "I do not wish to be free of you. I have been begging to stay near you always. It is *you* who wish to be free, *you* who desire another partner."

"Idiot woman . . ." Adam began furiously, about to

ask how she could be near him on a battlefield, and then the voices of the men entering the hall made him swallow what more he had to say.

Gilliane looked at his face, turned, and nearly ran to the stairwell. Adam had to lock the muscles in his legs to keep himself from running after her. It would be easy enough to explain how far from the truth Gilliane was when they were alone, he told himself. She would not remain angry. Anything could be explained except making her look a fool before her men, and he had avoided that. It did not matter if the men guessed there had been a quarrel, Adam thought, staring at the bread and cheese in his hand, so long as they did not know what it was about or who won. Finally, Adam raised his hand and bit into the cheese. He felt sick, but he chewed and swallowed, wondering what Gilliane thought she could accomplish by accompanying them to the battlefield.

No matter how Adam turned that, there was no sense in it. She might hope to subvert the men before they came to Wick, but once they had agreed to take Wick—no, Sir Edmund would never listen to her at all and Sir Richard would certainly consult Adam before he acted. Besides, even as headstrong a wife as his mother . . . But Gilliane was not a wife. The idea burst on Adam with a sensation of surprise because he was so committed to marrying her that he thought of her as his wife already and assumed she thought the same way. But Gilliane might not think the same way, and she might not be sure of him as a lover. *Another partner,* she had said. Could Gilliane be jealous?

The angry sparks began to die from Adam's eyes. Gilliane was so very beautiful that he had assumed she was aware of her effect on him. However, Adam was not particularly modest. He knew he had a substantial effect upon women. It was not impossible that Gilliane was jealous. That was funny. Adam choked on a mouthful of bread and someone pounded his back.

Absently, he mumbled thanks and drank the wine that was offered to him. If that was the answer . . . how delightful! But did it fit? Could even a jealous woman believe he was going to carry on an affair during an attack on a keep? Adam choked again. A jealous woman could think anything! They were more unreasonable than the totally insane, as he well knew.

Besides, Gilliane might not have thought as far ahead as the battlefield. She knew, he guessed, that he would not take another woman, not even a whore, while she was near and might know of it. He had complained bitterly enough of his frustration. Perhaps she thought he wished to ease himself at Sir Philip's keep. Adam grinned. That was not a bad idea at all! He heard Gilliane's men start to talk among themselves and the sound made him realize that none of them had said a word until that moment. Very wise, Adam thought, grinning more broadly. Very likely he would have snapped the head off any man who spoke.

"Lady Gilliane and I have decided that it would be best if she went to stay with my mother at Roselynde until we have Wick in our hands," Adam announced blandly.

"Er . . . yes," Sir Richard agreed, relieved by the restoration of his young overlord's usual good humor but not wishing by some inadvertent error to arouse his temper again.

"Unfortunately, Roselynde is out of the way for Leith Hill, and I do not wish to make the footmen march the extra fifty or sixty miles," Adam went on, pretending that he was unaware of the unease of the men. "However, we have compromised."

The *I* and *we* were deliberately misleading. The words implied that the difference of opinion between Adam and Gilliane was over the route to be taken and whether the entire armed force should accompany them. A compromise was possible on such a matter so that neither could be said to have won the argument. Adam could see the men relax and was pleased with himself. He had fixed their attention on a small matter that might arouse tempers but could not lead to the serious consequences for vassals and castellans that might be caused by a difference of opinion between their over-lady and her overlord on a basic subject.

By the time Adam had finished outlining his proposal regarding the movement of the troops, the men had almost forgotten the quarrel. Whoever proposed the plan was wise.

"Of course, you need not come to Roselynde if you would rather not," he said offhandedly. "If some or all of you wish to remain here, or with the men, I will have no objection."

Adam would have preferred that they stay behind. His first thought when he conceived of the idea of taking Gilliane to Roselynde had been that they could be alone on the ride and together in Roselynde, once he had explained matters to his mother. That delightful idea had to be abandoned, however. To announce to these men, so new in their fealty, that he was taking their overlady alone to a stronghold of his family could not help but rouse suspicion that some havey-cavey business was intended. Obviously, they must be invited to come also. Adam rather hoped that no one would think it worthwhile to ride the extra distance in the cold winter weather.

The hope was not fulfilled. All four men immediately announced themselves willing to come along. From their faces, they were more than willing; they were eager. Adam was a little surprised. It did not occur to him that Roselynde was one of the great places of the area, the resort of the most powerful and noblest men in the country, a keep about which these men had heard tales and rumors. Roselynde was not eminent or important to Adam, except for his affection for it and his happy memories of childhood there. He did not guess that Gilliane's men were looking forward to boasting to their neighbors that they had been visitors to Roselynde, rather than chance wayfarers, who would be welcomed by a steward and might never exchange a word with the lord and lady. They would be real guests.

Breakfast finished, the men went out to give orders to the troops. Meanwhile, word was sent to Gilliane to make ready to leave. Since she had been ready when she first came down in response to a message from Adam that he wished to speak to her in private, she merely rose from her chair and told Catrin to see that the traveling baskets were brought down to the pack animals. Perhaps, Gilliane thought as she descended the stairs, she would not ache so much now if she had not been so overjoyed when she received that first message. Adam had forgiven her for speaking out against his will, she had believed, and she had flown down to him.

"I have a plan," he had said, and Gilliane's heart had lifted with delight. He had discovered a way, she had thought, for them to be together. When they were folded in each other's arms, she was sure she could find a way to explain why he should not fight for Wick, endangering his precious person for something so much less valuable. Perhaps if thought were not so swift that she had time to hope so much, she would not have been plunged so deep in despair when she heard the plan. Adam had not forgiven her. He was putting her aside completely.

Driven desperate by fears she could not name, Gilliane had compounded her crime by arguing and pleading. How odd it was, she thought dully, plodding down the stairs and then across the hall to a window. Saer would have beaten her. Adam never touched her, but the pain she suffered was so much more agonizing that she would yield, would agree to anything. Only she did not think she would be given any opportunity to yield. Most likely, the whole argument had been a device to rid himself of her. This despairing conclusion seemed confirmed when Sir Richard, rather than Adam, came to escort Gilliane to her horse, and she drew a deep breath and braced her body. It was too late. Adam would not even permit her to beg pardon.

Sir Richard took one look at his overlady's pallid, set face and scented disaster. Adam seemed recovered. His rages were quick to rise and quick to cool. However, Lady Gilliane was still as angry as she appeared to be when she left the hall. Doubtless she would set Sir Adam off again. It was really too bad. The day after the abduction attempt Sir Richard had had high hopes of a match between the pair. Now if he did not think of some way to soothe Lady Gilliane, his expectation of a really strong bond to Adam's influential family might be ruined.

"I am sorry you are not pleased with Sir Adam's arrangements," Sir Richard said tentatively.

"Did Sir Adam say I was not pleased?" Gilliane asked, trying so hard to keep her voice from trembling and prevent herself from bursting into tears that she sounded cold as ice.

"No, indeed," Sir Richard assured her hastily, "that was my own guess. If I was wrong, please forgive me. I only meant to tell you how happy we all are to be invited to Roselynde. Such simple knights as we are might not have another chance to be guests in such a place. It was most kind of you, my lady, to think of us."

Gilliane lowered her eyes. Was she a hysterical fool, making a tragedy out of a simple, straightforward matter? Had Adam's intention all along been to bind her men more firmly to his purpose by impressing them with the power his family wielded? If so, she did not blame him for being furious with her when she cried she would not go to Roselynde.

Gilliane murmured something in answer to Sir Richard's compliment. He, seeing that she now looked far more thoughtful than sullen, said no more but merely led her to her mare and lifted her to the saddle. Gilliane was so deep in thought and so sure that Adam was still too angry to come near her that she did not look around for him.

Now that her mind had been jolted out of the state of despair her disappointment had brought about, gleams of hope appeared here and there. Adam had been annoyed when she argued against the attack on Wick, but there had been no anger in his face when he first broached the plan of going to Roselynde. Gilliane thought hard, recalling to mind every flicker of expression. No, he had not been angry. He had, in fact, looked pleased, enthusiastic, even a little excited. That was why her hopes had flown so high.

What a fool she was! Instead of discovering what Adam intended by the plan, she had fallen into a fit of disappointment, like a two-year-old denied a honeyed fruit. Suddenly Gilliane blushed deep red. Her simile was truer than she had first thought. Had she not been denied her sweet? Had she not thought Adam had made a plan to permit them to make love? When she realized that was not what was in his mind, had she not immediately assumed the worst? Even if he did not regard her as more than a casual mistress, he had wanted her very much all during the ride to Sir Edmund's keep. Surely it was ridiculous to think he wished to put her aside before satisfying that desire.

No wonder Adam had been so furious. She had mixed business with pleasure. When she should have been thinking of the best way to keep the men faithful and perhaps even overawe Sir Matthew into submission without war, she had been thinking of her body. Adam expected better of her than that. He had told her more than once that there were more important things than dinner. Now she understood more fully what he meant.

She must somehow redeem herself. She must think of ways to forward Adam's political purpose.

A qualm passed through Gilliane. Would she be allowed to speak? Would Lady Alinor allow her to associate with the other women? Would she regard her as something unclean and banish her to a separate place, perhaps even one of the outbuildings where the lowest servants—the women of dog boys and pigherds—lay? No, that was ridiculous. Whatever Lady Alinor felt, she could not treat Gilliane with contumely while her men were guests in the keep. Besides, how would Lady Alinor know that she had made a whore of herself unless Adam told her?

Would Adam tell? Would he keep her secret? Gilliane's spirits flew up, crashed down. She did her best to keep a rein on them, aware now of the fact that her imagination was dangerous to her. She was afraid to look at Adam, knowing he must still be angry because he would not come near her. But Gilliane was making her own grief. Adam was avoiding her only because he thought *she* was still angry. Each of her men rode beside her for a while, and that distracted her mind from Adam. They were all pleased and excited and spoke of Lord Ian and Lord Geoffrey. They were very great men, Gilliane was told. Lord Ian de Vipont was one of the closest friends of the Earl of Pembroke, who was Grand Marshal of England and guardian of the king. Lord Geoffrey FitzWilliam was the king's own cousin, his father being the natural son of old King Henry.

Unfortunately, this information did little to soothe Gilliane. She remembered the casual way she had treated Lord Geoffrey and Lord Ian when they were at Tarring, laughing and joking with them as if they were ordinary men. Doubtless they had written to Lady Alinor and told her that Lady Gilliane of Tarring was a bold hussy without respect or decorum. Much as Gilliane tried to control her overactive imagination, Lady Alinor of Roselynde began to form in her mind as a giantess, twelve feet high with a face of granite and eyeballs of flame.

CHAPTER NINETEEN

Tarring was a moderately strong keep, wide-walled and moated halfway around, but Gilliane's first view of Roselynde, gigantic on its cliff with the sea beating at its feet, merely confirmed her feeling that the mistress of such a place must be harsh and totally formidable. The first thin wedge of doubt about the rigid, fearsome creature she had created was driven in by the easy joy with which Adam was greeted as he crossed the drawbridge. From the towers and the walls, the men called down and those on guard by the lifted portcullis shouted questions, to all of which Adam bellowed genial abuse in reply. There was no lack of efficiency. The men were all where they should be and all alert, but there was a good-humored ease about them that bespoke long-standing contentment with their situation.

The attitude of the servants in the inner bailey also had its effect. Their greetings were softer and not so coarse, but there was no fear in their faces, no shying away from the armed men, no sidelong glances when their backs were turned to watch for a spiteful, ill-tempered blow. Adam came to help Gilliane down from her mare himself, but before she could say a word, an old man, although still big and strong, came forward. Adam turned immediately to embrace him and both began to talk a guttural gibberish that Gilliane recognized as English because Cuthbert spoke it to the men.

Absently, still talking to Beorn, Adam put out his hand to lead Gilliane in. Then Beorn turned away to see to the settlement of the small mounted troop that had accompanied them, and Adam called to Gilliane's men to dismount and come in and be welcome. He did not wait for them, but led Gilliane directly into the forebuilding and up the stairs, during which time she became so frightened that she could not speak. When they entered the great hall and had come about halfway across, the most beautiful woman Gilliane had ever seen in her life burst from a second stairwell and tore across toward them. Her flaming hair was all loose, streaming behind her as she ran, and her dress was not properly done up at the neck. She cast herself into Adam's arms, crying his name and kissing him all over the face.

Gilliane nearly fainted. If this was Adam's woman, what did he want with a blackamoor like herself? But although Adam clasped the woman fondly enough and returned her kisses, there was no tenderness in his voice when he spoke. Gilliane's senses stopped reeling. The beautiful redhead loved Adam, that was clear, but what he felt was still in doubt.

"What ails you, Jo?" he was asking. "You act as if I had been gone ten years."

"Adam, you wretch!" Joanna replied. "Three months is as good as ten years when we never heard one *word* from you. Why do you never write? And we sent two messengers who never returned. Mama and I were worried."

"Two messengers?" Adam repeated. "They never came to Tarring." He turned to look questioningly at Gilliane.

"No, my lord," Gilliane said quietly, too numb with shock to do anything but answer a direct question directly. "I am sure Alberic would have told me if someone had brought a letter for you."

Adam flushed slightly. He had had a brief flash of

suspicion that Gilliane had destroyed or concealed the letters, but he realized with shame that anyone who passed through the gates of Tarring while he was away would have been checked on by Alberic before he came into Gilliane's presence.

"I suppose either they never caught up with us—we have been moving from place to place—or else . . ." Adam frowned. "I hope there was nothing of importance in the letters, Jo."

Joanna had looked toward Gilliane, but now her attention came back to Adam. "No, only family news and Mama's request that you let us know whether you were dead or alive," she replied dryly. "Why?"

Adam grinned. "I am afraid I stirred up a hornets' nest around Lewes and around Knepp and Arundel . . ." He glanced back over his shoulder and saw Gilliane's men advancing toward them. "I will tell you later," he said softly. Then he looked at her with mock disapproval. "You are becoming a hoyden, Jo. Go set yourself to rights. You cannot greet guests half dressed with your hair all undone."

"You caught us dressing for dinner," Joanna gasped, blushed, gathered her hair into her hands and fled, crossing the path of another woman who was advancing with more dignity but also quickly. Adam left Gilliane's side to go forward, embrace, and be embraced, but Gilliane felt no shock of jealousy this time, only surprise. She knew this must be Lady Alinor because the facial resemblance between mother and son was striking. There, however, the resemblance ended. Lady Alinor was by no means twelve feet high; in fact, she was rather small, although sturdily made. Certainly she was no rock-hard giantess, and her eyes, far from flaming, were filled with tenderness. Nonetheless her voice was sharp.

"So help me, Adam, you are a disgrace to me and to your father. He was not an illiterate boor. Where you came by . . . Simon!"

The final word was an admonitory shriek, addressed to a child who had come running around Gilliane's men and now launched himself at Adam from some six feet away. Adam turned just in time to catch the boy in his arms. The child promptly swarmed up Adam's body, twisted around it, and seated himself astride his half-brother's shoulders.

"Will you fight me, Adam? Will you? I have a new sword and I am very good. Sir Guy says so. Will you?" the boy cried, bouncing up and down.

"Sit still, you little monster," Adam laughed. "How can I fight you if you break both my collar bones?"

"Simon! Is this how I have taught you to greet guests?" A man's deeper tones, touched with a comic hopelessness. "Simon, come down."

Adam put out his hands and grasped those of the newcomer. "Guy! I am glad to see you in good health. I thought by now this devil would have worn you to a thread or that you would have abandoned us in despair."

The stocky, sandy-haired man laughed again. "Well, I do sleep soundly of nights, but it is a great pleasure to teach so quick a pupil."

Gilliane stood quietly where Adam had left her, fighting tears. She had been transported back more than ten years to her own home. It had been exactly like this, she remembered with startling clarity, whenever her father had returned from a journey—the cheerful, contented servants voicing greetings, the happy women offering embraces, the child (herself) wild with excitement. But more than anything, the flood of warmth and affection and joy was what she remembered and had lost. This was a home. This was heaven, but she had lost it forever. For a time, the voices and laughter became a distant buzz in Gilliane's ears. Then she was startled into awareness by having her hand taken.

"So this is Lady Gilliane," Alinor was saying, and

the sharpness was gone from her voice. "I bid you welcome to Roselynde, my dear."

Lady Alinor already knew a great deal about Gilliane. Adam had not written, but both Ian and Geoffrey were excellent correspondents and had described the girl and her situation. They had also given Alinor full information on their doubts and their suspicions concerning Adam's predilection for Gilliane. Part of Alinor's concern when Adam had not written or replied to her letters was that he had fallen under the spell of a designing woman. She was at least as surprised by Gilliane's appearance as Gilliane was by hers. Alinor had been prepared for great beauty, but she had expected it to mask a hard shrewdness. What she saw in the huge dark eyes turned to hers was utter desolation.

The look was that of a lost child, and Alinor's heart went out to the girl who could easily have been the daughter she had birthed dead between Joanna and Adam. It was impossible to believe that Adam had mistreated Gilliane deliberately, but he was very heedless and might not realize he was frightening her. She looked pale and tired, too. That Adam! He thought all women were healthy mares like Joanna and herself, and this poor girl was probably not accustomed to riding all day and camping in the open.

"There is nothing to be afraid of here, my love," Alinor said softly. "Let me make known to you my daughter, Joanna."

Automatically, Gilliane curtsied while her eyes moved to the woman Lady Alinor was introducing to her. She almost forgot to rise from her bend. It was the woman who had embraced Adam so fervently when he arrived, although now her flaming hair was modestly hidden under her wimple and her dress was neat and proper. "Adam's sister?" Gilliane breathed, and then she blushed at her own stupidity. Of course it was his sister. He had often spoken of Joanna and, jealous fool that she was, Gilliane had not associated that with the love-name Jo. Also, Joanna had spoken of Mama. Who else could that have been but Lady Alinor?

The relief in the words Gilliane breathed and her blush clarified matters still further for Lady Alinor. She had seen Joanna's affectionate greeting and Gilliane had apparently misunderstood it. It seemed fairly clear that Gilliane was head over heels in love with her scapegrace son. That was most interesting in view of what Ian and Geoffrey had said about Adam's feelings. At present, Alinor could not judge those. Adam's attention had been on her, then on Simon, and now, still carrying the child, he was talking with the three men who had come with him, introducing them to Sir Guy and to Father Francis, who had come from his chamber.

As the thought crossed her mind, Adam lifted Simon from his shoulders and gave him to Sir Guy. Then he turned back toward them and said, "Gilliane . . ." The tone was compelling. There was something he expected Gilliane to do that she had not done. The girl swung toward him, her eyes wide, anxious. Poor thing, overwhelmed and confused as she was, how did Adam expect her to remember every nicety of convention? Lady Alinor was about to mend the slight breach in manners herself, but Joanna had already understood and leaned forward to whisper, "Introduce your men to Mama, Gilliane."

The kindness of the hint and the realization that Adam intended to support her position as overlady and thus as a gentlewoman of importance even within his own family restored a measure of Gilliane's self-possession. "If you will permit me, Lady Alinor," she said, "I would like to make known to you my vassal, Sir Richard of Glynde; and the castellan of Rother, Sir Andrew; and the castellan of Alresford, Sir Edmund."

"You are very welcome to Roselynde, gentlemen," Lady Alinor said, smiling and extending her hand to be kissed by each man in turn. "Sir Richard, I know you by name and by reputation. My first husband spoke most favorably of you to me. I know you lightened his heavy burden as sheriff of Sussex by your sound justice and wisdom."

Gilliane watched and listened with fascination as Lady Alinor found something personal to say to each man, set him at ease, drew him to talk, and soon had all the men smiling and comfortable. There was nothing haughty in her manner, yet Gilliane was sure no one would dare the slightest familiarity with her or fail to obey any order she gave. Joanna, having been introduced, was a quieter version of her mother. In another moment, Gilliane found herself, much to her surprise, drawn into the conversation. She was aware, however, that there were more servants bustling about the hall than there had been when they arrived and soon a very pretty maid said softly to Lady Alinor that the chambers and baths were ready if the gentlemen would like to be unarmed and made comfortable before dinner.

Baths for each guest! Gilliane blushed slightly with shame. She had not known enough to offer that to her guests at Tarring. Saer and his wife had never done so, but doubtless they were crude, dirty beasts compared to Lady Alinor. Adam had never suggested . . . but he was too kind to embarrass her by making a point of her omission. A middle-aged maid had approached Sir Richard and another made a curtsy to Sir Andrew, while the very pretty blond young woman who had spoken to Lady Alinor went toward Sir Edmund.

"What a slut that girl is," Joanna whispered in Gilliane's ear.

Every drop of color drained from Gilliane's face, and she was stricken mute. Joanna, watching the pair go off, did not notice.

"That is my maid, Edwina," she continued, giggling, before Gilliane could force either denial or apology through her stiff lips. "I am sure she arranged with Gertrude and Ethelburga which one she was to have before poor Sir Edmund had even climbed the stairs.

Oh, goodness, I should not have said that to you. You are his overlady. Do not tell his wife."

"He is not married," Gilliane managed to say.

"Have I shocked you?" Joanna asked contritely. "I am so sorry, but . . ."

"No," Gilliane replied hastily. "No, of course not. It was . . . I was surprised. The maids were all so frightened of Saer and Osbert."

"You need not worry about Edwina," Joanna assured her, smiling again. Then she turned away from Gilliane to grasp Adam firmly by the arm. "Come with me, piggy, and let me see if I can get the stink off you. I declare, if I had been on the windward side of the keep I would have known by the smell that you were coming."

"Oh, no!" Adam exclaimed playfully, backing away. "You are not going to get me in a tub again. You tried to drown me when I was a helpless babe. I remember."

"I did not try to drown you! I was washing your hair," Joanna protested.

"By holding my head under the water? Mama, did she not try to drown me? I want Gilliane to attend to me. She does not let the soap run into my eyes apurpose."

"Joanna *should* have drowned you," Alinor remarked sharply, with a swift glance at Gilliane's blanched face. "Do you not see how tired poor Gilliane is? You big ox, because you are never tired, you never think anyone else can be."

"I am not tired, madam," Gilliane said firmly. If Adam wished to show his mother and sister what she was by taking her so publicly to his bed, Gilliane was even ready for that.

Alinor suppressed a smile. Of course, Gilliane would say she was not tired. If Adam told her to pick up the keep, the idiot child would try to do it. More interesting was the sudden expression of anxiety that came over Adam's face.

"It was only a jest, Gilliane," Adam said quickly. "I was only teasing Joanna. You go with my mother and rest."

He turned away quickly then, as if shy of having his expression read. Alinor made no move, watching Gilliane follow him with her eyes. Perhaps she should have allowed the girl to go with Adam, Alinor thought. It is not only tiredness that is making her so pale. However, that opportunity was lost. Another would arise, or perhaps she could discover Gilliane's trouble and suggest a way of healing it. Whatever it was, was connected with Adam in some way. Alinor took Gilliane's hand and drew her up the stairs, talking gently of general matters in a way that required no reply.

Perhaps there would be no way to heal Gilliane's trouble. The girl loved Adam—but what if Adam did not love her? It could be that his initial attraction had been wiped out by boredom. If Gilliane was as shy and gentle as she seemed, Adam might have tired of a pretty face backed by nothing. So far, he had rejected every proposal of marriage made to him because the girls were empty-headed. That look of concern . . . Well, Adam was very kind. If he thought he had been too hard on anyone, he would be concerned. Alinor asked a few careful questions, but the answers told her nothing. Gilliane blushed when Adam was mentioned, but there was no sense of possession, of *he is my man,* in her voice or manner when she spoke of him.

Alinor's doubts about her son's feelings were resolved very quickly, but she received no answer to her basic question. In fact, Adam's conversation and behavior added to the puzzle. He was out of the bath and waiting in the hall for his mother when she came down to see if all was as it should be for her guests' entertainment. He strode forward to meet her, saying, "Thank God you did not bring Gilliane down with you. I want to talk to you about her."

"I bade her lie down. Perhaps she will sleep for a little while," Alinor said neutrally.

"Mama, do you think Gilliane is very frail?" he asked anxiously.

"*Very* frail?" Alinor repeated. "You mean in ill health?"

"Not that, at least . . . she does not cough or breathe oddly," Adam said, wrinkling his brow, "and she never complains or says she has pain or is tired, but Sir Richard is always telling me she cannot do this or that, and Sir Richard knows her longer than I."

"I will need a day or two before I can really answer your question," Alinor pointed out. "One cannot judge the soundness of a person's health on half an hour's acquaintance. Besides, after a long ride and the anxiety she must feel at meeting your mother . . ." Alinor let her voice fade suggestively, but the hint seemed to pass right over Adam's head and she continued more directly, "Why do you ask?"

"Well, I do not wish to kill my wife out of ignorance," Adam replied. "I thought at first Gilliane would have sense enough to say no if I bid her do too much, but she is like a willing horse, I fear, and will burst her heart before she denies me."

Lady Alinor was so stunned by the first sentence Adam had uttered that she had no room in her mind for amazement at how well he read Gilliane's nature. "Your wife," she gasped. "But did I misunderstand Ian? I was sure he wrote me that Gilliane had a husband living."

An angry shadow crossed Adam's face. "Oh, yes, Osbert de Cercy, but he is living only until I can lay my hand upon him."

"And has Gilliane agreed to this?" Alinor asked, carefully expressionless, wondering how she could have been so far wrong in estimating a character.

"No. She begged me to let him be," Adam replied,

renewing his mother's faith in her own judgment but making her wonder if her son was an idiot.

"Adam," she said, struggling to keep exasperation from her voice, "I am not trying to say that Gilliane does not love you because I have seen with my own eyes that she does—"

"Well, then," he interrupted impatiently, "why do you look at me as if I have two heads when I say I want her to wife?"

"Because a person can have a fondness for a man, wish him well, feel terrible guilt if anything should befall him, even if she does not love him."

"I do not understand you, Mama," Adam said, a worried frown wrinkling his brow. "You just said you were sure Gilliane loved me. Now you are saying she does not?"

"No, I am saying she may have a kindness for de Cercy and object to having him murdered—"

"Oh, no," Adam interrupted again. "Gilliane wants him dead all right. She killed one of his henchmen the day before yesterday and grieved terribly because it was not Osbert himself that she stabbed."

This light, good-humored announcement stunned Lady Alinor even more than Adam's statement—plainly somewhat in advance of actuality—that Gilliane was his wife. For a moment, Alinor gaped at her son, quite unable to formulate either of the two questions she wanted answered.

"Do not let that look of sweet innocence befool you," Adam remarked. "Gilliane is clever as a witch." Again a shadow of doubt crossed his expressive face. "I am only concerned for the strength of her body, not of her mind," he went on, "and if she will not tell me where to set the bounds of my use of her, I must ask advice elsewhere."

But Alinor knew that the latter part of what Adam said had nothing to do with his unease. Moreover, the fact that he was not willing to talk about it gave it greater significance. Could Gilliane's sweetness and anxiety be a sugared coating over something foul? Very likely that was what Adam suspected but could not bear to admit to himself. Had the coating cracked here and there and shown the putrid stuff underneath? Obviously, a consciously concealed evil would take more than a few words and looks to probe. Alinor set herself to discover, if she could, what had raised Adam's doubts. The most obvious place to start was this stabbing.

"Clever is as clever does," she said, "but a knife cannot be made by thought alone. What do you mean, she stabbed her husband's henchman? How did this happen?"

To Alinor's surprise, the doubt cleared from Adam's face. The anger grew plainer, but as he related the tale of Gilliane's abduction it was clear the anger was directed at himself. He rather glowed with pride at her courage and cleverness. Certainly, Alinor also approved heartily of Gilliane's actions under the circumstances. The only thing that puzzled her was the knife. A question about how Gilliane came to wear such a weapon pulled the stops on what she had told Adam about her life in Saer's keep and her fear of Osbert.

"Then why, if she hates him so much, did she bid you let him be?" Alinor wanted to know.

Adam blushed faintly and scratched his head as if he were about to admit something slightly shameful and puzzling but still a charming thing. "That is womanishness. Gilliane says he is a sly snake and will do me some harm I cannot guard against because I am not myself deceitful and dishonorable. She is not above being foolish where she is fond. Also, she gave me some farrago about her sin falling on my head if I killed him for her sake."

That was interesting. If Gilliane was deeply religious, she might be distressed by conceiving a desire for a man other than her husband. Alinor believed in sin and in punishment for it, but such things did not prey on her soul. She confessed her failings, did penance for them, and did not let them worry her further. Of course, a sin you could not repent was another matter. Obviously, if you intended to continue to love a man out of the bounds of wedlock, you could not be absolved of the sin. Alinor had faced the same problem and could understand. She, however, had considered that she was young and strong and not likely soon to die. Thus, it was only a matter of waiting until she married the man she desired. Then she could confess and say, truly, that she repented having loved him out of wedlock, do her penance, and be absolved.

It should not be very hard to convince Gilliane to think the same way, if that was her problem. The matter of killing Osbert was different. Alinor knew from Adam's face and manner that Osbert would die as soon as Adam caught up with him, even if the question of marrying Gilliane was not in point. In fact, there was no need to kill Osbert for that. The girl claimed she had been forced; thus, the marriage could be set aside easily enough. Since the French invaders were already in disgrace with the Church and publication of excommunication for them a daily possibility, the king's friends were sure of quick and favorable treatment on any Church matter. Peter des Roches would bring the petition of annulment to the pope's legate, Gualo, and he would pronounce the marriage void.

Alinor said nothing of that to Adam. Until she was sure that her son had not sensed real evil under Gilliane's sweet exterior, it was just as well they not marry. The legal impediment was useful because Adam was as stubborn as an ox. To caution him would produce little beyond a stronger determination to have his own way.

Still, nothing he had said so far implied any fault in Gilliane. Further questions produced the information that Gilliane was determined to rule her lands in her own right—a statement that surprised Alinor very much, although she made no comment upon it—and that Gilliane had agreed to take Adam as overlord—which did not surprise Alinor at all. That last piece of information, however, produced the first uneasy look since Adam had first commented on Gilliane's cleverness.

"Why should she not take you for overlord?" Alinor asked, really puzzled.

Adam looked past his mother into the flames of the great hearth. He wanted Alinor's advice very much, but he did not wish to prejudice her against Gilliane. So far, Alinor seemed more inclined to defend Gilliane than to blame her, and Adam did not wish to change that. He loved his mother dearly; more than that—he liked her. He did not wish to lose her friendship and her astute counsel. But he had to have Gilliane. If it came to a choice, he would choose Gilliane. He did not wish to have to choose between them. He wanted his mother and his wife to like each other well enough so that he could have them both.

"Mama," he said slowly, "I intend to marry Gilliane. I cannot think of anything—except, perhaps, if she herself should refuse me because she craved another man —that could hold me back from that purpose. I hope for that reason that you will take her as a daughter. Yet there is something . . . I hope you will not blame her overmuch nor take her in dislike, but I think you must know because I will leave her in your charge."

"Something I must watch her for or keep her from doing?"

"Yes, but . . . but I am not sure."

"Well," Alinor said sharply, "out with it. What do you see in her that is evil?"

"I think she favors Louis."

Alinor's eyebrows flew upward. This was what was distressing Adam? "There is nothing evil in favoring Louis. For an Englishman, it is stupid, but Gilliane is French. In any case, why should I care for that?" she asked, not laughing only because she was afraid she had misunderstood Adam. "I assure you, even if she does have a way to communicate with the prince, she will not be able to hand Roselynde over to him."

Adam did not respond to his mother's sarcasm. "But she says to me she will swear to Henry, blithe and free, and that her father was John's man," he said, following the train of his own thought.

Now Alinor understood. Adam thought Gilliane was lying, not only about her political purpose, but about loving him. He was wrong about the latter, although it might be the conflict between her love and the cause she believed in that was making her unhappy. There was a flaw in that reasoning. Why should Gilliane be attached to Louis's cause?

"You think she seeks to turn you away from the king and to the French prince? Why? What has she done? Has she urged you to join Louis?"

"No, never."

Having gone so far, it was useless to hide anything. Adam told about Gilliane's resistance to his suggestion that he raid Lewes and that he take the keeps of any vassals who were firmly committed to Louis. But, he pointed out, in other cases, such as winning Sir Richard to his purpose, she had given him most excellent advice. Such a contradiction was certainly peculiar, but Alinor was no more positive than Adam what it meant. However, she assured him with a smile, she would not dislike Gilliane over a political matter. What she would try to do was to explain that, if Gilliane desired both to hold her lands and marry Adam, she would have to abandon Louis. There was proof enough that Louis would never permit an estate like Tarring to fall into the hands of an avowed king's man.

Adam was not perfectly pleased with his mother's suggestion. To his mind it gave Gilliane too much leeway, but he heard Sir Andrew's voice asking for him and had time for no more than to warn Alinor that Gilliane's men knew nothing of either his doubts or his plans and that he wished to speak to Gilliane about marriage himself and she was not to interfere. Alinor's lips twitched. She would certainly say nothing to Gilliane until she was sure of the girl. After that, she would do what was best for Adam without worrying much about his wishes.

Joanna came down with Gilliane, who looked much better, just as the servants finished setting up for dinner. The scented bath she had taken had relaxed her. The quiet time she had spent in a well-outfitted chamber, Alinor's warmth and kindness, Joanna's easy jesting, all combined to make her realize her fears had been foolish. In addition, she had no time to dream up new terrors because her mind was fully occupied making note of the elegance she saw—the little tables set beside chairs, the embroidered cushions to add comfort, the goblet of wine and water set beside the bed to assuage the thirst of sleep. She noted, too, Alinor's manner and way of directing her maids. A glimpse of an embroidery frame holding a half-worked piece of exquisite design informed her that she had much to learn on that score also.

None of this did much to bolster Gilliane's ego, but it did not depress her, either. She knew herself very capable of learning such things and, if she had the materials, of producing a similar effect. Her only fears concerned Adam. If this was what he was accustomed to, was it the lack of such amenities at Tarring that had made him believe Gilliane was a lesser creature and could be used at will—as Saer used the maids? If so, it was only in his mind that she was dross. He had presented her with honor to his mother and had reminded her, when she herself forgot, that she was a woman of consequence, the mistress of a substantial estate.

Also, Adam's look when Joanna brought her to the table was first admiring and then questioning and anxious, certainly not angry or contemptuous. Gilliane smiled shyly. She knew she looked good. Joanna had brought her an exquisite dress, palest yellow over a darker gold tunic, all embroidered in gold that gave her skin a velvety glow. Beyond greeting, they said little to each other, although Gilliane was seated beside Adam. For one thing, Alinor dominated the conversation, which was her right and her duty. For another, Gilliane was busy absorbing the formalities of dining in a great house and taking note of the abundance and variety of dishes that were brought to the table.

Gilliane was appalled, thinking of the pottage, stew, roast, and savory that she had presented to her illustrious conquerors. Well, Gilliane resolved, she would not make that mistake again, any more than she would omit the offer of a bath or the placement of a drink beside each guest's bed. There would be cushions for the chairs at Tarring also, and she would learn the fine stitchery if Lady Joanna or Lady Alinor would teach her.

Her determination was bolstered by pride when Adam offered his mother a formal compliment on the meal and then commented that he had twice had a ragout in Tarring that was the match of anything presented to him anywhere.

"Then it must be close to angels' food," Alinor said tartly, but laughing. "I must tell you, Gilliane," she said, leaning across Adam, "that my son could chew raw oats like a horse and not notice the difference. When I made the mistake of stopping at Kemp, I was near starved to death, and poor Ian has often told me that camp rations have more savor than meals there. You must give me the making of this dish, if you will, for truly, it must be wondrous to draw Adam's notice."

Gilliane disclaimed anything special but said she would write down the recipe, and the talk ran pleasantly on cooking until they rose from the table. Alinor then asked what the gentlemen would like to do, but, before she made a suggestion, it was seen to be raining. That ended all thought of any outdoor exercise. A maiden newly come to Roselynde for nurturing was asked to play the lyre and the blond maid, Edwina, sang. Joanna drew Sir Edmund into a game of chess, noting with amusement that his attention was somewhat divided between his game and Sir Andrew, who was listening to the music with surprised pleasure. Adam seated Gilliane near his mother, beckoned to Sir Richard, and asked how many men he might borrow from Roselynde keep and hire in Roselynde town. Alinor heard Gilliane's breath draw in and, from the corner of her eye, saw the girl's pretty color had faded into pallor. Definitely something was wrong.

Alinor pretended she had noticed nothing and asked, "How long a term of service and how far from here must they serve?"

"Term of service? A month. If I cannot crack Wick in that time with a little more than five hundred men, I will need to call in my castellans on their forty days' service for an offensive war, but I will not do that until spring. The weather has held very well, but it cannot be trusted much longer. The distance? Twenty-five miles or a little under."

"And how soon will you need them?" Alinor asked.

"My lord," Gilliane put in, "are you forgetting Sir Philip?"

"Of course I am not forgetting him," Adam replied sharply. "I will leave for Leith Hill after lauds tomorrow."

Gilliane paled still more at the angry tone, but her voice remained steady. Better Adam should be furious with her than in danger. Every hour she could delay the attack on Wick was an hour of safety for her love.

"But," she said, "from what Sir Richard told us, Sir Philip is a man of very thin skin. If he believes himself slighted, he may refuse to join your action against Sir Matthew. Then you will have the choice of fighting him also, or of having your authority set at naught and attacking Wick without the addition of his strength."

"What the devil are you talking about, Gilliane?"

Adam snarled. "How will it slight Sir Philip if I go with your other men to—"

"My lord," Gilliane interrupted, knowing she would soon be unable to speak at all if Adam grew angrier, "you were born a man of great estate and Roselynde was your home. Thus, it is little to you, except for the joy and love you find here. But to me, it is a great honor to be a guest at Roselynde—as it is for my vassal and castellans. If Sir Philip is not invited to share this honor with my other men, will he not feel slighted?"

Alinor raised her brows and widened her eyes. She, like Adam, would never have thought of it, but Gilliane was right. Adam opened his mouth to make a curt denial and then closed it. Sir Richard nodded his head solemnly.

"Lady Gilliane has a strong point," Sir Richard said slowly. "And I will add this. From a feeling of insult, suspicion will grow. Sir Philip will soon begin to wonder what we were doing here at Roselynde and whether we were planning something to his hurt. He is not a bad man, but . . ."

"I see it now," Adam snapped. "I wish I had seen it sooner. Why the hell did you not mention it this morning, Gilliane?"

"I am sorry, my lord," Gilliane replied, dropping her eyes. "We had so little time and you seemed—irritated when I . . . I thought you had some purpose that made it needful to come here quickly."

Clever, clever, Alinor thought. Adam was quite right, Gilliane was clever as a witch. Not only did she point out a difficulty that everyone else might have overlooked but she did not crow over her cleverness and even took the blame for Adam's impatience and oversight without a hint of ill-temper. Alinor saw what was coming next, but held her tongue. Let Gilliane manage it if she could.

"Well, now that it is thought of," Adam remarked irritably, "what is to be done?"

"How far is it to Leith Hill?" Gilliane asked.

"I am not sure. Thirty miles, perhaps forty. Why?"

"Then it is not too far. A messenger could be sent in one day to invite Sir Philip here, since it is no more than a day's ride for him. You could blame your coming direct to Roselynde from Alresford on me. You could say that, although at first I thought I could manage, I found myself too shaken by my experience at St. Leonard's to continue."

"That is indeed the answer, Lady Gilliane," Sir Richard agreed enthusiastically. Sir Philip would not know this breed of woman any better than he had himself before he met Gilliane. He would believe she was prostrated by an abduction more quickly than he would believe she slew one of her captors, escaped, and talked calmly of how to win his service the next day. "In fact," he continued, "if you will trust me, my lord and lady, I will go as your messenger. That will prevent Sir Philip from wondering if the message is a trap."

"I begin to wonder if Sir Philip is worth the trouble," Adam remarked dryly.

"It is not so easy to deseisin a vassal as to put out a castellan," Sir Richard pointed out firmly. "Also, he is not only a good man of his hands and strong in action but is one who sees where the hands should be laid on and the action taken. Further, he does not like Sir Matthew. It will not be hard, I think, to induce him to bring as many as a hundred men—if you will bear part of the cost."

"That may be cheaper than hiring them from Roselynde," Alinor suggested.

Adam sighed. "Yes, I know. I did not mean it. The man must have his chance, just like any other. If you are willing to go, Sir Richard, I will be grateful. It will even save time because I can begin to recruit in the town."

"Do you not think you should send an invitation to Sir Matthew also?" Gilliane asked. Both men looked at her. "My lord, you just said each man must have his chance. Do you not think Sir Matthew should be told formally of my inheritance of the honor of Tarring—although doubtless he has heard by rumor—and also of what news we have about Lord Arundel and the treatment of the English by Prince Louis?"

"But that will warn him that we are coming down upon him," Sir Richard said harshly.

"I did not mean that!" Gilliane exclaimed, looking frightened. "I only thought that he might see which way the wind blows and—and there might be no need to fight at all."

A glimmering of an idea came to Alinor. She understood from what Adam had said—if Gilliane had told the truth—that Gilliane had hated or feared every man with whom she was closely associated since she had been made Saer de Cercy's ward. Naturally, she had not cared whether they lived or died, but her father had died in battle and so had Saer. If Gilliane associated fighting with death, it might be that she was only trying to prevent Adam from fighting, not trying to forward Louis's cause. Alinor had never put much faith in Gilliane's attachment to a political cause that could have little effect on her life. She was sorry for Adam, who, in spite of his irritation at having an oversight pointed out, had been delighted with Gilliane's cleverness and helpfulness. Now unease showed in his eyes again.

It was not an unease that Alinor would rush to dispel, even if she found her idea was right. Alinor, too, hated and feared war. She had waited all too often with a sick, heavy-beating heart for news of her loved ones. There were times when she could not look into her own eyes in the polished silver oval that served her for a mirror because of the terror that looked back at her. Her heart bled for Gilliane's fear. Nonetheless, if the girl could not master that fear, swallow it, bury it deep behind laughing lips and downcast eyelids, she was not the wife for Adam.

Subterfuge to prevent war, to encourage settlements by peaceful means, was good. If women did not engage in such subterfuge, there would soon be no men left, for they would all kill each other—half for fun, the other half for greed. However, emotional blackmail that left a man with a divided mind when he went to fight was an extra weapon in an opponent's hand. Gilliane might simply not understand that. If that were so, Alinor could explain easily enough. Then it would remain to be seen what the girl would do. By God, Alinor thought, such an explanation would answer both questions at once. If Gilliane's opposition to taking Wick came from her love for and fear for Adam—and if she cared more for Adam than for her own comfort—the opposition would stop at once. If Gilliane was incapable of setting Adam's welfare—either political or physical —ahead of her own, she would continue her attempts to dissuade him from bringing Sir Matthew to heel.

While she had been considering Gilliane's purpose, Alinor had been watching her son. He was not completely reassured by Gilliane's disclaimer, but in considering it, an idea had come to him and he began to smile.

"There is no reason why an invitation to Roselynde to meet his overlady should warn Sir Matthew of any danger to himself if it is phrased correctly," Adam said to Sir Richard. "Moreover," he added, smiling more broadly, "if he does not answer or refuses to come, he will have given us legal cause to move against him without further warning and without any challenge. What is more, since Wick is not more than twenty miles —it is less, in fact—we can move as soon as Sir Philip is here and has agreed to our plans. Even if Sir Matthew has taken fright from the letter, what could he do in a few days to bolster his defenses that he could not do if I sent a challenge?"

Alinor could see Gilliane draw breath to speak, but she interrupted her decisively, saying it was time to leave the men to plan the details of what they would do. Gilliane, Alinor said too positively to accept denial, needed her rest after the exertions and trials she had undergone.

"You have made yourself quite clear, my dear," Alinor stated, a warning in her eyes. "You do not find war an amusement, and war against one's own men is *never* profitable. I feel very much as you do, and I am sure Adam will respect your wishes to settle this matter without war if he can."

CHAPTER TWENTY

It was first light, the sun not quite risen, and it was bitterly cold in the women's chambers where the serving girls had not yet stirred the banked fires to life. Gilliane shivered when she threw off the covers, but she did not hesitate, merely clamping her jaws shut so that her teeth would not chatter. She drew on her stockings and a warm woolen shift hurriedly, covered this with a pale pink tunic, and pulled a soft rose cotte over all. The clothing was another gift from Lady Alinor and had been chosen because it became her dark beauty so well. Gilliane thought gratefully of Adam's mother, who had been as kind as any natural parent. Alinor had been much in Gilliane's thoughts all through the sleepless night she had just passed. All through the dark hours she had reviewed the conversations she had had with Lady Alinor that first evening at Roselynde.

"My dear," Lady Alinor had said, after drawing Gilliane into her own luxurious bedchamber, "I am about to speak very plainly to you because Adam tells me that you were raised in a simple knight's household, that all the women were mistreated there and had no affection for their menfolk."

The stricken expression on Gilliane's face told Alinor a good deal—if it was genuine. Alinor found it hard to believe it was not, but she repressed her sympathy. Adam was her son; her first duty was to him.

"Sit down, child," Alinor went on, her voice softening. What must be said, must be said, but there was no need to be harsh. "I am not going to scold you, but you must know certain things. Men of great estate must be warriors, and the men of our family are so by nature as well as by training. To keep vassals and castellans faithful, a man must be able both to defend and to punish them, and this can be done only by war."

"But . . ."

"There are no buts," Alinor said sharply. "The wider the lands a man wields, the more time he spends under arms. If he is not protecting his vassals against incursions by some other great lord, or settling a quarrel between his own vassals, he is putting down rebellion by men who wish to break away or to keep from him what is his due."

"For what?" Gilliane broke in. "For another ten shillings in rent? For a jewel to bedeck oneself? What good are rents and jewels to a dead man?"

"Do not be a little fool," Alinor snapped. "Tonight I adorned myself to do honor to you and to your men, but you have seen that I do not go bedecked in jewels, nor does my daughter, nor does Adam. On state occasions, Ian wears jewels because I force him; Geoffrey because he knows the value of the appearance of wealth. As to rents—do not speak scorn of them. They come year by year and bring with them power."

"Power? I do not desire power!" Gilliane exclaimed.

"Do you not?" Alinor asked cynically. "Then do you desire to be powerless? Yet I heard you stuck a knife in the neck of a man to free yourself from bondage. And do not speak to me of a middle path. There is no middle path. Either you keep or enlarge what is yours or you sink into a victim."

Victim! That was true. Gilliane closed her eyes. All her life she had been powerless—a victim. She would not endure that again. Yet if Adam must fight to keep her free . . .

As if she had read Gilliane's mind, Alinor continued, "In any case, it does not matter what you desire for yourself. Adam will be no man's victim for any reason —ever. Your lands lie close by his, and to ensure the peace of his own domain, he has taken yours under his hand. Will you nill you, he will bring your men into obedience—all of them. To allow the rebellious ones to go their own way would only breed rebellion in the others."

That was true also. "I see," Gilliane sighed.

"Do you see enough? I hope you understand that it is useless to quarrel with Adam about the taking of Wick and Bexhill. Moreover, there is more in this than rents and power. There is also the good of the realm at large. Matters are bad enough now with Louis weakening the hold of the king's guardians on the great lords so that they feel free to wage war upon one another. Can you imagine what it would be like if men like my husband and my son and son-by-marriage lost control of the men they lead? Every greedy, ambitious knight would attack his just and peaceful neighbors without fear of retribution. No man could hope for protection from the evil. Because Adam will crush Sir Godfrey and Sir Matthew—if they do not yield willingly—the rest of your men, and Adam's also, will be peaceful and obedient, perhaps for years."

"And perhaps not, in which case Adam will go out to fight again," Gilliane said bitterly.

Well, the girl did not lack for spirit, Alinor thought. When she is roused, she will speak. "Certainly," Alinor agreed, staring purposefully at Gilliane. "He will go out to fight even if they *are* peaceful and obedient. Adam *loves* to fight. If he does not need to fight for or against his vassals, he will fight in the king's war. And if that is ended, he will rush out to find tourneys to fight in. Adam is born and bred a fighter. So was his father."

"Who no doubt died in battle," Gilliane spat.

"No, he did not. He died in bed." Suddenly Alinor's

eyes were full of tears. "My poor Simon, my poor
Simon. How he hated himself for growing old and
weak." The tears rolled down Alinor's cheeks. She did
not sob, but Gilliane saw the suffering in her face. "All
the years we were married and he went to war and I
prayed and prayed for him to come safe home to
me. . . . If my prayers were answered, I will never forgive myself for them. He came home safe from battle—
to suffer and suffer and curse each day his eyes opened
upon. Better for him had he died in battle."

"You loved him," Gilliane whispered. She had not
realized that. Because of the sharp, forceful way Alinor
spoke of men going to war, Gilliane had believed that
Alinor could not feel as she felt.

Alinor wiped the tears away and smiled. "I love him
still. One does not stop loving just because a person
dies. And do not mistake me. I love my present husband also, and I fear for him. . . ."

"Then why do you let him go?" Gilliane breathed.
"Why?"

"Because I cannot stop him, or Adam or Geoffrey
either," Alinor sighed. "I have spoken to you of power
and necessity, but I, too, am a woman. Often and often
I have thought that if I could shut my dear ones into
this great keep and thus hold them safe, I would not
care if the world all around were utterly destroyed. But
then I knew that was what *I* desired. To me, what Ian
and Adam and Geoffrey desire is more important than
what I desire."

"And if they desire death, you will give them that?"
Gilliane whispered.

"Yes," Alinor replied bleakly. "They are not babes
to be protected against their wills. They are men of
sound mind and high spirit."

Then she sighed and smiled. If Ian heard her, he
would be hysterical with laughter at the notion that
Alinor would not interfere if he wished to do something
she believed was dangerous and unnecessary. However,

that was not the point. Gilliane was not knowledgeable enough yet. This was the first lesson. Others would come later. She took Gilliane's hand.

When they were settled in front of the fire, Alinor began once more. "There are times when death is not so great an evil. When Simon was so sick, I could have kept him living for some years longer, I believe, if I had kept him abed and given him certain medicines. That was what *I* desired. I wanted his warm arms, his wisdom, his tenderness. But my breath did not rasp in my throat, my legs were not swollen to twice their size and covered with ulcers, there was no stabbing agony in my arms and chest, my days were not one long lassitude of weariness harder to endure than pain. I did not hate my body for its failure. I let my Simon go. I let him crawl up the stairs and struggle to mount his horse—I let him die because that was what he wanted."

Gilliane's eyes were full of tears of sympathy, and she nodded mutely, caught up in Alinor's remembered grief.

"God willing, that is not a trial you will ever need to face," Alinor continued more briskly. "Adam and Ian and Geoffrey are strong men, and they do *not* desire death. They do not, even though it may seem to you that they seek it in battle. Adam, I know, does not even *think* of death when he thinks of fighting—and you must never, *never* put that into a man's mind."

The tears in Gilliane's eyes sank back to their source, unshed. "But if he has no fear—" she began.

"He will be ten thousand times more safe," Alinor cut in. "Do not equate fear with caution. Adam has been well trained by a man with great military aptitude, and his personal fighting skills have been honed and polished by the Earl of Pembroke, who was the greatest fighter of his day, and by my Ian, who is one of the greatest fighters of this day. Adam knows his own abilities down to a hair. Nor is he ignorant of what carelessness or recklessness can do. In the last two years,

Adam has been almost constantly in the field. You have seen the scars on his body. There are not many, and most are old, taken while he was still in training."

Of course, Alinor did not really believe what she was saying about her son. Thoughts of Adam's recklessness had given her many sleepless nights. However, Gilliane must believe Adam knew what he was doing or all this explanation would be useless.

"There is a new scar," Gilliane sighed.

Concern leapt into Alinor's eyes. "How bad? He seemed easy in his movement to me, and Joanna said nothing."

"Only a small tear in the skin," Gilliane assured her, both startled and relieved by the anxiety she perceived. She was now certain Alinor loved her son, a fact about which Gilliane had begun to wonder. "Nonetheless," she went on, "even if all you say is true, any man can be overmatched."

"Assuredly," Alinor replied, slow and deliberate, "and it is in that moment that it is most important he have no fear, no doubt, no other thing in his mind at all beyond his experience of battle. If at such a time the thought of death freezes a man's brain, how can his wits be flexible enough to espy any single brief chance of escape? If his thoughts are clogged with the knowledge that he will leave fear and grief behind—if he thinks of a weeping woman instead of his own safety—how will he be nimble enough to avoid the blows aimed at him?"

There had not been much color in Gilliane's face, for this talk was no lightener of the spirit. However, what there was drained away. "Oh, God," she breathed.

"A woman must hide her fear as best she may," Alinor went on inexorably.

"I understand," Gilliane whispered. "I understand." Then she frowned. "No, I do not understand. I heard you say you do not like war. You said it to Adam."

"No more do I," Alinor agreed in a more cheerful

voice, "and I do my best to keep my men from engaging in battles for the pure love of the sport—they *do* think of it as a sport, you know. However, I do not waste my breath or try their tempers by arguing against necessary action. You *know* Wick and Bexhill must swear fealty to you. Either their present holders must swear, or they must be removed and others chosen. This action is not sport, but necessity. You did right to suggest Sir Matthew be given a chance to do homage. If he does not, to think of other reasons to delay Adam will increase Adam's danger by giving Sir Matthew more time to prepare."

"I see that," Gilliane conceded unwillingly. She did see it, but she did not like it. "But if Adam should be hurt gaining these lands for me . . ."

"It is not for you," Alinor insisted, thinking only of easing Gilliane's guilt and not of how her words might be interpreted. "Had he found Neville, idiot and crippled, at Tarring instead of you, he would have done the same. He has taken Tarring and its men into his keeping for his own sake and the king's—and he will keep them."

At this point the talk faded from Gilliane's memory and was replaced by the doubts and jealousies those words had raised in her, the hopeless round of images that she probed for signs of Adam's intentions. It never occurred to Gilliane that Adam would marry her. She had not thought in those terms since she had so willingly given herself to him. Why should he marry her? All she wished was to be assured that he cared for her and would not cast her aside completely.

Had Gilliane even the smallest knowledge of men other than Saer and Osbert, she would have had no doubts. Unfortunately, she knew only the crude and open handling those boors gave the women they desired, the total indifference and even physical rejection they offered all other women. Adam, of course, neither rejected nor singled her out in any way when they were in company. Except that his eyes wandered to her once in a while, his looks and conversation were no more bent upon her than upon his mother and sister. Adam had been taught most firmly that a gentleman does *not* ogle his mistress when his attentions might embarrass her—but Gilliane did not understand this.

Over the four days they had spent in Roselynde, Adam had been polite and attentive. His manner toward Gilliane was about the same as that toward his sister when he and Joanna were not teasing each other with playful quarreling. Gilliane did not understand this, either. Much of Adam's time had been spent with the men. He had taken Sir Andrew and Sir Edmund hunting the day Sir Richard rode to Leith Hill. The next morning they had spent jousting and fencing, to Gilliane's suppressed terror and to Simon's ecstatic delight. In the afternoon, Sir Philip had returned with Sir Richard to do Gilliane homage. The messenger who had gone to Wick returned also, carrying, to Adam's heartfelt joy, an open defiance.

Gilliane, keenly aware of what Alinor had told her about useless argument, had forced herself to shrug her shoulders. She had listened to the war plans for a little while in silence, until Sir Richard growled that the greatest danger was that Sir Matthew might summon help or receive reinforcements from the French who used the harbor at the mouth of the river Arun.

"Cannot our ship—the one we took from the French —be used to block the harbor in some way?" Gilliane asked.

Sir Andrew, Sir Edmund, and Sir Philip gaped at her; Sir Richard nodded approval. He had not known about the captured ship, but that Gilliane should have captured one and now make so astute a suggestion about its usage no longer seemed strange to him. Alinor and Joanna began at once to talk about what armament the ship should carry. Adam laughed aloud and threw up his hands.

"I do not know why I bother my head. What do you say, gentlemen? Shall we go hunting tomorrow and let the ladies manage this little matter for us completely?"

"I beg pardon, my lord, if I have said something stupid," Gilliane offered. "I only thought . . ."

"Ungrateful dog," Joanna teased, "you are cross because Gilliane got in before you with a bright idea. Come away, Gilliane, we are spoiling their fun. If we say all the reasonable things quickly, they will not be able to chew the subject over all afternoon before they come to the decision we would have come to in ten minutes."

A very odd expression crossed Adam's face, but he said nothing when the ladies rose and left the men to their talk. Gilliane did not know whether she was glad or sorry. She had thought she would die of fear when siege engines and scaling ladders and the necessity of preparing hide shields against hot oil and pitch were discussed. It was a relief to be away from such talk, not to need to govern her face and hold her breathing steady. It was a real pleasure to be in the company of Joanna and Alinor, who kept her mind and her hands busy with talk of management of households and stitchery. On the other hand, she wanted to be near Adam every second before he went away. And she could not decide whether Adam's laughter had covered pleasure or anger or why Joanna had drawn her away.

The latter question was answered the following evening. Gilliane had not seen Adam at all that day. He had risen early to see the four men off. They were to lead the troops already under arms down to Wick, taking care that no offense be committed on the way. Adam would bring the men he had hired in Roselynde town and fifty experienced men-at-arms that his mother had offered to lend him from Roselynde keep. He would also bring extra supplies so that there would be no excuse for raiding. In addition, he would see to the armament and crewing of the ship. These arrangements had occupied Adam all day. He had not even returned to the keep to dine.

When he did return, Gilliane was sitting alone by the fire in the great hall. She did not notice him when he entered because she was stunned and frightened by a most peculiar byplay that had taken place a few moments before. She, Joanna, and Lady Alinor had been sewing and talking quietly when a maid came and whispered in Lady Alinor's ear. She had raised her brows, looked at Gilliane, and said firmly to Joanna, "You feel ill, Joanna. Come above and lie down for a while."

Joanna's mouth dropped open. She was breeding and it was true that she was sometimes uneasy in the morning, but she put in a full day's work, even riding out to the demesne farms when necessary. Her color was good; her voice had been easy; in fact, there was no sign of illness about Joanna. Before she could protest her mother's non sequitur and irrational remark, Alinor had seized her by the arm and drawn her forcibly out of her chair and across to the stairwell. Gilliane sat looking after them in blank amazement.

"Have you run mad, Mama?" Joanna asked as soon as she could master her surprise. Her voice, however, was low. She did not really think her mother was mad, merely desired an explanation. "Poor Gilliane—"

"Hush," Alinor said sharply. "I think I am giving 'poor Gilliane' exactly what she most desires. I want to see what she does with it. And hold your tongue," she went on. "I am not spying out of jealousy or morbid curiosity. I have a real purpose."

Adam was tired and cold and irritable. Although his arrangements had progressed smoothly, he was very much annoyed with himself. He had eaten his meal at an inn in the town, an inn he knew well for the excellence of its cookery and the greater excellence of its serving wenches. They were not new to him, for it was his custom to choose one of them for a bed partner when he was at Roselynde. Alinor refused to allow him to tumble the maids, not out of morality but because it was likely to arouse jealousy and quarrels among them. Adam had been looking forward to a playful hour or so that would abate the strain his unaccustomed celibacy was placing on his nerves.

To his horror, Adam had not been the least interested. He had eaten an excellent meal, teased all the girls, looked them all over carefully—and found himself colder than the winter weather outside. It was disgusting! It was infuriating! When he remembered how often he had laughed at Geoffrey and Ian for their purity; how he had disbelieved their protests that they did not want any other women, secretly believing them to be afraid of their strong-willed, jealous wives, he could only curse himself.

Thus, he had made some jesting remark and gone out to finish his business and to ride home in a black humor. To top his dissatisfaction, he saw a woman's skirt whisking into the stairwell just as he entered the hall. Adam knew the skirt and bit his lip with anger. Alinor had taken Gilliane away. Either his mother had become afflicted with an unnatural propriety or Gilliane had asked to leave the hall. Probably it was the latter. Damn Joanna and her warped sense of humor—telling Gilliane he was angry when she knew quite well he was barely restraining himself from kissing Gilliane publicly. Perhaps it was not that, anyway. Perhaps Gilliane thought he was making a jest of her suggestion about the ship in front of her men. Cursing all women and their inexplicable vagaries, Adam stamped over to the fire, threw his cloak on the floor, and cast himself into a chair.

If he could not have a woman, Adam thought, he could at least get drunk. Lifting his head to bellow for wine, Adam saw Gilliane in the chair opposite looking at him with an expression of astonished delight. She had been hidden while he crossed the hall by the high back of the chair and too involved with what Lady Alinor had done to notice his entrance. Indeed, Gilliane was so surprised by the realization that Alinor's action had been designed to give her a time alone— well, almost alone—with Adam that she hardly noticed the temper he was in.

"I was not angry that you thought of the ship," he said before she could speak. "I was pleased. Joanna was only teasing."

His voice, harsh with irritation in the first few words, softened as he spoke. Gilliane smiled and rose to pick up his cloak, dust it lovingly, and place it carefully folded on a stool.

"I am glad of that," she said softly, aware that Adam's eyes were following her.

"And I hope you do not think I meant to make jest of you before your men. Perhaps I should not have—"

"I never thought that," Gilliane interrupted, "never. You are always upholding me in their eyes." She came closer, as if his look were a rope that drew her, and he took her hand and kissed it.

"God bless your sweet temper," he sighed.

His physical need pressed upon him, but he was aware of the servants and did not draw her to sit on his lap. He was very glad now he had not taken one of the serving girls. Had his lips come from one of their mouths, he would have felt they soiled Gilliane's hand. Shyly, Gilliane touched his cheek and neck.

"How can my temper be other than sweet when I know you do me only good?"

"We are watched by the servants," Adam said softly, "kindly watched, but watched nonetheless. Go back to your chair and do not touch me or I will shame you and myself by seizing you here and now." His voice choked between a laugh and a sob. "You are killing me. And I will *not* make a scandal and a hissing in my mother's house. Ian would never forgive me for such ill-breeding." It was true, but that did not make it much easier for Adam to watch Gilliane retreat, and doubt pricked him again. "Why are you so displeased at the idea of taking Wick?" he asked.

"Because I—" Gilliane cut off the words "fear for you." *Never, never put fear into a man's mind.* She lowered her head to hide her eyes. "That is only selfishness, my lord. I do not wish to be parted from you."

The words were sweet, honey-sweet, but not what Gilliane had intended to say. Adam's bright eyes clouded. He wished she would say openly that she was Louis's adherent. Then they could talk about it instead of having this ugly pretense between them. It was useless to accuse her, Adam knew. Gilliane would only repeat that she did not care a pin for Louis. Well, perhaps she did not. That idea of hers about using the captured ship to guard the harbor had probably sealed Sir Matthew's fate. Then what was she hiding?

The lowered eyes had lifted again, and Adam saw in them a desire so wanton that it made all doubts irrelevant. Heat flashed across his loins, and he was grateful for the skirt of his tunic that hid the betraying bulge in his chausses. Then Gilliane closed the eyes with which she had been eating her lover. She bit her lips and folded her hands tightly together so that she would neither cry out nor reach toward him. And yet it seemed to her insane that out of good breeding they should deny themselves what the coming battle might tear from them forever.

Adam's mind was running along the same track. He had no fear of fighting at Wick, but he knew it might be several weeks before they could break the keep's defenses. And if he could not satisfy himself with the relatively clean serving girls of the inn, the filthy whores of the camp would surely not arouse him. He must have Gilliane. Damn the season. If it had been summer, they could have walked in the garden and found some privacy. Restlessly, Adam shifted in the chair, twisting slightly. He was rewarded for carelessness and impatience by a sharp twinge under his right arm. A smile of sheer delight overspread his face.

"Ouch!" he said rather loudly. "This is the tenth time today that wound has pricked me. Come to my chamber, Gilliane, and see if it is healing properly."

Gilliane jumped to her feet at once, and in the stairwell Alinor laughed soundlessly. "Oh, that sly, naughty boy," she said softly to Joanna, as she pulled her daughter up the stairs.

"There is nothing wrong with that wound," Joanna agreed. "I looked at it yesterday and thought it was near ready to have the stitches out." She held back against her mother's urging. "Mama, do you not think . . . I mean, Adam will take advantage of her. You know what he is, and Gilliane is so compliant to him . . ."

"Is that what Geoffrey takes of you—advantage?" Alinor laughed. "I thought he took—and gave—pleasure. Do not be a goose, Joanna. Did you see the girl's face? She is as hot for him as he for her."

Behind the closed doors of Adam's chamber the truth of Alinor's observation was being displayed. Adam had given Gilliane no time to ask about his hurt—not that she intended to. Fearful as she was for him, she knew an obvious excuse when she heard one. She was only aware of his need and the need for haste. They were close locked, kissing wildly, horribly aware that they had only a few minutes. To look would take no longer than that. They would have had more time if Gilliane could have brought in her basket of medicinals, but she did not dare fetch that from the women's quarters.

"Beloved, beloved," Adam was murmuring, "Let me —let me. I am afire."

She did not answer—when had she ever denied him? —only pressed her lips feverishly to his throat, his ear. Holding her fast with one arm, Adam tore at the string of his chausses, which fortunately was not knotted and came undone. It was not possible to get Gilliane's clothes out of the way so easily, and he had to release his hold on her to use two hands. It made no difference to the closeness of their embrace, for Gilliane clutched him all the tighter when he let go.

Now he had his tunic up and her skirt and he lunged forward, but they were too mismatched in size. Gilliane felt him against her, stretched up on tiptoe, but was still too short. Sobbing with frustration, Adam seized her thighs from behind and lifted her bodily. Without need for explanation or urging, Gilliane gripped his buttocks with her calfs, locking her ankles together for leverage as they joined bodies.

It was the wildest, most unusual mating Gilliane had ever experienced. The haste, the vulgarity of what she and Adam were doing should have shocked her. Instead, her passion was stimulated so that within moments she buried her face in the curve of Adam's neck, biting into tunic and flesh together to gag herself and muffle her cries as her body exploded into an agony that was pure pleasure. Vaguely, she heard Adam gasping and groaning softly, then whispering brokenly, "Gilliane, Gilliane . . . Oh, God. Oh, forgive me, forgive me, I cannot . . ."

Gilliane could not imagine what he was talking about nor could she summon strength to ask. She was only aware that her ankles had loosened their grip and that Adam's hold on her had slackened so that she was sliding down along his body. Instinct got her feet under her and they stood, swaying, leaning against each other, sighing with exhaustion.

"I am sorry, Gilliane," Adam said softly. "If we had five minutes more, I would try again, but . . ."

"What?" Gilliane mumbled, dazed but trying to respond intelligently. "What is it, my lord? I do not understand."

She had lifted her head from his breast and now he

could see her face. The glazed eyes, the half-parted lips told the tale without words. Adam chuckled softly.

"Nothing. It is nothing. I thought I had failed and left you discontent."

"I am never discontent when I am with you," she sighed. "Never."

That was true. Gilbert had often finished before her, but Adam woke such a fire that she was as quick as he or quicker every time. Gilliane sighed and shuddered, coming out of her waking dream of love to realize that had been yesterday evening. Now it was almost light, she was not yet dressed, and Adam was leaving that morning. She made what haste she could, but her cold fingers made slow work of fastening the tunic and cotte and Gilliane gave a worried look at the window in the antechamber where the light was already brighter. She did not wait to put up her hair, just threw the heavy chestnut waves back over her shoulders. It might take too long and Adam would be gone.

Tiptoe, Gilliane crept through the antechamber and out through the door. Her slippers were soft, but there was a whisper of sound when she crossed from the carpet to the wooden floor of the large central chamber. Lady Alinor rose quietly from her chair beside the hearth and followed, a discreet distance behind. She was almost certain Gilliane would make the perfect wife for Adam. Since the talk they had had, the girl's behavior had been impeccable. Alinor smothered a giggle. Perhaps impeccable was not exactly the right word for what had taken place in Adam's room—not that Alinor knew the details but the broad outlines were clear enough from Adam's sated and besotted expression.

With the men gone, Adam had made less effort to hide his feelings, not thinking it necessary since he had announced to his mother his intention of marrying Gilliane. Gilliane had been more reserved—or more exhausted. It might be true that Gilliane was not strong.

Alinor hoped it was only that she was not accustomed to so much physical labor. Often girls were required to do no more than sew a fine seam or walk about the keep overseeing others' work. Adam's wife would need to do much more. Alinor thought she would try to toughen Gilliane in easy stages over the next few weeks. From the dark of the stairwell, she looked out in the great hall. It was not very light yet, but to Alinor's dark-accustomed eyes, it was certainly light enough to see Adam's face as he looked down at Gilliane. Alinor bit her lip.

The anxiety that made Alinor bite her lips was on Adam's account. There were deeper emotions than sexual desire written on his face. Adam was committed to this woman only. If she were not suitable for him, Gilliane would have to die. If she died, Adam might eventually find another, but Gilliane would always be with him as Simon was always with Alinor. So Alinor bit her lip and willed Gilliane to say the right things. It was Adam's voice that came to her.

". . . not have come down to me, Gilliane."

"You did not forbid me, my lord," Gilliane replied, smiling. "I was very careful not to let the subject arise, remembering you forbade me last time."

Adam laughed. "It is just as well. You disobeyed me then and, I suppose, would have disobeyed me now. At least now you are warmly dressed and not shivering against a stone wall."

"Were you angry that I disobeyed you?"

"You know I was not. I would have gone to you, but I was afraid if I did . . ." He let that trail off, then asked, "What did you come for?"

"To fill my eyes with you. Oh, Adam, I cannot bear it when you go away." Her voice shook.

In the stairwell, Alinor stiffened. Adam put down the goblet of hot wine he had been holding and put his arm around Gilliane, pulling her against him. After a moment, he said harshly, "Gilliane, do not weep. You do not know what pain it gives me. I ask and ask and you never answer. Why are you so set against my taking Wick?"

The warnings rang through Gilliane's mind—a weeping woman clogs the spirit; men cannot be turned from actions of necessity; fear of death freezes the mind. She pushed herself away so she could look up into Adam's face, and she smiled with the tears on her cheeks.

"I do not care if you take ten Wicks. I only care that I am left behind to sew and be bored to death. Will you not take me with you, Adam? I will be quiet and good. I will not suggest anything or interfere between you and my men."

For the moment, Adam was struck dumb. Alinor clapped both hands over her mouth to smother her giggles. She had insisted often enough on accompanying her husband to unsuitable places, but never to a siege itself. However, there was no harm in this, provided the girl did not dissolve into tears again or have hysterics. Adam would be annoyed or amused or both at the same time, but it was not the kind of appeal that would distract him with worry.

"You will see," Gilliane went on quickly, encouraged by Adam's muteness. "I will be very useful. I can oversee the cooking and attend to the wounded men." Her voice wavered over those words and she hurried on breathlessly to cover the slip. "And I can wash your clothes, or see that they are done, so that . . ."

Having recovered from his surprise, Adam caught Gilliane to him so tightly that she squeaked with pain as she was crushed into the steel rings of his mail. Then he loosened his grip enough to kiss her long and hard. At last he released her lips and stared down at her with a bemused tenderness, fondling the thick waves of hair that had just the smooth, glossy red-brown sheen of a new-hulled chestnut.

"Then you will take me?" Gilliane breathed, not really believing it but beginning to hope.

Adam woke from his trance and burst out laughing. "No, of course not. Dear heart, you are the cleverest and the silliest girl at the same time. And do not begin to give me reasons why you will be useful and no trouble. You will be the greatest trouble to me because all the time I will desire to be with you instead of about my business. And with your men there, I will not even be able to look at you. Do you wish to kill me?"

"It does not kill me to be near you," Gilliane murmured reproachfully.

"Well, men are different," Adam chuckled. "A state of . . . of desire that cannot be satisfied is very uncomfortable."

He kissed Gilliane again, but lightly, and picked up his wine, drinking it more hurriedly as he saw from the gilding light that the sun had risen. He was not displeased by Gilliane's appearance of subdued resentment. She was jealous, he thought. That could do no harm. He set down the empty goblet, smiling.

"I must go, my love."

"Oh, wait," Gilliane gasped. "Tell me when you will return and . . . and what am I to do while you are gone?"

"How can I tell you when I will return? How can I know how fast Wick will fall? Within a month, perhaps a little longer if the weather holds. As to what—"

"Adam, write to me," Gilliane interrupted, "write often. I will—" Her lips tightened over the words *die with fear for you*. She swallowed and went on, with only the faintest tremor in her voice, "I will wish to know what you do and . . . and how the men behave and all such matters. Promise me you will write."

Alinor clapped her hands over her mouth again as she saw an expression of agony followed by one of resignation cross Adam's face. To take quill in hand was for him worse torture than having a tooth drawn. He sighed.

"Very well, I will write."

"Often!" Gilliane urged insistently.

"Very well, often," Adam sighed resignedly.

A faint chirrup of laughter forced its way between Alinor's hands. That was love, true love, total abject devotion. Nothing else could have drawn such a promise from Adam. The sound she had made was not loud, but Alinor dropped her hands and stepped out of the stairwell. Adam had quick ears and he would resent being spied upon even though he knew it was for his own good. Besides, the scene had gone on long enough. Gilliane had been perfect—enough emotion to show love and not enough to tear Adam to pieces—but there was no sense in putting too great a strain upon the girl. She would grow accustomed to partings—not that that would make them easier, but it would make her behavior more automatic and less of an effort. Adam's eyes lifted from Gilliane's face as Alinor emerged, showing he had heard her, but he smiled, thinking she had coughed or perhaps spoken to a maid on the stairs.

Still smiling, he looked down at Gilliane again. "As to being bored and what you should do," he said, "I assure you, you will not suffer any problem in either direction. My mother has never failed to make the fullest use of any pair of hands and feet available to her. You are more likely to be too busy to breathe than to suffer from boredom."

Gilliane flushed uncomfortably. It seemed dreadful that she should complain of fearing boredom in Alinor's company, but Alinor laughed and took her hand for a moment. Then she seized Adam by the ear and pulled his head down to give him a resounding kiss.

"Have a care for yourself, my love, and let me know from time to time that you are alive."

"Oh, no!" Adam exclaimed forcefully, turning to pick up his helmet from beside the empty goblet. "I have already promised to write to Gilliane. That is enough! If she receives letters, you will know I am well. And do not be reading my"—he almost said "wife's letters," but checked the words; this was no time to begin an argument about whether Gilliane was or was not his wife when she was married to another man—". . . vassal's letters. If I have something to say to you, there will be a special message."

"Yes, my lord," Alinor said demurely, making Adam guffaw.

But his attention had already wandered back to Gilliane. He stroked her hair, his glance gentle. "Do not drive my dove too hard," he murmured, "and do not let her fret."

On the words, before either woman could answer or react, he strode away. Gilliane started to run after him, but Alinor caught her arm and held her in a grip of iron, her other hand ready to clap across Gilliane's mouth if she should try to call out. She did not, only grew paler and paler, until Alinor thought she would faint. However, she did not do that, either, and, as soon as Adam was in the stairwell, Alinor drew Gilliane to the window from which she swiftly pulled loose the scraped hide.

"You can watch him mount from here," she said firmly, "and you can weep, if you will, but quietly so if he looks up he will not see or hear your crying."

But Gilliane did not weep. She stared down at Adam, who was calling orders and cursing the men cheerfully for this fault and that while his destrier was brought around, kicking and bucking and biting. Adam then cursed the horse, grasped the reins, delivered a sharp blow to the stallion's head, and swung himself into the saddle—whereupon peace was instantly established. Alinor shook her head. Simon and Adam had been able to work the same magic on those horses as her grandfather. Poor Ian and Geoffrey always had a few bad minutes curbing the beasts into obedience when they first mounted. She opened her mouth to say that to Gilliane, and was stricken by the girl's expression. Adam had just ridden out of the inner bailey.

"Come," Alinor said, aching for the agony she had seen in Gilliane's face. "We will go to the outer wall and you can watch him ride away."

Gilliane followed numbly, unable to speak or cry. All at once she knew she was abandoned in a strange place, completely alone, as she had been when she arrived in Saer's keep, naked to any abuse any person wished to inflict upon her. She was hardly aware of running through the bailey, across the inner drawbridge, across the outer bailey, and up through the dark tower. While on the stairs, she began to tremble with terror, sure she was being led to a prison or some dreadful punishment. Then she was pushed out into the open and a cruel wind bit through her clothes.

"There, look there."

Obediently, Gilliane looked as directed to see Adam riding down the winding road that led to Roselynde town where he would gather in the men he had hired and give final instructions to the captain chosen to sail the captured ship. The conviction seized Gilliane that when Adam disappeared, she would die, but she could not look away. Her life, her whole life was dwindling into the distance. Then, just before Adam disappeared and her life winked out, a warm cloak was wrapped around her, comforting arms enfolded her, and a kind voice said softly, "Child, child, it is not the end of the world. He will return. I swear to you he will return."

CHAPTER TWENTY-ONE

Osbert de Cercy had been well received in Lewes, where he was not well known. Saer had taken good care that his son not blacken his name among the neighboring gentry. In the town itself, there were whores and innkeepers who could have told tales that would have opened eyes at the castle, but it was not likely that their opinions would be asked. Osbert presented Louis's letter and was accepted as a welcome guest.

The castellan in charge of Lewes during the lord's absence was grateful for the attention Louis was paying his complaint. He was eager to be helpful in any way, and he answered all Osbert's questions as well as he could. After a time, however, he realized that the questions were far removed from the raid on the farm and were centered on the keep at Tarring.

"But what have the comings and goings at Tarring to do with who raided my lord's farm?" the castellan asked.

Osbert was a fool, but he was not stupid enough to reply *Nothing, but it is what I am interested in*. Besides that, he remembered Louis's warning about paying strict attention to business. Putting the two needs together, he said, "I believe it must have been Adam Lemagne who raided your land." In fact, Osbert did not have any such suspicion at all. He had hardly given a thought to the farm raid after announcing that Louis had sent him to discover who had committed the outrage.

The castellan began to laugh. "Why should Lemagne, who had just taken a rich keep, need to raid . . ." His voice faded, and then he looked at Osbert with respect. "By God," he burst out after another moment of thought, "you may be right!"

Far more surprised by the castellan's agreement than he had been by the initial laughter and rejection of the idea, Osbert said nothing.

"I should have thought of that myself," the castellan mused. "I knew your father had gone to make war on Lemagne—in fact, I warned him against meddling with that man. My lord made the same mistake—once. He is alive because after Lemagne had taken his revenge, my lord had sense enough to let matters lie."

"It is too late to worry about that now," Osbert said. His voice was tight with fear and his face pale, but the castellan thought it was rage that moved him. Tactfully, he went back to the original point.

"Your father must have stripped Tarring of supplies, and Lemagne had an army to feed. Yes, indeed, it was foolish of me not to think of it. Well, now, what do you wish to do?"

Osbert did not wish to *do* anything. He wanted the rents and honors that came with the lordship of Tarring, but he was afraid to do anything to secure them. Unwittingly, the castellan saved him again. While Osbert was attempting to think of a sensible reply that would not expose his cowardice, the castellan realized where this conversation might well be leading.

"I will give you all reasonable assistance," he added hurriedly, "but I will not join you in an attack upon Tarring—not without specific orders from my lord or from Prince Louis himself."

That was just the out Osbert needed. "If you will not,

you will not," he said with assumed irritation, and then he began to understand what the castellan had said.

His wild accusation had not really been so wild. The castellan really thought Lemagne might have been behind the raids that had so greatly enraged Prince Louis. So, if Osbert could prove Adam was guilty, Louis might be willing to take Tarring and return it to Osbert's control. Osbert's dull eyes lit with pleasure at the thought.

"The prince is most anxious to expose the guilty man because Lord FitzWalter has been blamed for the incidents," Osbert said. "It is not enough to think Lemagne is guilty. I must find proof, and that, I am sure, lies inside Tarring."

"It is tight shut and well guarded," the castellan responded. "You will find no easy way in without many men and much bloodshed."

"That is for the prince to decide," Osbert said hastily. "News can fly out of a place no matter how many bars hold the gates or men guard the walls. Do your merchants no longer do business with the town?"

"Merchants?" the castellan repeated. "Perhaps they do. Merchants care only for trade, not for honor, but what help can they be?"

"The keep is not besieged," Osbert pointed out. "Merchants doubtless go in and out. The men-at-arms come to the town to buy and drink and whore. Much can be learned from gossip."

A look of distaste crossed the castellan's face. Then he reminded himself that Osbert was bent on avenging his father's death. He himself would prefer less underhanded means, but it was not his business to judge a man with a personal grudge or one who was on Prince Louis's business. He put aside his disapproval and agreed that Osbert was free to deal as he liked with the merchants of Lewes.

It took Osbert more than a week to find the men he needed, but he eventually discovered a mercer of ill repute who had a brother, of even worse reputation, who had dealt in the town of Tarring and the port that lay south near the mouth of the Ouse. That brother had a grudge against Gilliane. One of the complaints brought before her had been against him, and she had forced him to make restitution to the man he had cheated. Moreover, when he complained that it was not a matter for her to decide but for the guild to which he belonged, she had summoned the guild master. To him, she had displayed the evidence and said, in no uncertain terms, that the guild had better exert more control over its members to prevent the public from being cheated. If it did not, she would withdraw the guild charter and enfranchise a new group of merchants.

This much she did exactly according to Father Paul's and Alberic's advice. Unwisely, Gilliane had not been able to bring herself to go all the way and insist that the dishonest merchant be expelled from the guild. He had a wife and children, she had said. Perhaps dishonesty had grown rife because Saer did not care to check it. Now that she had corrected him and shown him the consequences of cheating, the merchant might do better. At least, he should have one more chance. The merchant had done better; that is, he was far more careful in his practices. However, his profits had been cut severely. He did not forget that Gilliane had done him this harm. He did not forget, either, that she had saved him from utter penury, if not actual starvation—and he hated her more for her generosity than for her severity.

It was another week before the merchant of Tarring could come to Lewes at his brother's request. However, at about the same time that Adam settled his troops into siege position around Wick, several keepers of disreputable inns had the drabs who served and serviced the men-at-arms from the keep collecting information as well as money from their clients. Most of them were too dull and dispirited to wonder why the innkeeper should suddenly become curious about what Sir Adam Lemagne had been doing the previous month. They were glad to receive an extra penny for each tidbit of news. It was easy information to obtain. The men were delighted to talk about the exploits of their lord.

A few of the cleverer, more handsome women received more elaborate instruction. They were to find out, if they could, how thorough the gate guards were in examining the men and goods that came into the keep; how much care was taken to ensure that the men who came in went out again. Was there a careful check made on how many men-at-arms actually were in the keep? What was the relationship between the menservants and the men-at-arms? Were servants permitted into the guard towers and on the walls? Were there secret entries to the keep? If so, where were they? These women were warned to be careful in their quest for information. If the men grew suspicious, it would be the worse for them. On the other hand, if they discovered something of importance, they would be richly rewarded—after what they reported was found to be true.

By the beginning of February, it was quite clear that Adam had not only raided Lewes but had been responsible for using the battle cry "Dunmow" during the attacks. Then the Lord of Lewes wrote to his castellan that he would soon return. A truce had been declared between Louis and young Henry's guardians until Easter. Until that time, no war was to be waged and every man was to hold what he had in peace. Osbert was less pleased with this news than the castellan. He had no desire to meet the Lord of Lewes, who knew what had been said of him after the assault on Hertford.

What annoyed Osbert was that he had no real proof of what he knew about Adam. He had hoped that a piece of the loot from the Knepp or Arundel raids could be extracted by a whore from one of the men-at-arms. Nonetheless, he had actually had more success than he expected. It occurred to Osbert that if he went to report what he had learned to Louis, he could accomplish two purposes. He could avoid meeting the Lord of Lewes, and he would have a good excuse to taste in London more exotic pleasures than the simple town of Lewes could afford. Thus, Osbert set out for London to tell his tale to Prince Louis and to see if he could induce the prince to punish Lemagne for his crimes by depriving him of his lands and giving them to Osbert instead.

The warmth of the cloak around Gilliane, Alinor's kind voice and consoling arms, marked a new turning point in Gilliane's emotional life. She clutched at the support, slipping for a moment back into the time when she had been taken from her home and had clung to the woman who had been her nurse. Shaking, Gilliane braced herself for the instant of final horror, when she had been torn from those supporting arms. However, the horror was not repeated. The comforting embrace remained, the loving voice spoke more kind words.

"No harm will come to Adam. He is strong and wise in war. Anyhow, it may be days or even weeks before there is any fighting at Wick. First they must come to the keep and make camp and plan what they will do and talk with Sir Matthew. In the end, when he sees your ship in the harbor and how strong a force Adam has, and when Sir Richard has talked to him, perhaps he will yield. Then there will be no fighting at all. Gilliane, child, do not tremble so. Adam will return soon, safe and well."

Time readjusted itself. Gilliane was again in the present, and she realized she was not abandoned but in loving safekeeping.

"Come away, love," Alinor urged softly. "Perhaps in a day or two there will be a letter."

"You are very kind to me," Gilliane murmured as they returned to the great hall, but when Alinor had set her into a chair by the fire and given her a goblet of wine, she suddenly uttered a single sob and cried out, "I cannot bear it."

"You must bear it," Alinor rejoined sharply. "I tell you, Adam will come safe home."

"I did not mean about Adam," Gilliane said. "I . . . I have realized that I do not need to worry about outliving Adam. I . . ."

"Now, Gilliane," Alinor remonstrated, "that is a silly way to think. My daughter's husband was reported as dead, but he was not. He was lying badly wounded, a prisoner in France. If Joanna—who is nearly as silly as you but not quite—had taken her own life, what would have become of poor Geoffrey? Instead, she grieved, but when word came that ransom would be taken for Geoffrey, she was ready to go to heal him and bring him home. If Adam's wife—"

"But I am not Adam's wife," Gilliane cried, tears starting to her eyes, "I am only his whore. That was what I meant when I said I could not bear it. You have been so kind to me, and I . . ."

"Child," Alinor exclaimed, putting her arms around Gilliane, "you are no one's whore—unless that is what you are. If you love my son and are faithful to him in heart, in mind, in body, you are his woman, not his whore. A whore is for gold, for any man to handle. What has Adam given you—except his love?"

"But I am another man's wife," Gilliane whispered, scarcely believing what she had heard.

"Did you speak the truth to Adam about that marriage and about your feelings for the man?"

"Yes, oh yes. I killed Pierre, and I was glad, but, if only God had granted that it was Osbert instead, I should have spent my life seeking how to repay so great a divine favor."

Alinor could not help laughing. That was not the sort

of divine favor priests would accept willingly, but it seemed to be the kind Gilliane wanted. "Well, then, if you are resolved to be rid of de Cercy, why should you not be Adam's wife? You are gentle-born, you have a fine estate that runs well with Adam's own lands, the best of your vassals seems well pleased with Adam's management. It seems most suitable to me."

"Does it, madam?" Gilliane breathed. "You are very generous to overlook that I—I have given myself already, but Adam . . . I do not think Adam desires so light-virtued a woman as his wife. He . . . he . . ."

Alinor had been grinning again at the idea that Gilliane, who had apparently murdered a man with real enjoyment, should worry so much about bedding the man who would be her husband a little prematurely. The last part of Gilliane's halting statement brought Alinor's high-arched brows together in a frown.

"What do you mean, Adam does not desire you as a wife?" she snapped. "Has he said that to you? I will—"

"No," Gilliane cried, appalled at the anger she saw in Alinor's face. "Oh, please do not say anything to him. I do not care. I will be whatever he wants. If he is enraged and will not come to me, I—"

"Never mind that," Alinor insisted. "The only thing that could keep Adam away from you is if you hit him with a war ax. He is besotted. Answer my question. Has Adam said to you that he did not intend to marry you?" It would be just like that passionate fool of a boy to say something like that to test the child's love, Alinor thought furiously.

"No, but he said . . . we were talking of Gilbert's death and the marriage of rich widows . . . he said he had not married me."

Alinor nodded in satisfaction. She had not thought Adam would be cruel, and he had not meant to be. Gilliane was misunderstanding something that had pricked Adam's pride. Her attention was diverted by the mention of Gilliane's first husband. "By the by," she said, "how did Neville die?"

"He . . ." Gilliane's voice failed and she swallowed and tried again. "He fell from our bedchamber window."

"Fell?" Alinor asked sardonically, noting how Gilliane's color had faded, leaving her yellow and dull-eyed. "Did you push him out?"

"No!" Gilliane shrieked, drawing in on herself. "Oh, I would not—indeed, I would not—poor Gilbert."

The frantic denial might be owing to guilt as easily as to revulsion, but Alinor shrugged her shoulders. If a husband such as Gilbert de Neville had been forced upon her, she would probably have got rid of him also. There were kinder ways than pushing a witless cripple out of a window, but Gilliane might not know the peaceful efficacy of such drugs as hemlock. In any case, there was no danger to Adam in such a device. It would take a battering ram to shove Adam. Besides, Gilliane loved Adam; Alinor was sure of that. She had no quarrel with ruthlessness as such, and would applaud it if it were exerted to forward her son's purposes.

"Gilliane"—Alinor patted the shaking shoulders—"however Neville died, he is better off dead, poor thing. Forget it. It is past. Look up at me. I have something of import to say to you. Look up now."

"I did not, madam," Gilliane insisted. "I did not."

"No? Well, it is not important."

Gilliane's eyes opened wide. It was not important that she might have murdered her helpless husband? Not important that she had violated her vows of wedlock—not that she remembered making any? But then, what was important?

"What is important," Alinor continued, "is that you are a silly goose and Adam is a dolt! I know he does intend to marry you."

Alinor then related the conversation she had had

with her son about Gilliane's health. Before she was half done, Gilliane had realized Alinor was right. This was important. Her eyes were bright again and her cheeks flushed.

"Is it true?" she gasped. "You could not be so cruel as to hold out a false hope to me. You would not!"

"No, I would not, but in fairness, I must point out to you, my love, that you hold yourself too cheap. Not only Adam will desire you. You may pick and choose out of dozens of men if you will. You are not only very beautiful, but a woman of great substance—in fact, a rich widow."

An expression of revulsion came into Gilliane's face and she shook her head and put out a hand to reject and ward off a completely repellent idea. Alinor smiled. Clearly Adam was not grasped at out of fear and hopelessness but a true choice of the heart. The time of testing was over. Now Alinor must prepare her daughter-by-marriage for her role in life. "Child," she continued, "I hope you will not be offended, but if you are to be Adam's wife and the estates of Tarring are to be joined to those of Kemp—and since Adam's brother-by-marriage is the king's cousin and the Grand Marshal of England is our closest friend—you will be a very great lady. Forgive me if I say to you that you have much to learn."

"I am greatly aware," Gilliane sighed. "I have tried so hard to do what Adam expected of me, but I do not know how."

"There is no benefit in too-great modesty," Alinor reprimanded. "You seem to have managed the men-at-arms and people of Tarring well enough."

"But that was easy," Gilliane replied. "I only had to tell Alberic that I wished the punishments and judgments to be the same as those Adam would have delivered, and he told me what to say and I said it. Also, Father Paul told me what the custom was in the manor of Tarring. They did not know I was ignorant because

I told them that things were done differently in France. I do not know if that is true, but I did not think they would know, either."

"Very clever," Alinor approved, "but there will be times when Alberic and Father Paul are not by, and you cannot use that device when Adam is with you."

"But I will not need—I mean, Adam will give justice if he is there."

"No!" Alinor exclaimed. "They are *your* lands, *your* people. Adam will stand beside you, and if you need help—if it is a matter of honor between men—he will advise you, but you must remember at all times that you are a great lady. You *do* have much to learn." Alinor looked at the wide, frightened eyes. Her voice softened. "It does not all have to be learned today, child. We will go one step at a time."

There was very little to do at Wick, until the war machines had performed their work and breached the walls. Adam had time to read every word of Gilliane's letters and fret himself nervous over her wholly imaginary ill health. Fortunately, there was soon news that occupied Adam's mind. Ian wrote joyously that, although Berkhampsted had yielded after some hard fighting, Louis had apparently had enough. A truce had been declared and the prince had already withdrawn to London, leaving the army to break up at its own pace.

"This," Ian wrote to Alinor, "has not overly pleased Arundel, who has been here twice more and says Louis should have stayed to send the men away so that they would commit no outrage to violate the truce. You know this is unreasonable, but we are well pleased to see that Arundel finds everything the prince does unsatisfactory. Do not be surprised, my dear love, if we have him for a guest soon after Geoffrey and I return.

"Tell Adam," he continued, "that he should conclude his business at Wick as quick as he may. Although the truce does not bind an overlord from chastising a rebellious castellan in a general way, Lady Gilliane's case is a little delicate. Since her late husband was sworn to Louis, by strict law it might be considered that she is Adam's captive, not his vassal, and thus that Adam is violating the truce by taking Wick."

There was near a full sheet more of love and longing and small personal memories that told the tale of Ian's full heart. Alinor read and sighed with love, but her mind soon prodded her away from that delight. What should she do about Ian's message to Adam? She could, of course, write to her son herself and send a private messenger to him. That would spare Gilliane much pain, but was it right to spare her? The time for another testing had surely come. Could Gilliane steel herself to transmit a message that would thrust her lover into active battle?

Alinor bit her lip. Gilliane was a darling, exactly the kind of girl she would have chosen for a daughter-by-marriage had she been asked to choose a wife for Adam. She was as quick of wit as Joanna, not so stubborn, with as strong but a kinder sense of fun. Alinor had come to love her, and it was hard for her to hurt those she loved, especially gentle Gilliane. It was most unlikely that Adam would come to any harm in this action against Wick, but it could happen. If Gilliane had been the one to tell him he must begin the assault and he should by some ill chance be killed . . . Alinor closed her eyes and took a deep breath to ease the tightness in her chest and throat.

Life had to be lived. There was no easy path through it. She rose and went down to the hall, where she knew she would find Gilliane alone since Joanna had also had a letter and was in her own chamber savoring her husband's words.

"I have a hard task for you, my love," she said.

Gilliane looked up from her needlework and smiled.

"Do not tell me you still fear for my delicate health," she giggled.

"No, it is your tender heart I fear for. Listen to this." And Alinor read the pertinent section of Ian's letter to her.

The joy and teasing died out of Gilliane's face; her eyes grew large and glittered with tears. "Is it really my duty, madam, to tell Adam he must fight before he is ready?"

"He will not act before he is ready, sweeting," Alinor soothed. "Adam is too war-wise to endanger his men and the success of his enterprise by a hasty, ill-prepared assault. He will increase his efforts to *be* ready."

Alinor's bright hazel eyes met Gilliane's soft velvety brown ones, and the hazel eyes dropped. The tears spilled over Gilliane's lids and marked her cheeks. Gilliane knew Alinor was voicing a hope, not a conviction. Neither of them believed there was anything more Adam could do to hasten the readiness for the assault. He had written more than once, "I long for you. It seems to me no wall has ever been so stubborn to be breached." Gilliane had no doubt Adam was already doing all he could. Alinor came close and stroked Gilliane's cheek.

"Poor child," she sighed, "you need not write of this. I will. Perhaps I should not have told you, but, Gilliane my love, this will be your life. You must know and face it. I can shield you a little this time . . ." Alinor's voice checked. Gilliane was shaking her head in a determined way. Alinor's lips tightened. If that stubborn negation meant that Adam should not be informed of Ian's warning, Gilliane had learned nothing of political necessity. But Gilliane laid down her needle and wiped her eyes.

"Adam would expect me to write such things to him, would he not? If I failed in such a thing he . . . he might love me still, but he would not trust me as Lord Ian trusts you or Lord Geoffrey trusts Joanna. Is that not true?"

"Yes, child, that is true."

"Then I will write at once and . . . and is it proper for me to ask you to lend me a messenger, or should I . . ."

"It is perfectly proper, my love. The messenger will be ready when your letter is written."

CHAPTER TWENTY-TWO

Cedric Southfold, son of the man who had followed
Alinor's first husband all the way through Wales to
carry messages, took Gilliane's letter to Adam. He
broke the seal anxiously, knowing Gilliane would not
write before his messenger came to carry her letter
unless it was important. Naturally enough, the news
delighted him and sent him off to Sir Richard's tent to
pass it on. The other men were summoned to a war
council and to hear of the truce and Arundel's attitude
toward Prince Louis.

It was only after the plans for taking the keep had
been settled and Adam returned to his tent and reread
Gilliane's letter that he noticed its peculiarity. The hand
was hers. Adam had no doubt about that. However,
there was a stiff formality to the words that was not at
all like Gilliane's other letters. Those were written without art, just as Gilliane would speak, words of love
interspersed with bits of news and tales of daily happenings. This—there was not a word of affection in the
whole thing. That made Adam consider the meat of
the letter again, and his eyes went blank and cold.

Because it was the most natural thing in the world
for his mother and sister to relay such information
to Adam, he had not at first thought about how unlikely
it was that Gilliane should do so. Why should she
suddenly be urging him to take Wick when she had

378

been opposed to the idea all along? It was true that the last morning she had said it was only because she did not wish to part from him—she had said that the night before also—but it was not the whole truth. Gilliane had some reason she was not willing to confess for wishing Wick to remain in Sir Matthew's hands. Then why this letter?

The muscles around Adam's jaw bunched as he set his teeth. Gilliane had been forced to write. That was why the words did not sound like her own, and why there was no word of love. Alinor had somehow forced Gilliane to write that letter. Adam's eyes blazed with rage and he started up as if he would ride home to remonstrate with his mother and protect Gilliane. The motion was abortive, and he sank back. Adam knew Alinor was never cruel without a purpose. Perhaps this was a device to make Gilliane understand she was forever separated from Louis's party.

Whatever Alinor's reason, Adam could not like it. He could not endure the thought of Gilliane being forced to do anything. He could not endure the thought of Gilliane being unhappy at all. He stood up again, restless with the need to go to Gilliane and comfort her, assure her . . . Good God, assure her of what? That he would not take Wick?

With an explosive oath and a sinking heart, Adam emerged from his tent and began to stalk around the camp to make sure that all was being readied as swiftly and secretly as possible. Physical occupation eased the worst of his tension but did not reduce his desire to return to Roselynde. He would take Wick tomorrow, he determined. Then it would be too late for his resolve to be shaken, and he could go back to Gilliane with a quiet mind. Several times a cold finger of anxiety touched him when he thought that she, having failed in her purpose of controlling him by love, might receive him coldly. He would not permit himself to dwell on that, but he could not write his usual letter. He tried twice, but could think of nothing to say except angry accusations that if she loved him she would also love his friends and his political purposes. Since he himself realized that the shoe fit his foot also—after all, could she not point out that if he loved her he should also love Louis and the French—he threw the parchment aside and did not write at all.

After midnight it was easier because there was much to do. Men with faces and armor blackened softly carried the scaling ladders down to the ditch that surrounded the keep. Some of them crept down its sides, feeling their way slowly with great caution. There was no moonlight to help them or to betray them to the guards on the keep walls. Now and again a stone rolled or a man slipped. When that happened, all froze into stillness, scarcely breathing. Once a guard called out and raised a torch high. The flickering light illuminated nothing, certainly not the frozen men who even shut their eyes so that no chance gleam of light should reflect from their glistening eyeballs.

One by one the long ladders were passed down. Then, with even more care, the men began to climb the sides of the earthen mound that was topped by the stone walls of the keep. Two thirds of the way up they stopped. The foot-ends of the ladders were passed up. Then footings were dug—slowly, carefully the earth was loosened, scooped out a handful at a time, and laid silently aside. It was near four in the morning before all the ladders were set and ready. The men crouched beside them, wrapped in their cloaks, shivering, breathing softly on their hands to warm them, cursing war in winter. No one dared speak; they hardly dared breathe. Each knew that the fate of the man who made a sound that warned the keep would be far worse than a quick, clean death in battle.

When all was ready, the whole army drifted by twos and threes to the edge of the ditch. Quiet was still the order, but if warning should be given now it would not be so serious. If the guards on the walls should raise the alarm and call out the men in the castle, Adam's troops were instructed to rush down the ditch, help raise the ladders, and join in the assault at once. No one needed to speak a word. Everything had been explained very clearly the previous day. Adam hurried along the edge, tapping the shoulder of the leader of each group and pointing downward. He knew that the silence could not last more than a few minutes longer. Sooner or later a man would slip and bring those ahead of him down with him, or a man would sneeze or cough.

All in all, they were luckier than Adam expected. He had almost made his way back to the central group where he was to meet Cuthbert before the alarm was given. It rang out on the opposite side of the keep—Sir Andrew's men, Adam thought. It would be likely. They were not as well disciplined as the others, being accustomed to getting around their not-too-clever master. It did not bother Adam at all that the warning had been given. He had been growing impatient for the real action to begin.

"Go! Go!" he shouted, throwing off his cloak and running back toward his own station.

Noisily and far more rapidly now, the men slid and scrambled down the ditch. As Adam reached his own group and began to climb down the slope, he could hear the men ahead grunting and gasping as they lifted the heavy ladder against the sharp gradient. Crashing down among them, he lent his own enormous strength to the task, first pushing from underneath, then climbing up beside the tall, wavering ladder and pulling at it while others pushed from behind. A step at a time Adam climbed and pulled, his muscles cracking with strain as he balanced the effort of two men on the opposite side.

Above on the walls there were shouts. Resinous torches were flung over to fall on the slope of the mound and light the places where the men struggled to raise the ladders so that the archers could aim their bows. Adam bellowed for his men to stamp the torches out. It was true that the action would mark their presences, but without light the arrows could only be fired in a general direction. The men who were immobilized by the effort of lifting the scaling ladders into position would otherwise make too-excellent targets.

At last the ladder was up. Adam began to climb. The faster he made it up the ladder, the less likely it was that the defenders of the keep would be able to push it over. Just behind him he could hear Cuthbert. The man had a little wheeze in his breath when he was exerting himself strongly that betrayed his presence to those familiar with him.

"Lord," Cuthbert gasped, "watch your head!"

Adam ducked aside and, as something swished over his head, twisted his hand to seize the sword that had been hanging from his wrist by a leather thong. He struck out with it carefully, thrusting rather than swinging so that he would not crack the sword against the stone. It was a good sword, his father's, made of Eastern steel. It would not shatter like the less well-tempered metal of the men-at-arms' weapons. Nonetheless, slamming its honed edge against a stone wall would do it no good. As the point connected with something soft and shoved it backward, Adam laughed aloud with joy. They were up!

After that it was all play to Adam. In fact, no one met much difficulty. The walls were cleared very easily because they had taken the keep so much by surprise that Sir Matthew himself and most of his men were not ready. The gate towers were taken, the drawbridge over the ditch let down. However the taking of the walls was only the first step. The great keep itself was still in Sir Matthew's hands and could be held far more easily than the walls. There were food supplies in the lowest level and wells for water. If the defenders shut themselves in, they could probably hold out for weeks or months before they began to starve. Adam's advantage was that eventually they would starve and, since he held the outer portion of the castle, he could make terms with the town so that it would seem as if the action were over and there were no violation of the truce. Moreover, supplies for his men could be brought in by ship from Roselynde so that the end would be sure. Adam would have no need to lift his siege because *his* men were starving.

However, Adam did not wish to wait for Sir Matthew to yield or for the war machines or tunneling to open a way into the keep. It was too dark still to see much, but from the battlement he could hear the sounds of many men. Apparently, Sir Matthew had not yet withdrawn into the keep. Adam breathed a prayer of thanks and bellowed for the archers to hold their hands. Although they could not see to aim, they could shoot down at random, hoping to strike targets among the massed men. Then Adam passed the word for Sir Richard to come to him at once. When the vassal arrived, breathing heavily from running and anxiety, Adam told him that Sir Matthew must be kept busy and infuriated.

"There is an old grudge between you. Do you re-awaken it. Insult him. Speak ill of whatever he loves— true or not is no matter."

"Gladly, my lord, but why?"

Adam grinned wolfishly. "So that I can get as many men as possible down from the walls again and massed just out of sight of the drawbridge before he can see what we are about. I will also fill the two towers with men. If we can keep him in the bailey, we will have a chance to rush him."

"Good." Sir Richard's eyes glittered. "If he yields he will go out scatheless. Let me but come hand to hand with him . . ."

"Do you think you can drive him into such a frenzy

that he will agree to single combat?" Adam asked hopefully.

Sir Richard laughed bitterly. "I do not need to drive him into a frenzy for that. He will suggest it himself, but—"

"Accept for me," Adam interrupted with enthusiasm.

"No!" Sir Richard exclaimed.

Adam looked disappointed. "Do you claim prior right?"

"I have prior right, I suppose, but no man in his right mind would accept a challenge from Sir Matthew under these circumstances. His treachery—"

Adam laughed, cutting off Sir Richard's explanation. "Once known as treacherous, a viper's teeth are drawn. Man, this is the best chance of all. Accept for me, and you, who know his ways and what he is, can take measures that he cannot work his will."

"My lord, do not be a fool," Sir Richard pleaded. "This man is not stupid. He knows I am here. Anything I suggest he will quickly devise some evil to counter."

Adam's eyes were straining down toward the forces below in the bailey where shadowy movement was now visible. "There is no time to argue," he rumbled. "Quick, challenge him before he becomes more suspicious. And do not worry about me. I am well able to take care of myself. No, I will have no more words with you. If you will not do as I ask, I will challenge him myself—yes, that will be even better. I will challenge him myself."

Without waiting for an answer, Adam turned away and hurried around the wall, pausing to speak to Cuthbert. Sir Richard looked after him very briefly, then came forward to the inner edge of the rampart. It was still not light enough to see clearly, but in a very short time it would be impossible to hide the fact that the force on the walls was being thinned drastically. Adam was right. If their device was to be successful, he must divert Sir Matthew at once. He shouted down, demanding that someone go and drag out Sir Matthew, who was doubtless shivering in the safest place in the keep, so that he could dictate terms to him.

This was a deliberate slander. Sir Matthew was no coward and was well to the fore among his men, directing the plans for defending the keep and, if possible, expelling the invaders. Although the walls had been taken, Sir Matthew's position was far from hopeless. He had had time to estimate the number of men Adam had with him. He knew that the majority of those men should now be on the walls. If most of Adam's men were on the walls, the only way down was through the towers with their narrow stairs and entrances. Adam's men could come out only a few at a time and would need to face Sir Matthew's entire force in the bailey. What was more, if Adam's attack seemed to be succeeding, they could still retreat into the keep and try to hold out until help came.

It was not surprising, therefore, that Sir Matthew answered Sir Richard's insulting demand that he come forth with even cruder insults. Both the language and the imprecations the men addressed to each other became fouler and fouler. Adam twice paused on his round of the walls to listen, treasuring up the filthy and downright impossible things each man was saying about the ancestry, upbringing, family, habits, skill, and character of the other. Adam had thought he was well educated in invective, but now he realized he had been consorting too much with mealy-mouthed gentlemen like his stepfather. The only comparably original things he knew how to say were in English—a very coarse tongue.

Nonetheless, Adam had not forgotten the purpose of all this obscenity. He was pleased with the way Sir Richard had drawn out the shouting match to give him time to instruct the other leaders and the masters-at-arms. It was clear, however, that the insults were reaching a peak. Adam gave a last, low-voiced command, and began to run to the tower opposite where Sir Richard stood. He heard Sir Matthew, seemingly completely out of control with rage, shrieking a challenge at Sir Richard and asking what guarantees he wanted for his safety. He heard Sir Richard roar with laughter filled with contempt, and bellow back that Sir Matthew's shit had more value than his promises, since the shit might grow vegetables—if it did not poison them —whereas the promises had no use at all.

At this point Adam reached his goal. "I am Adam Lemagne," he called, "overlord to your liege lady, Gilliane of Tarring. Sir Richard says you are a treacherous cur, and I have good reason to believe him a wise man. Nonetheless, to spare further bloodshed, I will take up your challenge. If you win, I will withdraw; if you yield to me, we will take your keep. What guarantee will you offer me that you will meet me honestly, body to body?"

Sir Richard stared open-mouthed, too surprised to protest. Adam was speaking in what, for him, was falsetto—a boy's shrill tenor. The sound was near-sexless and gave no conception of the deep chest and huge body that Adam's normal bass rumble evoked. In fact, the voice brought an instant image of an eager, light-boned boy. Sir Richard gritted his teeth over laughter. Adam was skirting a dishonorable pretense. To conceal his physical capacity in such a way—since he could not be seen—was almost the same as concealing a weapon. Still, there was really nothing to laugh about. Pretense or no pretense, Adam was as a lamb to the slaughter. His fighting ability would avail him little against Sir Matthew's treachery.

In a last effort, Sir Richard cried out, cutting across Sir Matthew's promise that his men would withdraw around the side of the keep where they could not rush out suddenly. He warned Adam not to trust Sir Matthew's word.

"I do not need to trust it," Adam's falsetto snapped back pettishly. "When I come down into the bailey, I will be able to see whether the men are there or not."

"My lord," Sir Richard protested, "there are—"

"Oh, very well," Adam interrupted hastily, preventing Sir Richard from saying aloud that there were many places men could hide in the bailey, "let me bring ten men to guard against surprise and do you do the same, Sir Matthew. And do you, Sir Richard, hold your tongue."

Adam knew perfectly well that men would be concealing themselves in sheds and other hiding places around the bailey. He suspected that Sir Matthew had been using his argument with Sir Richard in a similar way to his use of it. Most likely Sir Matthew had been sending groups of men into places from which they could ambush any enemy who entered the bailey. Adam did not care about that. The bulk of the men would have to retreat as Sir Matthew promised. Those in concealment would be watching their master for his signal to attack. Meanwhile, Adam's own men could quietly get into position. Presumably, with man-to-man combat going on right before them, Sir Matthew's troops would not notice immediately, even as the light grew stronger, that the walls were nearly empty.

Just as Sir Richard opened his mouth to protest again—in spite of Adam's admonition—Sir Edmund seized his arm and began to talk. Sir Richard listened, glancing distractedly over at the other tower. He could not see well enough to be sure that Adam had already gone down, but he suspected it. He kept shaking his head at what Sir Edmund was telling him, remembering with a sinking heart that Adam was only eighteen years old.

"My God, my God," he whispered at last with tears in his eyes, "we will never be in time."

It was too late for vain regrets. Sir Richard pushed his way down the steps of the tower past the close-

packed men who waited for the next order to attack.
They were in good spirits. The excellent way the surprise had worked and the ease of taking the walls had
lifted their morale. As softly as he could, Sir Richard
unlatched the heavy door and opened it a bare crack.
Shadows moved in the shadows, but he did not think
Adam had stepped out of the other tower yet. This was
confirmed a moment later by Sir Matthew calling mock-
ingly to know whether Adam had lost his courage and
changed his mind. Sir Richard set his jaw. This time
Sir Matthew would not win. If Adam fell, Sir Richard
intended to take the keep despite Adam's promise to
withdraw.

The high voice was suddenly speaking from the doorway of the other tower, complaining that there were too
many shadows moving in the bailey, and then saying
arrogantly that if Sir Matthew did intend treachery the
agreement would be abrogated. Sir Richard swallowed,
wondering whether Sir Edmund and Sir Andrew had
got down the ladders and organized the men near the
drawbridge. And what of Sir Philip, who was to lead the
men out of the other tower? Would he suddenly take a
pet and refuse to do his part?

"Where are you?" Adam cried suddenly. "Light a
torch so that I may see you and how many men you
have."

Now he sounded uncertain, as if fear were conquer-
ing the boy's bravado that had driven him to answer
Sir Matthew's challenge.

"So that your archers can shoot from the walls?" Sir
Matthew rejoined.

"Do not be silly," Adam answered. "If a single arrow is loosed, you need only throw down the torches
and move away. It will soon be light enough for my
archers to shoot, anyway. If you will not light torches,
I will consider that you intend treachery. I will consider
the arrangement broken."

So well was Adam playing the part of a vainglorious

boy who was regretting a situation he had unwisely
created that Sir Richard began to feel uneasy. He knew
Adam well by now, but would Sir Philip understand
the pretense? At least Adam had managed to convince
Sir Matthew and win his point. A torch sprang to life.
No arrow flew. Another torch was lighted. Sir Richard
ground his teeth. Adam had made a bad mistake. The
torches showed five men to each side of a single man,
Sir Matthew, but their light, contrasting with the darkness around, effectively increased Sir Matthew's advantage by making the men he had hidden more invisible.

Before Sir Richard could cry a warning, ten men had
come out of the door of the other tower. They came
forward slowly, shields on their arms and swords drawn
but lowered.

"Well," Sir Matthew drawled, "where is this great
hero who was so quick to offer to meet me?"

"Tell your men to draw aside as mine do," Adam
cried. "I need room to fight."

Sir Matthew began to laugh. "You need to come out
first!" Perhaps he would not need to signal the men
in hiding. It seemed as if this little loudmouth had
trapped himself. Contemptuously, he told his men to
withdraw a suitable distance. Adam's men-at-arms kept
pace with them.

"Make ready," Adam threatened, his voice shaking
uncontrollably with laughter. "I come."

Sir Matthew barely raised his sword, and Adam did
come—a bull's mad rush out of the shadows by the
tower door, across the bailey, between the two groups
of men. His sword was swinging as he came, bellowing
now in his true voice, "Lemagne! Lemagne!"

It almost worked. The force of Adam's first blow
slammed Sir Matthew's shield, hastily raised at a bad
angle, into his head. The next stroke knocked Sir Matthew's sword out of his hand, taking some fingers with
it. Had Adam had time for one more swing, he might
have beheaded his opponent then and there and ended

the battle. Unfortunately for Adam, Sir Matthew's men were loyal. They did not waste time waiting for a signal that would never come. In fact, only surprise had kept them from attacking earlier.

The ten in the open leapt toward their staggering master and the giant pursuing him. Out of the shadows at least fifty more charged. Adam's guards had converged on him as soon as Sir Matthew's men moved, but, as Sir Richard burst from the tower with his contingent, he could not help crying out in horror. Adam and his ten men had disappeared as suddenly as if they had all been struck down with a single blow.

CHAPTER TWENTY-THREE

Adam's letters had arrived with remarkable regularity from the time he left until the day after Gilliane sent him Ian's suggestion that he hurry along the taking of Wick. There should have been a letter the following day. When it did not arrive, Alinor soothed Gilliane's growing nervousness by laughing at her. What did she want, Alinor asked, perfection on earth? It was near a miracle that nothing had happened to delay the regular arrival of letters up to this time. Horses did go lame. Messengers' minds did wander so that accidents occurred. Perhaps the letter would come a day late. Perhaps the accident the messenger had encountered was serious or fatal. In that case, the letter would not arrive at all.

This was so reasonable that Gilliane had to accept it, although her rebellious heart fluttered periodically with fear. Had she been idle, Gilliane would soon have been hysterical, no matter what reasoning Alinor used, but Alinor was too wise to permit that. She would have invented work for the girl had that been necessary but, fortuitously, it was not. Ian and Geoffrey were already on their way to Roselynde and the Earl of Pembroke had written to say he was on his way, too, bringing a number of unnamed but important guests. Gilliane thought she had been well occupied before, but now she scarcely had time to breathe as a great keep geared up for high-level visitors and entertainment.

Nonetheless, as the days passed and no letter arrived from Adam, Gilliane's eyes grew huge and haunted. Joanna pointed out gently that, if Adam were in the final stages of preparations for taking the keep, or even if he were engaged in negotiations over its yielding, he might not have time to write. He was not like Ian or Geoffrey, who could dash off a few lines without effort or thought. For Adam, writing was a real task that required time and quiet.

The words might have produced a more calming effect if Gilliane had not seen the anxiety in Joanna's own eyes. That was another lesson. Joanna was almost as fearful as she, but it did not stop her from performing every duty. Gilliane forced herself to follow that example. Although she started and looked anxiously at every manservant who moved toward her with hurried steps, she did everything necessary quickly and efficiently. It was both harder and easier because the fear she felt was very different from that with which she had been familiar all her life. For the first time, it was purely fear for someone else. Previously, even Gilliane's fear for Adam had been mixed with fear for herself because, with his death, her security would be lost and she would again have been prey for any man. Now Gilliane knew she herself was safe, safe forever. Lady Alinor had accepted her, and the people of Roselynde cared for their own.

It was strange, under the circumstances, Gilliane thought as she sewed doggedly at a rich green gown that would bring out the bright lights in Adam's eyes, that this fear should hurt so much more. It was a constant leaden weight she dragged around wherever she went, a constant ache in her throat and chest, a constant sick hollowness in her belly. Equally strange was her ability to endure, to smile at the servants who had done their work well, to discuss with apparent interest the subtlety to be prepared for each course of the dinner, to examine the cattle and pigs in the pens and decide which should be first slaughtered and which fattened for a few days longer. Strangest of all was the genuine joy Gilliane felt for Joanna and Alinor, whose men were safe and on their way home. Gilliane would have thought that this knowledge would only increase her own bitterness, but it was not so. She wondered whether she would feel the same when Ian and Geoffrey actually arrived.

That question was answered the following night, long after dark. The guards on the walls had just about called a warning that many men were approaching the keep when Ian himself reached the moat and demanded admittance. The castle sprang to life. The hall blazed with torches; servants threw on their outer clothing— if they had not been sleeping in it for warmth; Alinor and Joanna ran in bed robes with free-flowing hair to greet the kingpins of their lives. Gilliane found to her relief that she was touched by longing, not racked by envy. Her single doubt was about what to do. She did not wish to intrude on the fierce embraces and passionate questions of greeting, but she did not wish to appear sullen or uncaring, either.

The second question was resolved as pleasantly as the first. A few minutes were spent in clutching their men, in assuring themselves that they were well and unhurt. Then both Alinor and Joanna asked for Gilliane. A maid was sent running to fetch her if she was awake. The maid had not far to go, for Gilliane was in the stairway, waiting uncertainly. She came forward eagerly when summoned, to be embraced tenderly by Ian and warmly by Geoffrey who, of course, knew everything their wives knew about Gilliane—except that Alinor had not written that she, as well as Geoffrey, suspected Gilliane of murder. That, Alinor thought, was one of those things men would not want or need to know. It might give them the wrong impression of Gilliane's character.

Minutes later even the dreadful fear about Adam was eased. While Geoffrey was asking some questions about Tarring, Alinor was pouring out the story about Adam to Ian. Geoffrey soon was listening more closely to that than to Gilliane's reply to his question because he made no comment on that but remarked, "Surely you cannot think it odd that Adam did not *write*. When did he ever do so?"

"Every two or three days to Gilliane since he left here," Alinor answered significantly.

"On regular days?" Ian asked quickly.

"No, my lord," Gilliane replied, "the days might vary."

"When did you send him Ian's news?" Geoffrey wanted to know.

"Five—no, it is morning now—six days past," Gilliane said, watching Ian's face desperately for a sign.

Ian did not notice. His eyes sought Geoffrey's, and Geoffrey's lips moved slightly as if he were counting. Still watching him, Ian said, "There is a day, perhaps two, I cannot account for."

"It is Adam we want accounted for," Alinor snapped, "not the days."

Geoffrey smiled at her and at Gilliane. "It is Adam we are accounting for." Then he turned back to Ian. "You are thinking of your own ways, Ian, of saying to a vassal you have known for twenty years, *Sieve me out this keep*. Adam would not do that. He will examine the place and people for himself. He does not know Gilliane's men too well and also . . . well, it is hard even for me to trust the judgment of my men, compared with my own."

"There, you see?" Ian said, also smiling at Alinor and Gilliane. "There is nothing to trouble your beautiful heads about. Naturally, Adam would not write the day he was preparing for an assault, nor on the day the keep was assaulted. If they had failed, he would have written to give that news and perhaps to ask me what next to do. Thus, since you did not hear from him, the assault was successful."

"Then, knowing how much Adam loves to write, I would guess he told himself it was not needful because he would be home as soon as his messenger," Geoffrey added.

"But he is not home," Gilliane whispered.

Ian put his arm around her. "Child, you will see him tomorrow, I expect, although late." His lips smiled, but a faint anxiety showed in his eyes. "And if he does not come, I will ride over myself and see what is delaying him. Likely he is trying to be sure the loot is evenly divided or there is some problem of arranging the governance of the keep. Do not think about it anymore. I will bring him home with me."

One other cause of delay had occurred to Ian. Adam might be badly wounded. If he was out of his head with fever, he could neither write nor give orders to send to Roselynde for help. Even if he was not out of his head, he might not permit news of his hurt to be sent to Roselynde. Knowing his mother, Adam would understand that she would come to him at once, battleground or no battleground, and likely enough she would bring Gilliane with her. Heedless Adam might be, but not so heedless as to want the woman he loved to come into such danger—or his mother, either. He would hide news of his hurt until he could be brought home.

The only thing that prevented Ian from rushing off that moment to make sure his darling boy was not dying was the character Alinor had given Sir Richard. Whatever Adam said, Sir Richard would have sent for help if he thought Adam might die of his wound. Thus, if Adam was not, as Ian really believed, merely trying to be sure no cause for quarrel rose among the men who had taken the keep, he could not be mortally hurt. In that case, it would be crueler to frighten Alinor and

Gilliane by rushing off in the middle of the night than to leave Adam where he was for another day.

No one except Gilliane rose early the next morning. Ian and Geoffrey had been too busy consoling themselves and their wives for their three months' absence to have closed their eyes much before the sun rose, and, when they finally opened them, were so delighted with the change in their situations that they felt obliged to pay down new tokens of their devotion. Gilliane busied herself with putting the last touches to the preparations for receiving their guests and, in fact, was only just in time. Well before noon a very large troop of men bearing the banner of the Earl of Arundel was reported approaching Roselynde from the east.

Poor Gilliane had no idea what to do. She was embarrassed to interrupt Alinor or Joanna, who had so recently received their husbands back into their arms. On the other hand, she was well aware that the lord and lady of the manor should be on hand to welcome so eminent a guest. She did not even know whether the guards at the drawbridge and portcullis would obey her order to allow Arundel to enter. That decided her. Gilliane had been sufficiently well instructed in politics by now to understand that offending Arundel would be far worse than interrupting even the most passionate lovemaking. She sent a maid up to tell Gertrude that Lady Alinor must be informed the Earl of Arundel was on his way.

As it transpired, Gilliane could not have warned Alinor in time even if she had not delayed a few minutes to think. As she turned away from the maidservant she had instructed, she became aware of a large red-faced man striding toward her across the hall. His cloak was not only lined with fur but faced and collared with it. His armor was of the finest. The helmet he carried was worked with gold wire. His surcoat was elaborately embroidered and even showed the flash of a precious stone set here and there around the neckline. This could be no one but the Earl of Arundel.

Gilliane's first impulse was to run away. She had never in her life spoken to so high a nobleman. What if she should offend him? She was all the more terrified because she knew how important the man was to Adam's political cause. Fortunately, before she could act on this cowardly impulse, two ideas came to Gilliane simultaneously. It would be more offensive for no one to greet Arundel than for her to behave awkwardly. The latter could be blamed on the forwardness of a silly girl; the former could only be the fault of Lady Alinor and her family.

The second thing Gilliane remembered was Lady Alinor's reiteration that she was a great lady and must behave like one if she wished to be worthy to be Adam's wife. With that in mind, Gilliane stepped forward a few paces, dropped a full curtsy, and produced a shy smile because the gentleman looked quite as much taken aback as she had felt.

"Lady Alinor?" he faltered, knowing quite well it could not be. He had not seen Lady Alinor for many years, but she must be much older than this girl and she was not easily forgotten.

"No, my lord," Gilliane replied softly but firmly. "I am Lady Gilliane of Tarring. I bid you welcome to Roselynde and beg your pardon for that Lady Alinor and Lord Ian are not here to greet you. Lord Ian and Lord Geoffrey arrived very late last night. May I take your cloak? Will you be seated? May I offer you wine? Food? A bath?"

So intent had Gilliane been on Arundel himself that it had never occurred to her to wonder how he had come into the great hall without even a servant to run ahead and warn of his arrival. Ian might have left instructions with Beorn to admit the Earl of Arundel, but his coming would still have been announced. This had not yet penetrated Gilliane's confused thoughts so that she was taken completely by surprise when, having handed her his cloak and politely refused refreshment until his hosts should join them, Arundel turned to look over his shoulder.

"I can see why you are so assiduous to make Lady Gilliane's men obedient to her," Arundel remarked with a broad grin.

Gilliane's eyes followed his and she gasped, first turning pale, then red with joy. Adam was standing behind and to the side of Arundel. She could not understand how she could have missed seeing him, but her intense relief struck her mute and froze her expression. Adam tore his eyes away from her to reply to Arundel and blushed hotly under the older man's grin. That made Arundel laugh aloud. Adam grew even redder. Alarm overcame Gilliane's paralysis at the sight of the way Adam's eyes were sparkling.

"Please do sit down, my lord," she said to Arundel, as she stepped past him. She turned to gesture toward a high-backed, cushioned chair, which also brought her between Arundel and Adam. "And may I have your cloak, Sir Adam?"

The color receded from Adam's face and he put a hand to his cloak clasp, only to drop it again. "My armor is not fit to be seen," he remarked in a rather strangled voice.

Gilliane was by then facing him fully so that Arundel could not see how pale she became at those words. Adam did not see it either because his head had turned to his mother, who had just entered the hall.

"What do you mean, Adam?" Alinor cried as she came across to them.

Just behind her, Ian asked simultaneously, "Are you hurt, my son?"

"Not at all," Adam replied to Ian and smiled at Alinor. "As a result of a small stratagem, I got rather covered with mud and blood—not my own, not my own. And when we had taken the keep, I laid the armor aside. I never thought to *say* to clean it. You know Alberic has always done that, but Alberic is not with me. Cuthbert is a good fighting man, a fine master-at-arms, but he has never served a nobleman without squires. So . . . Well, he will not make that mistake again, but I did not wish to waste more time this morning and wore it as it was."

Assured of her son's well-being, Alinor fixed her attention on other matters. Her eyes had flicked from Adam's face to Gilliane's. It would be just as well, she thought, if Arundel were not treated to a fainting maiden or an emotional outburst from Adam who, in spite of his smile, had dangerously bright eyes and a suspicious whiteness around the mouth.

"Would you go and see Adam made decent, Lady Gilliane?" Alinor asked politely.

"Yes, madam," Gilliane replied very low.

Adam glanced at her, looked at his mother—but Alinor had already directed her full attention to Arundel and was welcoming him, apologizing for being late in greeting him, thanking him warmly for honoring Roselynde with his company. He answered her briefly, his mind plainly elsewhere. Adam turned away to move toward his room, feeling sick. He was sure his mother had refused to meet his eyes deliberately, and Gilliane was pale and stiff, seemingly unwilling to accompany him. Her greeting today, so cold and formal, was a sad contrast to the way she had run to him at Tarring, heedless of everything, even the danger of startling his destrier. In addition, as he walked away, he heard Arundel come out with what was on his mind.

"Lady of Tarring, eh?" he said to Alinor. "She must be well found in land, if I remember Neville's holdings aright. And a very pretty girl, too. What would you say—"

"She is bespoke already, my lord," Alinor interrupted quickly, laughing. "Surely you did not think me so behind-hand that I would not affix the honors of Tarring to our family?"

Adam winced. He would murder his mother! She of

all women should have been wiser than to speak in those terms in front of Gilliane. Did she not realize that, although softer of manner, Gilliane was just as fiercely possessive? No wonder Gilliane was pale and angry. If she thought Adam wished to take what was "hers, to her" she would have no part of him. Well, he had better say nothing of marriage until he had a chance to prove that, to him, her person was more important than her estate.

Gilliane had not once looked at Adam since he disclaimed being hurt. She knew she would not be able to control herself if she did, and she remembered how set Adam had been about not making "a scandal and a hissing" in his mother's house. Servants had followed them into Adam's chamber and, without speaking a word to him, Gilliane handed a maid his cloak and, when she had it off, his hauberk to a man. There was already a fire in the room. Gilliane had bid the servants light it that morning to convince herself that Ian was correct and Adam would be home that day. She sent the other man to have a bath brought in, and, while this was being fetched, busied herself in the chests, picking out suitably elegant garments.

"Gilliane . . ." Adam began.

Still she would not look at him. She sent the last maid off to fetch the chest of medicinals.

"I am not hurt," Adam insisted crossly, "and I do not want a bath." But Gilliane paid no attention, following hard on the heels of the maid. "Wait," Adam ordered harshly.

Gilliane could not disobey a direct command, and stopped at the door.

"Gilliane . . ." Adam began again.

Before he could say another word, she had pushed the door shut and flung herself at him. Adam uttered a grunt of surprise at the impact, staggered back a step, and grasped at Gilliane to keep his balance. She clutched him tightly and Adam yelped.

"I thought you said you were not hurt," Gilliane cried, keeping her face buried in his chest.

"I am not. My men were a little too enthusiastic about protecting me, that is all. There was an attempt at treachery and the idiots knelt on top of me while making a shield wall. Never mind that. Gilliane, why will you not look at me?"

"I dare not. The servants will be back in a few minutes. Let me go, Adam."

Adam could not help laughing, although he was puzzled and suspicious. "It was you who flung yourself at me," he remarked. "And the servants need not come in if I bid them stay out. Kiss me."

"No," Gilliane insisted, pressing herself against him eagerly but keeping her head down. "Please do not kiss me. Please. I will rid us of the servants, but they will see from the hall if the bath is sent away and we do not come out. Adam, please! A bath can take as long as one likes."

That was an excellent notion. Adam remembered distinctly the way Gilliane had used a bath as an excuse in Tarring. However, he found her behavior confusing in the extreme. She bid him let her go, yet she was the one who was embracing him, his arms barely around her. She clearly intended to couple with him—there could be no doubt of that from what she had said—but she would not look at him. Adam knew Gilliane to be very passionate. Could she be eager for the lovemaking and angry at the same time? That was not impossible. Adam had experienced it himself with two of his mistresses. He was tempted to laugh at Gilliane but knew that would make matters worse, and certainly it could not help if he thrust her away as she said she wished.

"Gilliane," he began yet again, "tell me—"

There were sounds at the door, and Gilliane pulled free of Adam's lax grasp and went at once to fling it open. The maid with the chest of medicinals tripped in, followed almost immediately by the men carrying the

huge tub and a train of other men lugging buckets of
hot and cold water. Gilliane became very busy bidding
this man and that pour to make the water right. Adam
watched, his lips twisted and his glance fulminating.
Color began to rise in his face and, at last, after the
fifth testing of the water, he suddenly bellowed, "Gilliane, get these people out of here. I want to talk to
you."

There was an anxious stiffening among the servants,
but none made the mistake of running away. Adam had
followed the custom of the house—a custom made
necessary by the fact that Lady Alinor was the true
owner of the property and both her husbands had been
scrupulous in recognizing her right. Adam thought little
of that. Partly his response was habit; partly it was
courtesy. Gilliane had summoned the servants; Adam
would not make her look small by sending them away
as if she had no right to do what she had done. Had
he really been angry, he might not have been so careful,
but he was as much amused as irritated by her dithering.

Without glancing at him, Gilliane made a swift gesture of dismissal. As the door closed, she was back in
his arms, sighing reproachfully, "Could you not have
waited five minutes more, my lord? I would have found
a reason to send each away separately so it would not
have been known we were alone here."

Whatever Adam might have replied to that was lost
because Gilliane finally did look up at him, and there
was such love and desire in her face that he forgot completely everything but their nearness. "Every night," he
muttered, "every night I dreamed of this," and fastened
his lips to hers.

"Will you bathe first, my love?" Gilliane asked when
they came up for air.

Adam shook his head and plucked at her wimple.
"Take that cursed thing off," he urged. "I wish to see
your hair."

As her fingers busily did Adam's bidding, Gilliane's

brow wrinkled in a frown. "The water will be cold later," she warned, "and someone must bathe or it will be seen the water is clean. What could we have been doing?"

"Everyone will know what we have been doing," Adam murmured between kisses on her cheek and chin and throat, while his hands fumbled at the neck fastening of her gown. "Do you care?"

"No," Gilliane sighed. "I am yours for whatever purpose you desire me. But—but, Adam, your mother says you wish to wed me."

She felt Adam's body stiffen under her hands and her breath caught. Gilliane had also heard Alinor's answer to Arundel's half-begun proposal to contract Gilliane, presumably to one of his sons or nephews. At the time it had made no impression on her, since her attention was totally fixed on getting Adam alone so that her passionate regard for him would not be blatantly displayed before Arundel and the servants. Now the words suddenly came back. What if it was Alinor who wanted her to be Adam's wife—for the very reasons she had given Arundel—rather than Adam who desired it?

"There is no reason for you to marry me, Adam," she said quietly.

"Do not be a fool!" he exclaimed, wishing he could have smothered his much-beloved mother before she had opened her mouth. "I do not want—"

Gilliane could not bear to hear him say it. "Let me remain Osbert's wife," she cut in desperately, "and keep me with you. I will be content with that. I swear I will be content, so long as you do not put me away."

"Little idiot," Adam said, crushing her tightly against him. "How could I put you away when you burn in my heart and my brain every minute of the day and night? I need you. I must have you—you and only you. I do not care for anything else."

Although there was a little sad core deep inside her, Gilliane smiled. Whatever reason Adam had for not wanting her as a wife, it did not seem to be lack of love. She would think no more of it. She would accept the joy of loving him and being loved and let all else happen as it would. Only . . . Even as Adam pushed her face up to kiss her again hungrily it occurred to Gilliane that, if he did not intend to marry her, it was important not to give cause for public scandal—and to send away a bath full of clean water after they had been closeted alone together in Adam's chamber for so long would be too good a tale for the servants to keep to themselves. Arundel's people would be sure to hear of it— and any other servants who accompanied the other expected guests.

Gilliane yielded her lips willingly and savored the embrace, but, when Adam broke free to begin removing the remainder of his clothing, she said, "Adam, I will not deny you. I will never deny you, but it was you who said to me we must not make a scandal and a hissing in your mother's house. If the bathwater goes out clean, the servants will think it a fine jest. Arundel's servants will hear of it also, and then . . ."

He flung his tunic away and began to unlace his shirt, saying, "Yes, yes, I will bathe, but later. For God's sake, Gilliane, I have been hungry for you for near a month."

"But the water will be cold. You will take a chill. Five minutes, Adam. In five minutes, I can wash you."

For a moment, his eyes flashed anger, but he knew she was right, and he knew also that she was as eager for him as he was for her. He eyed the bath malevolently. "If you had not ordered that accursed . . ." His voice trailed off and the sparks of rage in his eyes were replaced with a mischievous glow. "Come in with me," he laughed. "It will serve all purposes. We will not even rumple the bed."

Gilliane eyed the bath with trepidation. It was a large tub, a long oval, about twenty inches high smoothed and polished and oiled to prevent splinters. However,

Adam was a very large man and the tub, owing to her fiddling with the water temperature, was rather full. Gilliane doubted that the tub would hold both of them. She was absolutely certain that, if they did what Adam obviously intended, most of that water would end up on the floor. She looked up from her slightly startled perusal of her fate to see Adam, free of his clothing, laughing at her.

"But, Adam," she protested feebly, "I do not see how . . ."

Nonetheless, Gilliane had her cotte off before she finished the sentence. The idea was rather appealing. She had always taken a sensuous pleasure in the feeling of the warm water of a bath lapping around her body. The idea of that pleasure added to the delight Adam was offering interested her greatly. Still, as she tried to conceive of a position that would fit them and the tub, she began to laugh.

"You will not drown me, will you?" she giggled as her underdress and shift followed the cotte.

"Only in love," Adam replied, getting in.

That surprised Gilliane. She thought she would get in first, but she was content to leave the management of so novel an operation in Adam's hands and slid off her shoes and stockings without further argument. Trustfully, she put her hand into the hand Adam held out to her. His eyes were alight. He was sitting upright somewhat forward in the tub and directed her to slide her legs around his chest under his arms and place her feet behind him. It would have been impossible, because no person can stand at such an angle, but Adam had a firm grip on Gilliane's hands

Now, Gilliane swung free, supported by Adam's powerful grasp on her hands. He leaned forward suddenly and buried his mouth in the mass of glossy curls that hid her mount of Venus. Gilliane gasped with surprise and pleasure at his tongue's invasion, but the pang of joy undid her. Her knees buckled, sending her down upon Adam with a tremendous splash. She was not hurt because she landed on the flat of his thighs above the knees and from there slid down slowly. Both of them were giggling helplessly, but the laughter did not quench passion. Rather, it added its own stimulus so that when their mouths met a flame leaped between them that even oceans could not quench.

CHAPTER TWENTY-FOUR

The deception Gilliane and Adam had practiced was not in the least successful, partly because the bath they took was probably the longest known for a keep in midwinter, partly because Gilliane's clothes, discarded too near the tub, were soaked and Adam would not let her put them on lest she catch cold. Excuses enough could have been found for the wet garments—there was water over everything and Adam was known to be playful when taking a bath. No information could have been obtained from Catrin, who brought her mistress dry clothing and was the only one to know she was naked when the dry clothes arrived, because she was devoted and close-mouthed. However, nothing but the truth could explain the expressions with which Adam and Gilliane finally emerged from his chamber.

No one minded. No one said a word to them, even in jest. When Arundel raised his brows, Alinor laughed indulgently. "They are very young," she whispered. "After all, she is not a maiden and has nothing to lose. Also, she has been greatly afraid lest harm come to Adam while he was in her service."

Nothing could have suited Alinor better. She had sent Gilliane with Adam for the purpose of clarifying their relationship because Alinor had realized, even as she said Gilliane was bespoken, that she would have to tell Arundel the truth about the forced marriage to de

Cercy and confess that Gilliane was not yet free to marry again. Too many people knew the situation existed, and Alinor was afraid Arundel might hear of it from someone else. She did not want even the faintest shadow cast on the veracity of the men and women of Roselynde. Once the story was out, Arundel would know Gilliane could not be betrothed to Adam, and he might have some hope of winning her estates for a member of his own family. But if it was made plain that Gilliane was already Adam's mistress, Arundel would no longer consider her available.

In any case, such minor matters were soon completely forgotten. When the Earl of Pembroke arrived, all attention was focused on the state of the realm. Arundel was somewhat apprehensive. His parting with Pembroke the previous year had been rather acrimonious, Arundel shouting that oaths to a man who constantly violated his own could not be considered inviolable, and Pembroke shouting back that a man's honor was his own and what others did was no excuse for dishonorable behavior. There was, of course, no trouble at all. Alinor had already written to Isobel, Pembroke's wife and her long-time friend, that Arundel was expected at Roselynde and that, if her husband handled him properly, Arundel might be won back to Henry's cause.

In fact, Pembroke's own eldest son, William, had rebelled and joined Louis, only recently returning to his loyalty to Henry and his father.

Young William had been apprehensive when he approached his father, but he was received with joy. Wiser heads than his, Pembroke said dryly, had been confused by King John's atrocities. The only shadow that fell between himself and his father was ephemeral and led to a firmer understanding between them. This occurred when Pembroke summoned his son out of the castle given into his keeping and bade him come along to Roselynde. Instantly, the guilt-scarred pride of the young man was touched and he asked angrily if his father felt he could not be trusted.

"Do not be an ass," Pembroke growled testily. "If I did not trust you, this is one meeting to which I would never bring you. We will be planning how best to win back the coast. Do you think I would invite anyone I did not trust? Everyone makes mistakes, William," he said more gently. "Forget yours, except as it has taught you a lesson. Fortunately, it turned out none so ill."

"Then what do you want me for?" the young man asked, less aggressively but still suspicious. "I am no sailor, as well you know, and I do not have any knowledge of those parts."

"If you will listen for five minutes without jumping down my throat to drag out words that are not there, you will find out. I want you to convince Arundel, who we hope will be at Roselynde also, that the king will not be ill disposed toward him if he should wish to repudiate Louis, and I want you to convince him also that he must not speak ill of John to young Henry. He may say what he likes to me and to Gualo, but not to Henry."

"Oh." William's face cleared. It was altogether reasonable that he should be useful in calming the fears of others who wished to be received but felt they might be scorned or insulted. "I will, indeed, but surely, Father, Arundel will not speak ill of John to the king. John was Henry's father, and—"

"There is no telling what a blockhead like Arundel will do. He would only be trying to justify his own actions, but . . . I cannot say anything to him at all, except sweet words, because . . . well, think how you take fire before I even say a word. Do you be careful what you say to him, also. His soul will be just as sore as yours—soothe it with the balm you most desire for yourself."

Pembroke did not forget his own advice. He greeted Arundel as if a whole year had dropped out of time, as if there had never been any argument between them on the question of loyalty to a bad king, as if they had never been opposed in battle. At first nothing at all of a political nature was said. It was perfectly honorable to meet your opponents in battle as friends during a truce. It was young William who started the ball rolling by announcing to Arundel that he had left Louis's service. Louis had violated his oath to stay in England, William said hotly, and thus freed his followers from their oaths to him. Arundel might be a blockhead, but he understood the usages of war. He knew Louis's action was no violation of his oath, unless he did not return to England. Arundel, however, did not make the obvious point and later it was seen that he was in close talk with young William.

"I think we have him," Ian said softly, and Pembroke nodded in satisfaction.

"Nor will he waver again," Geoffrey remarked, his golden eyes thoughtful. "Also, he will be active in casting Louis out. He is not merely trying to protect himself against all chances."

"Matters look most hopeful," Pembroke agreed. "I have heard from good sources that Louis had some trouble making his way from London to a port that would supply him with ships."

Adam grinned. "The most direct route is Kemp, but he has never tried that. I have just closed the mouth of the Arun to Louis, also—and Arundel smiled on me. I met him by chance on the road and told him Wick had fallen. Soon I will close off Bexhill."

"Not until after Easter," Pembroke warned.

"No," Adam agreed, "but not because it has anything to do with the truce. Bexhill is my vassal's honor and her vassal defies her. Still, I could do nothing until the new year in March. Gilliane's men have already given near their forty days' service for this year, and I will not ask them to serve again if I can avoid it. Thus, I plan to move against Bexhill after the first spring planting, but I would be very happy to serve the king in this and will move when you bid me—if the matter is not too long delayed."

"I thank you for the king," Pembroke replied, his eyes fond as he looked at the worthy heir of his dearest friend. "Hold by your own present plans. I will let you know if some need of Daubeny's should necessitate a change."

"Who is this Daubeny?" Ian asked. "I scarcely remember the man. I thought you wrote he would come with you."

"That was intended until I heard Arundel was coming also. I know that even if he does not come back to us, he would not act the spy apurpose, but . . ."

Pembroke did not need to finish that. The others nodded understanding. Arundel might not intend to betray them, but he might well say something without realizing its significance. Even if Arundel did return to his fealty to the king, he was not the safest person in the world to entrust with secret plans. There might well be in his household or entourage those who were in Louis's pay. Arundel would never watch for spies. He did not engage in such practices himself, and was unlikely to think that anyone else engaged in them.

"As for Daubeny," Pembroke continued, "he was warden of the islands of the narrow sea before Eustace drove him out. I bade him wait a few days longer. He will sail to Roselynde harbor as soon as I send him word we are ready. You need not mistrust Daubeny. Because he knew John so little, he loved the king well. He came to me as soon as he heard of John's death to swear fealty to Henry."

Ian's brow wrinkled. "You say he loved John well, but I do not remember him to have been in any war of the king's. How—"

"He was, Ian," Geoffrey interrupted. "I know him. He is of the sea and directed the gathering and sailing of the king's fleet. My father and I were much in contact with him when we sailed against Damme and in those other actions on the coast. He is a good man and knows the sea like a fish."

"The sea? Our trouble is here on land," Ian protested.

"We will soon be big enough to solve the problems in England . . . if Louis can obtain no more help from France. The Church is doing its part. The pope has sent strong letters to Philip, and Gualo hears that the king has yielded to the Holy Father's threats. Besides, Philip does not care for England. He hated old King Henry and all his get, but I do not think he feels much against the children, especially John's son. Now that Louis's enterprise is beginning to cost more than it can bring in, Philip has lost interest."

"Yes," Ian agreed, "Philip always had a keen eye for what was worthwhile, and from what Simon said to me, it was Richard that Philip really hated."

"He was always rather contemptuous of John," Geoffrey added, "and the Battle of Bouvines seems to have cured whatever remained of his hatred because he now has someone to vent it upon."

There was bitterness in Geoffrey's voice. He had been wounded nigh to death at the disastrous Battle of Bouvines and would always walk crookedly because of it. Ian looked at him anxiously, but there was nothing of self in Geoffrey's face. He regretted the lost battle, the comrades who were dead and those who were still shamefully imprisoned, treated like animals. His own injury meant little to him.

"Whatever Philip's reasons, he is none so eager to support this venture any further," Pembroke went on. "If, in addition, we close the narrow sea so that ships are lost to France, Philip will soon actively forbid any help to Louis rather than simply be indifferent."

"That will take some doing," Ian remarked sardonically. "Ever since Eustace the Monk quarreled with John and took Louis's silver, we have near been locked in our own ports. Trade with the Low Countries is down to nothing, and Alinor is having fits at the loss in her revenues from Roselynde and Mersea. It has given me some work also," he added dryly. "Our fisherfolk are faithful and give us warning, but if they did not, we would have reavers ashore all along the coast."

"Yes, well, that is what is to be discussed with Daubeny. There is some money now for fitting out a fleet. If he is willing—and I believe he is eager—to take charge of it, we may solve that problem."

"I do not believe Daubeny can conquer Eustace," Geoffrey said. "The Monk's successes and the liberties he allows his followers have attracted a very large number of captains. They are all little more than pirates, but they obey him because if they do not, he turns the others on them. Their profits are high, too, since they prey on all shipping and on the rich coast towns."

"That will be as it may," Pembroke replied with a shrug. "I do not expect to run before I walk. It will content me if Daubeny can capture or sink enough French ships to make Philip forbid the supplying of the French force here, and if he can protect enough of our ships and those of the Low Countries to bring trade closer to normal."

"Most reasonable," Ian agreed, but without much interest. He did not have Alinor's passion for profit, and, although he was a brave man, the thought of fighting at sea gave him a definite sensation of chill.

"It is very interesting, indeed," Geoffrey remarked with far more enthusiasm. He liked sea duty. "But what is our part in this? Does Daubeny wish to recruit from among Lady Alinor's people?"

"That, of course," Pembroke replied, "but far more important is the assurance of safe havens for him if he must run from a greater force or seek harborage in a storm."

"Ah, I had not thought of that," Ian confessed. "This is the right place for such assurances. Among us here,

we hold harbors enough to make the attempt reasonable. Wales is safe, of course."

"But too far from Louis's usual path and too poor to
make it of much interest to Eustace's reavers," Geoffrey
commented.

Pembroke nodded. "And Cornwall, which is also
safe, is much the same. By the time Daubeny reached
those places, he could be wrecked or taken a dozen
times. Portsmouth is the last harbor to the east that is
the king's—aside from Dover. But Dover is so often
under siege that it is not a sufficiently reliable haven.
The four other of the Cinque Ports are even worse. The
mayors and people incline toward us, but the fortifica-
tions are held by men who have sworn, although they
are now doubtful, to Louis. They are near ready to
come to us, but they desire some assurance that the
French will not send a large fleet against them."

"And so you go round and round." Ian laughed, a
little bitterly. "Daubeny needs harbors, which the
Cinque Ports will furnish if Daubeny first offers assurance that he will preserve them from attack by Eustace. But he cannot promise this until they promise
harborage and repair facilities."

"What is more, even Portsmouth is not safe with
Roselynde sitting where it sits," Pembroke remarked.

"What?" Ian exclaimed. "Are you mad, William?
When has my faith wavered that you should consider
Roselynde a threat?"

"Not I. I have sworn myself blue in the face that
you are true as steel, but Daubeny has eyes and ears
among the sailors and he has had reports of a French
ship sitting in Roselynde harbor. Not only that, but
sailing out with armed men."

"A French ship?" Ian's eyes bulged. Had Alinor's
lust for profit or her desire to have a foot in each camp
led her to consort with Eustace?

"It is not a French ship," Adam said hastily. All
three men turned toward him and he laughed irrepress-

ibly at their puzzlement. "It was a French ship but is now ours," he explained. "I mean it is Lady Gilliane's." He described the capture of the ship and the use to which it had been put since then.

Pembroke smiled at him. "Lady Gilliane has had a remarkable change of heart in political matters. She came to fix Louis's power over Neville's property and has become devoted to Henry instead. I wonder why?"

The teasing was meant as a compliment to Adam's male attractiveness, but it touched a sore point. "Because those are the terms on which she continues to hold her lands of me," Adam said rather harshly.

"Do you mean she has not had a change of heart?" Pembroke asked, rather startled. "Why, you have just told me it was she who ordered the French ship taken."

"I do not know," Adam replied unhappily, regretting that he had betrayed Gilliane. "She has never acted in any way other than in complete compliance with her oath to me. I do not know what makes me doubt—other than that she is a woman and oaths mean very little to women."

"Alas, we all know that," Geoffrey said, grinning, "but I do not think you need to doubt Lady Gilliane. My wife says she has no political particularity—which is also common to women—and Joanna sees clearly."

Geoffrey did not say that whatever Adam believed in, Gilliane would believe in, but the faint smile on his lips and the cock of his brow made Pembroke nod. Adam's doubts were a young lover's nervousness. Adam flashed Geoffrey a glance of gratitude, wondering whether Joanna had really said that or whether Geoffrey had sprung to the defense of Gilliane as he would to that of any member of the family. There was a feeling of comfort in that and the tight look on Adam's face eased.

"In any case," he said, "you may count on the harbors below Wick and Tarring. Unfortunately, they are not large, but we can give succor and supplies to a few ships—so long as Daubeny and his men commit no outrages. I do not wish to exchange one set of reavers for another."

Pembroke accepted that with a shrug. "That is another reason why Daubeny comes here. It will be best if all is clear and open—what help he may count upon and what obligations he will be under." His eyes wandered across the hall to where his son was still talking with Arundel. "I wish he would decide one way or the other and be gone," Pembroke said softly. "If Daubeny must wait too long, doubts may be raised in him."

The wish was fulfilled with surprising promptness. Even as the words left Pembroke's lips, young William moved away from Arundel and gestured for his father to take his place. The next day Arundel returned home to discuss matters with his own vassals. He had no doubts about their enthusiastic reception of his change of heart. They, too, had become more and more dissatisfied with their relationship with the French prince and his followers. So sure was Arundel of his men's reaction that he had already made a definite date for his reception and swearing to the young king. Pembroke sighed with relief and dismissed the matter from his mind. Arundel would not break his word.

The meeting with Philip Daubeny took place little more than a week later, and its conclusion was equally satisfactory. By the end of February, Eustace was no longer having things all his own way. Daubeny could not muster as many ships as the Monk, nor were his as large, but many of the men who sailed them were bitter victims of Eustace's raiding and they fought ingeniously as well as hard. More merchantmen ventured into safe English ports as their confidence increased that they would not be attacked when they sailed out again. Lone ships of Eustace's fleet did not return to their home port with increasing frequency. The narrow sea was no longer a safe and private road for them.

Moreover, the English coast grew less and less hospitable. At one time any of the Monk's ships could sail into almost any port east of Portsmouth and demand supplies. Now, if the ships were not well manned and very wary, they were sometimes refused with contumely; sometimes the ships were attacked as they tried to sail out of the harbor; sometimes they were welcomed with apparent friendliness, and, when suspicion was lulled and stores were being loaded, they were attacked.

The truce with Louis ran out at Easter, but Louis was still in France and his men were still roistering in London. Pembroke did not waste this opportunity. He took nearly all of the castles held by Louis's adherents in Surrey, Sussex and Hampshire, including Saer de Quincy's own stronghold in Winchester. Pembroke did not deceive himself that he could hold all these places, but they were stripped of supplies and gold and everything else of value, which went to buy more men for the young king. "Besides," Pembroke said to Adam and Geoffrey, who had gone with him for "something to do," "I prefer the war be fought on the ground of Louis's vassals rather than Henry's."

Gilliane was again frightened, but Adam's letters came every few days without fail and the dreadful terror that choked her life came only in little spurts now and again. At the beginning of April, Geoffrey and Adam returned, unhurt and completely delighted with the good time they had enjoyed, as well as with the loot that bulged the bags and baskets their pack animals carried. Word had come that Louis was on the coast of France, preparing to return to England. The temporary holders of the castles Pembroke had taken were all warned. They were to exact as high a toll in life and goods as they could from Louis's men, and then yield up the places. Stripped as they were, with the new crops barely in or only a few inches high and winter stores exhausted everywhere, the keeps would be as much a burden as an asset to their new captors. Men like Geoffrey and Adam had been dismissed to attend to their own concerns while Pembroke waited to see what Louis would do so that he could lay his own plans.

In London, Osbert was not sure whether or not he was glad Louis was on his way back. His funds were running dangerously low, and he had found a growing reluctance among the resident lords to receive him as a guest. Thus, he certainly needed the prince's patronage. Louis had not received him before he left England, having far more pressing business. Osbert was reasonably sure that the information he had about Adam being the one to blacken FitzWalter's name—although it was very stale news by now—would bring some reward. The lack of funds had also impressed upon Osbert the absolute need to get Tarring back into his hands. It was the only source of income available to him. He knew that it was impossible to return to France. Now that his father was dead, his brother would be far more likely to kill him than to support him. Tarring it must be, even if he must fight for it.

At that idea, Osbert shuddered and his mind squirmed away from the images of pain and terror inherent in an assault. Oh, he would not mind watching. There was pleasure in watching others scream and writhe. But when Osbert felt himself endangered, his sense of enjoyment failed. There must be some other way to regain what was rightfully his. Yet, he knew there was not. If Adam had left the old mercenaries, there might have been a chance of bribing them, perhaps by allowing them to raid and loot the port town. The information from the whores had closed that door, however. Alberic's men were proud of their master, their discipline, even of the respect in which they were held by the townspeople. There might be one or two bad apples in the contingent that held Tarring, but . . .

Osbert's mind swung back to the thought of bad apples. Surely there must be some way to take Tarring by trickery. But what good would one or two men be? Most of the troop believed the sun rose and set on their master. Besides, even if a traitor should allow a few men in by a secret route, the others would fight bitterly and Osbert wanted no part of that. In addition, Osbert was not at all sure he trusted his informants or those who said they did not love Adam. Perhaps they would take a bribe and then run with the information to their master-at-arms. Then a trap could be laid for those entering, and if Louis's men fell into that trap . . . Osbert shuddered.

Still, the idea of getting men into Tarring by trickery lingered. Only, as often as it recurred, the knowledge that it would not prevent a battle from taking place and that, since it was his keep, Osbert would be expected to lead that battle, dimmed the luster of the notion. Two conditions had to be fulfilled before treachery could work to Osbert's satisfaction. First, he had to be out of the battle itself. Second, Adam's men had to be immobilized somehow, so enough of Louis's soldiers could get into Tarring to win a battle. In fact, the best solution would be to find a device that would force Adam's men to yield without fighting at all.

That was it! The first answer that proposed itself was that Adam should be taken prisoner and used; that is, the men should be told Adam would be tortured or killed if they did not yield. Osbert dwelled on that lovingly for a time, especially on what he would do to Adam when his men had yielded and left the keep. He would not kill him . . . no. But Gilbert de Neville would be considered whole of body and mind compared to how he intended to leave Adam. Unfortunately, practicalities imposed themselves on this lovely daydream. Taking Adam prisoner would be as near impossible as taking Tarring single-handed. In addition, the thought of Adam anywhere near him, even in chains, terrified

Osbert so much that his bowels loosened and he had to seek the waste shaft.

Fear of Adam sparked memory. Legally, Adam held Tarring only as Gilliane's overlord. Osbert was stupid but not stupid enough to believe Adam would yield Tarring if Gilliane were dead; however, certainly Adam would prefer to keep her alive. The Church was a powerful enemy, and Osbert believed the Church would support his claim because of the marriage contract he possessed. Thus, if he could take Gilliane prisoner, Adam's men would have to yield to save her.

Osbert realized this plan was as full of holes as an aged cheese, but there was a seed of hope in it because it did not make him sick with fear. He turned the ideas over and over in his mind until they began to look more and more hopeful. First, he realized it would not be necessary to bribe any of the men-at-arms to get into Tarring. He could get a few of his own men into the keep with very little difficulty. Tarring was not under attack, and, although the guards at the entrance were alert, they did not closely inspect the merchants who entered or the serfs from the outer farms bringing in supplies.

Entrance would be easy, but where the men would hide, how they would seize Gilliane and what they would say to the men within the keep was near impossible to devise. Even Jean would not be able to do what needed to be done. Besides, Osbert did not really trust Jean anymore. Ever since Gilliane had escaped from Pierre, and Pierre had somehow been killed, Jean had been different—sullen and suspicious. Then, a really brilliant notion came to him. He could enter Tarring himself. Fear flicked him, but it died down quickly. The thing must be done while Adam was away, of course. There was no chance of discovery by Adam's men, for none of them had ever seen him. He knew where to hide. He knew the keep well. He knew just how to handle Gilliane. Had she not been quiet and docile

all the time he was near to control her? That fool
Pierre had somehow relaxed his vigilance and lost his
power over Gilliane. Osbert was not at all sure how it
had happened, but he was certain it was Pierre's fault.
Gilliane was nothing.

Another brilliant flash came to Osbert. Everyone
would consider it a very brave act to enter Tarring with
only a few men. The ugly rumors about him, the nasty
looks and contemptuous remarks would be stilled. He
giggled. For those lame-brained oxen who were good
only for hacking each other apart, it would be dangerous. Those idiots would not know how to get into
the women's quarters without being noticed or how to
frighten or hurt a woman so that she would consent
to call the guards away from the small postern. Two of
Osbert's men could then pretend to guard it and, instead, let in Louis's troops. Again he giggled. If he had
to get to the women's quarters without being noticed,
he could not wear armor and could not be expected to
join the fighting.

A frown replaced the smile of delight that had been
wreathing his features. There might be some danger
after all. He was sure he could get in and force Gilliane to obey him, but what if Adam's men did not
care about whether he killed her and refused to yield?
They could not sneak a whole army in through that
postern. Then he smiled again in relief. With Adam
gone and with no fighting in the vicinity, there would
not be many men-at-arms in the keep. Also, with no
alarm, only the guards would be armed. Louis's men
could fall upon the others before they could protect
themselves. Really, only a small troop would be necessary.

Osbert thought and thought, refining his plan until
he grew so fond of it, so secure in his belief that he
could do the thing, that his confidence carried over to
Louis when he finally obtained audience with the prince.
Louis was beginning to regret heartily his treatment of

the English barons. It had lost him the young William Marshal, Arundel, Warrenne, their vassals and a number of lesser knights. Although he was still not ready to see any power pass into English hands, he had sharply curbed the tongues and manners of his French adherents and was eager to do anything he could to please FitzWalter, de Quincy, and the others who still held by their oaths to him.

Thus, he listened more attentively to Osbert than he might otherwise have listened to so contemptible an individual, and actually gave some thought to the idea he proposed. He summoned FitzWalter and told him Adam Lemagne had been responsible for the insult done him. More, he assured FitzWalter that he would do all in his power to obtain vengeance for him and urged him to listen to Osbert's suggestion. Again Osbert detailed what could be done and his confidence grew stronger because of Louis's belief in him. Then Louis proposed that if Osbert succeeded he would give the overlordship of Tarring to FitzWalter, if FitzWalter would accept Osbert as his vassal to hold Tarring.

Everyone was happy with this notion. Osbert would have Tarring—he thought. FitzWalter knew he could remove Osbert and put his own man into Tarring at a few hours' notice any time he decided to do so. Louis thought that it would not even be necessary to remove Osbert. He could send a knight along to "help" Osbert in case he could not lead into battle the troop that took the keep. The knight would remain and "help" Osbert manage Tarring so that Louis's will rather than Fitz-Walter's would be done—in case a difference of opinion should arise between him and FitzWalter. All thought hungrily of the good, if small, port below Tarring. Secure ports were growing harder and harder to find on the southern coast.

FitzWalter raised the first practical objection. He pointed out that Osbert's scheme depended upon Gilliane being alone in Tarring. According to what Osbert had said, she was not now in the keep, and how did they know that Adam would not accompany her when she returned? Louis agreed that they would have to wait until Gilliane was alone in Tarring but, he added with a smile, if Adam should return with her, he would not long remain.

"From all I have heard of Lemagne, he is a man of war. There will be war enough in this realm to draw him away from Tarring—that I promise you."

CHAPTER TWENTY-FIVE

When Adam returned from "amusing himself" with taking keeps from Louis's supporters, he found a good deal of business awaiting his approval. Sir Richard had been left in Wick. When he had seen Adam apparently fall under the onslaught of Sir Matthew's hidden men, Sir Richard had been determined to avenge his young overlord. He was so full of the rage of grief that he hacked his way through Sir Matthew's guard and killed the man outright, even though Sir Matthew was injured, weaponless, and could not defend himself. Later, when the fighting died down and the dead were pulled off the living, he found Adam at the bottom of the heap, gasping between pain and laughter but quite unwounded. Adam had gone down deliberately and his men had been instructed to kneel above and around him with their shields raised to form a near invulnerable defensive "turtle."

In his joy at finding Adam unhurt—except for the bruises caused by Cuthbert and another overenthusiastic man kneeling right on top of him in their desire to be sure he was safe—Sir Richard did not question the stratagem. It had served its purpose excellently. Sir Edmund and Sir Andrew had had time to enter the keep over the drawbridge; he and Sir Philip had rushed from the towers without loss, while all attention was on subduing Adam and protecting Sir Matthew. Only

later Sir Richard wondered whether the stratagem had
been even cleverer than he first thought and designed
to accomplish a deeper purpose. Adam knew his men
loved him. Adam knew Sir Richard hated Sir Matthew.
Had Adam wished to be sure Sir Matthew would be
killed and therefore allowed everyone to believe he was
dead? Did he not expect that rage and grief would drive
someone to kill Sir Matthew without thought of ransom
or giving him a chance to yield?

It was not a question Sir Richard had any intention
of asking his overlord. Again, it was something that,
possibly, just skirted complete honesty. Nonetheless,
added to the performance in falsetto voice, the whole
thing gave Sir Richard a great feeling of confidence. It
seemed to him that it was scarcely necessary to worry
about the future. Quite aside from the fact that the
king's party seemed in a fair way of gaining the upper
hand, Sir Richard was growing quite sure that Adam
would find a device to keep them all safe, no matter
who eventually won the war.

Thus, when Adam had settled what to do with Sir
Matthew's wife and children and had seen the loot
divided properly, Sir Richard had been willing to remain at Wick, sieve out the hired men-at-arms to find
a new troop to hold the castle, and, in general, arrange
for the administration of the land and the port that
Wick controlled. Sir Edmund and Sir Philip had been
freed to return home with their share of the booty. Sir
Andrew promised to stop at Glynde and make sure that
Sir Richard's wife and second son, who had been
called home while his father and elder brother were
away, were well and faced no military emergency. A
month had seen the end of all the necessary tasks. Wick
seemed quiet and ready to accept its new master. Sir
Richard now wanted to go home. He had the priest in
the town write to Roselynde to beg Lady Gilliane to
choose a castellan to hold Wick.

Adam raised his eyes from Sir Richard's letter, which

had remained unanswered awaiting his arrival, and looked at Gilliane. "It is your keep," he said neutrally. "Do you have someone in mind to be castellan of Wick?"

In Gilliane's mind, Alinor's strictures rang, echoing Adam's statement. *They are your lands, your people.* Obviously, Adam expected her to choose a castellan or he would have immediately suggested someone himself. But how could she name someone? She did not know any noblemen, except the men she had met at Roselynde, and they were all too exalted personages to be castellans for her. Then desperation spurred her keen mind.

"I did think that perhaps Sir Richard's son—if he has done well by Tarring—would be suitable. If you think him too young, my lord, I am afraid you will have to choose for me. I am sorry to seem so useless to you, but I beg you to remember that I know very few people in this country."

A mixture of emotions held Adam momentarily silent. Alinor looked with pride on her protégé. Geoffrey and Ian nodded sharply.

"If the relation between father and son is loving, you have made a shrewd choice, Gilliane," Geoffrey remarked, with a lift of his brow. "The one will be hostage for the good behavior of the other. Sir Richard will be more loyal for the upraising of his son, and the young Richard will be more assiduous in his duties and careful of his honor to give credit to his father. What is more, when the old man dies, you will have Wick available for a fresh bestowal."

Flushing slightly because he suspected Geoffrey had spoken at length to cover his own muteness, Adam said, "They are very loving, and Sir Richard is a fine, honest man. If the son follows the path set by the father, I must agree that Gilliane has made a good choice."

"I hope he may," Gilliane put in, "but I know no

more of him than you do, my lord. If you have another you would prefer to hold Wick, I will yield most readily to your better knowledge."

She was aware that Adam had been surprised and uneasy at her choice and sought to placate him, but her wildest guess could not have fallen upon the reason. Adam had been pricked by jealousy. When he had asked Gilliane to name a castellan, he had half feared she might put forward someone unknown to him who was Louis's man. He did not really think this would happen, but could not resist testing her. What he truly expected—since she could have appointed anyone while the letter lay at Roselynde unanswered—was that Gilliane would say she knew nothing about the matter and leave it in his hands. Even Alinor and Joanna left such decisions to their husbands.

What Gilliane had said was a pleasant/unpleasant surprise. The pleasant part was encompassed by the facts Geoffrey had pointed out and the pride Adam felt in Gilliane's judgment. This was tempered by the promptness with which she had put forward a candidate who could be considered her man rather than Adam's. No doubt that was a result of his mother's meddling— setting into Gilliane's mind that he desired her lands to add to his heritage. Adam hoped she would have forgotten that, but this suggestion proved that the problem was still in the forefront of her mind. Gilliane did not trust him. Probably that sweet offer to defer to his opinion and accept a man of his choice was a test for him, as he had been testing her. The clever witch! Now, even if he saw a fault in young Sir Richard, he would have to hold his tongue. To put forward his own candidate—his right as her overlord—would convince her he wished to rule her lands.

Then the green-eyed demon rose up to add trouble to that already in Adam's mind. Adam did not see any fault in young Sir Richard, but how could Gilliane know that? It was Adam who had ridden the demesne

with the young man and taken him into the town clustered around the harbor. Had Gilliane also found time,
when Adam was not by, to discuss the management of
Tarring keep with young Richard? If she had, how did
it come about that she had never mentioned his name
until this moment? Was it not suspicious—the way she
said she knew no more of him than Adam did?

Adam took hold of himself while his mother dis-
coursed to Gilliane on the advantages and disadvan-
tages of maintaining the same castellan in a keep for a
long period of time. If Adam permitted himself to believe Gilliane desired Sir Richard's son, he must believe
her truly a whore. Only that forenoon when she went
to his chamber to unarm him, she had come to him as
if she wished to swallow him whole instead of only
swallowing his shaft. She was not a drab who would
display the same hot desire for every man who paid.
Adam knew he had never seen, not once, not for a moment, a single look of interest in Gilliane's eyes when
they fixed on another man—not even his stepfather.
She could be just so fine an actress, she was so clever
. . . No! Gilliane was not a whore!

"There is one trouble only with your choice, Gilliane," Adam said slowly. "If we draw young Richard
from Tarring, we will leave it with only Alberic, and—"

"Oh no, my lord. I will go to Tarring," Gilliane cut
him off promptly.

Adam cast a glance of such fury at Alinor that she
almost cried out in protest. Then she laughed. "No,
Adam, we have not quarreled, Gilliane and I, nor have
I pressed her to such hard labor that she feels the need
to flee Roselynde—do you, my dear?"

"Of course not, madam," Gilliane laughed. "I love
Roselynde, and I hope that I will someday be permitted to come again."

"Do not be silly, child," Ian said, smiling. "Come
whenever you like. You need no invitation from us
any more than Adam needs an invitation. You will be

welcome to me and to Alinor whenever you can spare us your company."

"Nonsense, Gilliane," Alinor said at the same time. "You are well beloved here and you are welcome at any time for as long as you like. But you are quite right that it is time for you to return to Tarring. There are many things to which young Sir Richard could not possibly see. I dread to think what muddles the maids have made in weaving and sewing, and you must look to your fields and see over the spring planting so that you can judge what the harvest will be. Otherwise, child, less will come into your granaries than should."

While Alinor described what Gilliane should look for and the best relationship among quantities of barley, wheat, oats, and rye and how she might consider rearranging things if a good balance was not achieved, Adam regained control of his temper. He had never suspected a quarrel between Gilliane and his mother, nor had he thought Alinor had worked Gilliane too hard. Gilliane's desire to return to Tarring had seemed part and parcel of her suspicion that he wanted her lands. Now, again, he was trapped. He could not protest, or he would confirm Gilliane's fears that it was Tarring he wished to have rather than Gilliane.

Adam had hoped to leave Gilliane safe in Roselynde while he went to capture Bexhill. Tarring was a strong keep, but Adam feared that, once he aroused Louis's adherents at Pevensey and Hastings, they might attack Tarring to draw him away from Bexhill. If Gilliane had been at Roselynde, he would have left Tarring to defend itself, merely sending an observer from time to time to make sure the keep was in no danger of falling. With Gilliane inside, Adam was not sure he would be able to hold to this plan. And here was his idiot mother encouraging Gilliane to go home when she knew perfectly well he would be making war in the vicinity.

As his instant anger and panic subsided, Adam realized that Alinor had probably thought the matter over and felt there would be no danger. It was true that Tarring was out of the way of the main action. If Louis's men were not all in the field retaking the keeps Pembroke had seized, they were far more likely to attack him directly than to seek to draw him away by an elaborate subterfuge. Besides, Sir Richard at Glynde was only five miles away and would be glad to show thanks for the favor done his son by sending regular patrols to keep a watch on Tarring. Bexhill was near enough for Adam to defend Tarring with Sir Richard's help and maintain the attack on his objective. Those were calming thoughts, and the notion of being with Gilliane at Tarring while men and supplies were gathered was even pleasanter.

Adam had managed that quick coupling this morning and was in no physical need, but he was finding that such animal satisfaction was the least of his desires. He wanted to *be* with Gilliane, to sit idly by the fire in her bedchamber and talk easily of the estate and the realm and their own plans. He wanted to lie beside her and gaze upon the dark glow of her skin, the red-brown nipples like glossy buds on the summit of her round breasts. He was growing to hate the hurry and the guilt, the need to hide what everyone knew was taking place but politely ignored. He wanted a wife and the right Geoffrey and Joanna had to lie abed together in lazy contentment after their lovemaking. At least in Tarring, he could have something more than the stolen quarter-hours propriety kept them to in Roselynde.

Thus, Adam pushed aside his fears of leaving Gilliane alone in Tarring and joined willingly in the discussion of when the move should be made. That matter settled, the ladies went off to their various duties around the keep and the men remained, idly talking by the fire. Geoffrey yawned widely; he had greeted Joanna as avidly and at considerably greater length than Adam had greeted Gilliane.

Ian grinned at him. "I know that was not only owing to boredom, but do not worry about being too quiet here." Geoffrey snapped his mouth shut and began to protest, but Ian waved him into silence and continued. "I have had a letter from Peter des Roches. He desires that you should come to him, bringing Joanna, as soon as possible. The king, it seems, is most anxious to hear the details of what took place at the Battle of Bouvines. Perhaps Peter wishes to bask in your glory."

"There was not much glory about me at Bouvines," Geoffrey remarked dryly. "All I got from it was a walk like a crab."

"Well, yes, Peter may have been thinking of that, also. Everyone who was there mentions you, how fiercely you fought—yet you were sore wounded." Ian looked at Geoffrey thoughtfully. "Henry is twelve years old now and exceedingly desirous of leading his own army. Peter doubtless counts upon you to be able to hold the balance between making the boy a coward and making him a daredevil."

Geoffrey began to laugh. "You mean I may praise war all I like while being a horrible example of what comes from war. The Bishop of Winchester was ever a subtle devil."

"Now, now, one must not call a bishop of God's Church a devil," Ian remonstrated, also laughing. "Especially when I know he desires to do you good. It would be very wise for you to go and let your cousin know you and bind him in love. Peter knows that this is the time to make a lasting bond with the young king. He is, I hear, very clever and will appreciate your seeing eye, Geoffrey."

"I agree it is a good time to fix our interest with Henry. Yes, indeed, and I am grateful to Peter des Roches for the invitation. I will tell him so." Then he turned to Adam. "Do you want me to carry your appeal to Peter? If it were not that—"

"What appeal?" Adam interrupted blankly.

"Well, I suppose it will be Gilliane's appeal, really, for an annulment of her marriage. I know you are determined to kill this Osbert de Cercy, but God knows when you will be able to get at him. If he is as lily-livered as you believe, he may even have run back to France after his father's death. Surely, you will not wait forever to marry the girl. If she should get with child, it would not be fair to her. I had my doubts in the beginning, but I have none now. Joanna says——"

"Good God, what an idiot I am!" Adam exclaimed. "I never thought of it. Can you believe I could be such a fool as not to realize the marriage could be annulled? Why, why did I not ask Gilliane to write to the Bishop of Winchester from Tarring? Curse me for a fool! Now it is too late."

"What do you mean, too late?" Ian asked in amazement. "Surely, you cannot believe Gilliane is unwilling. Adam! I saw how she greeted you." Suddenly he frowned and said more slowly, obviously reluctantly, "Are you unwilling? Have you changed your mind or do you feel that she . . . that because she . . ."

"No!" Adam exploded furiously. "It is nothing to do with me, even if I were unwilling—which I swear I am not. It is my dearest wish to marry Gilliane—but even if I were unwilling, you know I would wed her after what has passed between us. Gilliane will not marry me—at least, not at this time."

"You are mad!" Ian said forcibly.

"Adam, I do not know what crochet you have taken," Geoffrey put in, "but I tell you the girl is top over tail in love with you. Joanna says she scarce breathes waiting for your letters—although what she can make of such scrawls or what good she can get from so few words I cannot tell. Why do you think she would refuse marriage?"

"Because Mama told her I wanted her lands," Adam said grimly.

"Do not be ridiculous!" Ian exclaimed.

Geoffrey drew in his breath but said nothing.

"I do not mean that Mama used those words to Gilliane, but she must have spoken of how well the lands run with mine. Also, I heard her myself when she was speaking to Arundel say that she would not be so behind-hand as to fail to fix the Neville estates into our family. Gilliane heard it, too. She was so angry she would not look at me for near half an hour, until I . . . well, never mind that."

"Are you sure?" Ian asked. "She does not seem at all that kind. She is so gentle."

"She is gentle enough," Adam agreed bitterly. "She will not rail at me nor throw things nor stamp her feet and shout as Mama does. I know that. Simply, she will excuse and delay and find contrary reasons . . . she will not marry me. She all but said so. She said . . . no, never mind what she said, but the sense of it was that she loved me but would not have me for a husband."

"Now, that does not make sense," Geoffrey ventured, "although I must admit that it is most unfortunate Lady Alinor was constrained to make that statement to Arundel in Gilliane's hearing. And it is not surprising the girl should be angry, but if she loves you . . . you are already her overlord, and you—"

"I do not know what is in her head," Adam interrupted. "Do you know why Joanna does the things she does? I have tried to tell Gilliane that I desire only her, that she may rule Tarring and her men as she chooses—within reason and within the bounds of her oath to me and mine to Henry—but she will not listen."

"What do you mean, she will not listen?" Ian asked.

Adam blushed. "She . . . er . . . diverts me."

Geoffrey bit his lip to suppress a smile. Joanna often "diverted" him from topics she did not choose to discuss that way. To look to Ian was no help. He was showing such deep interest in the servants who were setting up tables for a meal that Geoffrey imagined Ian was also often "diverted" from his purpose in a similar manner. It was not really funny, however. Somehow Adam would have to convince Gilliane he did not wish to reduce her to a powerless puppet. It was a difficult problem made more complex by the past treatment Gilliane had received, and it might take a while to accomplish.

"Then I had better not do anything about an annulment. Once it is granted, she will be meat for the table of any man who can seize her," Geoffrey said slowly.

"I know," Adam sighed. "The thing is, I do not wish to force her again. Once we were wed, she would see I was no different, that I would remain fond and, within reason, let her go her own way. But to fright her again by forcing her . . ."

"No, do not do that," Ian urged sincerely, "and not for her sake, my son, but for your own. It is a thing that curls round and round in a man's mind and taints the sweetest kisses with sour doubt."

"How would you know?" Adam asked with a bitter laugh.

Ian looked past him. "I did not force your mother—well, you know Alinor is not the woman to yield to force—but your father was only a few months dead when I married her, and she loved your father deeply, Adam. There were circumstances . . . John had a grudge against her and I wished to protect her. I . . . er . . . overpersuaded her. I could not forget it. I was a fool. When Alinor accepts a thing, she accepts with a whole heart, but I kept remembering and I twisted her words and looks in my mind until I near ruined us."

"Mama loves you now," Adam assured him anxiously.

"Yes, I know that," Ian replied. "But I made much grief for both of us. Do not worry about it. It is long past. I only told you so you would not make the same mistake."

"But what *am* I to do?" Adam pleaded.

"Perhaps Lady Alinor or Joanna—" Geoffrey began.

"No," Ian interrupted. "At least, not yet. Gilliane loves them and clings to them—poor child, she never had a mother or sister. Adam would be forever wondering whether she married him for their sakes or for his own. Take her back to Tarring, Adam. Do as I do with your mother. Stand behind her while she deals with her people. Take her to Kemp and show her how you rule your own and still treat her with great respect, even when she is in your stronghold. Then ask her outright, assuring her she will still rule her own. I will have copies made of my contract with your mother and of Joanna's with Geoffrey. Let her read them and know that you will sign a similar contract with her. She loves you, Adam. She will yield."

An almost identical conversation took place in the women's quarters the next day while Joanna was helping Gilliane to pack. Ordinarily, Catrin would have packed, but Gilliane had been about to leave behind all the gowns Joanna and Alinor had given her, so Joanna was overseeing a repacking that included the gifts. The discussion began casually enough, with Joanna suggesting that Gilliane send Geoffrey a copy of her marriage contract with a deposition by the castle priest that she had been forced, married without her approval or knowledge. She assured Gilliane that no difficulty would ensue. The Bishop of Winchester would carry the matter before the papal legate, and Gualo would issue the annulment. To her amazement, Gilliane burst into tears and sobbed that Adam did not wish to marry her.

"I know your mother desires it and that you are willing, also, because of the lands, but Adam—"

"That is impossible," Joanna interrupted. "Do not tell me that Adam does not love you!"

"Love? Perhaps," Gilliane sighed, wiping away her tears. "He desires me, that is true, but he was shocked when I told him your mother felt we should marry."

"Nonsense," Joanna exclaimed. "He was the one . . ."

Joanna did not finish that. Adam would not be the first man to change his mind when he found he could have without marriage what he thought he would need to marry to obtain. Moreover, Joanna knew Adam was free enough with any married dame who ogled him or responded to his advances, and she had seen the contempt in his eyes when those women were spoken of— although he himself never admitted or implied any intimate relationship. But such women were a far cry from Gilliane. Gilliane was not of easy virtue. She never looked at another man—not even at Ian. It was cruel and wrong if Adam did not see that. It was cruel and wrong for Adam to punish Gilliane for loving him too well.

"It *is* nonsense," Joanna repeated. "I will speak to him. It is ridiculous—"

"No," Gilliane begged, "no, please. I do not care. If you tell him he is wronging me, he will leave me. I will die! Please!"

Seeing the terror Gilliane felt, Joanna dropped the subject. She was not of a hasty disposition like her mother, and she was prepared to let the situation develop on its own. Particularly after Gilliane and Adam left the next day and Joanna revolved the matter in her mind, she became more and more convinced that Gilliane was mistaken. Adam had never once looked at her with contempt. His face showed desire, admiration, tenderness, teasing affection, occasionally a flash of doubt or anger—never contempt. He must intend marriage. Gilliane had misunderstood some word or look. It was odd that Adam said nothing to her, but he had spoken outright of marriage to Alinor. Joanna smiled. Silly girl. Adam would never go back on his word. Let them work it out for themselves, Joanna thought. The fruit will be all the sweeter for the salt tears that watered the tree of love.

For Adam and Gilliane, it was an easy trip home. They stayed with Arundel one night—on their best behavior, a polite and proper overlord and vassal. The picture was marred a little by the blushes of both under Arundel's heavy-handed teasing, but his wife soon curbed his tongue. The next morning they rode to Wick and Gilliane spoke to Sir Richard on the subject of giving his son Wick to hold. His gratitude and delight promised well for the future of Wick, and for Gilliane's relationship with father and son. He would stay, Sir Richard agreed, until his son came, and put him on the road to good management. Adam and Gilliane spent the day riding the demesne, speaking to the bailiffs and the people of the town, and Adam made sure it was Gilliane who asked the questions and received the answers. The people were still nervous and worried, but that was common when a new overlord took hold, and Gilliane could see that if young Sir Richard was as careful as his father, all would prosper.

The next day they rode to Kemp, where Adam found that Robert de Remy had gone for a few days to Telsey, all being safe and quiet at Kemp. Adam presented Gilliane to his servants and gave orders that they obey her as they would obey him—or else. He then left Gilliane in the keep and rode out to see how matters went in his absence. Gilliane knew she had no rights in Adam's household, but the maidservants flocked around her with questions and appeals, and when she saw the disorder to which all things had come in two years without a mistress, she could not bear it. She started with the sheared wool and stalks of flax, divided, assigned tasks to be performed, sharply settled questions and arguments about whose duty each task would be. Spinning was ordered, the yarns spun in the past examined and accepted or rejected; weaving projects were examined, planned and designed.

Long before her work in the women's quarter was half done, an outdoor maid crept trembling up the stairs to beg the lady if she would be so good as to come to the cooks. Memory stirred in Gilliane of Ian's and Geoffrey's complaints of meals, ill cooked and ill served in Adam's keep. Wondering whether Adam would be offended, but unable to resist the plea, Gilliane went down. A sight of the kitchen sheds nearly made her faint. Such filth! Such waste! Such disorder! Only rigid self-control and self-reminders that these were not her people restrained Gilliane from ordering them all soundly whipped. Her compressed lips and flashing eyes had almost as violent an effect. Perhaps the cooks had expected quick advice on how to flavor a dish; what they got was quite different. A clearance and cleaning were made of two sheds and a portion of the cooking utensils while Gilliane returned to the maids. An hour later she descended to approve the cleaning and to give recipes and instructions on what to cook. Later she came down again to taste and to order more of this and a touch of that to be added.

When Adam rode in, he found the hall set for dinner, the servants mostly seeming to know what to do and when to do it. The service did not move with Roselynde's or Hemel's greased perfection, but it was a far enough cry from the usual madhouse that had prevailed at Kemp that Adam noticed.

"Tsk, tsk," Adam said in Gilliane's ear. "I see I have not broke you of the habit of muddling about with dinner. Food, food, food—all you think of is food."

But publicly he thanked and complimented Gilliane. Aside from the brief teasing, his manner was formal. Except for that teasing and the fact that Adam's eyes were very tender, Gilliane would have been frightened out of her wits. As it was, when Adam took her no further than the stairs and kissed her hand formally in parting with her for the night, tears of mixed gratitude and frustration filled her eyes. It was marvelous that

Adam would not dishonor her, even before his servants, but she wished . . .

The gratitude was a little marred by fear. Was it his reputation or hers with which Adam was concerned, Gilliane wondered. Could he be tiring of her? Neither his looks nor his conversation added to her doubts. On the ride from Kemp to Tarring, Adam was as attentive as any woman could wish. Propriety had to be maintained before Sir Richard's son, but after he left, Adam still only bowed over Gilliane's hand at the stairs. Then fear overwhelmed her and she clutched at him.

"You swore you would not put me aside," she whispered. "Are you tired of me already? Why will you not come up with me?"

Adam knew quite well that he should say he wanted a wife, not a mistress. That if Gilliane did not feel she could trust herself to him in one way, why should she trust him in another? He should have pointed out that if she was willing to share his bed, she should be willing to share all things. Instead, heat washed over him as he looked into her lovely face, flushed with embarrassment and desire. His loins tightened and his knees felt weak.

"It is not my right to come into your women's quarters without your permission," Adam said huskily. "I have been waiting and waiting for you to ask me."

He should have said that it was she who rejected him, she who had no faith, believing he wished to rob her of her lands and her pride. Instead, he pushed her back into the stairwell and kissed her until she shook with desire. They came into the women's quarters handfast, and Gilliane did not care. These were her people, and she would deal with them if so much as a glance was cast askance. That thought flickered through Gilliane's mind, but she never realized how much the thought marked the great change in her in a few short months. After that she thought of nothing besides the deep pleasure of undressing slowly, of caressing Adam and having him caress her without hurry or shame, of the slowly building feelings that drifted over this part and that of her body.

Then there was the big bed, fresh made, sweet scented, and more slow caresses, sweet, idle words, kisses that wandered from fingertip to breast tip, steel-hard hands so light, so gentle, as they fondled a beloved body. There was time for Gilliane to touch also, to giggle and have her laughter broken by passion and giggle again at Adam's reaction to kisses that did not aim at his mouth. Excitement grew and deepened. There was neither anxiety nor weeks of deprivation to drive it into a flashing explosion. The five-day abstinence had built appetite but had not pushed it out of control. The need Gilliane felt for Adam and he for her was hot and steady, like the bright red core of a long-burning Yule log.

There were, this time, no sparks and flashes, no cataclysm of sensation, over too soon. When Adam mounted Gilliane, he arched above her, his lips gently on hers, his shaft touching, entering slowly, so slowly, while both pairs of eyes shut languidly to hold in the exquisite relief and fulfillment. He withdrew as slowly, Gilliane sighing softly at the loss of his pulsing warmth and simultaneously thrilling with joy at the knowledge that her satisfaction would be renewed. Withdrawn, renewed; each time the core of heat grew hotter, as if a steady breath of air flew into the heart of the burning log. Still there was no urge to hurry, no need to find culmination before they should be interrupted.

Nonetheless, each time Adam thrust a little harder, a little quicker, sighing and then moaning softly with each movement. The image of heat grew more intense. Behind her closed eyes, Gilliane could imagine her whole body deep red with lust, then orange as her excitement intensified. Then, at last, a sharper pleasure stabbed her, as if a yellow tongue of flame found a crack in her smoldering body. That stab of fiercer joy, like a split in a log that allows an exit to trapped air and therefore provides for a renewal of the substance that supports fire, broke Gilliane's quiescence. She cried aloud, arched herself upward under Adam's weight. The single tongue of flame changed to a sheet of fire, flashed over her whole body, encompassed her, yellow and then white-hot, an agony of delight. She heard Adam groaning above her, higher, higher, until his voice broke.

There was further joy—no hasty uncoupling, no need for shamefaced straightening of garments. There would be no others waiting, with eyes carefully averted from their faces, lest they see too much. Aware of his weight, Adam turned on his side, lifting Gilliane with him and supporting her on a powerful thigh so that their bodies could remain joined. When eventually they slipped apart, they still lay nestled together. Adam made a lazy comment about a chair in the hall that needed mending. Gilliane riposted, with soft laughter, that chairs were not made to support oxen, but that she would see that it was strengthened, and all the others, too. There was an easy silence, a gentle kiss. Gilliane reminded Adam that she had been cleaning out the lowest level of the keep. The servants had discovered some arms and armor in a dark corner. Likely, they were too rotted to be of use, but would Adam look and see if any could be salvaged?

Both thought longingly that this was what marriage should be, hot and sweet, passion mingled with the small tasks of every day and with time enough for everything. Neither could spoil the ease and sweetness by speaking of what each feared the other did not desire. It must be enough for me, Gilliane thought. Let me not be so mad as to lose all my joy for a few words mumbled by a priest. I will have her, Adam resolved. I will give her these few weeks, until I return from Bexhill. Then I will force her, if I must, despite what Ian said. He feared my mother still loved my father and did not love him. I know Gilliane loves me.

It will be different for me. But the idea lay heavy and cold in Adam's mind. He did not want to force Gilliane into anything. He did not want a wife who would watch him fearfully for a change of heart or a desire to steal her heritage.

CHAPTER TWENTY-SIX

Adam and Gilliane had almost three weeks of near-perfect joy. Except for odd moments now and then, both forgot they were not husband and wife. Adam strewed dirty garments over Gilliane's neat bedchamber, played silly tricks on her, lost his temper and roared over nothing as was his habit when he was perfectly at ease. Gilliane picked up the dirty garments, scolded him, laughed at his jokes, yielded, made him laugh, or even, a few times, gave him his own again to cure his bad temper. They were not too much nor too little in each other's company. Adam was recruiting and training men for the assault on Bexhill, changing and improving the machines and defensive armament of Tarring; Gilliane was molding Tarring, its demesne, and the town it controlled into as close an image of Roselynde as she could make it. Her methods were not identical with Alinor's, but the results were equally good.

The port was not really Gilliane's, of course. It had a charter and was governed by its mayor and aldermen. When things ran smoothly, Gilliane had little contact with the townsfolk and was not terribly interested in their doings. She had enough to occupy her among the people directly under her control. Thus, she was not aware of a special visitor in one merchant's house. She was aware that the merchant brought goods to the castle with greater frequency than others in the town and that his prices were lower and that he seemed desperately eager to please her. Since Gilliane recognized him as the merchant she had both punished and saved, his behavior did not seem unusual to her. It was logical that he should be both grateful and eager to prove that his practices had changed for the better.

Life was easy and sweet in Tarring, undisturbed by the news that came regularly from Roselynde. Geoffrey had managed to convince the young king that, at present, his presence on the battlefield would be a great danger to his men. As an example, he pointed out how, when his own father had thought only of saving him, Salisbury had been struck down. Bouvines was lost anyway, Geoffrey agreed, but something might have been saved if Salisbury's attention had not been distracted. If every leader was thinking more of the king than of the battle, disaster must ensue. Geoffrey and Joanna had then gone home to Hemel where Joanna would lie in near the end of June. After the family news, Alinor reported briefly Louis's success in reoccupying the castles Pembroke had taken while the prince was in France. This was expected and did not trouble Adam; he continued his preparations for the attack on Bexhill.

Osbert listened to the merchant's and the whores' reports on Adam's progress and licked his lips with anticipation. His plans had been enlarged after he had reported the object of Adam's warlike preparations. His own part remained unchanged, but, when the position of Bexhill had been pointed out, it had seemed reasonable to Louis that Lemagne should be punished for his activities against Lewes and Knepp and for the shame he had caused FitzWalter.

With Pevensey less than ten miles to the west and Hastings not much more than six miles east, it would be easy enough to fall upon Lemagne from both directions and smash him like a roach. They would not need extra men. The garrisons could be stripped from

Pevensey and Hastings for the day or two that would be needed to attack and defeat Lemagne with the help of the garrison of Bexhill. Their advantage would be increased because Lemagne would not expect any attack. He would reason that Louis's forces would all be occupied with destroying Pembroke's work and in the new attack upon Dover that Louis had begun.

This device would regain for Louis not only Tarring itself but Kemp and Wick and, indeed, all the properties Lemagne controlled. An additional security and advantage would be that Louis himself would be near at hand to see that nothing went wrong. The prince had not forgotten the danger and embarrassment he had undergone when he tried to leave England in February. He had resolved to take Dover once and for all, and ensure himself both an escape route, if necessary, and free entry for reinforcements and supplies. Since Dover was only about forty miles from Hastings, Louis could have news within the day of Lemagne's doings and could swiftly order attack or change the plans to suit the situation.

However, Louis was not to have everything his own way. As soon as the prince invested Dover, gracing the siege with his own person and swearing publicly that he would not move from that place until it was his, Pembroke put his own plans into operation. He had determined, as his first move, to clean out any stronghold of Louis's that thrust into territory largely loyal to the king. In pursuit of this plan, he instructed the earls of Chester and Ferrars to besiege Mountsorel and sent out summons to the other vassals of the king to join him in Newark on the first of May to give Mountsorel the *coup de grâce*.

Adam received this summons on April twentieth and cursed luridly for ten minutes before he shouted for the priest to write summoning letters to his own men. He dictated the text quickly, having the wording by heart, adding fresh only where and when they were to meet him. Then, while Father Paul set about writing the correct number of copies, leaving blank the place for the name of each man, Adam began to count up the force each would provide. Suddenly, the blasphemies he had been uttering, which had been making Father Paul wince, although he had sense enough not to make any reprimand, and making Gilliane wring her hands because she did not understand why Adam was so angry, ceased. Adam's eyes began to sparkle with pleasure rather than flash with rage and smiles replaced grimly gritted teeth.

"The dear old devil," he exclaimed, "he remembered I wished to take Bexhill."

"Then you do not have to go?" Gilliane breathed.

"Oh, I must go. That is of no account. What is important is that he called me to bring no more men than my own castellans will provide. Also, the times fall in excellently. I summoned Sir Richard and the others to come on the last day of May, you remember."

"Yes, I remember," Gilliane replied, trying desperately to hide her disappointment and fear.

Adam looked at her doubtfully. Was she going to try to keep him from answering this summons? "You agreed it was the best time, with all the spring planting finished and before the first haying so that the men pulled off the land would work no hardship on the crops," he pointed out.

"Yes," Gilliane agreed. She had accepted that date because it was the latest Adam would agree to.

"Well, then, you must see why I am pleased. My term of service for this summons will run only until June tenth, and I am sure Pembroke will allow me to substitute Robert de Remy for myself for the last ten or fifteen days. Thus, this summons will not interfere at all with my taking of Bexhill."

"No, I see," Gilliane said in a strangled voice, and turned away.

She made blindly for the nearest wall chamber where

she could pretend to busy herself with something—
anything—until she could choke down the fear that had
risen up to blanch her face and restrict her voice. It
would be worse, alone in Tarring, than it had been
when Adam left from Roselynde, where she had Joanna and Alinor for exemplars and comforters. In the
privacy of the wall chamber, tears and terror made her
even blinder so that she could not see the storage chests
and she stumbled ahead until she walked right into
the wall. There she clung, pressing her face against the
cold, rough stone. Her heart was hammering so hard
that she could hear nothing except the blood pounding
in her ears. She was not aware that Adam had followed
her until he spoke.

"I will not endure it," he snarled. "When you accepted me as overlord, you accepted the fact that I
was Henry's man. What is it that binds you to Louis?
That makes you weep and quarrel with me each time
I act against his good?"

The sound of Adam's voice made Gilliane jump as
if he had lashed her with a whip, but what he said
made no sense at all. "Louis?" she gasped, turning and
leaning back against the wall. "Who is Louis?"

"What lunacy is this?" Adam bellowed. "Do you
think me an idiot, that you can hide your wishes by
pretending you do not know I speak of the Prince of
France?"

"What has the Prince of France to do with me or
you?" Gilliane shrieked, completely unbalanced by
Adam's rage and her own fear. "What do I care for his
good or ill? If I weep and quarrel, it is only to stop
you from running to war. May a pox take Louis! I do
not care if they all die of a pox—Louis, Henry, Pembroke, Sir Godfrey, all! All! Only let them cease from
tearing you away from me."

This time there were no modest, downcast eyes, no
soft murmurs of excuse, no reason. Even Adam could
read no pretense into the naked fury of Gilliane's

response. In that moment, what Geoffrey had assured him, and his mother, and Joanna, was hammered home and Adam realized what an ass he had been. It was true Gilliane had opposed the taking of Wick and Bexhill—but those were the places that would not yield except by war. Whenever Adam's purpose could be accomplished by peaceful means, Gilliane had aided and encouraged him most enthusiastically. In fact, several times when he would have resorted to force to bring her men to heel, Gilliane had shown him a way to lead them willingly to loyalty—which was far more detrimental to Louis's cause in the long run than subduing unwilling men. Geoffrey had struck it right, as usual. Gilliane had no political particularity.

As that thought and what she had said came together in his mind, Adam choked. "My love," he said softly, but in a voice shaking with laughter as he gathered Gilliane into his arms, "it is most unkind of you to wish the pox on a sweet child no more than twelve years old and on an old man who loved my father and who loves me and, even though he summons me to war, will do his uttermost to protect me. You may have the others—for all of me, both Louis and Sir Godfrey may take the pox and die of it, and have a bloody flux and suppurating sores, too."

"Very well," she said, smiling amidst her tears, "I will withdraw my wish that a pox take those you love, but I cannot love them—not now when it is to serve them that you leave me. I swear I will love them well every moment we are together."

Adam hugged her tight and then loosened his grip, but he had felt her trembling and he understood. "Then to engage your love for those who love me, I will keep you longer with me by a few days. I must go north, and I know Louis is at Dover, so the way past London is not dangerous. What would you say to bide with me as far as Hemel? Geoffrey is doubtless summoned to Mountsorel also. It would be good for Joanna, breed-

ing as she is and heavy now, to have you with her.
My mother desired that she stay in Roselynde, but she
would not. She insisted that Geoffrey's child be born
in Geoffrey's keep."

Half Gilliane's trouble flew away when she knew she
would not be alone. Nothing could completely remove
her anxiety, but to know she could share it, and that
she might be able to lighten Joanna's spirit or be of
use to her, made it possible to conceal the occasional
stabs of terror that continued to torture her. She was
very busy in the few days she remained in Tarring. The
keep was to be thoroughly cleaned while she was away
and was to be shut tight, only the bound serfs and a
few men-at-arms remaining. No one was to be permitted to enter for any reason—no supplies to be
bought or merchandise to be accepted.

When this news trickled down to Osbert, he nearly
had a fit. His patience had been sufficiently tried when
Adam idled at Tarring for so long. He had believed
that the attack on Bexhill would begin soon after Adam
and Gilliane arrived. Had it not been that Louis was
besieging Dover and might take it into his head to
order an assault at any time, Osbert might have returned to the prince to report to him. Had he sufficient
money or any rich friends there, he would certainly
have returned to London. As things were, he had to
stay where he was. He was at least safe from battle
and had sufficient food and drink. Although he knew
this would be an excellent time to assault Tarring, he
did not send a messenger to say it was bare of defense.
There would be no excuse for him to avoid fighting in
this situation—and Adam would be free to take Tarring
back again. He had no choice but to wait until Gilliane
returned.

The most industrious pressure on the whores who
spied for him produced no answer to the question of
when this would happen. The men-at-arms who had
been left in the keep knew nothing, except that in case

of any threat they were to ride for help to Sir Richard at Glynde. No one would dream of telling servants or men-at-arms the plans of their master unless they had some duty directly connected with those plans. Thus, no one bothered to inform them that Gilliane would return to Tarring on the twenty-seventh or twenty-eighth of May to prepare for the arrival of her men on or about the thirtieth.

Adam left Gilliane with Joanna—who greeted her with tears of joy and relief—on April twenty-eighth. He hurried north the same day, because Joanna told him that Pembroke was camped at Northampton, only thirty miles away. The quicker they had enough men to storm Mountsorel, Adam thought, the quicker he could get leave to go about his own business.

Nothing, however, works as planned. Within each party there were traitors, and Pembroke's intentions were no secret to Louis. Naturally, Pembroke was not ignorant of this fact, but he was relatively sure Louis was set on cracking Dover and that the prince could not be diverted from this purpose by an attack on an outlying castle that was not even held by a Frenchman. Mountsorel was one of Saer de Quincy's keeps—a dower property of his wife.

What Pembroke had not counted on was the bitterness of the English rebels. When the news of the siege came to de Quincy, he asked for leave to bring help to his castle. Louis denied this, saying he could not believe it necessary. Lincoln, a keep of the same type, had been besieged for months and still showed no signs of falling. Saer said nothing just then, although it was plain that he was not pleased, but when the news came that an army was assembling to aid the besiegers, de Quincy exploded.

First Louis tried to calm him by promising him the next equivalent keep they took. That brought Fitz-Walter to his feet, red with fury, to scorn the promise. Louis, he pointed out, had never given an English

baron anything. Even Hertford, to which FitzWalter
had a clear and valid claim and for which he had
fought, had been handed over to a French land-seeker.

"We shed our blood on which the vermin who follow
you from France batten and gorge themselves," de
Quincy roared. "What you lose is our loss—who has
paid me for what was reft from Winchester?—but what
we gain is gain for you and your French maggots alone.
Not this time, my lord. If I stand by you longer, my
children will be worse starvelings than the creatures you
have brought to fatten on our lands. Better for me to
yield myself prisoner to the king. He might take my
head, yes, but I would at least be able to bargain for
my children's welfare—and be able to trust the bargain
would be kept."

"When I gave fealty to you," FitzWalter added, "you
swore to be my good overlord and save me from
injury. I wonder now whether your love or John's hate
has done me greater hurt."

Apparently, this time matters had gone too far to
be mended with sweet words. Inwardly, Louis swore
to be avenged for this stupidity, which might cost him
Dover, but he knew he would have to satisfy de Quincy
or lose the English party en masse. He agreed that an
army might be mustered to relieve Mountsorel. Having
a finger, FitzWalter and de Quincy promptly tried to
bite off the hand. They demanded that Louis come
himself, that the siege of Dover be lifted and the whole
force march north. They argued that Dover could not
be taken with half the men anyway, while the whole
army could accomplish much in the Midlands.

This suggestion threw Louis into a rage. He had not
forgotten the campaign of the previous autumn. They
had taken some keeps, true, but they had lost almost
as many in the south, which was far more important to
Louis, being richer, more populous, and of easier ac-
cess to France. He had nearly been trapped in England, in fact. Perhaps that was what the English lords

wanted, believing he would be more in their power
that way. They could go and take their own men, he
allowed, but he would not leave Dover until it was his.
His anger did not produce the result he expected. Fitz-
Walter answered roundly that they had helped him win
fifty castles (which was an exaggeration, but no one
worried about that). If he would not help them protect
one—which was his duty as their overlord—let him
give them twenty-five of what he had gained and let
him see if he could take even one more without their
help.

Neither could really afford to lose the other, in spite
of harsh words. Eventually a compromise was reached.
Louis convinced them he could not go; he had sworn
an oath not to leave Dover. However, he would send his
deputy, the Count of Perche, with enough of his troops
to make up six hundred knights and twenty thousand
footmen.

By April thirtieth, this army was approaching St.
Albans. Terrified villagers, fleeing the undisciplined
force, which was permitted to loot and raid as it liked
on the road north, warned Joanna. Gilliane watched her
color fade and her hands go protectively to her swollen
belly. Then she drew herself up and snapped orders to
the master-at-arms.

"Let fifty men, in two bands of twenty-five, all
horsed, go to patrol the south and east borders of the
lands. They are not to kill *all* the looters. Drive some,
especially the badly wounded and those you will maim
by chopping off their hands, back toward the main
force. Let it seem as if there are as many men here as
when my lord held the lands with Lord Ian. If there
are too many, or if it is seen that the main force is
coming here to Hemel, return at once."

"Yes, lady."

"On your way out, send me the chief huntsman and
two messengers."

While Joanna explained the situation to the huntsman, Gilliane wrote two notes reporting the movement of a large army northward. The messengers were dispatched with the notes to be delivered either to Adam or to Geoffrey. This was all they knew at the moment, Gilliane wrote. They would send more news as soon as they had more information. Meanwhile, Joanna bid her huntsman hide his men in various places where they could see the keep.

"If we are attacked," she said, "you must go seek Lord Geoffrey and Sir Adam, who will be with the Earl of Pembroke's army. Try first at Northampton, and if you do not find them there, follow their trail until you come to them. Give them the news that we are besieged and that I, and Lady Gilliane with me, will hold the keep at all costs until they can come to us."

Offense, warning to Pembroke, and an appeal for help arranged, Joanna turned to defense. Those men who were left in the keep were told their stations. The menservants were gathered and stations appointed for them also. They could throw stones, help push ladders from the walls, wind crossbows, heat and pour pitch, sand, and oil. Barrels of these were raised to the battlements, layers of stones laid ready for fires to be lighted upon. Arms were gathered and distributed, even to the unskilled, and such armor as was available dealt out.

Amid all the signs of a defense against hopeless odds, even when twice bands of looters escaped Joanna's patrols and approached the keep so that troops had to be sent out to fight them, Gilliane was not aware of any fear, except her anxiety over Joanna's condition. With regard to her own safety, she felt no qualms at all. When she had time to think about it two days later, after all danger of being attacked had passed and Hemel was back to normal, Gilliane laughed heartily.

"I have been afraid all my life," she explained to Joanna, who wanted to know at what she was laughing, "and now I am never afraid—or, at least, never afraid for myself. I am afraid for Adam, of course. No, do not tell me it is silly, that he is a better fighter than any man you have ever seen. It does not matter."

"I was not going to say that," Joanna replied, smiling. "I know it does not help. Adam tells me I need not fear for Geoffrey, but I do. And I fear for my little one also. But me? I can take care of myself. Why should I fear for myself? Even if Hemel should fall, Geoffrey would come, or Ian or Adam or Mama."

"Yes, I suppose that is why I have changed," Gilliane said slowly. "There was no one who would come, before I knew Adam. But it is more than that. It is something in me. I never thought before that I could take care of myself. Now I think I can."

Pembroke had heard of the army advancing on Mountsorel before Gilliane's notes reached Adam and Geoffrey. To avoid being caught between two fires—the garrison in the keep and the advancing force—he ordered the earls of Chester and Ferrars to raise the siege and retreat to Nottingham. They would then be north of Mountsorel, whereas Pembroke at Northampton was south of it. If they could catch the rebel force in an untenable position, they would attack. For the moment, however, that army was so spread out that little would be gained by chasing one small group after another. Meanwhile, more summons were sent out and some men delayed on the way were still drifting in to swell Pembroke's army. It was still a waiting game, but Pembroke was not discouraged. Louis's men were ripe for mischief. They would not sit still at Mountsorel.

That decision was being echoed inside Mountsorel. The Count of Perche, never tactful, sighed that after this wild goose chase he supposed there was nothing to do but return to Dover. Then he made some acid and unwise remarks about de Quincy's anxieties. "In the future," he suggested, sneering, "it might be just as well to send a horde of servants with painted jerkins to drive the English away. Since they never stay to fight, they would never know the difference. A fine waste of men and money it has been to bring six hundred good knights and twenty thousand seasoned footmen to chase a bunch of timid hares."

Although de Quincy and FitzWalter had little love for Pembroke, they smarted under the insults directed at the English. Coupled with Pérche's comments about de Quincy's anxiety for his property, the remarks seemed as much directed at them as at the men who had retreated from their approach.

"The victorious French," de Quincy remarked dryly, "have not made much headway with Dover."

Perche frowned, then shrugged. "There are exceptions to every rule, but de Burgh at Dover seems to be the *only* exception to this one."

"That is all you know of it," FitzWalter taunted. "A simple woman has kept your constable of Arras fuming and biting his nails at her gate for months. I heard she even spit in his eye."

"That was not the constable of Arras," Perche snapped, and then, realizing he had betrayed his knowledge of Nicolaa de la Hay's spirited resistance, he raised his brows. "It is no surprise she can hold out," he sneered. "All Gilbert de Gant has is a few hundred men. How long do you think she would resist us? Or do you hesitate to assault Lincoln's walls?"

"We?" de Quincy threw back in Perche's own tone. "*We* have been begging your master to finish off these centers of infection, but he is so desirous of securing a route of escape from the 'frightened hares' of Englishmen that he will not move ten miles from the river in London or the seaports of the coast."

That remark was not accepted with good grace, but, when the wrangling over insults died down, it was clear that both parties were essentially agreed. Since they had been deprived of a chance to do the king's party an injury at Mountsorel, they would do them a worse injury by taking Lincoln. At least their long march would not have been wasted.

Pembroke had the news that Louis's men were on the march through the vale of Belvoir toward Lincoln on May twelfth, and the old man wept with joy, sinking down on his knees to raise his hands in thankful prayer. "I would thank God fasting," he said to those around him, smiling grimly, "but I will need my strength to fight."

In attacking Lincoln, the French and rebel force would be placing themselves in exactly the same position the English had retreated from at Mountsorel. In fact, they would be in a worse position because Lincoln was in an area largely controlled by the king's adherents. Nottingham, Newark, and Sleaford were all loyal keeps and could serve as havens in case of defeat or provide reinforcements if a few hundred more men could turn the tide toward victory.

Everyone was cheered by the news. Many wished to pursue the force up the valley of the Belvoir, but wiser heads prevailed. The French foot soldiers were the refuse and scum of the country, swept out of the prisons and alleys and forced into Louis's army as much to rid France of them as to help in the taking of England. To discipline them was near impossible, even if their leaders had desired to do so. Also, because the region was king's country, they were actively encouraged to loot. It was, in fact, necessary to the lives of these men, who, poor wretches, were often sent to England without enough clothing to cover their bodies—although some kind of arms was given to them. The situation was much the same as when the army had advanced on Mountsorel. Once they had arrived at Lincoln, however, they would be gathered together. Furthermore, when the baggage animals were unloaded, it was less likely that the French could retreat with their goods so that the possibility of loot for Pembroke's men would be greatly increased.

Pembroke, therefore, took his men wide after gathering in Newark and continued north so that they could come at Lincoln from the northwest. On the night of May nineteenth, Pembroke, attended by his son William and Faulk de Breauté, rode to the Earl of Salisbury's quarters to thank him for coming in such haste halfway across England. There he found Ian, Geoffrey, Adam, and Peter des Roches regaling themselves on roast venison—William of Salisbury, being an old campaigner, had thoughtfully carried with him a stag's carcass and several small barrels of wine. Pembroke nodded in satisfaction as he accepted one of several pieces of meat held out to him on eating knives. He had rather hoped to find this group together. If they agreed to his plans, he would have a formidable bloc of opinion behind him, which would cut down any chance of wrangling over who should do what.

Adam and Geoffrey rose hastily and proffered their stools to Pembroke and de Breauté. Salisbury shouted for his squires to bring blankets and skins to sit on and three more cups of wine. Geoffrey made some jest about the young sitting at the feet of the wise, and Peter des Roches convulsed everyone by hastily hiding his feet under his stool and complaining that he refused to lend his feet for such a purpose. If that big ox Adam sat at them, he explained, he would be crippled for life. Somehow, amid the laughter, the slight feeling of constraint that lingered between those who had been steadily faithful to the king and those who had wavered disappeared.

For the few who were not familiar with Lincoln, Ian described the town and keep. These were separated, as were Roselynde keep and Roselynde town, the keep on a high plateau above the town, which was surrounded by the old Roman walls to the east, west and north. To the southwest lay the keep itself, and southeast, opposite it, the cathedral. The town had long been in the hands of Louis's partisans, yielded against Lady

Nicolaa's will by the bishop, and Gualo had given permission to treat the renegade churchmen who preached to and supported the French as common enemies. De Breauté, who was even more familiar with the area, added some details, including the fact that there was a small postern door in the west wall through which, with Lady Nicolaa's permission, they could enter the keep. Peter des Roches offered himself as ambassador to Lady Nicolaa, to gain permission for entry, but Pembroke objected.

"It will take too long," he said. "If more than one man at a time could come through the gate, de Gant would have forced it long ago. Either we would be attacked while waiting to enter the city, which would mean we would be at a disadvantage because they are many more than we are—"

"It will not do to mount an assault on the walls," de Breauté said.

To that, there was instant agreement. De Breauté had been accused of many things during his lifetime, most of them with justice—he had been called cruel, devious, dishonest, grasping, irreligious and immoral—but there were two things no man had ever said of him. No one had ever impugned either his loyalty or his courage. He was, in fact, brave to the point of foolhardiness. If Faulk de Breauté said Lincoln's walls could not be assailed, they could not.

"I never thought of the walls," Pembroke agreed, "but we came to break into Mountsorel. We have engines of war with us and ready. Let us attack the three gates."

Adam groaned softly. He knew what that meant. They would sit around for weeks waiting for the rams to batter down the gates, which would be constantly reinforced by those inside the town. Probably it would take so long that the attack on Lincoln would begin just when Adam should be back in Tarring to lead Gilliane's men against Bexhill. On top of that, they would be bored to death, the only excitement when archers shot at them from the walls, or . . .

"Oh, I say," Adam burst out. "Archers!"

"Archers? What use are archers against the gates of Lincoln?" Pembroke asked.

Adam blushed. He was well aware of being the youngest present, and also aware that, if his father and his lord had not both died and the land not been in a state of civil war, he would still be a squire rather than a knight leading a considerable following.

"Not for the gates, but inside," he answered quickly. "Sir Faulk says we can go in. At least we should be able to disrupt the attempts to break into the keep."

"Yes, indeed," de Breauté assented heartily. He did not love to sit in front of a town battering at its gates any more than Adam did. "Not only that, but once you have blocked all three gates so that they can neither escape us nor ride out to attack us, perhaps we can assault them from within."

The three younger members of the group applauded this suggestion with great enthusiasm. Salisbury, Pembroke, and Ian looked sourly at their sons who so eagerly embraced the idea of risking their necks climbing roofs to shoot arrows and fighting afoot through winding streets, which provided many easy ambushes. Still, the idea did have great merit—de Breauté was an astute and experienced military leader—and it was even possible that a group from the castle could fight its way to one of the gates and open it. Geoffrey made that suggestion. The others leapt on it with joyous additions and amendments. All three fathers—two of the body and one of the heart—opened their mouths simultaneously to forbid such rash actions.

"I will allow them to do nothing that will endanger them without adequate recompense," Faulk assured them.

The assurance changed no one's sentiments because Faulk was not a cautious fighter, but it stopped the fathers' tongues. Soon after, the impromptu conference came to an end and all left together to join a general council of war. This was quite brief, everyone having had just about the same notion of what should be done. There was little to discuss except which parties should attack which gates, and acceptance of the plan to cull out the archers of each group and send them with Faulk and his contingent into Lincoln keep through the postern door. Adam, Geoffrey, and William Marshal promptly offered themselves and their men to accompany him.

As events occurred, the anxious fathers were both right and wrong. Conflicting opinions among Louis's men—the French scorning the advice of the English and the English unwisely keeping information from the French—permitted Pembroke to begin his operations at the gates without any opposition and without the withdrawal of any of his enemies. Faulk de Breauté's entrance into Lincoln through the postern door on the west side was also accomplished without difficulty. Thus, it was still quite early in the morning on the twentieth of May when Geoffrey and Adam unlimbered their longbows, strung them, and went out on the battlements to bedevil the attackers as best they could. Faulk had decreed their position, pointing out when they wished to accompany most of the other archers down to the roofs of lower buildings that their mail would make them clumsy and a danger to the other men.

It was just as well they and a number of other knights of Faulk's retinue who were skilled with the bow did remain. Nearly all the French noblemen and English rebel barons were with their men in the open area between the front of the cathedral and the wall of the keep, which was being battered into collapse by mangonels and trenchbuts. The rain of arrows from the battlements and roofs did far more damage than had been expected. Men and horses alike were struck. A few of the horses fell, screaming; many tried to bolt where there was no room to run, or bucked and lashed out with hooves and teeth, panicking other horses that had not been wounded. Men fell also, some struck by arrows and some thrown by their frantic mounts; they were crushed under their own horses or kicked by others, as were any footmen near the beasts. In only a few minutes, there was bedlam and chaos where an army had been massed for attack.

Faulk was not one to ignore such an opportunity. He called together those knights of the castle and of his own who were not on the walls and rode out to make hay among the disordered invaders while he could. On the walls, Adam and Geoffrey cursed their own skill because it had kept them from hand-to-hand combat, which both preferred infinitely to long-distance assassination with a bow. However, they were soon freed from bondage to their longbows. As Faulk's men became intermingled with the besiegers in violent action, it was as likely an arrow would hit a friend as a foe, and the archers ceased to fire.

Adam and Geoffrey leaned forward to watch enviously the progress of Faulk's attack. This, unfortunately, was not going well. In spite of the confusion and damage caused by the archers, there were so many in the opposing force that Faulk himself was surrounded and in imminent danger of being made a prisoner. Shouting with mingled consternation and pleasure at the idea that they would get into battle after all, the knights on the battlement rushed down to mount their horses and ride to the rescue.

Meanwhile, Peter des Roches, who was as eager a warrior as any despite being Bishop of Winchester, had taken a party on a tour of inspection. He had, thus far, had no chance to take part in the active fighting, although his embassy to Lady Nicolaa was very nearly equally hazardous. The lady did not love churchmen, since the town of Lincoln had been yielded. She recognized Peter, however, as one who had never wavered in his faith to the crown, and listened to him. Now Winchester was looking for a way to contribute to the battle. Instead of a route for a charge, he found an old gateway in the wall north of the keep itself but with entry into the town. The gateway had been blocked with mortared stone, but this was crumbling and in no condition to resist a battering ram. Whether the French knew of the weakness in the wall, Winchester had no idea, but obviously they were far too busy just now to think of defending it.

Messengers were sent to Pembroke. A ram was brought around. By the time Faulk's captors had been ferociously reft of their prize, it was apparent that his rescue had not really been of much importance. The body of the king's forces was pouring over the rubble of the old gateway. For a brief time, perhaps a half-hour, the fighting was fierce. As a chronicler was to write a few years later, "Then sparks of fire were seen to dart, and sounds as of dreadful thunder were heard to burst forth from the blows of swords against helmeted heads." Strangely enough, that was all it amounted to, a great deal of sound and fury, signifying nothing.

The next day Geoffrey wrote a full description of the battle to Joanna. "It was more like a mock battle at a fair than a real thing. Between the first and third hour after sunrise, the whole action—including looting the French baggage train, the town, and the churches—whereby I have some new and very pretty trinkets to bestow upon you, my dearest love—was over, and we were finished and seated, eating and drinking, at tables by the ninth hour. There was so much noise and confusion, such screaming and rushing and clanging of arms, that I would have expected my horse to be wading to his knees in blood."

Geoffrey paused to look at the window behind him and shake his head in wonderment before he dipped his quill again. "Instead, out of this travailing of mountains, not even a mouse was born. There were some hurts among the common soldiers, but even among them, only one was killed. Of the noble party, Reginald Crocus was slain by a mischance. That would have been the full tale of losses on both sides, but when the Count of Perche—a proud and stupid man—was called upon to yield, being completely surrounded, he cried out that he would not give up his sword to the English, who were all traitors, even to their own king. Adam and I were there together and we laughed at such vainglory, as did most who were by. But one, doubtless touched to the quick because he had wavered in his faith, leapt forward before the rest of us could disarm that silly fool and pierced him through the eye. The thrust went to the brain and Perche was dead upon the instant. It is too bad. He would have brought a rich ransom.

"I must say, however," Geoffrey continued, "that we have so many prisoners—more than four hundred knights—that the anger at the waste of Perche was not much. This, in fact, is why I am not writing to say that I am on my way home to you, beloved. Pembroke left us at once to carry the good news to the king and the legate Gualo. My father, Chester, and Ferrars are charged with the division of the spoils and the prisoners. I would not stay for that, except that I do not like the way my father looks. He, like the knight who fell upon Perche, remembers too often that he once turned his back upon his brother and would not serve him. His awareness arouses uneasiness in Chester and Ferrars, who do not see that his guilt is for the past and fear some future act. I am, therefore, his hands and feet and mouth again for this time. However—"

At this point Adam strode into the chamber where

Geoffrey was writing to inform him that there was more good news. "A man just rode in to say that Pembroke had word the knights holding Mountsorel have fled. We came to take it, and we have—without ever going near the place. Anyway, Ian has been told to go with the sheriff of Nottingham and see that the place is razed to the ground, so I will have to escort Ian's prisoners to Roselynde."

"I will take them," Geoffrey offered, "if you want to get about that business at Bexhill."

"No. I have to bring my own prisoners to Kemp anyway, so it is not far out of my way. Besides, I think you should be home with Joanna as much as possible just now. She is due to lie in next month, is she not?" Adam saw Geoffrey's eyes cloud and his mouth tighten. Death in childbirth took about one third of the women delivering their first child. "Oh Lord," Adam said, "I did not mean there was anything to worry about. Joanna is just like Mama—slow to get with child, but fast and easy to deliver them, you will see."

"I hope you are right." Geoffrey bit his knuckles. "I swear I had rather go through Bouvines again, even knowing what would come of it."

Adam had a sudden horrible sinking of heart. He was not worried about Joanna, in whose strength and good health he had the infinite, unreasoning faith of a younger brother, but he suddenly saw himself facing the same situation, and he did not have equal faith in Gilliane's strength and health. Had Gilliane's mother died in childbearing? He shook off the thought. He would do no good to anyone by adding to Geoffrey's anxieties by showing his own fear.

"Well," he said, "do not tell Joanna that, for God's sake. I know it drove Mama wild when Ian hung over her, asking every minute how she felt and pacing the floor a month ahead of time."

Geoffrey could not help laughing. He, too, remem-

bered Lady Alinor's barely controlled impatience with
her husband's fears. She was pleased that he loved her,
but she preferred other demonstrations of it. Of course,
it was Lady Alinor's sixth or seventh lying-in, which
made a difference. Nonetheless, Adam was right. He
had better not frighten Joanna by appearing frightened
himself.

"You are right," he confessed, "but who told you of
it?"

"I was at home for Mama's lying-in with little Alinor,
who died. My lord had that first spell of sickness, and
there was naught for me to do on his lands. Mama used
to beg me to make Ian ride out or practice at arms. I
was only jesting when I said he asked every minute
how she felt—of course he did no such thing—but he
watched her. It teased her, yet she wanted him near
also."

"Yes. Joanna was not overjoyed at this summons—
but then, she always hates when I ride to war."

"That is common to all women. At least," Adam
amended with a grin, "to all of them that do not *hope*
a war will make them widows. Which reminds me"—
his happy smile was replaced by a frown—"I must
write and tell Gilliane I am still alive. Do you have
another piece of parchment and a quill?"

Gravely, but with a quivering lip, Geoffrey drew
another large sheet of parchment and a fresh quill from
the writing desk beside him. Adam groaned, then turned
to Geoffrey with an ingratiating smile.

"You have already written the tale of the battle,
have you not?"

Since a full sheet and a half written in Geoffrey's
neat script were lying on the table, he could not deny
it, although he longed to do so. It would have afforded
him considerable amusement to see what Adam would
make of a battle description. He was forced to nod.

"Good. Please tell Joanna to read that part to

Gilliane—and do not tell me Gilliane will want to see it in my own hand. Perhaps she will, but a woman can be spoiled too much."

With those words, Adam drew his knife and severed a small section from the parchment, dipped the quill and began to write. Geoffrey bit his lip. The twisted contortion of Adam's face could not have been increased by the agony of having the barbed head of an arrow torn out of his flesh. Geoffrey could not resist adding to his letter a description of his brother-by-marriage's struggle with that most recalcitrant of all enemies—a pen. After that, however, Geoffrey's good nature prevailed and he begged Joanna not only to read the battle description to Gilliane but to assure her it was not owing to lack of love or good intention on Adam's part that he did not write his own. In all this time, Adam had committed two lines to the parchment.

"Beloved, we won with great booty. I am safe, entirely without any hurt. I must carry my prisoners and Ian's to our keeps."

At this point Adam looked up at Geoffrey. "You can, if you will, do a favor for me, Geoffrey. If this business of the prisoners is delayed above a few days, I will not have time to ride back to Hemel to fetch Gilliane and still reach Tarring before the last day of the month to greet Gilliane's men. Could you spare two days, say on the twenty-seventh or twenty-eighth of this month, to see Gilliane safe home? Then, even if I were late by a few days, she could explain to the men."

"Of course. There can be no favor in it. You escorted my wife further, and under worse conditions."

That was formal, if sincere, but Adam frowned. "Do not be so sure of worse conditions. There will be bands of escaped survivors of this battle roaming the entire land between here and the south coast like starving wolves. We took most of the knights, but you know many of the foot soldiers escaped. Otherwise, I would not trouble you to escort Gilliane. Her husband might even be . . . good God!" Adam jumped to his feet. "Perhaps de Cercy is one of the prisoners. I must go see about that."

CHAPTER TWENTY-SEVEN

Adam's hopes were not fulfilled as Osbert was still ensconced in the merchant's house in Tarring town. He was enraged, impatient, near to giving up hope of achieving his objective. He was still there only because he had no place else to go and Louis was still, as far as he knew, at Dover. In this supposition, Osbert was utterly mistaken. The "fair" at Lincoln was a disaster of such magnitude that Louis's hopes for the conquest of England were, if not dead, mortally wounded. FitzWalter and de Quincy had been taken prisoner. Great numbers of English rebels, those who were not also prisoner, promptly deserted Louis and either locked themselves in their keeps, in the hope they would be overlooked by the king's retribution, or rushed to Pembroke, Gualo, or Peter des Roches to beg for peace and mercy.

There could no longer be even the slightest chance of taking Dover and, as besiegers, the French were now in far greater danger from their position, which was exposed to attack by the king's forces, than the besieged. Louis fled to London, where the fears of the populace that had welcomed him from the beginning, the great walls, and the river route to escape would permit him to treat for peace in relative safety. Naturally enough, he did not give a single thought to Osbert, who was a contemptible minor cog in a wheel already broken and useless. And Tarring, being already of Henry's party, lay quiet and undisturbed by news or rumor of danger.

On the evening of the twenty-seventh of May, Gilliane returned to Tarring with Geoffrey. He was somewhat concerned that there were no more than thirty men-at-arms in the keep and offered either to leave her his troop or stay until Adam arrived. She refused with thanks. Under the circumstances, it was incredible that Tarring would be attacked. Who was there to attack it? Furthermore, Sir Richard was five miles away with troops all ready to march against Bexhill. Even if the unthinkable should happen and some army under a renegade knight should try to loot the keep, Sir Richard could be with her in two hours.

On the other hand, Geoffrey could not travel safely without the twenty men who had come as an escort. Nor would Gilliane consider keeping Geoffrey with her. Joanna was plainly near term, large, unwieldy, uncomfortable, and eager to be rid of her burden. Alinor was coming from Roselynde to be with her daughter, but she had not yet arrived when Gilliane and Geoffrey left Hemel. He hid it as well as he could, but Geoffrey was in an agony of anxiety about leaving his wife alone—although what he could do to help Joanna, Gilliane thought with concealed amusement, was beyond her comprehension. Still, Joanna wanted him near, Gilliane knew, and she would not have kept him even if she was worried, which she was not.

Accordingly, Geoffrey rode off at the first moment it was light enough to see on the morning of the twenty-eighth. An hour or so later Gilliane sent a messenger into town to inform merchants who had been holding orders of spices and silk cloth for her that those items might be delivered to the keep. Within minutes of that messenger's departure from the house of the merchant where Osbert lived, another messenger rode off to bring Louis's order to the castellan of Pevensey that his garrison should march upon Tarring. Osbert added that this should be as soon as possible, but certainly within the next two days, as it was uncertain whether Lemagne would return and bring more men. At present, he wrote, there were fewer than fifty men in the keep who could use arms.

Actually, Osbert was nearly sure Adam would not come to Tarring. There were no men in the keep he would want to take with him to Bexhill and no supplies for war. For what, then, should he come? To Osbert, it was incredible that a man should wish to see a particular woman and go out of his way for that purpose. But what if Adam did return after Tarring was in Osbert's hands? Pevensey's men could not remain long; they would be needed in their own castle. While the merchant concocted a message to Gilliane that he was waiting for a shipment, which he expected the next day or the day after, and would bring her order as soon as fresh spices arrived, Osbert rethought his plan. All in all, it would be best to kill Gilliane. Then the lands would surely be his, and there could be no chance that she would run away or be stolen from him.

The only difficulty he could perceive was that the leader of the force from Pevensey would know she had been alive when the keep was taken. Some people were stupid about the murder of a woman, and there was also that silly thing about not inheriting the lands of a person you killed. He would need some excuse, Osbert knew. If only he could order Jean to kill her and then accuse Jean of the crime and have him executed for it . . .

No. Osbert sighed and put the idea aside. Jean was too clever to be caught in such a trap. Besides, Jean would be needed to lead the troop from Pevensey to the postern. The few other men Osbert had did not know its position. He would need to deal with Gilliane himself, and he would not have much time for it, either. Once the guard had been drawn away from the postern door and replaced with Osbert's man or men, he would have to kill Gilliane before the men from Pevensey arrived. Yet he could not kill her where the servants could see. They had always taken her side, and that idiot cripple's, and Osbert would be alone and unarmed, although he would have a sword hidden under his cape. Neville's servants . . .

With the name of the man he had murdered, revelation came to Osbert. He had his reason and his method all laid out and ready. Of course, Gilliane would confess to him that she had murdered Neville and would then leap to her death from the very window from which her husband had been pushed. The murder, he could say, had eaten into her soul, and, when she saw her second husband—for whom she had murdered her first—in the very spot where she had committed the crime, it had been too much for her. Osbert hugged himself in glee. Everything was going his way.

Osbert's ignorance of the happenings at Lincoln was not general among Louis's adherents. Days before his messenger arrived at Pevensey keep, its castellan had ridden off to London to consult with his master. Osbert's messenger was, therefore, directed on to London. The man had some idea that the message he carried was urgent, but he liked his master no better than anyone else who served him. He deliberated briefly, then threw the letter into the nearest ditch. He would go on to London, but only to discover what had really happened. If it was as great a disaster as rumors at Pevensey indicated, he could best hide himself there, take other service, or escape. No thought of returning to warn Osbert ever crossed the messenger's mind. Not by deed or word or look had Osbert ever given a sign of caring what happened to him; why should he care what happened to Osbert?

Rumors of the defeat at Lincoln had spread wider than the castlefolk of Pevensey. At Bexhill, Sir Godfrey had also heard that Louis had suffered a setback.

To him, the tale was minimized as much as possible, but he had to be told. "Do not believe the rumors of a disaster," his informant wrote. "The country to the north is of no real value and the prince's hold upon the southern shires remains strong. London is also entirely his, and while he holds London his cause cannot fail ultimately." Far from giving Sir Godfrey reassurance, these words made him most uncomfortable. He, for one, was not at all sure that the prince's ultimate purpose was the same as his own.

The letter to Sir Godfrey arrived on the twenty-fourth. On May twenty-fifth, Sir Godfrey sent out his eldest son and two younger brothers to make certain inquiries. By the twenty-eighth, he knew the true scale of Louis's defeat, and that nearly every keep that was not in the hands of one of Louis's Frenchmen had already yielded to Pembroke or was in the process of negotiating with him. He had been prepared to resist Adam by battle, counting on help from Pevensey and Hastings. Now he realized he would get no help from them if Adam came to Bexhill. However, if Adam came and he yielded, it was possible that, after Adam rode away, Louis's men would use that excuse to take Bexhill. Probably Adam would come back to help him, but he might not. He might think it better to let Louis's men put him out and then reclaim the keep in Gilliane's name when the war was over. Then he could put his own castellan in it.

The only solution seemed to be for Sir Godfrey to go in person to Adam and yield to him. Pevensey and Hastings need know nothing about it, and, if he were well received, that would be the end of the matter. He would still have Bexhill. There was no real reason for Adam to put him out. He had not answered Gilliane's letter announcing her inheritance and reminding him of his oath to her, but he had not actively defied her. He had not paid his rents, either, but he could bring money for that with him. If only Sir Adam were older, Sir Godfrey would have been more sure of his reception. An older man would have understood that he had had to lean toward Louis with his property placed as it was. After all, Neville's other vassals had gone along with the change in political affiliation as well as he. Even Sir Richard . . .

There Sir Godfrey's thoughts paused. A few minutes later he was dictating to his clerk a letter informing Sir Richard that he was going on the thirtieth of May to Tarring to yield himself to Adam's mercy through Lady Gilliane's mediation. He begged Sir Richard to come with him to intercede for him and explain that this would be the best solution to the problem. Sir Godfrey's two brothers and his son would remain in Bexhill so that Adam would have no profit if he took Sir Godfrey prisoner or even killed him.

Sir Richard received this missive at breakfast on the twenty-ninth of May. He looked out across the hall of Glynde keep and sighed. Sir Andrew, a late sleeper, was snoring in a wall room. He had arrived the previous day with his hundred men to accompany Sir Richard and his hundred to Tarring on the morrow. Sir Richard did not doubt that Sir Edmund and Sir Philip were also on their way. His son had been excused from this service because Wick was too newly in his power for him to leave it safely. So here they were, four hundred men in addition to those Adam would bring, all converging upon Tarring to fight Sir Godfrey. And Sir Godfrey was coming meekly to do homage. What was that old song about the king marching his men up the hill and then down again? What a waste of money hiring the extra men had been.

Then, suddenly, Sir Richard smiled. Ah well, Adam was never at a loss. Probably he would think of something profitable to do with the force. Lewes, for example. Lewes was in the hands of the French, and it was uncomfortably close to Tarring and Glynde. Also, the Lord of Lewes was almost certainly absent at this time. And Lewes was very rich. Possibly it would be wise to insert a thought about Lewes into Adam's mind before he thought of something less profitable to do with the men he had summoned. Yes, and Sir Godfrey would wish to prove his loyalty. He had doubtless hired men also to defend his keep. Perhaps Sir Godfrey would like to offer his men to a good purpose—like clearing the French out of Lewes. Sir Richard began to eat again with excellent appetite. He and Sir Andrew would ride south tomorrow to meet Sir Godfrey, as he had requested, and he could explain his idea.

On the same morning, Osbert sent men to watch the roads east of Tarring. As soon as they saw a large force of men approaching, they were to come back and warn him so that he could go into Tarring keep and open it for his allies. He did not expect anyone that day, and spent it joyously rehearsing how he would deal with Gilliane and trying on his merchant's disguise, adjusting the hood this way and that so it would shadow his face and conceal it from any servant who might know him. He did not fear recognition by the men-at-arms because most of them were new. He fooled with the hood for some time but was not satisfied with the result and eventually bethought himself of a particularly rich bale of cloth. That would be a double defense. He could hold it so that it obscured his face and also say it was too precious to spread in the hall with the other goods.

Osbert was surprised when his men returned that very night with the news that a small group was encamped on the banks of the Cuckmere. It seemed rather soon for the castellan at Pevensey to respond and the number of men seemed too small. Still, Osbert thought, he had told them there were only thirty men in Tarring. There could be no reason to camp on the Cuckmere, so close to Tarring, if not to wait for Jean to lead them in. If Lemagne showed up later when there were so few men . . . Osbert shrugged. Once

Gilliane was dead, he could change sides. During his stay in town, he had discovered that Adam was far from a monster. From the tales he had heard, the man was a fool, so lenient to the people that they got away with a modest profit in their dealings with him. He had even *given* food to some. Osbert shrugged off the problem of Lemagne. He had been a fool to let the cowards who escaped from the battle at Kemp frighten him. Anyone as soft as Lemagne could be dealt with. Meanwhile, everything was going well. Tomorrow Tarring would be in his hands.

The evening of the same day Adam arrived in Kemp. Had he been alone or with his household troop, he would have dropped his prisoners in Sir Robert's lap and ridden straight on to Tarring to spend the night with Gilliane. He could not do that because he had with him a large force of footmen, whom he had picked and chosen from among the soldiers taken at Lincoln. Those he had chosen were English-born mercenaries who had been in the service of the rebels. These common men had no political opinions and, seeing no hope of further employment with their late masters, were quite satisfied to take service with Adam.

They were good fighting men and had been accustomed to discipline, although the license they had been permitted to practice recently had shaken their standards. Adam marched them from Lincoln to Roselynde in three days with strict orders not to loot or rape along the road. They were promised that food and other necessities would be provided. The first evening two men had been executed for raping a woman, and five had been flogged within an inch of their lives for stealing. However, a plentiful meal was prepared and served, and Alberic and Cuthbert went around the camp and saw that every man had a blanket and a pair of leather boots.

The second night there were some floggings also, but

less severe, for minor infractions. An equally plentiful meal appeared and Adam himself walked through the camp with the leech beside him inquiring about wounds, sore feet, and general health, and seeing that the men were treated and dosed to the best ability of the leech. The third night no stern disciplinary measures were required. Cuthbert had sharp words with one new-hired man and knocked him down for an insubordinate grimace, but generally speaking, the men were shaping up. Adam sent word around that if behavior continued good, there would be feasting and drinking at Kemp, his own stronghold, the following night. The new men had come one hundred and thirty miles in four days, after a humiliating defeat; they deserved a rest.

Bitterly resenting the inconvenience, and vowing he would make Gilliane suffer for it before she died, Osbert rose and dressed in his disguise just before dawn on May thirtieth. By the time the sun rose, the merchant and his assistants were at the drawbridge of Tarring asking for permission to enter. They were unusually early, but they were received readily because the merchant was well known in Tarring. No one looked particularly at those who entered with him. Since the merchant's goods were valuable, cloth and rare spices and medicinals, he also asked for and received permission to go up to the hall to lay out his wares.

Outside the keep in a sheltered position, Jean dismounted from his horse and waited. His instructions were to stay until the guard was changed, and then ride to the men encamped on the bank of the Cuckmere and lead them to the small wood not far from the castle. Meanwhile, two of the merchant's assistants helped him carry the parcels up. One of these assistants was genuine, in case someone like the priest should ask questions about the goods; the other was Osbert. Two other assistants, both of them Osbert's men, led the horses around to the back where the stables lay. Osbert, smiling broadly in the concealment of his hood, unpacked a particular bolt of cloth and made for the stairwell. It was still early enough that the servants were in considerable confusion. Some were putting away bedding; others were drawing on clothing; still others were staggering down to the bailey to wash, to snatch some food from the cooking sheds, to obtain a cup of ale as an eye-opener. No one noticed Osbert, which was just as he planned it, and this increased his confidence in the efficacy of his plans.

All continued to go perfectly. One maid called a question as Osbert entered the large upper hall, and he mumbled that the lady had asked to see this bolt of cloth in her chamber. With his hand across his mouth and the cloth as well as his hood obscuring his face, no one knew him. He passed unchallenged, laughing to himself, into Gilliane's room. There, luck favored him once again. Catrin was right near the door, her back to him, bending to put something in a chest; Gilliane, just finished dressing, was seated at the polished metal that served as a mirror, fastening her wimple, too intent for the moment to notice him.

Stimulated by success to greater success, Osbert dropped the cloth, closed the door quickly, drew his sword and struck Catrin over the head with the flat of it so hard that she fell unconscious to the ground. That was an accident. Osbert had meant to kill her, but he was so awkward with the sword that the weapon turned in his hand and the edge did not strike her.

"Do not scream," he hissed at Gilliane, who had leapt to her feet at the sound of Catrin's fall. "I will do you no harm."

For one moment, Gilliane was paralyzed with surprise and terror. Tarring had been taken! In the next instant, she realized that was impossible. Her window was wide open. Through it she could hear the ordinary morning sounds of the keep. Moreover, Osbert was without armor, and——her eyes moved to the floor near

him—he had been carrying a bolt of cloth. Somehow
Osbert had gotten into Tarring by trickery. Then the
man who would have been a symbol of the devil to Gilliane had he not been so contemptible in his evilness
began to advance upon her, and her eyes widened.

Owing to aching heads—the result of their new master's generosity and fulfillment of his promise—Adam's
troop was a little slow getting started on the morning of
the thirtieth. The sun was up by the time they were
formed in ranks and ready to move. Word went out
that this was all Sir Adam's land. If they looked crooked
at a woman who was unwilling, they would be drawn
and quartered; if they stole, they would lose both hands.
In fact, it would be safest not even to step on the grass
by the side of the road until permission to do so was
granted. There was no laughter at Alberic's jest. The
newly hired men were not sure it was a jest, but they
were sure that this master kept his promises—both for
good and ill—and expected to be obeyed.

Although he was eager to see Gilliane, Adam had not
rushed them. His own head left something to be desired,
as he had fought over the whole silly debacle at Lincoln with Sir Robert and the most congenial of the
prisoners. He had felt it necessary to ease their grief
and humiliation with liberal potations of wine, and,
naturally, one could not allow guests to drink alone.

On the banks of the Cuckmere, Sir Godfrey and Sir
Richard had met and were having a very fruitful discussion. They were interrupted by shouts, and as they
leapt to their feet they heard the sounds of a brief pursuit
and a scuffle. Moments later a slightly battered Jean
was dragged into their presence and thrown down at
Sir Richard's feet by his master-at-arms, who said suc-
cinctly that the man had asked for the castellan of
Pevensey. At the name, Sir Richard's and Sir Andrew's
swords were drawn. Sir Godfrey turned a pasty yellow.
Sir Andrew's master-at-arms had alerted the men, John

of Glynde continued, and Sir Godfrey's men were surrounded.

"But if this is a trap for the men of Pevensey to know where to find us, my lord," John of Glynde went on, "I would say Sir Godfrey's men know nothing of it."

"And neither do I!" Sir Godfrey exclaimed. "On my life, it is no such thing. Louis's people have more to think about than your two hundred men."

That was true. What was more, how could Sir Godfrey know Sir Richard would bring more than ten or twelve with him? How could he know Sir Andrew would be at Glynde? Sir Richard had not particularly expected it, although it was not much of a surprise because Sir Andrew often broke his journey to Tarring at Glynde. Although Sir Richard's sword remained bare in his hand, his eyes moved from Sir Godfrey to Jean. That sly wretch had recovered from his shock of surprise and resolved in seconds to throw his master to the wolves to gain a hope of preserving his own life. Without prompting, he disclosed the entire plot.

Sir Richard was not much inclined to credit Jean's tale, but he did not dare discount it, either. Lady Gilliane might be in danger. To ignore such a warning, even from so unreliable a source, was a violation of his oath to serve her. Another factor leading Sir Richard to favor action on Jean's tale was that strategically he would be better off in or near Tarring, even if men from Pevensey were bent, for some unknowable reason, on war with Adam. Sir Edmund and Sir Philip should be arriving at Tarring sometime this very day, if they were not there already, and so should Adam himself. All things considered, even if Tarring had been taken and Jean was trying to lead them into a trap, with the force he had and the men who were due to arrive, the trap might be sprung on the trappers themselves.

"Bind and guard this man," Sir Richard directed John of Glynde. "Order the men to make ready at once to march for Tarring."

"But if Sir Godfrey is a traitor . . ." Sir Andrew sputtered.

"I do not think it, Andrew," Sir Richard soothed, "but you will watch him for me. Sir Godfrey," Sir Richard continued, turning to him, "I do not disbelieve you, yet you must understand that we can take no chances. I will not ask you to give up your sword, but I must ask you to order your men to surrender their weapons. You know me. Upon my honor, if this is not a trap of your making, you will go free and your men with you, whatever the outcome of your meeting with Sir Adam."

Sir Godfrey was stubbon, but he was neither mad nor an idiot. If he refused, Sir Richard would have no choice but to order his own men to disarm Sir Godfrey's force. Sir Godfrey himself would be made a prisoner, and all would be lost. Biting his lips in fury, he agreed. His men were disarmed and ordered to ride in small groups between larger groups of Sir Richard's and Sir Andrew's troops. Sir Godfrey rode beside Sir Richard with Sir Andrew just behind. For some time, they went in silence until Sir Godfrey asked what Sir Richard intended to do if Jean's story was true.

Sir Richard looked at him speculatively so that Sir Godfrey wondered whether he would refuse to answer, but after a moment he said, "I think I will simply present myself at the gate. I know the man-at-arms who was left in charge. If he greets me and my troop is permitted to enter, I will so do. Then, if Lady Gilliane is not in the hall to greet me, I will go up to her, assuming the man did speak the truth and she will need help."

"But what if it is some kind of trap?" Sir Godfrey asked nervously.

"Sir Andrew and his men will remain outside to give warning to Sir Adam and also to see that no one gets out," Sir Richard answered indifferently.

"That may not do you much good," Sir Godfrey warned.

Sir Richard smiled at him. "I hope to live long yet, of course, but it is no great matter if I should not. If I should die in Sir Adam's service, he will avenge me and will see that my wife and children are protected— aye, probably better than I could protect them myself. He is that kind of man."

Sir Godfrey thought that over for a few minutes, then said, "Whatever happens at Tarring, I swear I had no part in it, but I would like to come in with you. I will even give you my sword if you desire and unarm myself. The thing is"—Sir Godfrey smiled wryly—"I think I would have more chance, disarmed and caught in a trap, than with Andrew. To explain to him . . ."

"Very well," Sir Richard laughed, "we will go in together. Keep your sword and your armor. I cannot be in worse trouble if this is a trap of your making. If it is not, likely you can do me some good." They came over a low rise, and Sir Richard looked down at Tarring town. "It looks quiet enough," he remarked, signaling the men to turn right to avoid the town and head toward the keep above it.

Two miles away to the west, Adam gestured for Alberic to come up to him. The ride from Kemp in the fresh spring air had cleared his head, and he was suddenly impatient to see Gilliane. He had been content in the company of men over the past month. There had been moments of frustration, of unfulfilled physical need, but these were easier to bear than in the past. Partly this was because Adam's days were so full of strenuous activity that he was tired by the time he sought his bed. Mostly, however, it was because his mind was quiet, because he knew that when he came back to Tarring, Gilliane would be there, as eager for him as he was for her. The weeks of living together easily as husband and wife, even though the union was not yet official, had drawn the poison of doubt out of him.

Neither his love nor his passion was less strong. When

he thought of Gilliane, he wanted only to be with her, to talk to her, to laugh with her, and the blood still rushed to his loins. Now, however, the sensation made him happy. He smiled even while he cursed the situation that prevented him from satisfying his need. There was a contentment in his memories of long, loving nights abed, of companionable days. The fever, anxiety, and bitterness were gone, and Adam could long for Gilliane as Ian and Geoffrey longed for their wives, with aching desire but with confidence. The uneasy craving, the half-shamed mental writhings that sought a way to *get* Gilliane were over. A brief memory of those hasty, crazy couplings made Adam laugh.

Then Adam realized that with the arrival of Sir Richard and the others, he would be back in the old situation. No, he resolved. Enough was enough. It was at that point that he signaled Alberic to him and gave him instructions about bringing the footmen to Tarring. He would ride ahead with Cuthbert and a few mounted men. He would have this matter out with Gilliane right now and announce to her vassals and castellans his intention of marrying her as soon as her marriage contract to Osbert could be annulled. Once the contract was written and they were formally betrothed, there would be no need to hide their relationship. Although the Church insisted that betrothal was not marriage and a priest's blessing was necessary, Gilliane's men would not be so strict.

Sometime earlier, Gililane rose from her knees beside the still-unconscious form of Catrin, whom she had bound and gagged according to Osbert's instructions. The operation had taken a long time, and it had taken Osbert a full ten minutes to get her to begin. At first Gilliane had stared blankly at her husband, her lips moving slightly, her hand clutching the crucifix that hung around her neck. Osbert had spoken soothingly to her, assuring her over and over of his good will. He was afraid her fear would rise out of bounds and that she would begin to scream in hysterical terror despite the threat of his naked sword. Her screaming would be dangerous. The sound would carry through the open window and bring curious servants even if he silenced her quite soon.

For Osbert's purpose, the naked sword was an empty threat. He did not dare inflict any wound on Gilliane until after she had dealt with the guards at the postern. He did not dare knock her unconscious, either, for fear she would not regain her senses in time to serve that purpose. Thus, he had to convince her he meant her no harm. He could afford the time to talk to her softly. It would take time for Jean to reach the camp of the men from Pevensey, and then more time for them to arrive at Tarring.

Finally, Gilliane's hand dropped away from the crucifix. Osbert took that as a sign that her panic had subsided into submission. He ordered her to drag Catrin away from the door and bind and gag her. Gilliane had just looked at him when he gave the order. Osbert resumed his soothing, but it had no further effect.

"I will have to kill her if you do not bind her," Osbert said at last.

He intended to kill Catrin anyway, but he did not want to do it then because the sight of the blood might send Gilliane into hysterics. Slowly, very slowly, as if she were drugged or half stunned, Gilliane did as he ordered, binding Catrin's mouth with a veil, her wrists with another, her feet with a third. Osbert watched, but he had no fault to find with Gilliane's work. He did not realize that the cloth was so soft, so loose woven, and the veils so thick, wound round and round Catrin's wrists and ankles, that if the woman pulled strongly everything would loosen and the knots would roll over her hands and feet to set her free. He only noticed that, after her first wide-eyed stare, Gilliane did not look at him. That gave him only satisfaction. It fed his conviction that Gilliane was terrified into docility.

Osbert was more mistaken about his second conclusion than about the fact that Catrin was well tied. Gilliane's face and form were unchanged, but Osbert did not know the new woman inside the old shell. It was not fear that made Gilliane grip her crucifix and pray, but joy. God had delivered her enemy into her hands, and she had thanked Him full measure and overflowing. Her slow reactions were not a result of paralysis but of thought. What in the world did Osbert expect to accomplish in a keep filled with people who Gilliane knew would spring to her defense?

Gilliane did not need to wonder about it long. Osbert told her. Since he knew how long it would take for the troop from Pevensey to arrive, he could not resist boasting of his cleverness to Gilliane. At first she stood quite still, her eyes on the maid near her feet. As the plan unfolded, she closed her eyes and took her lip between her teeth. From time to time a shudder passed through her body. Osbert preened himself on her acceptance of the inevitability of his victory.

What was really agonizing Gilliane was her struggle with mirth. She did not know which was funnier—the fact that Osbert did not know of the defeat at Lincoln and, therefore, that no one could be coming from Pevensey, or that, even if there were men coming, her vassals and castellans were converging on Tarring in considerable force that very day. If the men Osbert's scouts had seen were not merely a French force fleeing to safety in London and were from Pevensey, they would be caught between Tarring keep and Gilliane's men.

Gilliane would have laughed aloud in Osbert's face, except that she wanted to keep him off his guard. God had delivered him into her hands, but she had not yet decided how to kill him and did not want to lose any advantage she had. Gilliane was no expert in battle tactics, but she understood that his overconfidence and belief in her submission were two strong weapons in her hands.

Unfortunately, at this point Osbert decided it was time for Gilliane to play her part in the scheme and draw the guards from the postern into the stable where Osbert's men would overpower them and take their armor. He announced this in a voice of such calm, bland certainty that he surprised Gilliane out of her rigid self-control. Helplessly, she burst into laughter, gasping, "You ass! You braying, long-eared ass!"

Had Osbert not been exactly what Gilliane said, the mistake would have cost her dear. She was at the moment close enough for him to grasp her, and she might have suffered severely for her lack of control. There are places to hurt a woman that do not show when she is clothed. However, Osbert was as much surprised by Gilliane's reaction as she had been by his stupidity, and her understanding of her mistake and her reaction time were quicker. Before the full implications of what Gilliane had said sank into Osbert's mind, she had scrambled across the bed and was safe on the other side, hidden from him by the bed curtains.

Osbert uttered a shriek of rage and rushed around the foot of the bed after her. In his fury, he might well have used his sword, forgetting his need and his purpose. However, Gilliane knew the effect of frustration on Osbert. She had often been pummeled and kicked when his father or brother had denied him something. After attaining the temporary sanctuary, Gilliane had wasted no time in seeking something with which to defend herself. Her knife was across the room in a chest behind Osbert, which was just as well because Gilliane would have grabbed for that instinctively and it would have been no defense against a sword.

Since she knew her usual weapon was beyond reach, Gilliane's mind was free. She needed something long and strong to hold Osbert off. Even as she cursed herself for being as big an ass as he, she grasped the candlestick that held the night candle by the bed. It was taller than she and strong enough, being made of twisted bars of wrought iron. It also had the advantage of a long, sharp point upon which the thick night candle was impaled. Gilliane tore off the candle and threw it into Osbert's face as he came around the end of the bed. It was then that the disadvantage of the candlestick became plain. It was far too heavy for Gilliane to use as a weapon. She could tilt it forward and keep Osbert far enough away. She could even lift it and thrust with it briefly, but it was much too unwieldy and unbalanced to be held for any time or swung freely to block sword thrusts.

For a man of ordinary courage and skill, the candlestick would not have been much of an obstacle. If he wanted Gilliane alive, he had only to sheathe his sword, wrench the candlestick from her grasp, and grab her. If her death was his aim, he could grasp the candlestick in his left hand and swing his sword freely with his right. Osbert, however, made a rabbit seem like a lion in comparison to himself. Moreover, his mind was fixed into his own daydream of success. He had worked everything out to his own satisfaction, over and over for months. It had to come out that way. More particularly, he could not believe that Gilliane would oppose him.

Gilliane was so furious with herself that, as soon as the immediate need for self-defense had been satisfied, she began to cry with vexation. How could she have been so stupid! Why had she not simply agreed? As soon as they came into the bailey, Osbert would have been seized by her men-at-arms. He could not have walked out of her chamber holding a sword in his hand. Even if he pressed a knife against her, she could probably have got away without being hurt. No merchant would dare touch or hold the lady of the manor. Every manservant in the house would have fallen upon Osbert in outrage. Gilliane had not thought about it because she did not want Osbert taken prisoner by the men-at-arms. She wanted to kill him herself!

Osbert had been hissing obscenities at her. Now he changed over to threats. Gilliane's eyes roved wildly, seeking a better weapon. She did not see that, but through the parting of the bed curtains she saw the latch of the door lifting. It was too late! Someone was coming. She would be rescued, but Osbert would be taken prisoner. Adam would challenge him, but Gilliane knew Osbert would never agree to fight and Adam would probably not simply order him to be killed. If only she could prove that Osbert was a murderer. He could be judged and executed for that—but there was no proof.

"Murderer!" Gilliane shrieked in frantic frustration, just as the door opened. "Do you think you can stand by that window, where I saw you throw poor Gilbert to his death, and tell me to obey you? I would rather die!"

"Poor Gilbert!" Osbert sneered, so intent on Gilliane that he did not see the door open and the two men standing transfixed on the threshhold. "What if I did throw him out? He was dead already, really. You cannot call throwing a corpse out of a window murder."

"He was not!" Gilliane cried. "He was getting better!"

"If you cared so much," Osbert snickered, with a nasty grin, "why did you not denounce me?"

Gilliane had not heard another sound from the door and dared not glance at it again. She assumed a maid had opened it and, seeing Catrin bound or Osbert with a drawn sword, had fled to bring help. She was surprised that the woman had not cried out, but was grateful for that because it gave her one last chance to rid herself of Osbert.

"Because I wish to kill you myself!" Gilliane screamed, taking a good grip on the candlestick and charging forward suddenly.

She had the point against Osbert's chest and had actually borne him backward a couple of steps. Knowing what a coward he was, Gilliane had hoped shock and fear would make him drop his sword. Instead, he swung wildly with it. He did not strike Gilliane, but, in ducking, she lost her grip upon the candlestick and stumbled to her knees. A double roar of rage from the doorway brought a scream of terror from Osbert and made him abort the second blow he had aimed at Gilliane. Desperately, Gilliane got to her feet and grasped the candlestick again. She was just in time to prevent Osbert from running to hide under the bed. He uttered a second scream of fear and did drop his sword, but it was too late for that. Sir Richard and Sir Godfrey charged, their intentions unmistakable. One blow struck him, but glancingly. Gilliane lunged forward again fiercely. Backing away, screaming hysterically, Osbert toppled against the sill of the open window and went out.

Gilliane, Sir Richard, and Sir Godfrey stood panting, staring at one another. Before any of them could gasp out a single word, a familiar bellow came up from the bailey below.

"Adam!" Gilliane cried, and burst between the two men to run headlong down the stairs.

Since Adam had run equally precipitously upward, they met in the hall. Sir Richard and Sir Godfrey, following behind Gilliane as swiftly as they could, were treated to the interesting sight of an overlord clasping his vassal to his breast and covering her with kisses, between which he asked disjointedly what had happened and whether she was unhurt, and never gave her time to reply because of kissing her again. Equally disjointedly, Gilliane strove to tell Adam about Osbert. He could not really follow what she said, there being scarce time for two consecutive words before his mouth closed on hers once more—and Gilliane made no effort to change the situation. To her way of thinking, it was far more important to kiss Adam than to explain what had happened to Osbert.

Eventually, however, Gilliane got Osbert's name out. "Osbert!" Adam roared. "Was *that* de Cercy?"

As Adam rode into the inner courtyard, he had seen a man fall from the window of Gilliane's chamber. Sensibly, he had not stopped to investigate who it was but had rushed up to discover whether Gilliane was in danger. The dead man, whoever he was, would not go away.

"He sneaked in disguised as a merchant," Gilliane gasped.

"He nearly killed Lady Gilliane," Sir Richard exclaimed.

"He admitted murdering de Neville," Sir Godfrey growled.

Adam's head swung from one to the other and fixed on Sir Godfrey. "Who the devil are you?" he asked.

"This is Sir Godfrey, come to do homage to Lady Gilliane," Sir Richard began. "He—"

"Come to do homage?" Adam roared. "Now? After I—"

"Sir Godfrey is welcome to me now and at any time," Gilliane said, loud and clear.

Adam's face turned a fascinating shade of purple. Sir Godfrey gritted his teeth but did not reach for the sword he had sheathed. It was too late for that. If Sir Richard had been able to talk to Sir Adam in quiet circumstances, perhaps he would have seen reason. In the midst of all this furor, so young a man was bound to act hastily.

Gilliane stiffened. This time she had gone too far. Adam would certainly beat her. She did not care a bit. Let him. Sir Richard would not let him kill her, and Adam would be sorry for it later. When he saw her bruises, he would give in and accept Sir Godfrey. That would keep him out of one battle at least.

"He is *my* vassal," Gilliane added, breathing hard

but keeping her voice steady and standing her ground. "And I do not choose to have my vassal's land destroyed by war if he is willing to swear and be loyal."

"No, of course not," Adam bellowed. "I am not an idiot! But what the devil am I to do with near a thousand men . . . ?"

Sir Richard was the only perfectly calm member of the group. He had some experience with Adam's quick temper and, by now, nothing Gilliane did surprised him much. The final oversetting of his conventional views of women had been the sight of his gentle overlady rushing on de Cercy with that candlestick. He understood Adam's fury, too. If he had summoned his vassals and expended sums on hiring mercenaries, he, too, would be having a fit. Fortunately, he had already considered the problem.

"Lewes," Sir Richard said loudly.

There was a startled silence. Adam looked blankly at Sir Richard; then a beatific smile illuminated his face while his color rapidly returned to normal. If Gilliane, who understood quite well what had turned Adam's rage to pleasure, could have got at Sir Richard with the candlestick, she would have pushed him out the window as cheerfully as she had pushed Osbert out. However, she was, as Alinor promised, growing hardened. She was not less afraid something might happen; merely, she was no longer certain Adam would be lost to her. Thus, she could bear her fear. Sir Godfrey was also watching Adam, caught between anxiety and hope. If he had understood what the young overlord said, he was safe. This was confirmed at once.

"Lewes," Adam repeated. "Ah, yes, Lewes. Indeed, you are welcome to me, Sir Godfrey. I presume you would have no objection to doing your service now in the taking of Lewes?"

"None at all, Sir Adam," Sir Godfrey hastened to reply. Lewes was well away from Hastings and Pevensey. No one would have to know he was involved in any attack on it. Quite cheerfully, he began to tell Adam how many men he could furnish.

"If you will pardon me, gentlemen," Gilliane interrupted icily, "there is a small matter of housekeeping I must see to. Someone must sweep up my late husband and throw him away. Really, we cannot have dead bodies littering the courtyard. Now that I am a widow, I must look to my reputation."

There was another silence. Sir Godfrey looked stunned. Sir Richard frowned disapprovingly at Gilliane for such levity. Rage lit up Adam's eyes again.

"Reputation?" he snarled. "What do you mean by that?"

Gilliane had not meant anything specific. She was simply annoyed at the three men standing there, totally intent on something she hated, seemingly having dismissed from their minds an event that was of monumental importance to her. She did not need to reply; the question was rhetorical and Adam was continuing hotly.

"It was you who would not hear of an annulment so we could marry. I swore a dozen times that I did not desire to take your lands or lessen your power, but you would not trust me. I will bear it no longer! I desire you as my wife, not my mistress. I will not creep to your bed like a sneaking cur. You can make what terms you like for the disposition of your lands, but before I leave this keep, I will have you married to me—will you, nill you."

Needless to say, Adam was being unjust, although not consciously. He had never mentioned an annulment or marriage to Gilliane, but he had argued the matter over with himself so often, supplying the answers he thought Gilliane would give, that he was quite sure she had refused him more than once. Gilliane, however, had not the slightest inclination to protest against this injustice. Heaven had been offered to her. She was not about to question the kind of platter upon which it was being served.

"Oh my dear, dear lord," she breathed, "you have surely been misled by some stupidity and lack of understanding in me. I will marry you gladly, even right here and now with my vassals as witness, without any contract at all."

"Will you, Gilliane? Do you mean that?"

"Let Father Paul be summoned and he may marry us at once," Gilliane urged.

Although this was scarcely a normal procedure, Sir Godfrey and Sir Richard held their tongues. Sir Godfrey did not care much for a female overlord, but he would not say anything to endanger his newfound rapport with Adam. Sir Richard had no doubts of Gilliane's safety in Adam's hands, and besides, he was convinced she was well able to take care of herself. Adam hesitated for a moment. He had in his possession a contract written exactly like the one his mother had devised for her own marriages, except that the names of the people and properties were different. He had intended to use it as an inducement, since it safeguarded the rights of the contracted woman. Then he signaled a servant and bid him fetch the priest to the chapel immediately. Let Gilliane believe she had given up all for love. It would be a sweet thing to hold in his heart forever, as would her joy when he showed her the contract and she realized she had lost nothing.

So Gilliane was married for the third time without the smallest preparation or ceremony. This time she did not care. She could have been naked and bedaubed with filth, so long as it was Adam who held her hand and gave the responses. However, she was not ill dressed. In anticipation of the arrival of Adam and her men, she was quite elegantly gowned. Moreover, she found she was to receive a bride-gift—for the first time. While Father Paul made ready, Adam had sent a servant to retrieve a certain chest from Alberic. This, after he had kissed his new-made wife, Adam opened. Gilliane gasped. Rubies and diamonds were hung about her neck, fastened to her wimple, slipped on her fingers and up her arms. The contract was pressed into her hand.

"There is a copy in French, my love. Read it, and you will see you have lost nothing," Adam murmured. "Beloved, you have only gained a willing slave to serve you forever."

"I do not want it," Gilliane whispered, pushing the parchments back at him. "I do not need it. Dear lord, how could you think I ever mistrusted you?"

That was sweetest of all, but Adam firmly bade her take it and sign. "You do not need it to protect you from me, but it will protect our children—a second son or daughters. Sign, beloved. I believe you never mistrusted me. It was my own fault."

The contract was signed and witnessed by Sir Richard and Sir Godfrey. Later it would be signed by Sir Edmund and Sir Philip also, and Adam intended to have it witnessed also by Pembroke and the Bishop of Winchester. He kissed his wife again, hungrily. He had been away from her for a month. Gilliane was eager also, but she had no intention of being swept into a hurried coupling, marred by the knowledge that her men were waiting impatiently below for them to have done and come back to more important business. Not on her wedding day. They had waited a month; they could wait a few hours longer until night, until there would be time for love, for sweet words, for unhurried caresses. Thus, when Adam turned aside, intending to lead her upstairs, Gilliane slipped out of his hold.

"Where do you go?" he asked sharply as she curtsied and backed away. "Sir Richard will see to the removal of de Cercy."

Gilliane dimpled with mischievous laughter. "I will be grateful to him for it. Even dead, Osbert is an abomination to me. However, as a married woman, my reputation as a housewife must be upheld."

"What?" Adam exclaimed, and then began to laugh also. "No! Do not tell me I have not yet broken you of that habit. Do you mean to say you are thinking of dinner again?"

"But yes, my lord," Gilliane insisted gently. "I must see to dinner. Surely a suitable feast must be prepared for my wedding day."